Deadly Little Lies

STEPHANIE DECAROLIS

ONE PLACE. MANY STORIES

HQ
An imprint of HarperCollins*Publishers* Ltd
1 London Bridge Street
London SE1 9GF

www.harpercollins.co.uk

HarperCollins*Publishers*
1st Floor, Watermarque Building, Ringsend Road
Dublin 4, Ireland

This paperback edition 2022

1

First published in Great Britain by
HQ, an imprint of HarperCollins*Publishers* Ltd 2021

Copyright © Stephanie DeCarolis 2021

Stephanie DeCarolis asserts the moral right to be
identified as the author of this work.
A catalogue record for this book is
available from the British Library.

ISBN: 9780008462123

MIX
Paper from
responsible sources
FSC™ C007454

This book is produced from independently certified FSC™ paper
to ensure responsible forest management.

For more information visit: www.harpercollins.co.uk/green

Printed and bound in the UK using 100%
renewable electricity at CPI Group (UK) Ltd

To my mother, and in memory of my grandmother.
Thank you for giving me wings and believing I could fly.

"Three may keep a secret, if two of them are dead."
~ Benjamin Franklin

Poor Richard's Almanack

Prologue

The cries of the sirens pierce through the frigid night air before the forest lights up with splashes of red and blue. Emergency lights bounce between the trees and illuminate the wet earth, slicked with a kiss of fallen leaves.

We stand there, watchers in the trees, like a coven of witches. But we've traded in our dark cloaks for skin-tight dresses, flowing blonde curls, and swaths of red lipstick pulled over sparkling white teeth. We are the most dangerous kind of predator—the kind that is designed to look like prey.

None of us dares to move as we watch the slumbering campus jolt to life, knowing that we were the ones who summoned the lightning before we retreated into the forest.

"No one can ever know," I say breathlessly, my voice escaping my throat in a jagged whisper.

I look around at the others, all staring straight ahead, the blue lights reflecting in their wide, glassy eyes. No one replies, but I know that they will follow my lead.

They always do.

Chapter 1

Now

I run down the stairs of the train platform, the dingy gray cement marred with black stains of decades-old chewing gum and ground cigarette butts.

I hear the metallic doors of the subway train slide open, and I pick up the pace, the nylon strap of my messenger bag slipping down my shoulder. I can feel the sweat building under my arms, my feet sliding in my shoes. This is not at all the glamorous life I'd envisioned when I decided to go to law school.

I make it onto the train just as the doors grind closed, and drop into a plastic seat. I twist my hair up into a bun and secure it with the thick, black rubber band that is perpetually looped around my wrist. I lean my head against the grimy wall behind my seat and briefly close my eyes, letting out an exhausted sigh.

It's the laughter that jolts me back to attention, a peal of it ringing across the crowded train car, so familiar and yet so foreign that it sounds like an echo from a former life.

My eyes follow the sound to a group of girls huddled near the door. They're turned to face one another, their ranks forming a closed circle. I take in their short dresses that hug their slender hips, the spiked heels, their long hair set into rolling curls that bounce along with the rumbling train car.

I try not to stare, but I suppose it doesn't matter. I doubt any of them will even notice me sitting across the aisle. Their world is still sparkly and new. The thirty-two-year-old woman in her sensible court shoes will surely blend into the background scenery, barely registering on their radar. And yet, they feel so familiar to me. I know them. I was them. In a different life, one I've tried so hard to put behind me. These girls have no idea what's coming.

"Is this seat taken?" I hear a voice ask. I see a larger woman pointing to an empty seat behind the group. She shuffles nervously on her feet as the girls turn to face her, setting their sharp eyes on her. I can see her the way they do, the way I was trained to, if I allow my mind to go back there. I'm certain they've clocked the way her thighs strain against her worn slacks, the way her hair has come loose from its bun, the freed tendrils clinging to her neck in the sticky underground heat.

Or maybe I've gotten it all wrong. Maybe these girls are nothing like we were. Perhaps I'm just projecting, overlaying a film reel of my own memories over the scene before me. But then one of the girls smiles, and I know. The corners of her mouth tick upward into a predatory grin that makes my gut twist.

"It's all yours," she says, all saccharine insincerity.

I watch the girl move closer to her friends, deeper into the pack. But she doesn't leave the woman enough space to maneuver into the seat, forcing her to wedge herself between the girl and the other commuters, her discomfort on full display. The girls put on a show for everyone in the train car and made sure they had front-row seats. It could have been unintentional, and to any other onlookers it probably appeared that way, but I know better. I know the game; I was once a player.

I feel my stomach churning with a mixture of disgust, at the girls, at myself, at the person I was. It's a bit like being in recovery.

It's taken me a long time to put my past, that life, behind me. And yet all it took was spotting a group of girls who looked vaguely familiar to bring it bubbling back up to the surface.

When the train finally arrives at my station, I make my way out onto the platform, and bound up the stairs, back to the surface of New York City, desperate for some fresh air.

A yellow taxi whizzes down the avenue, which is lined with brownstones and waifish trees trapped behind painted fences. Even nature is contained in my neighborhood, forced to fit into convenient, preordained spaces. The people who live here would never tolerate anything unruly, anything wild.

I jog up the stone steps that lead up to my own brownstone. Okay, so it isn't really *mine*. My husband, Jason, and I rent a postage-stamp-sized apartment on the first floor of a brick townhouse in Chelsea. I'd dreamed of living here, in New York City, for as long as I could remember, but I sometimes forget why I ever thought this place was so magical. How I'd ever convinced myself that living here would transform me into someone stronger, better ... worthy. I still feel like a dandelion hiding among daisies, a weed growing in this manicured garden.

Jason reminds me constantly that we could afford a much bigger place if we only moved out of Manhattan. But I like the anonymity of living in a city surrounded by so many people that I can blend into the crowd. In a city like New York, everyone has their own lives to lead, their own stories to tell ... their own secrets to keep. Mine is just one more, lost in a sea of voices.

I stop for a moment, my hand resting on the tarnished brass knob on our glossy, black front door. I know that on the other side, Jason will be waiting for me, a smile on his face, ready to ask me about my day, my cases, my life. I need to collect myself before going inside, to tamp down the memories that have been threatening to push through the surface since my experience on the subway. Jason doesn't belong to that world, to that part of me.

Sometimes I can't believe people like him still exist in this world—people who haven't yet been broken, people who are just plainly … nice. Especially when my own nicety is now spoken like a foreign language: each syllable pondered, a stuttering fluency. But I need to be the person Jason married, the person he deserves, the person I've worked so hard to become. I have to banish the old me back into the shadows where she belongs.

"Hey, Jules!" Jason exclaims the instant I walk through the door. He's in the kitchen, a wok in his hand, tossing stir-fry as though he's auditioning for a role on a celebrity cooking show. "Dinner is just about ready."

I smile, trying not to think of the mess he's inevitably making in the kitchen. "Smells great," I say instead. And it does. Cooking is only the latest in Jason's long line of hobbies that he seems to have mastered without breaking a sweat. He's like *them* in that way. Things come easily to him. Perhaps it's what drew me to him from the beginning. He possessed something I spent so long trying to emulate, something I could never have. "I'm just going to get changed first."

Jason gives the contents of the wok a showman-like flip. "Sure thing."

I close myself in the bedroom and shove my clothes into the hamper. It wasn't always like this. It wasn't always so hard for me to be the kind of person Jason deserves, the woman he fell in love with. As I dig some more comfortable clothes out of my dresser, I think back to the early days of our relationship, to the champagne dinners, the carefully packed picnics in the park, the effortless happiness I found for the first time in him. When Jason walked into my life, I felt as though I'd been given a second chance. He is a light in my world—the only thing that is sometimes bright enough to banish the darkness of my past. He has become my shelter from it, my redemption. If someone like Jason can see goodness in me, then perhaps someday I might too.

But memories, they can be such mutable things, can't they? Always changing and shifting like the colors in a kaleidoscope.

Because the woman I was then, so full of happiness and bursting with new love, I remember her so vividly at times that I can almost convince myself that she was real. But she wasn't. Not entirely anyway. She was a hopeful illusion, a cobbling together of half-truths and good intentions meant to bury something much darker. But some things, they're just too big to stay buried for long. The past, this secret I've been concealing all these years, has begun to push its way up through the foundation of our marriage like roots of a poisonous tree. When I take the time to look closely enough, I can see the cracks it's drawn in the facade of happiness that I've created, and I sometimes wonder how much more damage it can withstand before it all comes tumbling down.

I shake away the thought and yank a T-shirt down over my head. *Jason and I will be fine. I'm not that person anymore.*

I'm about to step out of the bedroom when I hear my phone buzzing inside my bag. I debate ignoring it—surely whatever it is can wait. *But what if it's the office?* I should probably check, just in case it's something important.

With a sigh I turn and fish my phone out of my bag to check the home screen. I find that I have one new email from an address I don't recognize: JennyTeller@gmail.com. I open it quickly with trembling fingers. The email contains only one line. Two simple words:

Remember me?

But they are enough to make me drop the phone as if it had scalded me.

I don't know who sent me this email, but I know it wasn't Jenny Teller.

Because Jenny Teller is dead.

Chapter 2

Then

"Jules, honey, are you sure you don't need us to stay?" Mom asked as she picked up her purse off the bed in my new dorm room.

"It's fine. I'm fine. Really," I told her, suddenly not feeling quite so sure.

My eyes swept over the room, its sterile white walls, the two narrow twin beds and the matching wooden desks pushed along either side of the room, a small window set into the back wall, which looked out onto a lush green lawn four stories below. This was everything I'd dreamed of, wasn't it? I'd been envisioning this day for years. The day I started at Westbridge University. I was so sure that its ivied walls were going to transform me into someone new. Someone who mattered. I just wasn't sure who that might be yet.

I thought back to my high school days, to the aching loneliness I felt. Aside from my best friend, Kelly, no one seemed to notice I existed. I grew up in a small town in Ohio, where everyone had known each other since kindergarten. Our standing in the social hierarchy was hashed out in those early days on the playground.

I was quickly labeled the smart one, the quiet one, someone not worth looking at twice, and in a town like that, there was no room for me to shed the label that felt emblazoned on my forehead and become someone new.

I moved through the hallways like a ghost while the glossy-haired girls with the easy smiles and the soft laughter sauntered by in their pleated cheerleading skirts with ribbons tied around their swishing ponytails. It felt as though there simply wasn't enough sunlight for all of us to blossom, and so I was left in the shade, dwindling behind the brighter blooms. But I was sure Westbridge would be an open field, where I would have the space to discover who I wanted to be and grow into someone worth noticing.

And I'd worked so hard to get here. My parents could never even dream of affording the staggering Ivy League tuition, and they'd been adamant that I would not bury myself under a mountain of college debt I'd never be able to climb out of, and so I knew that a scholarship was my only hope. I gave up so much to be here—choosing studying over parties, honors classes over hanging out behind the gym, and so as nervous as I was watching my parents walk out of my new dorm room, my bed freshly made with my brand-new sheets, this wasn't the time to get cold feet.

"I *was* hoping we'd at least get to meet your roommate," Mom said, sounding disappointed. The other twin bed in my room had already been made, if you could call it that. There was an aqua blue comforter tossed over the worn mattress, a few unpacked suitcases stacked in front of the closet.

"You're in luck then," a voice from the hallway filtered in over her shoulder. "Hey, Roomie."

That was the first time I saw her. Tori Sullivan. She was cool in a way I never knew existed. She was so different from the cheerleaders who ruled my high school with Starbucks cups in their hands and Michael Kors bags on their shoulders, but I could immediately tell that she wasn't like me: Tori wasn't a girl who had ever been overlooked. Her brown hair was highlighted with

9

caramel streaks, and a tiny diamond stud glinted from her nose. She wore a pair of jeans that probably cost more than everything my mother had just neatly folded into my dresser, and they were artfully torn at the knee. An olive-green canvas duffel was flung over her shoulder, and she stood with her hip jutted to the side, gum crackling between her teeth.

"I'm Tori," she said, extending her hand to first my mother and then my father. It amazed me how self-assured she was around adults, as if she was already certain of her place in this world. I suppose she was.

"This is Juliana," my father said by way of introduction, clamping his large, warm hand over my shoulder.

"Hi," I muttered, giving Tori a little wave. I found myself immediately intimidated by her.

"Hey, Jules."

Some of the tension eased from my shoulders. She'd already given me a nickname, and it felt like being taken under her wing.

"We're going to have so much fun," Tori said with a wink, gum still clicking behind her teeth.

"Well, we'll leave you girls to it," Mom said, ushering my dad out of the room. I no longer felt the same jangle of nerves watching them leave. I had Tori, *and we were going to have so much fun.*

As Tori unpacked, with a torrent of classic rock bellowing from her laptop behind her, I texted Kelly:

My roommate is so freakin' cool!

She responded instantly.

Phew! Thank God you didn't get stuck with some weirdo!

Kelly had applied to Westbridge with me but wasn't accepted. Instead, she'd decided to attend a local commuter college in Ohio to stay close to her boyfriend, Owen, who planned to take over

10

his father's sod business. She didn't have to worry about room-mates, and we'd spent the summer talking about how nervous I was to be moving in with a girl I'd never even met.

"What if she's a total weirdo?" Kelly had mused as we lay on our backs on the trampoline in her backyard, fireflies weaving lazy loops above our heads.

"You mean like one of those people who get up at five a.m. to go running?" I added with a laugh.

"No, more like Ms. Minton … Have you seen her bug collection in the science room?"

We giggled, our heads touching, our hair splayed out beneath us like halos, hers brown, mine blonde.

But Tori was none of those things. She was better than I'd ever imagined.

"Wanna check out the campus?" Tori asked, pulling me from my thoughts.

"Sure," I replied, sliding off my bed.

Tori pulled on a pair of high-top sneakers and then looked at me appraisingly, as if she was just then seeing me for the first time. "You're really pretty," she said, almost quizzically, as though the thought had taken her by surprise.

It had taken me by surprise too. I never thought of myself as pretty, even though I've always been naturally slim and Kelly frequently told me that my blonde hair was "to die for"—much nicer than her "boring brown".

"Thanks," I replied shyly, feeling a flush rise into my cheeks.

"Come on, I'll show you around."

Westbridge University was nestled into scenic Tompkins County in upstate New York, just outside the town of Ithaca. It was surrounded by other schools: Ithaca College, SUNY Cortland, Binghamton University, and its Ivy League rival, Cornell University. All within a stone's throw of Westbridge's front gates.

When I'd sat in my bedroom back at home in Ohio filling out my application to schools in New York, I'd envisioned skyscrapers and brownstones, yellow taxis and double-decker buses. But Westbridge, approximately a five-hour drive north of Manhattan, existed in a different world. It was a world of rolling hills covered in leafy trees sporting a bursting fall palette in hues of yellows, oranges, and fiery reds. It was a bucolic place of scenic gorges, waterfalls, and hiking trails where quaint bed and breakfasts opened in full swing when the air grew crisp in the fall to accommodate the flood of "leaf peepers" who flocked to the area.

Though I couldn't yet see the invisible boundaries that carved up the state, I quickly came to learn that upstate New York, which apparently according to any *real* New Yorker was anything north of New York City, may as well have been a different state entirely. The topography of Manhattan, each neighborhood a city of its own, was even more complicated. One address meant you were someone to be envied, but a residence a few blocks away meant you were someone to be pitied. I had a lot to learn about my new home.

Tori walked me past the Hillview Dining Hall—"The Hill" as she called it—the main fountain at the center of campus, the open quad where a pack of guys were already tossing a frisbee, and finally the library. I wanted to poke my head inside, to smell the books, the dizzying array of literature lining its stone walls. But I could tell that Tori wasn't so interested in this particular part of the tour. She pointed to the grand building casually, a barely acknowledged blip on her radar. I made a mental note to go back there later, on my own.

"How do you already know your way around campus?" I asked, in awe of this girl who seemed to know everything there was to know.

"Oh, my cousin went here. I used to visit her all the time. The parties were unreal."

God, Tori is cool. I'd never been to a college party, and the few high school parties I'd attended consisted of nothing more than a bunch of idiot jocks serving warm, frothy beer in their parents' backyards.

"We got, like, so lucky to be in Nickerson Hall," Tori explained. "It's the coolest dorm on campus."

"Really?" I had no idea that one dorm was better than the others.

"Yeah, it's supposed to be the party dorm."

I swallowed hard hoping Tori didn't notice. I wanted to experience college and everything that came along with it: the parties, the friendships, the nights we'd tell stories about for years to come, but I wasn't sure how I felt about living at the center of it. What if I couldn't keep up?

"Yo! Tori!" a deep voice rang out.

I turned to find a cute guy jogging in our direction.

"Hey, Nate," Tori replied, sounding almost bored.

"Who's your friend?" he asked, turning his gaze on me. Nate was incredibly hot: a square jaw, thick dark hair, and toned biceps under a tight gray T-shirt. I didn't know how Tori seemed to be so unaffected by him, while I could feel my own cheeks set ablaze just because he threw a look in my direction.

"This is my roommate—Jules." Her gum clicked, a rapid staccato. "Nate, Jules. Jules, Nate."

"Hey," Nate said distractedly, his fleeting interest in me already long gone. His eyes were fixated on Tori, and I could see something there, a longing that she refused to return. "Just wanted to ask if you were going to the party at the Beta house tonight."

"I don't know. I might." Tori shrugged. "Haven't decided yet."

"Think about it," Nate said with a wink before kissing Tori lightly on the cheek and making his way back to his friends.

Tori rolled her eyes after he'd left. "Nate Porter: notorious player, one-time bad decision that I can't seem to stop making."

I blushed. "Did you go to high school with him?"

"No, he went to Morrow Prep. I went to Brighton, but I used to hang out with some of the Morrow guys sometimes."

I nodded along knowingly, even though I didn't have the faintest clue about the intricate social nuances surrounding the finest preparatory schools. "Are you going to that party?" I asked, wondering how I'd feel about being alone in my dorm room for the first time if she did.

"Maybe. You wanna come?"

Me? I almost asked the question out loud before biting back the words. Tori existed in a different social stratosphere and I never anticipated that she might extend her hand to lift me up with her.

I shrugged my shoulders, hoping I didn't seem too eager. I was starting to understand: girls like Tori weren't playing the same game as the popular girls back at home, where all they had to do was hike up their skirts and boys in letterman jackets would circle them like lions. At Westbridge, the rules were entirely different. It wasn't enough to just be desired; if I was going to keep up, I had to learn to desire nothing in return.

Chapter 3

Now

This can't be. Jenny Teller. Just seeing her name in print is enough to make my world spin.

"Dinner is ready!" Jason calls in.

"Just a minute," I yell back, trying my best to sound normal.

My thumbs hover over the keyboard on my phone. I know who I have to call, but it feels almost surreal, as if I'm stepping back into the past. I feel a rush of nerves, and yet … sadness. I once thought nothing of calling Tori Sullivan. She'd been my closest friend, and now I don't even know if she has the same number. Thanks to social media, we've been able to keep tabs on one another's lives from afar. I watched from the sidelines as she married a man named Matt, and then when they welcomed their daughter, Mia, who must be nearly one by now. It feels so strange to know her so well, and yet, not at all.

But before I can bring myself to dial her number, the phone rings in my hand, Tori's name on the screen.

"Jules, it's Tori," she says, her voice urgent but sure. "I know it's been … a long time, but I have to know. Did you get it too?"

"I did …" I reply, biting my lower lip anxiously. Though a small, selfish part of me feels a sense of relief that I wasn't the only one who got Jenny's email. At least I wasn't alone. *But then again, I never was.*

"It's so fucked up," Tori whispers breathlessly.

I have to assume that Matt must be nearby, and even after all these years, after all the things we've missed, I know she wouldn't have told him about Jenny.

"Why would someone do this?" she asks.

"I … I don't know. But listen, my husband, Jason, is in the other room. We can't talk here. We should meet up. Talk in person."

"Okay. Fine," I can hear the annoyance in Tori's voice. She isn't used to being told to wait. "It's gotta be tomorrow though. We need to figure out what's going on. I'll text you the address of a restaurant in midtown. We'll meet there after work. Around six o'clock, okay?"

"Okay, see you tomorrow," I reply quickly. I end the call abruptly as Jason appears in the doorway.

"Everything okay, babe?" he asks.

I rearrange my face into a pleasant smile. It's second nature by now, this ability to slip into someone else, someone designed to show the world exactly what it wants to see.

"Yup, I just got a call from an old college friend. She wants to get together for drinks tomorrow after work."

"Oh, that's so nice! I feel like you never talk about your college days."

That's an understatement.

"I'd love to meet some more of your friends," Jason adds.

"Sure, maybe," I reply, though the thought of Tori and Jason being in the same room makes the muscles in my shoulders tense. "Let's see how tomorrow goes first. It's been a long time since I've seen her."

"Of course," Jason says, scooping a spoonful of rice onto my plate.

I try to envision it, my new life overlapping the old. I imagine it going as smoothly as ocean waves crashing onto a stone jetty.

I have no doubt that Jason would find a way to win over Tori. He's just one of those people everyone seems to love. We can go out to dinner, and by the end of the night he has three new best friends and an invitation to play golf. He talks to everyone—the bartender, the older gentleman seated next to us at a baseball game, a stranger on the train. There's a warmth about Jason, an easy charm that people seem drawn to. No, it's not Jason I'd have to worry about … it's me.

Who would I be if I had to make my world big enough to fit both Jason and Tori? They know me as entirely different people. I've always felt torn in half, the person I was clashing against the person I'm trying to be. It leaves very little room to figure out who I am *now*, to figure out how to navigate the world and feel like a whole person.

Jason and I sit down to dinner and he fills me in on the details of his day at the office. I try to pay attention as he laughs through the words, telling me a story about a co-worker who got stuck in the elevator. I nod along, smiling in all the right places, but behind the facade my mind is reeling.

"You sure you're okay, Jules?" Jason asks.

"I'm fine," I reply, taking another sip of my wine. I feel heady with it, a dull thrum buzzing in my ears.

"It's just that you've barely touched your food."

I look down at my plate. I guess I've had more to drink, and less to eat, than I realized. I watch myself pushing the chunks of meat around my plate with my fork on rote as if my hand was being controlled by someone else.

"Oh, yeah, I'm fine. Just have a lot on my mind with work," I lie. *What's on my mind has very little to do with my job, and everything to do with Jenny Teller.*

Jason nods sympathetically and resumes chatting. "They actually had to call the fire department to rescue him!"

I try again to focus on what he's saying, but I can't. All I can think about is my phone, which is still lying in the other room, calling me like a siren luring a mariner to a watery grave.

"I'm sorry," I interrupt, "I just need a second."

"Oh sure, no problem," Jason replies, as I push away from the table.

I walk toward the bedroom, quickly snatching my phone off the bed, before closing myself in the bathroom with it.

It's still there. The email. I'd almost hoped I'd imagined it, but I knew I hadn't.

I stare down at the thumbnail photo of Jenny that popped up next to her email address. Frozen in time at eighteen years old. As much as I've tried to forget that time, that girl, every detail rushes back with pointed clarity as I look at her face. I feel my mind shutting down, like a floodgate closing before my whirling, angry memories can crash over me, pulling me under.

My breathing becomes shallow, and I can feel sweat pricking my palms. Before long it feels as though the walls are closing in on me, heaving with the past.

I hastily close out of my email app. I can't look at that photo, that name, any longer. Once it's off my screen, I immediately feel calmer, my head clearer. This is probably just some sick freak playing a cruel joke. I tell myself that tomorrow I'll talk to Tori and she'll know exactly how to handle this. She always had the answers. Tori and I will get to the bottom of it, and by tomorrow it will all be over. But deep down inside, I hear a voice—*her* voice—telling me that this is far from over.

Chapter 4

Then

I stepped back from the mirror and scrutinized my outfit choice for the hundredth time. Behind me, dresses, which my mother carefully hung in my closet only a few hours earlier, were scattered on the floor like empty husks. None of them seemed right for my first college party. I knew that I only had one chance to make a first impression. *I just wish Tori was here to give me some guidance.* She left over an hour earlier with promises to return with a fake ID for me. She, naturally, already had one. We wouldn't need it for the Beta party, she'd explained, but we might want it if we checked out the bar scene afterwards. A frat party *and* college bars all on my first night at Westbridge. This outfit needed to be just right. I shimmied out of a pair of jeans that felt as though they were cutting off circulation to my feet. I needed to do better.

I reached back into my closet and pulled out a sapphire blue bandeau dress and tugged it over my head. I had to sneak it into my room. My mother would have had a heart attack if she saw any of the clothes that Kelly and I secretly accumulated over the summer. My mom had taken me back-to-school shopping, purchasing rows of cardigans, cotton T-shirts, and knock-off-brand jeans, and then I had done my own shopping with the money I'd earned babysitting and from my shifts at the local library.

Not bad, I thought as I smoothed my new dress over my hips. I slid my feet into a pair of towering heels, another acquisition that my mother was blissfully unaware of, and rimmed my eyes with coal-black eyeliner before the full-length mirror mounted to the wall.

"Well look at you," Tori said, leaning against our doorframe, her arms folded over her chest, a crooked smile playing at her lips.

The sound of her voice made me jump. I still wasn't used to sharing a room. As an only child, I'd never had to do it before. It just felt so … intimate. I took in Tori's outfit: the same torn jeans, a cutoff Pink Floyd T-shirt, a choker necklace snaked around her slender neck. I felt heat rise up into my chest and I watched as red splotches bloomed on my chest in my reflection. I'd gotten it all wrong.

"Do you think I should change? I probably should …"

"No, don't," she replied reassuringly. "Seriously. You look hot."

I still felt unsure. Tori looked so effortlessly cool, while there was definitely nothing effortless about me. But she'd said I looked hot. I'd never been one of the pretty girls before. It felt like being welcomed into a secret society, and I wasn't going to ignore her advice. *Tori would know best, wouldn't she?*

"Okay," I said tentatively. "If you're sure."

"I'm sure. Here, this is for you." She handed me my new driver's license. "Your name is Sarah and you're twenty-two."

"Perfect," I replied, sliding the invaluable bit of plastic into my tiny cross-body bag.

"One last thing," Tori added, pulling a small glass bottle from her bag and pushing the door to our room closed behind her. "Time to pregame." She unscrewed the top of the bottle of Bacardi and took a swig. I looked around like a criminal about to rob a bank. Drinking alcohol was forbidden in the dorms and I was certain that the resident assistant was going to burst in at any second and write us up. But when Tori passed the bottle in my direction, I took it.

I put my mouth to the rim, which was still warm from Tori's lips, and mimicked her long, measured swig. The rum burned the back of my throat and I coughed involuntarily. It wasn't my first drink—Kelly and I would sometimes sneak her mom's wine coolers, or nurse warm beers at lame high school parties, but I'd never taken a shot straight from a bottle of liquor before.

"*Now* you're ready," Tori said, hardly able to suppress a smirk. "Shall we?"

* * *

Tori and I joined a gaggle of other girls in tight skirts and spiked heels outside of the Beta house, their colt-like legs white in the moonlight. We were all shivering against the crisp evening chill, but we weren't going to cover our carefully selected outfits with coats, as if showing deference to the elements was a sign of weakness. Bare shoulders and exposed midriffs took priority over comfort.

Tori lit a cigarette, the glow from her lighter momentarily casting spectral shadows over her face.

"You smoke?" I asked, hoping I didn't sound like a Goody-Two-Shoes. But I didn't like the idea of living with someone whose clothes would always trail in the stench of stale cigarettes.

"No, only when I drink," she replied with a shrug, as if that was an important distinction. She let out a long plume of smoke and it rose above our heads in curling tendrils.

Finally, it was our turn at the front door. The Beta house was an old colonial home, which reminded me of the photos we'd studied in high school of southern plantation houses. It was one of several similar houses that lined Main Street, each with bold Greek letters fastened to the facade. The inside of the house was lit with a warm glow that seemed like a welcome reprieve from the cold night.

"Ladies drink free," a boy in a backwards hat and a green sweatshirt told us as we neared the doorway. He stamped my hand and then Tori's, and handed each of us a red Solo cup. "Punch is in the kitchen," he added with a wink.

"We won't be drinking the punch," Tori told me after we'd gotten inside. She had to lean in close to my ear to be heard over the roar of the music and the excited cheers of boys playing drinking games in the dining room.

"Why not?" I asked, all round-eyed innocence.

"Never drink the punch. You don't know what's in it. I don't trust any of these assholes and neither should you."

My eyes grew even rounder. *Was she suggesting that someone may have spiked the punch? Weren't these our classmates? Our colleagues?*

"I didn't mean to scare you. You'll be fine. I promise. I've got your back." Tori looped her arm through mine. I liked the feel of her warm skin against mine, the intimacy of her claiming me as her own. "Let's hit the keg."

We made our way into the kitchen, where another boy in a green sweatshirt was pumping the top of a dented silver keg. Tori handed him our cups and he filled them to the brim.

I took a sip of my beer, the foam clinging to my upper lip. I watched as Tori did the same, her quick tongue darting out to collect the foam.

A crowd of people pushed into the kitchen, everyone vying for their turn at the keg. Before I realized what was happening, a pair of strong arms materialized around Tori's neck. It was Nate, who was now standing behind her and whispering something in her ear. Tori's lips curved into a cat-like smile and I knew that whatever he was saying to her was exactly what she wanted to hear.

Tori leaned her head back against Nate's muscular chest,

relaxing into his touch, and I suddenly felt as though I was intruding on an intimate moment.

I wandered away from Tori, feeling a bit unmoored, but not wanting her to think I was too clingy, that she'd have to babysit me.

I made my way into the living room, and that's when I saw her for the first time: Emily Jane Wiltshire. She was sitting on the back of a couch, long legs crossed at the thighs, seemingly holding court while worshipers fell at her feet. Her head was thrown back in laughter, her thick blonde hair, which looked like spun gold, cascading down her back. She was wearing a petal pink dress—something cute, sweet, something that my mother would have loved to see me wear—and her mane of hair was held back by a thick, velvet headband. She was the girl every guy wanted to corrupt and every girl wanted to be.

I watched as the boys, arms folded under Greek letters, hung on her every word, all of them looking at her with hunger in their eyes. She smiled sweetly at each of them in return, a suggestion of what could be, but a promise of nothing.

"Ah, I see you've found Emily," Tori said as she reappeared at my side, Nate no longer draped over her shoulders.

"You know her?" I asked incredulously.

"Yeah, we went to Brighton together. I think you'll find that just about everyone knows Emily."

"And who is that with her?" I asked, discreetly nodding my head in the direction of a stunning girl seated to Emily's right. She had long, chocolate brown hair that cascaded down her back in neat curls, wide, round eyes, and a bright-white smile. She was wearing a tight black dress and cherry red lipstick that matched her glossy manicure. A slim black choker encircled her slender neck.

"Oh, that's Vanessa Holland, though everyone calls her Nessa."

"She went to high school with you too?"

"Yup, another one of Brighton's finest. She and Emily are attached at the hip. It's rare to find Em without her loyal sidekick."

23

It was hard to imagine someone like Nessa being anyone's sidekick. If sex was a person, it would look like her: racy curves, long glossy hair, and a sultry, seductive grin. But next to Emily, everyone else's light was forced to dim.

"Looks like you're about to meet Em," Tori said as Emily deftly leapt down from her makeshift throne.

"Oh my God! Tori!" Emily squealed, planting flighty air kisses on each of Tori's cheeks. "I'm so glad you decided to come after all."

I watched as Tori transformed before my eyes. The cool girl, the tough girl I'd met earlier instantly disappearing as she slipped into a new role.

"Of course I came! I wasn't going to miss our first big night out!"

"Yay! I can't believe we're all here at Westbridge together! Just like we always talked about!" Emily squeezed Tori hard.

It appeared that they were much closer than just classmates as Tori had seemed to imply.

"Oh, this is my roommate—Jules," Tori added as she pulled away from Emily's embrace.

I offered her a smile, unsure what to do with myself. Something about Emily made me instantly feel like an outsider, as though I was kidding myself that I ever thought I could be one of them.

"Hey, Jules," Emily said, giving me a wave with a wiggle of her pink polished fingers. Her eyes diverted to me for the briefest of moments, and I could feel her sizing me up, taking instant inventory, before she turned her attention back to Tori.

The room felt colder when the warmth of Emily's spotlight was no longer trained on me, and I immediately felt cast aside. A child's toy no longer entertaining. I didn't know it yet, but that was her power: she fed off other people's envy of her, and she knew how to draw it out of you, to make you feel beneath her and yet grateful just to be in her orbit.

"Ugh, you wouldn't believe the roommate I got stuck with,"

Emily told Tori. "A total freak. But at least we're all in Nickerson Hall. I'm going to see if I can get our rooms changed around so Nessa and I can room together. Totally unfair that we weren't put together to begin with. I, like, totally requested it months ago."

"I'm sure you'll find a way," Tori replied with a roll of her eyes.

"I always do," Emily said with a wink.

I'd only just met her, but I already believed that to be true. There was nothing Emily couldn't have. And just like that, I was drawn in, lured to the light that glowed from her golden halo like a moth to the flame.

Chapter 5

Now

I swirl the red swizzle straw in my watered-down drink, the ice clinking against the glass, condensation beading against my fingers. It's a vodka seltzer. I wanted something heavy on alcohol and low on calories. Probably a holdover from my college days. Always afraid that gaining one ounce was what would push me from my precarious perch on the social hierarchy.

The restaurant Tori chose turned out to be a rooftop lounge in midtown Manhattan with low couches, dim lighting, and eighteen-dollar cocktails. The name sounded familiar, but I don't think I've ever been here before. Though I can easily imagine Tori hanging out here with the friends I've seen her posing with on Facebook, the ones from her job at the PR company who still have their fingers on the pulse of the latest trends, even in their thirties. After Westbridge, after what happened, I was no longer part of that world.

I see Tori before she sees me, picking her way through the bar. There's still an edge to her that makes her stand out in a crowd, a whisper of something dangerous in the way she strides through the crowd so purposefully on long legs. I find myself thinking that she's still the same person she was in college, or at least she seems to be. Because I know, more than most, that people aren't always who they appear to be.

As Tori nears my booth, I suddenly register that Nessa is trailing in her wake. *She must have gotten the email too.* Of course she would have. She was there that night too. Nessa is still as beautiful as ever, her signature red lipstick staining her lips under round hazel eyes. From what I've gathered from social media, she's an actress now, having performed in a handful of off-Broadway shows, but I'm certain that she's really just biding her time, waiting for her big break in the music industry. Singing was always her true passion.

From the outside, we probably look like any other group of friends in their thirties, meeting up for cocktails after work. But that couldn't be further from the truth. In a way, I suppose we're more strangers than friends now. Although that's not quite right either, is it? No matter how much distance we've put between us, the past, the secrets we kept, are threaded through our lives like twine, binding us together. A long time ago, we became sisters bound by blood, and despite how much time has passed, that bond can never really be broken.

Tori slides into the booth across from me, dropping into the seat with a thump. She shimmies out of her light jacket, which is wet with rain. Nessa settles herself next to Tori, and she does so far more delicately, sitting primly on the edge of her seat, not a hair out of place.

We look at one another, studying the faces that were once so familiar. I can see them, the girls they used to be hovering beneath the image of the women they are today. The past is never truly gone. I wonder if they can see me too, if they can see not just who I was, but who I've tried to become in the years since we last saw one another.

"It's gross out there," Tori announces. "It started to pour as I was walking over." The front of her hair, which must not have been protected by her hood, hangs together in thick strands. She rakes her fingers through her tossed mane, which is now a warm auburn color.

This is what we've been reduced to. Three semi-strangers talking about the weather.

"Not to rain on this parade—" Nessa begins.

"Ha." Tori laughs dryly. "Sorry, couldn't resist."

How easy it is to fall into old patterns, to slot back into the roles we designated for ourselves so long ago.

Nessa rolls her eyes. "But I can't sit here and chitchat about the weather." She lowers her voice to a whisper. "I'm freaking out here."

Of course she is. Nessa was always the nervous one of the group.

"Well, I'm gonna need a drink first," Tori says, raising one hand in the air. Gold bangle bracelets jingle on her slim wrist.

A waitress appears at our table almost immediately. I don't think she could be older than twenty, with wire-rimmed glasses, and thick frizzy hair knotted into a rough braid that sits on her shoulder in a clump. *We would have eaten her alive.* I'm immediately ashamed at myself for even thinking that way. Being around Nessa and Tori has a way of bringing old habits to the surface.

Tori orders herself a Jack and Coke, and Nessa requests of glass of cabernet. I ask for a refill of my drink as well. I already know I'll be needing it.

"So I assume we all got it then?" Nessa asks nervously as we wait for our drinks. "The email?" Her eyes dart around the room as though Jenny Teller might be lurking somewhere in the shadows.

I nod in agreement.

"It's so fucking sick though, isn't it?" Tori adds, an angry edge to her voice. "Like, what kind of person would find this funny?"

"I don't think it was *meant* to be funny," Nessa replies, her blood-red nails tapping on the tabletop anxiously. *Click, click, click.*

I suck down the last drops of my drink. "Do you guys think

it could be … her?" It's the question we've all been thinking but have been too afraid to speak aloud.

"You mean … Emily?" Nessa replies.

"Well, I certainly don't think she meant *Jenny*," Tori says, her voice dripping with sarcasm. "*Of course* we're still talking about Emily. Even after all these years, everything always comes back to Emily."

"Well do you think she's the one who sent these then?" I ask, a little more firmly now. Tori always turned to humor in stressful situations. It was her means of coping. Perhaps it still is. But we need to stay on track. This meeting isn't a cheerful reunion; we're here for a reason.

The waitress returns to our table, sliding our drinks in front of us on small, square napkins. Her presence breaks the tension that hangs over our table, and, unaware, she smiles brightly before walking away.

"I don't think it's Em," Tori says. "It doesn't feel like her style."

"Anonymously toying with people?" Nessa huffs. "Sounds just like her style to me."

"I agree," I reply. "Though this would be particularly messed up, even for her. She was there that night too."

"Who could forget?" Tori grumbles into her drink.

"Well, if you don't think it's Emily, then who the hell could be doing this?" Nessa asks, her eyes flitting between me and Tori.

I shake my head. "I honestly don't know."

"The list of people from Westbridge who weren't especially fond of us isn't exactly short," Tori quips. "It could be any of them."

Silence falls over us like a blanket of snow while we consider what this means: we have no idea who is targeting us.

"Look, this is stupid," Tori says, taking control. "It's just an email. Some jackass playing a cruel prank." She pulls out her phone and her fingers nimbly move across the keypad. "There. Done. I deleted it."

Nessa and I lock eyes over the table.

"I suggest you two do the same," Tori adds.

Nessa and I each slide out our phones and follow Tori's lead. Seeing the tiny thumbnail photo of Jenny again sends a cold chill down my spine, and I try not to let my eyes linger on it as I hit the "delete" button. *Poor Jenny, ignored even in death.*

The moment the email disappears from my screen, I feel liberated. I hadn't realized exactly how heavily its existence had been hanging on my shoulders.

"Done," I announce.

"Me too," Nessa says.

"Good," Tori responds. "Now let's enjoy these drinks and get on with our lives. I, for one, have had enough of a walk down memory lane."

She raises her glass in a toast, and Nessa and I lift our own glasses to meet hers.

We each take a sip of our drinks, and it feels cool and refreshing on my tongue. And then we hear it—all of our phones vibrating on the table at the same time. I know before I even look at my screen what is going to be waiting for me: "You have one new email from Jenny Teller."

Did you think I'd be so easily forgotten?

Chapter 6

Then

"Are you coming, Jules?" Tori asked, her hands stuffed into the front of her navy blue Westbridge hoodie.

"Yeah, just a sec," I replied, as I finished applying a lick of mascara. I never wore makeup in high school. It felt like a waste of time. But at Westbridge, it seemed like the girls woke up in a full face of makeup. Products carefully applied to make it look as though all their beauty came naturally.

"It's just a football game—you know that, right?" I could see Tori rolling her eyes in her reflection over my shoulder. Tori never seemed to fuss over her appearance as much as I did. Probably because she didn't need to. She was naturally pretty, and that coolness about her, that intangible thing that sets some girls apart from the others, came effortlessly to her.

"I know, but it's homecoming. Literally *everyone* will be there."

"Well at this rate, we'll be the last to arrive."

"Fine, I'm finished. Let's go." I pulled my own home-team sweatshirt over my head and smoothed it out over my skinny jeans. My feet were tucked into a pair of wool-lined boots that had cost me a decent chunk of my savings from my summer job at the library, but it seemed like I was the last to know that they were the must-have item on campus this season.

"Let's do this then," Tori said as she led the way out of our dorm room.

As we trekked through campus, a cool breeze whipped around us. It was only early October, but there was already a sharp chill in the air. I shoved my hands into the front pocket of my sweatshirt and felt thankful that I'd purchased the boots after all. Tori and I walked past masses of students dressed in all combinations of blue and white, their Westbridge pride on full display, as they sipped from plastic cups and made their way toward the football stadium. Shouts of "Go Hawks!" and upbeat music with a thudding baseline filtered through the campus. Everyone seemed to be buzzing with excitement. People, like me, who had never cared about football before were eager to fill the stadium.

I knew that homecoming was about so much more than football. It was about where you sat, who you shared drinks with, and who you'd leave with after the game. As the first major social event of the year, homecoming was where we would all be sorted into our designated roles. We'd be assigned our social labels that would follow us for the rest of our college careers.

"I texted Em," Tori told me, raising her voice to be heard over the crowd and the music, which grew louder as we neared the entrance to the stadium. "She and Nessa are already inside. They saved us seats."

I tried to keep the look of relief off my face. Emily saved *us* seats. We were only about a month into the semester, and due to my association with Tori, I'd had lunch, or gone out to parties with her, Nessa, and Emily a few times, but Emily hadn't seemed to warm to me. In fact, it hardly seemed that she'd noticed my presence at all. But at least she'd remembered to save me a seat at homecoming.

I followed Tori through the crowded stadium. A boy in a

backwards hat bumped against my shoulder as we climbed the metal stairs. A splash of beer sloshed over the side of his plastic cup and wet my sleeve. He didn't seem to notice. Or if he did, he didn't bother to apologize. Well, I wasn't going to let it get to me. Not at homecoming.

We finally spotted Emily, her hands wrapped around a steaming paper cup full of hot chocolate, marshmallows bobbing lazily on the surface. Emily waved us over, patting the empty space on the cold metal bench next to her and Nessa.

She was wearing a crew-neck Westbridge sweatshirt with a matching navy blue headband, and at the bottom of her long, crossed legs were the very same boots I was wearing. *I really am glad that I splurged on them.*

"Hi, girls," Emily said with a little wave. That's when I noticed her nails, painted a glossy blue and white. I looked over at Nessa, who had chosen a white knit sweater and a Westbridge blue scarf, and noticed that she had the same custom manicure. I could picture Emily and Nessa huddled together sharing a bowl of popcorn while they painted each other's nails. I felt a pang of jealousy surge through me. It wasn't that I didn't like living with Tori, but she wasn't the "give each other mani-pedis and giggle about boys" type. Besides, there was something so intoxicating about the idea of being a part of Emily's inner circle, about the prospect of being that close to her—as though by sheer proximity some of the magic she possessed might be passed on to me.

"Did we miss anything?" Tori asked as she settled into her seat and dropped her bag at her feet.

"Nothing at all," Nessa replied. "Just some football."

"But I *like* football," Tori said.

Emily arched one of her sculpted eyebrows and took a sip of her cocoa.

"Did your roommate come to the game?" I asked Emily, trying to strike up a conversation.

"Who, Jenny? Yeah, she's here somewhere." She rolled her eyes. "I think she's sitting with some of the other losers a few rows back."

I turned around, trying to be discreet. There was Jenny, her limp, black hair hanging lank at her shoulders, shielding part of her face. I'd met her a few times in passing when Tori and I went by Emily's room, usually to collect Emily on our way to lunch at The Hill or for a night out. Jenny always looked the same: hair greasy, her clothes one size too big, her eyes semi-hidden behind smudged glasses with odd blue frames, always downcast as though she was afraid to be noticed. She never asked to join us, and we'd never extended the invitation. I felt a little badly about that, but I certainly wasn't going to be the one who invited her along when it was clear that Emily hadn't wanted to include her.

Today Jenny was sitting with a few other girls I recognized from our hall: Beth, the wiry girl with the perpetually rosy cheeks who always had a flute case in her hands; Abby, Nessa's roommate, with the unruly curls and puppy fat that poured over the waistband of her jeans; and Lizzy, the mousy girl with horse posters all over her dorm-room walls.

Jenny caught my eye and I gave her a small wave, hoping Emily wouldn't notice. Jenny returned the gesture with a shy smile before I turned back to my group. I should have been sitting with Jenny, and I knew it. The natural order of things would have put me on that bench wedged between Beth and Abby. I was keenly aware that the only thing separating me and Jenny was the random twist of fate that I was assigned to live with Tori. I doubt Emily would have given me a second glance had Tori not already given me her stamp of approval. But as long as I was with Tori, she tolerated me.

The game was exhilarating, even though I didn't really follow the rules. Tori tried to explain the concept of "downs" to me, but I couldn't seem to grasp it. Though, to be fair, I wasn't really paying attention. My focus was split between the game and watching Emily out of the corner of my eye. The way everyone already seemed to know her, exchanging waves and smiles as they passed by, the way she took dainty sips from her cocoa, and the way she'd lean over to Nessa every so often, whispering something into her ear that made Nessa smile deviously. I wondered who they were talking about, who across the arena had caught their eye, and I wondered whether I would ever be truly welcomed into their fold.

I tried to follow Emily's gaze as she said something to Nessa that made Nessa giggle, but it was impossible. I couldn't decipher who they were looking at. The stadium was packed with students as well as alumni, some attending with their spouses and children.

I tried to picture my future self here with a handsome husband at my side, maybe a little daughter on my lap, but I just couldn't conjure up the image. Their faces wouldn't slide into focus. However the future played out, I hoped I'd still be sitting here with these girls, women by then. I pictured us as older versions of our current selves, reminiscing about our college days and laughing about all the fun we'd had. I hoped we were just at the beginning of a lifelong friendship. The kind my mom shared with her best friend from high school, the kind where our kids would grow up together, the kind where nothing would ever come between us.

* * *

Westbridge won the game, not that I'd spent much time watching it, but that meant all of the frat houses on Main Street were throwing lawn parties. Kegs were set up under glowing porch lights, and swarms of students wearing Westbridge blue crowded the streets. It felt as though the whole school had come together to celebrate. Well, *almost* the whole school. I'd seen Jenny and her friends heading back to the dorms before the game even ended. They hadn't said a word to us as they passed by us in the bleachers.

Emily linked her arms through Tori's and Nessa's, leaning her head on Nessa's shoulder. I trailed one step behind feeling notably out of place. I wondered later whether Emily had done it intentionally, as a subtle reminder that she, Tori, and Nessa were a unit. They shared a history that I wasn't a part of.

I could imagine them in their prep school uniforms: Emily sitting cross-legged on her bed, a fan of college brochures spread out before her; Nessa lying at her side, headphones slung around her neck; and Tori, with her shirttails untucked, pretending to be uninterested. But she *was* interested. They all were. I'd come to learn that as Brighton graduates, they would each have had their pick of schools, and yet they'd planned to come to Westbridge together. The only thing that wasn't a part of that plan was me: the tagalong. The scholarship kid who couldn't quite keep up.

I quickened my pace to catch up. I didn't want to be so easily forgotten.

"So I guess the school wouldn't let you switch rooms then?" I heard Tori say. I'd missed the earlier part of the conversation, but I already knew they were talking about Jenny. Emily had been talking about it for weeks: how she'd requested that she and Nessa be moved into a room together.

"No. They said they don't reallocate the rooms after move-in day, which is, like, totally ridiculous. Why do they care so much about who I live with? I asked Jenny if she would switch rooms with Nessa. She likes Nessa's roommate—Abby—well enough, I think. I've seen her and the other weirdos hanging out in the student lounge sometimes. But the little Goody-Two-Shoes refuses." Emily sighed heavily. "It's like she *wants* me to be miserable."

I could immediately sense that Emily wasn't accustomed to being told "no" by anyone.

"You know what they say," Nessa interjected. "You might catch more flies with honey, Em."

Emily seemed to ponder this for a moment before a smile spread across her face. "You know, Nessa, I think you're right."

Chapter 7

Now

"Now I'm *really* freaked out," Nessa says dropping her phone onto the tabletop with a clatter. "Why is this happening? Why now?"

It's a good question, one I've considered myself many times over the last twenty-four hours. And this latest email brought me no closer to figuring out the answer.

Nessa lowers her voice to a whisper before she continues. "What happened with Jenny was … what? Ten years ago?"

"Almost thirteen," Tori corrects.

"Right, so why is this all coming back up now?"

I don't have an answer to give her, and it appears that Tori doesn't either. She shakes her head slowly back and forth, a look of bewilderment on her face.

"I don't know why this is happening," Tori eventually responds, her words slow and measured. "But I think we just need to ignore it and whatever asshole is messing with us will eventually get bored and move on. It's just a few emails. We can't fall apart over this."

Nessa and I lock eyes over the table. We nod in agreement with

Tori, but I can tell that neither of us are certain that sticking our heads in the sand will make this problem go away.

"Jules? Is that you?" a voice calls over the murmurs of conversation in the restaurant. I nearly jump out of my seat, whipping my head around as though Jenny might be seated at the bar. I know she couldn't be ... *could she?*

I breathe a sigh of relief when I see that it's only my friend Claire. Claire and I met at the gym when we both signed up for a hot yoga class and instantly regretted it. We found ourselves sneaking out early, sweat dripping down our backs. We were giggling like children tiptoeing out of the class while trying to avoid the instructors' judgmental glare. After a few more chance encounters at the gym, Claire and I became friends.

I don't have many women in my life who I can call friends. After everything that happened at Westbridge, I had a difficult time putting myself out there, meeting new people. I kept to myself in law school, focusing entirely on my studies. In contrast to my life at Westbridge, by the time I got to law school I just wanted to blend into the background. I was there to earn my degree and move on with my life.

Claire is the first person I've met since college who I could tentatively call a friend. We'll sometimes meet for drinks after work, or Jason and I will go out to dinner with her and her husband. She's wonderful: happy, supportive, and generous, never thinking twice about picking up our tab on her AmEx Black Card. But aren't friends meant to share secrets? That's what Emily always said. And I can't share mine with Claire.

"Hi, ladies," Claire says as she approaches our table.

I feel panic setting in as I watch my new friend, the only untarnished friendship I have, venturing so close to my past. It's like watching a fish wander into shark-infested waters.

"Claire, hi!" I say a bit too brightly. "What are you doing here?"

She looks at me oddly, her eyebrows knitted in confusion. "I come here every month for happy hour to meet my old NYU sorority sisters." She nods toward a group of women seated near the bar before a cluster of half-filled wineglasses, their long legs folded over barstools, heads thrown back in laughter. "I'm sure I must have mentioned it to you before?"

"Of course. You have," I suddenly recall. No wonder the name of this restaurant sounded so familiar. "I don't know where my head is today."

Claire turns toward the table with a warm smile. "I'm Claire," she says with a wave.

Tori and Nessa introduce themselves. I can see it happening. The moment Tori, Nessa, and I slip into old roles. When we pull on the mask and we're the happy, lucky women we want the world to see once more. Just three old friends meeting for drinks.

"We were all friends in college," I offer by way of explanation, and then quickly change the subject before Claire has the chance to ask any more questions about why I'm sitting here with two women I've never once mentioned. "How's the baby?"

Claire has a little boy, Charlie, who is about the same age as Tori's daughter. She showed me photos of him, his big gummy smile and wispy blond hair, the first day I'd met her. "Isn't he just darling?" she'd said. "But he's the reason I'm back in the gym doing crazy things like hot yoga!" she joked, patting her toned, flat stomach.

"Adorable as ever," Claire replies now. "Though I really do need to find a new playgroup for him or something. It's getting so boring sitting at home with him every day. Is that terrible to say? Maybe I'm just an awful mother, but I feel like a caged animal in that apartment!"

I don't know how she could possibly feel trapped in her penthouse apartment. It's larger than the squat, one-story ranch house I grew up in. But I smile and nod sympathetically, as if I have the first clue what it's like to care for an infant day in and day out.

"Tori goes to a great playgroup, don't you?" Nessa volunteers. A part of me has always known that Nessa and Tori stayed in touch all these years, but it still stings to hear it confirmed. That

Nessa knows all of the tiny details of Tori's life, that I was the only one left to fend for myself after everything that happened.

"Yeah, you'd love it. I'll write down the info for you," Tori says as she fishes a pen out of her purse. She scribbles her number and the time and date of her next Mommy Meet-Up on a cocktail napkin. "You should definitely come!"

I cringe at the thought of Tori and Claire spending time together without me. About the things they might talk about, about the bond they might form. They belong to the same world, Tori and Claire, and I know how easy it is to be edged out of a group like that.

She hands the napkin to Claire who holds it reverently, as though she's just been given a winning lottery ticket. "I can't tell you how much I appreciate this! Good mom groups are so hard to find," she says, tucking a lock of ash blonde hair behind her ear.

I wonder how much she spends every month to keep her blonde bob looking perfect. My hand wanders to my own hair, and I toss it over my shoulder to hide the split ends.

"Anyway," Claire continues. "I'll let you ladies get back to your evening. I'm so glad I ran into you though!" She waves the coveted cocktail napkin like a white flag.

Claire flits off to rejoin her friends, and Tori, Nessa, and I let our masks slip once again, the mood suddenly somber in Claire's wake.

Because the truth is that as much as it may appear we have in common with Claire—just former college friends meeting at a trendy bar for cocktails—we have much bigger problems than finding a decent playgroup on the Upper East Side, and we all know it.

* * *

It's late by the time I get home and I change quietly in our darkened bedroom before I slip into bed next to Jason. He instinctually throws his arm over me, and I can feel his warm body pressed against my back, protective even in his sleep.

It's one of the things that made me fall for Jason, his instinctive drive to protect me. It's just who he is. And maybe I felt in need of protection. I'm far from a damsel in distress, although that day, the day I met Jason, I suppose I was.

It was just after I passed the bar exam, and I was waiting on the subway platform for my train to arrive and whisk me off to a job interview at a firm I didn't particularly want to work for. It had rumors of being an "associate mill" where they'd chew you up and spit you out within a year or so, leaving you burnt out and disillusioned with the legal profession. But jobs were tough to come by, and it's not like I had much of a social life to give up by that point anyway. And so I was standing on the cement platform, listening for the familiar sound of metal wheels screeching through the cavernous underground tunnels, when I felt a sharp pain in my shoulder blade. An elbow, as it turned out, jammed into my ribs.

I turned around to see a fight breaking out between a group of teenaged boys, backpacks slung loosely over their backs, sinewy arms shoving against puffed-up chests. They were scowling at one another in that way teenage boys do when testosterone has taken over their sensibilities, when their fiery anger and overinflated pride prevent them from thinking rationally. I tried to back away, but I felt the bumpy yellow divider under my foot—a warning to passengers that they are venturing too close to the edge of the platform, hovering over the twisted metal tracks below.

I looked for a way to get back toward the wall, to safety, but I couldn't get around the boys. I felt my heartbeat growing ever more rapid as the fight escalated. The boys were shouting at each other, their fists flying. They hadn't even noticed I was behind them, my heels drawing nearer to danger.

I heard a train approaching at my back, and I made to turn around, but just at that moment one of the boys crashed into me, his backpack colliding with my chest, knocking the breath from my lungs. I felt myself losing balance, and I knew that this would be the end. I was about to fall underneath the incoming train. And for a brief moment I thought that maybe karma had caught up with me, maybe I'd had this coming. But then I felt Jason's strong hand grip my upper arm, righting me on my feet. He'd pushed his way through the fight and came to my rescue just in time. He'd saved my life, and it felt like a second chance.

I clung to him, this stranger on a crowded train platform, the only one who seemed to notice that I'd felt the cold fingers of death brush against my skin that day.

"Are you all right?" he'd asked as I finally pulled my face away from his chest, mortified that I'd soaked his pale gray shirt with tears.

"Yeah, yes, I'll be fine. I … I can't thank you enough."

"It was nothing," he said sounding sincere, as though he rescued women on the subway every day of his life.

But it wasn't nothing. Not to me. I looked up at him, my eyes watering, my face streaked with tears, and it occurred to me that I must have looked in quite a state. I felt my cheeks flush, and I wasn't sure why. I didn't even know this tall, handsome man with the black rectangular glasses and the mop of dark wavy hair. And yet, this was the closest I'd been to any man since … before.

"Please. You must let me repay you somehow," I replied. "At least let me buy you a coffee?" By then I'd already given up any thoughts of making it to my interview.

"You know," he said, "coffee sounds great."

We walked out of the subway together, Jason still holding on to my arm as I couldn't seem to stop shaking after the shock I'd had. We walked to a little café on the corner, and I bought us each a coffee and blueberry scones.

We sat and talked for a long time, and I felt myself relaxing, smiling, more than I had allowed myself in quite a long time.

Finally, Jason looked at his watch. "I'm really sorry, Jules, but I have to run. I have a meeting to get to this afternoon."

"Of course. I didn't mean to take over your day." I felt my cheeks flush again.

"Believe me, I'd rather stay here and continue talking to you."

I pushed the last bit of pastry around on my plate. "I know I've already said it but thank you again. For what you did back there. A scone hardly feels like sufficient repayment."

"How about dinner then?" he'd said. "A real date with you, one that doesn't start off with you in tears, feels like a fair exchange."

"Oh … I, yes, I'd love that," I stammered. And I found that it was true. For the first time in a very long time, I was interested in someone again.

"Tonight then?"

It seemed fast, but I already couldn't wait to see him again.

"Yes," I'd said, writing down my number for him.

As he turned to walk out of the café, I felt myself smiling at his receding form and I couldn't seem to stop.

I wish I could still muster up those feelings now. I wish I could push the past back into the recesses of my mind where I've tried to keep it locked away for so long. I want nothing more than to snuggle into Jason and drift off to sleep. But I already feel a new distance growing between us, the secrets piling up like an insurmountable barrier. If only I could tell him what's going on, maybe then he'd understand why I wriggle out from underneath his arm, choosing instead to be alone with my thoughts, but I can't. There's so much about me that he still doesn't know.

I lie with my eyes open, staring into the darkness, willing sleep to come, but it evades me, slipping through my fingers like a darting minnow.

Chapter 8

Then

"You should go for the red one. With your dark hair, it'll really make it pop," Emily said.

Jenny stared at her reflection in the mirror, holding up one of Emily's many designer dresses. It had a low V-shaped neckline, and it was cinched at the waist with a narrow gold belt.

Tori, Nessa, and I sat cross-legged on Emily's bed nodding along agreeably.

Jenny thumbed the hem of the dress, the satiny fabric sliding between her fingers. "I don't think I could wear something like this," she said.

"You totally can. Tori did an amazing job with your hair—we'll just add a little makeup and you'll look like a total knockout," Emily replied confidently as she scrutinized Jenny's image in the mirror. "Why don't you try it on?"

"H—here?" Jenny stammered.

"Sure, we're all friends, right?"

I could tell Jenny was uncomfortable, shifting her weight from foot to foot, but then she caught Emily's gaze in the mirror, the rest of us sitting behind her, her loyal entourage.

I felt my stomach twist for Jenny. I wouldn't have wanted to change in front of everyone either. The others did it all the time. They'd try on each other's clothes, pulling off their tops to reveal lacy bras over full breasts and tanned, flat stomachs. They were so comfortable with their own bodies, and with each other's, that they never seemed to give it a second thought, though I supposed if I looked like them I might have felt the same way. But I didn't. My skin was a milky white and all of my child-like cotton bras had been purchased by my mother at the only department store in my hometown.

Jenny slipped off the oversized T-shirt she'd been wearing, letting it fall to the ground. Her thin arms were quick to cover her bare stomach as she shimmied into Emily's dress. It hung loose on her willowy body, made for the soft curves of someone like Emily.

Emily looked at Jenny appraisingly. "It's a little loose, but here, I can fix that." She pulled a pin out of a ceramic jewelry box atop her dresser and began to adjust the dress at Jenny's back.

Jenny's hands flew to her small breasts, which were nearly exposed in the process. "Oh, please don't pin it," she said. "I wouldn't want to ruin the dress."

It occurred to me that Emily's dress was probably more expensive than anything Jenny had ever worn before.

"Don't even worry about it," Emily said casually. "I, like, never wear this anymore."

I saw Jenny's cheeks redden. Emily's flippant attitude about an expensive dress probably only made Jenny feel more out of place in it.

"What do we think, girls?" Emily said, turning to us, her eager audience.

Tori gave Jenny two thumbs up.

"Ohh, I'll do your makeup!" Nessa squealed, pulling a matte

black tube out of her purse. Inside, I knew, was her favorite lipstick, a deep velvety red.

Jenny looked to me, her eyes locking on mine, desperate for approval. "You look really pretty, Jenny," I said sincerely. She smiled shyly, though I could tell she was starting to feel it: that rush that comes with being noticed.

"Just one more thing," Emily added as she whisked Jenny's thick blue glasses frames off her face.

Jenny squinted her eyes, blinking rapidly. "But I need those."

"Ugh, fine, we'll bring them," Emily said with a sigh, shoving the frames into Jenny's purse. "But you might want to consider contacts."

Nessa did Jenny's makeup, applying mascara to her lashes and the perfect shade of red to her lips, while the rest of us took turns sipping from a bottle of vodka that Emily produced from the bottom drawer of her dresser. I was starting to get more accustomed to the sensation of alcohol warming a trail from my throat to my stomach and could now manage a few sips without wincing embarrassingly.

Emily turned on some music and she danced around the room, her pleated skirt rising into the air as she twirled, revealing her white, lace panties. She looked so free, her arms outstretched, her face angled toward the sky, gold hair swirling around her, and I wondered in that moment what it might be like to feel so unencumbered. It was a foreign concept for me, who was constantly worried about how the rest of the world saw me. I could never seem to lose myself the way Emily could.

"There! Done!" Nessa announced.

Jenny walked over to the mirror and studied her reflection with an awestruck look on her face. She'd been transformed into someone else, someone who belonged at Emily's side. I didn't realize it then, but I had too.

* * *

We walked out into the hallway giggling and laughing, all of us feeling fuzzy from the vodka. The thin strap of the little black dress I'd borrowed from Nessa slid down my bare shoulder. I picked it up, and Tori pushed it back down again with a laugh. Even Jenny was smiling. She really was quite pretty when she smiled. I hadn't noticed before.

"Jenny?" a voice called from the student lounge.

I turned to see a game of Monopoly set up on one of the lounge tables. Abby, Lizzy, and Beth—Jenny's friends—were hunched over the board.

"You look … different, Jen," Lizzy said.

"Thanks," Jenny replied, already a little unsteady on her feet. I couldn't tell if it was the borrowed heels or the alcohol. She looked like a fawn taking its first steps. Bambi lost in the woods.

"Are you going out?" Beth asked, her eyes growing round. She was wearing pajamas printed with teddy bears holding red balloons.

Emily rolled her eyes and sighed impatiently.

"Um, yeah, we're going to this party downtown …" Jenny replied, once again looking down at the floor.

"At, like, a bar?" Beth asked incredulously.

Jenny nodded.

"How are you even going to get in?"

Emily huffed. "She's with us. That won't be an issue. Besides, look at her, no bouncer alive is turning her down tonight."

Jenny's cheeks burned a crimson red, nearly matching the shade of her borrowed dress.

Emily looped her arm through Jenny's. "Come on, girls. We don't want to be late."

We crammed into a cab that was idling outside of our hall. We piled into the back, a tangle of bare legs and stiletto heels. Nessa sat on Tori's lap, leaning her head backwards out the open window. She closed her eyes against the evening air, smiling as her dark hair whipped around her, shining in the moonlight.

She looked wild, reckless. That was back when we believed that we were invincible, that tragedy could never touch us. We didn't think anything could.

The club was crowded, warm bodies, damp with sweat, pressed against one another as the music pulsed in our ears. It was so loud that I could feel the bass thudding in my chest.

Nate somehow spotted Tori in the crowd and pushed his way through the throngs of people dancing, making out, and throwing back shots with their groups of friends.

He kissed Tori on the cheek and then yelled something that I couldn't hear. I saw his mouth working, but I couldn't make out what he was trying to tell me.

He mimed taking a shot, and I finally realized that he was asking if he could buy us a round of drinks. Tori was already nodding in agreement. I wasn't sure I needed another drink, but one more couldn't hurt, right? Jenny looked to me. I could tell that she was already drunk and didn't want the shot.

"You don't have to," I yelled, leaning in close to her ear.

"It's okay," she yelled back. "I'm fine."

She gave Nate a thumbs-up.

He smiled at us before he made his way to the bar. He returned only moments later with handfuls of thick shot glasses brimming with amber liquid. I didn't know what was in those glasses, but I was starting to think that maybe one more shot *could* hurt.

But then Nate's friends appeared behind him with matching shot glasses in their hands. "These are my buddies, Steven and Alex," he shouted.

Alex. He looked familiar, though I couldn't quite place him. He was wearing a backwards hat, soft dark curls poking out from underneath, and his strong arms and broad chest strained against his baseball T-shirt.

He looked at me and I felt myself blushing. I willed myself to be cool, to stop looking so desperate, but my cheeks betrayed me.

"I think I know you," Alex said, looking at me inquisitively.

I shrugged and locked my eyes on his. I tried to mimic Emily's confidence, her feigned innocence.

"Oh! You're the girl I spilled my beer on at homecoming!" he suddenly recollected. "Man, I'm so sorry. I tried to apologize but by the time I put the rest of my drink down and turned around, I couldn't find you."

"It's cool," I said, hoping I did, in fact, sound cool.

"Nah, it was my fault. Lemme get you a drink," he replied.

Is he flirting with me? Is that even possible? Alex was officially the hottest guy who'd ever spoken to me, never mind hit on me.

"How about a shot?" I said, taking one from Nate's outstretched hands.

I don't know where my sudden burst of confidence came from. Maybe I was emboldened by Alex's attention, or maybe it was just the alcohol talking, but in the moment I felt like I was on top of the world.

Alex clinked his glass against mine and I threw my head back, swallowing it down with a practiced ease that I didn't actually possess.

"I'm Alexander. But everyone calls me Alex," he said.

"Juliana. But everyone calls me Jules." I'd only just learned his name, and I already knew I was in trouble.

* * *

As the night wore on, the crowd began to thin and Alex and I found a space at the bar. I leaned against it, feeling the sticky wood against my exposed back. Alex stood in front of me, his arm wrapped around my waist as we talked. He was so close to me, I could smell the whiskey on his breath, feel his leg pressed between my thighs.

Tori had spent most of the night making out with Nate, and Nessa and Emily were on the dance floor, their bodies writhing against one another making every man in the bar salivate. All except Alex. He didn't seem interested in anything but me. And I was reveling in it. I could feel the power shifting into my hands as Alex leaned into me. I could feel how badly he wanted me as he looked me up and down, his eyes lingering on my breasts, which pressed against the thin material of Nessa's dress. There was something so delicious in being desired by a man who once upon a time wouldn't have even noticed I existed.

"I want you so badly," he growled into my ear as his hand slid up the back of my head, his fingers splayed in my hair.

I smiled wickedly.

"Do you have any idea how beautiful you are?" he all but moaned.

I did. In that moment I felt it. Maybe for the first time in my life. But I wasn't going to give in to him that easily.

I also wasn't going to tell him that I was a virgin. It wasn't that I was opposed to having sex exactly. It was more just that it hadn't happened. The closest I'd ever come was letting Billy Matter, a round-faced band geek with shaggy hair and worn sneakers, kiss me at our junior prom. It had been such a horrible experience, his thick, wet tongue sitting in my mouth like a slug, that I hadn't cared much to do it again. I thought maybe something was wrong with me, I thought maybe I just wasn't interested in sex. But it turned out I was wrong. I was *very* much interested in sex. My body burned with it. I felt it pulling at me, an unfamiliar tingle, that I'd never known before.

Alex leaned in closer and I knew he was going to kiss me. I could see it unfolding before it even happened: his hand in my hair, his warm lips, and I wanted it so badly that I felt hollowed out with it. He started at my neck, his kisses gentle grazes at first before becoming more intense, greedy. I let my head loll back, my neck bared to him, inviting him to go further.

As he made his way up to my jaw, and just nearly my lips, I heard a familiar voice at my side.

"Well, well, sorry to interrupt, you two," Emily said, a Cheshire-cat grin on her face. Her cheeks were flushed a sweet, cotton-candy pink from dancing, and perspiration glittered on her chest. Behind her stood a man I'd never met before, his arms snaked proprietarily around Emily's waist as he eyed her hungrily. He seemed older, more refined, with stubble darkening his square jaw.

"Jenny is a bit of a mess," Emily added, pulling her full pink lips into a pout. "I think she had too much to drink, the poor thing." She pointed to the edge of the dance floor where Jenny was leaning against a wall, her head down, her hair a black veil across her face.

"You'll take her back to campus, won't you, Jules?" Emily rested her head against the man's chest.

I wanted to say no. I wanted to tell Emily that Jenny wasn't my problem. But I also didn't want Alex to think poorly of me, selfishly refusing to help a drunk girl back to her room, and I knew none of the others would volunteer to go in my place. Tori and Nessa were still on the dance floor, their arms around their partners of the moment.

Emily didn't even wait for my response before she waved Jenny over to us.

"You're the best, Jules," Emily said, as Jenny gripped my arm, struggling to stay on her feet.

I lead Jenny outside to hail us a cab. *Fucking Jenny.* I was about to have a moment with Alex before I was torn away to babysit. *How did she become my responsibility? I hardly even know her!*

"I'm sorry, Jules, I didn't mean—" Jenny started, before promptly falling to her knees and vomiting into the street.

Chapter 9

Now

Jason yawns awake, an exaggerated sigh. He folds his arms behind his head, his bare chest just visible above our white, down comforter.

"You're up early," he says questioningly.

"Yeah," I reply. "Couldn't sleep." What I don't tell him is that I've been up most of the night tossing and turning, Jenny's words rattling around in my head. *Did you think I'd be so easily forgotten?* Or that I slept fitfully when I did sleep, images of my time at Westbridge haunting my dreams and startling me back to reality, which is becoming nearly as frightening. Because the truth is, I *haven't* forgotten, as much as I've wanted to. Not for one single day. Jenny was there with me when I graduated. She was there when I got my first job at a law firm. She was with me on my wedding day, at what should have been the happiest moment of my life as I walked down the aisle to a misty-eyed Jason who thought he was marrying the girl of his dreams. I've never been able to put what happened to Jenny behind me.

"Well since you're up ..." he says suggestively, sliding his hand over my thigh. I recoil instinctively, and I can all but feel his ego deflate. This part used to be so easy for us, the intimacy. We just fit together, Jason and I. Sometimes it feels like he knows my body better than I know it myself. It's as if he's in my head while we're having sex. But my head is not in the right place right now, and I'm afraid to let him in, not when I know that there's so much I'm holding back.

I know Jason. I know that he likes milk and sugar in his coffee, I know that he hates pulp in his orange juice, I know he loves football and craft beer and medium-rare steak. He's uncomplicated, my husband—what you see is what you get. But he doesn't know me in the same way. Not all of me anyway. I know he believes that he does, but in reality he fell in love with the pieces of me that I've offered up to him, the bits I thought were worthy of his love. But the part I've kept hidden—the darkness I fear still clings to the core of me—I've always worried that once he sees it, he won't ever be able to look at me the same way again. And I just couldn't bear that. Jason is the only person who has ever made me feel like I might be okay. But right now, I'm afraid that I can't keep the ugliness hidden, not with thoughts of Jenny, of the past, set loose in my mind.

"Or not then," Jason says, pulling back his hand. I can tell he's hurt.

"I'm sorry, babe." I put my hand over his on top of the comforter, hoping to soften the sting of my rejection. "I'm just exhausted and I have a lot on my mind with work. I have a huge deposition coming up this week and I don't feel prepared." The lie slips right off my tongue.

"Is that what kept you up? Don't stress, Jules. You always find a way to pull it all together." He squeezes my hand reassuringly.

My stomach churns with guilt over lying to him. Kind, trusting Jason. But I don't have any other choice. How could I tell him about Jenny—the real Jenny *or* the impostor? Maybe I should have told him when we first met. Before he fell for me, before I fell for him, certainly before we got married. But it was so hard to shatter the image he had of me. I wanted so badly to be the woman he thought I was, the woman I saw reflected back at me when I looked into his eyes, that I thought maybe I could pretend just for a little while. I promised myself I'd tell him the truth soon. But the longer I put it off, the easier it became to ignore the past and live in the present with him, to become the person he thought I was.

I didn't want to fall for Jason at first. I told myself that I didn't belong with someone like him, someone so wonderful and kind. I told myself I didn't deserve him. But he made it so easy to fall in love with him.

On our second date, Jason told me he was taking me for a special dinner at his favorite place in the city. I'd put on a sexy black dress, one that clung to my hips and accentuated my figure. I was on a mission to impress him after I'd been in such a state the day we met. I paired the dress with a pair of buttery leather heels. They were the nicest shoes I owned, and far out of my budget at the time, but they were my gift to myself when I'd graduated law school. I'd never even worn them out of my apartment before. I didn't go out much in those days. At least not anywhere that required stilettos. But when Jason rapped on my door, I found him in a black knit sweater, his thumbs hooked into the pockets of his jeans. He rocked on the heels of his sneakers and let out of long, deep whistle of appreciation.

"Wow, you look … amazing," he'd said. "Though, I hate to tell you, severely overdressed for this particular dinner."

"It was a little hard to plan, considering you refused to tell me where we were going," I replied playfully.

"You're right. I should have warned you. You're going to want more comfortable shoes."

Where could he possibly be taking me that would require practical footwear?

I poured Jason a glass of wine from the uncorked bottle that was chilling in my refrigerator. It belonged to my roommate, a girl I'd met through an online posting seeking a roommate for a vacancy in her two-bedroom apartment in Brooklyn. We generally kept to ourselves, each living our own quiet lives, but I didn't think she'd miss just one glass.

Jason sipped his wine, and I ignored the tiny wince he'd reflexively made at the wine that was, in all likelihood, sour.

I walked into the bedroom, which was only a few steps away from the living area where Jason sat on our ugly, brown suede couch, his ankle casually crossed over his knee.

I tried on a number of outfits, discarding the rejected items onto my bed. None of them felt right for a date. Not with Jason, the first man I actually felt a connection with in years. Feeling defeated, I pulled on a cream-colored turtle-neck sweater, black jeans, and a pair of tall black boots with flat soles. I ran a brush through my hair, which had become tangled after trying so many outfits. But after a few strokes with a paddle brush, it had a healthy shine and fell about my shoulders in soft waves. *Not bad*, I thought, studying my reflection appraisingly. I looked like someone who might actually belong with a man as handsome and charming as Jason.

I walked out of the bedroom and stood before Jason, suddenly feeling a little shy under his gaze. But he smiled warmly, a dimple appearing in his left cheek, and I immediately felt the tension easing out of my shoulders.

"I think I like you better this way," he said, making me blush.

We walked out of my apartment building arm in arm. It was early December and there was a wintry chill swirling through the city. Not the kind that reaches deep into your bones and keeps you shivering under your down parka, but a gentle frost that turns the tip of your nose a rosebud pink and feels as refreshing as peppermint.

Jason raised one gloved hand into the air to hail a cab, which immediately pulled over to the curb. A lucky break in my part of town. We slid onto the bench seat in the back of the cab. The warm interior smelled of worn leather.

Jason directed the driver to Central Park. The taxi crawled through the city streets, crowded with tourists wanting to see the holiday attractions, but I didn't mind. I stared out the window, mesmerized by the glittering Christmas lights, the city polished with tinsel. I caught my reflection in the glass, my face surrounded by the glowing lights, and I felt truly happy.

Christmas has always been my favorite time of year. When I was a child, my father and I would go chop down a tree together, and later my mother and I would string popcorn and cranberries into long strands to wrap around it, cups of hot cocoa steaming at our elbows as we worked. They were some of my happiest memories. Before everything had all gone so wrong. And driving through the decorated city with Jason brought back those same nostalgic feelings.

When the taxi arrived at Central Park, Jason took my hand and helped me onto the sidewalk. Horse-drawn carriages lined the road waiting for passengers to huddle under the wool blankets inside. I took off one glove and stroked the muzzle of a gray and white dappled horse. It felt as soft as velvet beneath my fingers. The horse huffed, its breath escaping its nose in a frosty puff, making Jason and me laugh.

Hand in hand, we strolled past artists painting cartoon-like portraits, street vendors selling touristy souvenirs, and carts offering warm, soft pretzels, the smell of burning coal wafting through the air. Finally, we reached a hot dog stand and Jason stopped.

"Here it is," he said. "My favorite dinner spot in all of New York City."

At first, I thought he was joking, but then he turned to the man behind the stall and ordered two hot dogs.

"You want relish?" Jason asked me.

I wrinkled my nose. "No, thanks."

Guess he wasn't kidding.

"Thanks, Leon," Jason said, handing over a few crumpled-up bills to the vendor.

"For you, anytime," Leon replied with a prideful grin.

Jason handed me a hot dog and a white paper napkin.

"Shall we?" he asked, again offering me his arm.

I linked my arm through his, taking a bite of the warm hot dog. It was surprisingly delicious, and Jason smiled at me knowingly.

As we walked through Central Park together, fat white snowflakes began to fall between the lacy elms that had been wrapped in soft white twinkle lights. We talked about our families, about our plans for the holidays, about everything and nothing.

And while we walked, I watched him, silhouetted against the landscape of the city, snowflakes clinging to his hair, and the streetlights casting a silvery halo over his form. He seemed too perfect to be real.

"Shall we go somewhere to warm up?" he asked. I nodded in agreement as he laced his gloved fingers through mine.

We walked to a quaint little bake shop, its front windows bordered with twinkling lights and frost, where Jason ordered us two steaming cappuccinos and a huge slice of red velvet cake. The decadent cake melted in my mouth, and I savored the taste as much as I was savoring this incredible evening with Jason.

We must have sat for hours in that bake shop. We were so wrapped up in one another, that we'd completely lost track of time. I'd forgotten that the rest of the world existed, just for a moment. It wasn't until we heard the jangle of the shop owner's keys as he swept up the floor, subtly hinting that it was time for him to close up, we realized that we'd probably overstayed our welcome.

By the time we reemerged onto the city streets, New York City had been transformed. Its once cold, sharp edges were marshmallow soft under a blanket of fresh snow. Its grime hidden under a layer of pristine white. It felt like the city and I had both been given a clean slate that night, like anything was possible. I looked up, watching the snowflakes drift lazily between the towering buildings around us, and it felt as though we were in a snow globe. In that moment everything was perfect.

Until it wasn't. Jason escorted me home after our date, kissing me for the first time in the chilled December air, our noses cold and our eyelashes wet with snow, and I felt a shock run through me. An electrical current that I hadn't felt in a very long time. And it brought me back to that time, back at Westbridge, when it all began to go wrong.

"Goodnight," I said, breaking the spell.

"When can I see you again?" he asked.

"I … I'm not sure." My cold hands fumbled to open the door.

"I'll call you." His voice was resolute. "I really like you, Jules."

The truth was, I really liked him too. I didn't want to admit it to myself, but I was already falling for him. Even then. I told myself that I'd tell him the truth eventually. When the time was right. But when is the right time to tell your husband that you're a terrible person?

Chapter 10

Now

I climb out of bed and begin to get ready for work, splashing cold water on my face and brushing my teeth. I put on a pale gray suit with a pencil skirt and a fitted jacket and brush my hair until it shines.

I study my reflection in the small medicine cabinet mirror. *Who am I now?* Am I still the same girl I was back then, back at Westbridge? I've tried so hard to leave the past behind me and to become someone new, someone better, but I can't help but feel like it still clings to me, its dark claws sunk deep into my skin. When I look at myself now, I see the lawyer, the wife, the woman who has trained herself to smile even when she doesn't want to. But I can also see the girl I used to be, a shadowy specter peering over my shoulder. *Is it really possible to start over? To change? Or are we all destined to be haunted by ghosts we thought we'd left behind?*

Jason steps into the cramped bathroom behind me and brushes my hair off my neck before kissing it softly.

"Are you sure you're okay?" he asks. "Something seems different with you lately."

59

Can he see her too?

"I'm fine," I reply, a little more abruptly than I'd intended to. I can't help but feel on edge.

"I'm going to shower then," Jason says with a sigh, as he lifts his shirt over his head.

I hate that there's tension building between us, that it's my fault. I make a promise to myself that as soon as I deal with these emails, I'll make it up to Jason.

I finish putting my things together and start my walk to the subway. It's unseasonably warm for October today, and if things were different, I might have slowed my pace and enjoyed the last remnants of warm sunshine before the harsh winter months set in. Although it's been a long time since I've been in school, this time of year will always remind me of freshly sharpened pencils, new backpacks, and the sound of leaves crunching under the soles of carefully selected school sneakers.

By the time I finish my commute—another trip whizzing beneath the streets of New York City—and arrive at my office, I find that I can't bring myself to step into my office building. Behind the massive door leading into the minimalist lobby and its glass elevators, waiting to whisk me up to the twenty-seventh floor to the Law Offices of Miller & Marquee, life is proceeding as usual. Everyone else blissfully unaware that I'm standing on a precipice, dangerously close to falling over the edge. I know Tori said that if we just ignore Jenny's emails this will all be over soon, but in this moment I can't shake the dark sense of foreboding that washes over me, telling me that nothing will ever be the same again.

"After you, Ms. Daniels," a deep voice says. It takes me a moment to register that he's speaking to me. Even though Jason and I have been married for nearly three years, his last name, at least to the extent that it's used to refer to me, still feels foreign to my ears.

I changed my name immediately after we returned from our

honeymoon in Hawaii. I couldn't drop my maiden name, Johnson, fast enough. I was Mrs. Jason Daniels. Juliana Daniels. A new name, a new start, a new me. *Or so I'd hoped.*

"Oh, thank you, Mr. Barrett," I replied, quickly snapping out of my daze and hurrying into the lobby ahead of my boss. Mark Barrett is a hefty man with perpetually ruddy cheeks, and a reputation for lacking in patience. Today he's wearing a dull brown suit and the remnants of his breakfast seem to have landed on his tie. I hear him breathing heavily as he struts behind me toward the elevator. I'm dreading the prospect of sharing an elevator with him, having to make small talk in the notoriously slow elevator as it crawls up twenty-seven floors. I never know what to say to Mr. Barrett. Mark. I don't even know what to call him. The other associates and I refer to all of the other partners by their first names, but Mr. Barrett is different. Despite his disheveled appearance, he generally insists on formality, his mouth always turned down into a scowl as if he anticipates that the world will inevitably fail to meet his rigorous standards.

The elevator doors slide open and I stick my hand out to hold them open while Barrett makes his way toward me. I'm tempted to let go, to bash the "door close" button and pretend I hadn't seen him, but instead I smile reverently as he squeezes past me. Before long, we're alone in the cramped elevator car with nothing but the sound of his breathing to break the silence.

"So. Ms. Daniels." The commanding sound of Barrett's voice snaps me to attention, my spine straightening at the mere mention my name. "I've heard talk that you're going to be considered for partnership this year."

This is not news to me. I've been working hard for this promotion, and I knew it was being floated around by the senior partners for possible consideration at their annual partnership meeting in a few months, but hearing Barrett speak it out loud makes it all the more real.

"That being said," he continues, "before I cast my vote, I'm going to give you an important assignment. Consider this a trial run."

I don't know whether to be excited or insulted. I settle on grateful. Barrett only works with a small group of cherry-picked associates. He rarely trusts anyone else to touch his files. "Thank you, Mr. Barrett. I really appreciate the opportunity."

He snorts derisively before stepping out of the elevator and into our office suite. I notice that this time he doesn't hold the door for me before he skulks down the hallway and into his corner office.

I step into my own office, with its pale green carpeting and stark white walls, and settle in behind my wooden desk that's an obvious imitation of real mahogany. My officemate, Andrew, isn't in this morning. He has a deposition today and will most likely be out of the office for most of the day. Which is probably for the best. I like Andrew, but we tend to chat when we're both in the office, a welcome reprieve from the stress of our jobs, but I already know I'm going to have enough difficulty focusing today as it is.

My phone stares up at me from my desk. Its screen black and cold. But I can't stop thinking about the email that's sitting inside of it. I can see my mirrored reflection in the dark screen, but it feels as though it's Jenny's face that is staring back at me, her eyes blank and unforgiving.

My hand slowly reaches out for the phone, but just as I'm about to switch it on, to delete yet another of Jenny's emails, Barrett's deep, booming voice makes me jump.

"Ms. Daniels. Here is the file you'll be working on." He has an accordion file tucked under one arm as he steps into my office. I watch him curiously as he pulls the door closed behind him. As a general rule, the doors to the associates' offices remain open at all times. The partners like to be able to walk by and see that we're hard at work at any given moment.

"I think you'll find that this is a special case," Barrett continues.

"And our client is relying on our discretion. I hope that I can rely on you as well."

It's a strange introduction to a case file. *Don't all of our clients rely on our discretion as their attorneys?* But, then again, Barrett is a strange man and I need his vote in favor of my partnership, and so I nod solemnly as he places the file on my desk.

"Of course. I understand," I reply.

"I'm giving you the relevant medical records. Familiarize yourself with the facts of this case, and then I'll be requesting your help preparing a motion for summary judgment."

A motion for summary judgment on a file I've had no previous involvement with will be a big task, but I can't turn down this opportunity to get on Barrett's good side.

"Sure. I'll start looking it over today."

Barrett nods curtly and leaves my office as quickly as he appeared.

That's it. With this new assignment on top of all of my other cases, I can't afford to be distracted today. Whoever is sending these emails can't get in my way of making partner. I know Tori said to just ignore it, but I feel like I'm being terrorized by my own phone and I need to put a stop to it.

I consider blocking the email account, but as soon as I see the now familiar email address, the thumbnail photo of an eighteen-year-old Jenny, a wave of anger washes over me at this faceless, nameless person who is dragging up the past I worked so hard to put behind me. And so instead, I open my email app and type out a reply to Jenny's last email:

Who is this?

I stare at my phone as if I expect the answer to come instantaneously. But my inbox is eerily quiet. I refresh the screen, and see the little wheel spinning endlessly. *Come on already.* Finally my inbox loads. No new emails.

Shaking my head, as if I could loosen the tension prickling under my skin like raindrops, I drop my phone into my bag. Out of sight, out of mind. Or so I tell myself.

I spend a good portion of the work day poring through Barrett's new case file. It's a wrongful death case, wherein our client, an anesthesiologist, is being sued for allegedly administering the incorrect dosage of anesthetics while the plaintiff was undergoing a complicated heart surgery. This isn't my first case regarding the administration of anesthesia, and it's a fairly routine defense: we'll ask our expert witness to review the medications administered and determine whether the plaintiff was given the appropriate dosages in light of his height, weight, and any preexisting conditions. I can't imagine why Barrett suggested that this case in particular was so special.

The photocopied records Barrett gave me are dog-eared and jumbled, probably having passed through numerous associates' hands during the life of the case. After a few hours of combing through the voluminous file, I grow frustrated and decide to request the original hospital chart from the file room instead. At least I know *that* will be in some semblance of order as we have a duty to maintain any original records in the condition in which they were given to us. I dial down to the file room and place my request. A few moments later, a file clerk drops it on my desk.

I get back to work, combing through the chart. It takes me some time before I see the inconsistency, but once I do, it feels as though it's leaping off the page at me. The original operating report lists Nurse Nancy Ravit as having assisted during the surgery. But I don't recall seeing her name in the version of the records Barrett had given me. I flip back through the photocopied records and find the operating report—it lists one Gabriella Marion as the surgical nurse. The name "Nancy Ravit" is nowhere to be found.

I dial the extension for Barrett's office.

"What is it?" he barks into the phone.

"I just wanted to follow up on something I noticed in this file. The nurse, Nancy Ravit, did anyone interview her?"

Barrett hesitates for a fraction of a second, but it's enough to make my antennae stand up. "Where did you …? Never mind. It doesn't matter. That name is completely irrelevant to this motion. I need you to focus on the task at hand." He slams the phone down with a click.

Something isn't adding up. Why would there be two versions of the same operating report? The two reports are identical with the exception of the name of the surgical nurse. I think the issue through … If I was on the other side of this case, I'd be trying to track down any witnesses who were in the operating room the day that the plaintiff died. But in my review of the file, I didn't find any deposition testimony from Nurse Ravit. No affidavits, no subpoenas, or any other mention of Nurse Ravit at all. It's as if, as far as the plaintiff's attorney is concerned, Nurse Ravit never existed. *I wonder if that was the point.*

This time I decide to check the file room myself, taking the elevator two floors down to the cavernous room stuffed with rows of accordion files identical to the one on my desk. Each case is assigned its own coded number, and it takes me a few minutes to find the remaining files on Barrett's case on the dusty shelves, and even longer still to find what I need: the copy of the hospital chart that we would have been required to provide the plaintiff's attorneys in the early stages of this case.

I pull out our discovery exchange, a thick slab of paper bound together by a sharp metal fastener. I slide to the floor with the heavy document in my arms and lean my back against the cool metal filing shelves. I flip through the pages in the dim overhead lighting until I find the operating room records. Just as I suspected: the version of the records we disclosed to the opposing counsel lists Gabriella Marion as the surgical nurse. The name "Nancy Ravit" is glaringly absent.

The records must have been altered in an effort to conceal

Nurse Ravit, a potentially important witness, from the opposing counsel. Stunned, I flip to the end of the discovery response to find that it was signed by Mark Barrett, Esq. himself, not one of the associates as would usually be the case with a routine exchange of records.

I make a photocopy of the doctored operating room report, putting the discovery exchange back where I found it on the shelf. I then retrieve the original hospital chart from my office and make a copy of the real report. I know that I'm going to have a decision to make: do I report Barrett, and by extension our client, who most likely had something to do with this as well, or do I keep my mouth shut—violating my ethical responsibilities as an attorney but securing the promotion I so desperately want?

I pull out a plain manila envelope and drop the two versions of the records inside. I want to take the weekend to mull over the decision.

As I shove the envelope into my shoulder bag, I see my phone lying inside. I can't believe I managed to forget about it for so long.

I switch on the screen to discover that "Jenny" has replied to my email. I open it with trembling hands.

You're asking the wrong question, Jules. It's not who I am that you should be worried about, but what I'm going to do next. I know you lied about what happened that night. You all did. And until you tell the truth, this isn't going to end. I will destroy your perfect lives, piece by piece. It will be a fun little game.

Just like the ones you and your friends used to play. You remember those, don't you?

I scroll to the bottom of her email to find a photo that rips the breath from my lungs.

It's a photo of the five of us: Me, Tori, Nessa, Emily, and Jenny. All of us smiling, wearing dresses with hems that are too short and heels that are too high. I remember that night. The night of the

Valentine's Day party. Jenny was wearing a blue dress borrowed from my closet. The same one I'd worn my very first night out at Westbridge. We'd walked out into the night with vodka on our breath and trouble in our eyes. We looked so happy, so free. If only that hadn't been the night that destroyed Jenny Teller.

Chapter 11

Then

"So, are you gonna see him again?" Emily asked, her chin propped on one hand as she leaned over the dining-hall table.

"I ... I hope so," I replied, feeling far less bold than I had the night I met Alex.

"You two seemed really into each other the other night. But you haven't heard from him?"

"We didn't exchange numbers or anything." I could hear a wisp of defensiveness creeping into my voice. The fact that I hadn't heard from Alex was already nibbling at my insecurities, and to hear Emily say it out loud, in front of everyone, got my back up. But she was smiling at me innocently, with a dreamy look in her eyes, as though she was genuinely interested in my love life. I wondered whether she had done it intentionally—found a loose thread and pulled at it just to see how far I'd unravel. But that was unfair, I thought. Emily hadn't ever been cruel to me. It was just my own insecurities whispering in my ear.

"Tori could have Nate give him your number, couldn't you, Tor?" Emily asked, turning to Tori who seemed far more interested in her grilled cheese sandwich than hearing another word about Alex. I'd probably driven her crazy talking about him since that night at the bar, and after nearly a week of hearing about our "almost moment", I was sure she'd had enough.

"Sure," she offered between bites.

I felt my hopes soar.

"Might look a little desperate though," she added.

And I felt them crash back down again, ashamed of myself for *being* so desperate.

"Well, I'm sure you'll see him again," Nessa offered, her voice warm and reassuring.

Jenny stared down at her salad, pushing leaves of lettuce around her plate but barely eating more than a bite. She'd been spending more time with us lately. Lunches at The Hill, watching *The Bachelor* on Monday nights in our pajamas and slippers, a bowl of popcorn passed around the group, but she'd been quiet, even by Jenny's standards, since that night at the bar. I think she was embarrassed by how drunk she'd gotten.

"Hey, Jenny," a quiet voice said, pulling our attention to the head of the table. Abby stood there, holding a tray of food: a greasy-looking burger, a plate of fries, and a pile of cookies. We looked up at her from our seats at the table, at an angle that, as Emily would say, was not particularly flattering for her "pudgy face and upturned nose". It didn't help matters that her mane of dark, frizzy hair seemed particularly unruly that day, giving her the appearance of being even larger, or that she was wearing a T-shirt that was just a touch too tight, revealing the outline of the fleshy bulge of her stomach curving over her jeans. "You're not having lunch with us today?"

"Uh, no, I uh … I just ate with the girls," Jenny replied.

"Oh, '*the girls*'. I see," Abby remarked. "Well if you ever feel like hanging out with your *friends* again, you know where to find us." Abby walked away, her chin turned up, as she made her way across the dining hall to join Lizzy and Beth in a forgotten corner of the room.

"What's up with Flabby Abby?" Emily said, garnering snickers from the rest of the table. I cast my eyes over at Jenny. She smiled along dutifully, but I could tell that she didn't find Emily's remark particularly funny. To be honest, I hadn't either.

After lunch, Tori, Nessa, and Jenny had classes and I planned to go to the library to get a head start on a research paper I had coming up for World Literature 101. We parted ways outside of The Hill, and I shoved my hands into the pockets of my coat, my head bowed, bracing myself against the fall breeze that seemed to grow colder with each passing day.

"Jules, wait," Emily called. I stopped in my tracks, curious as to what she could possibly have to say to me. Emily rarely spoke to me at all, and certainly never outside of the presence of the rest of the group. "I don't have classes for the next few hours. Do you want to come back to my room and hang?"

A small voice in the back of my head reminded me that I had classwork to do, but I quickly silenced it. "Sure, sounds great."

* * *

"So, you really like him then?" Emily said as she hugged one of the fluffy throw pillows adorning her bed.

I picked up a matching pillow and pulled it close to me. "Yeah, I mean, I guess. I just met him …" I tried to sound casual. As if my night with Alex was nothing special, something that happened to me all the time, the way it surely did to Emily.

"He's cute, I guess," she conceded with a shrug. "I just don't see the point in settling down so early in the year. We just got here. Who knows who else you might meet. And college guys are just so … immature."

I nodded in agreement, but I think Emily could tell I was feeling disappointed that she hadn't given me her approval. I don't know why it mattered so much to me, but it did. It was as if she could sense my desperation for her acceptance radiating off me in waves. The problem was, she needed nothing from me in return.

"What about that guy you were with at the bar the other night?" I asked, deflecting. "Are you going to see him again?"

"Who, Nico? I thought it was just going to be a one-night thing but, I don't know … maybe," she replied, her eyes sliding upward as she seemed to mull over her options. "But that's different. Nico's not a college guy—he owns that new club downtown. Making these hookups a more regular occurrence could come in handy." She winked.

"Oh," I said, unsure how to reply. I'd never met anyone who was so cavalier about sex before. But what did I know? My perspective on the matter was admittedly narrow. The only person I'd ever really talked to about these kinds of things was Kelly, particularly leading up to our prom night when she and Owen booked a hotel room and planned to sleep together for the first time—a decision they'd spent months discussing, treating it with almost sacred reverence.

"But," Emily pressed on, gently resting her hand on my arm, "if you really want to see Alex again, I'll make it happen."

"You really don't have to. I don't want to look desperate or anything," I responded, picking at my thumbnail. "Maybe Tori was right. I should probably just leave it. If I'm meant to see him again, I will."

"I'd never make you look bad," Emily replied solemnly, her eyes locking on mine. "You trust me, don't you?"

"Of course I do," I replied without a moment's hesitation.

She smiled sweetly, before reaching into her nightstand and pulling out a handful of nail polishes in little glass bottles. "Do you want to do matching manis for tonight?"

"Sure," I responded. I'd made it. I was being welcomed into her inner circle. It felt like being ordained.

Emily chose a cotton-candy-pink polish for us, and as she

spread the first lick of glossy wet paint onto her nails, she asked, "Are you going to hook up with Alex if you see him again?"

"Oh … I … I don't know …" I stammered. I was caught off guard by her question and I wasn't sure how to respond. *Should I tell her that I'm a loser who'd barely ever been kissed? Or do I pretend that sex is no big deal?*

Emily looked at me as though she could read my thoughts, her sharp eyes probing my internal struggle.

"You *have* hooked up before, haven't you?" she asked.

I knew it was a test. That the answer I gave her would forever shape her view of me, and I desperately wanted give her the version of myself that she wanted to see.

"Of course I have," I said cavalierly. I reasoned that it wasn't a lie. I *had* let Billy Matter make out with me junior year, and some people would call that hooking up. I knew she meant sex, of course she did, but I told myself that it was just a little white lie, just stretching the truth a bit. But I don't think Emily believed my version of the truth. She looked at me almost pityingly.

I rushed to fill the silence, to fix my mistake. The words tumbled out of my mouth before I could stop them. "Well, I haven't had *sex*, but I've done, like, everything else. And really that's only because I hadn't found anyone worth sleeping with at my high school. But I totally would with the right guy."

"Good," she replied, seemly satisfied with my answer. "Because someone like Alex Caldwell is going to be expecting it, you know? We're in college now. Guys don't want to just, like, make out or whatever."

"Totally," I replied, my stomach churning with nerves at the thought. As much as I'd felt ready to sleep with Alex at the bar the previous week while I was drunk and feeling uninhibited, in the light of day the prospect was a little more frightening. And knowing he was *expecting* it made it even more anxiety-inducing. *What if I'm awkward? What if I'm not good at it? … What if I don't want to?*

"There are just *so* many girls here, and college guys have the attention span of two-year-olds. If they aren't getting what they want, they'll get bored." She blew on her nails, pretty in pink. "If you want to lock Alex down, you're going to have to give him what he wants."

"Definitely," I agreed, nodding along and hoping I sounded more confident than I felt.

"And, Jules?" Emily said as she passed me the bottle of nail polish. "Thank you for telling me your secret."

My virginity wasn't a *secret* exactly. It just wasn't something I'd wanted to advertise. I considered correcting her, but then her pretty blue eyes locked on mine.

"Real friends are meant to share secrets," she said.

And I decided that I wanted us to share mine.

Chapter 12

Now

I rush out of my office, nearly colliding with Andrew in the hallway.

His imposing frame blocks my path. The other associates jokingly call us the "odd couple", as I'm sure we do look quite mismatched: he with his towering height and broad shoulders set against my short stature and petite frame. But we hit it off the moment we met, a friendship forged in the trenches of Miller & Marquee. Which is fortunate, given how much time we're forced to spend together confined to our little office.

"Sneaking out early on a Friday, Jules?" he teases.

"No, I … well, yeah. You caught me," I concede, trying to sound lighthearted. I briefly consider confiding in Andrew about the discrepancy I discovered in Barrett's file. I trust him as a colleague, and I want someone, anyone, to tell me what I should do. *Even though a small voice inside of me reminds me that I already know …* But right now, I have more pressing concerns. Namely, Jenny.

The walls of this office feel like they're closing in on me, the air itself is suffocating, and I just want to get outside. Away from prying eyes, so that I can call Tori and tell her about the latest email, about the photo.

"Well, good for you. You never leave early."

I grit my teeth and force a smile. "Have a great weekend," I reply.

I make it all the way to the elevator bank, miraculously managing not to run into anyone else. I press the call button for the elevator and wait impatiently for it to arrive, the toe of my shoe grinding circles into the carpet.

Out of the corner of my eye I see Barrett approaching. He's at the far end of the hall, but it looks as though he's spotted me and is heading in my direction.

Come on, not now. With every passing moment I'm getting increasingly anxious to speak to Tori, and I'm just not prepared to discuss Barrett's file with him yet. Surely he's going to want to know my thoughts on the motion he asked me to prepare, but I need more time to think. I need to organize my thoughts before I decide what I'm going to do about this file, and I know I won't be able to think clearly until we come up with a plan to handle the Jenny situation. Right now my head is swimming, and I just need to get out of here. Now.

Mercifully the elevator arrives, and I dash inside. I vaguely register Barrett raising one arm and calling after me, but pretending I hadn't seen him, I press the "door closed" button and the doors grind shut before he manages to catch up with me.

The elevator begins its descent and I lean my back against its cool glass walls. *What the hell do I do now?*

When I finally step back out onto the city street, it's crowded with rush-hour commuters walking hurriedly down the cement sidewalks. A taxi blares its horn, and a city bus rumbles by. The sounds of this city, normally the faded soundtrack of my life, a gentle cadence in the background of my day, suddenly feel overwhelming, as though the city itself is angry, its usual hum growing to a mighty roar. My heart pounds in my chest as I will myself to calm down. *Everything is going to be okay. It was just words on a page, just a photo.* But it wasn't just any photo. It was a photo of *that* night. Someone, somewhere, knows what I did. I suddenly feel like I'm going to be sick.

I rush down the sidewalk, feeling my body being jostled by the passing crowds, like a tiny boat being tossed around by an angry sea. After I get about a block away from my office, far enough that I probably won't be spotted by any of my co-workers merrily on their way to a Friday happy hour, I collapse onto the nearest bench and dig my phone out of my bag.

I call Tori, my foot tapping anxiously against the sidewalk as I wait for her to pick up. "Come on, come on," I mutter under my breath.

"Thank God," I say breathlessly the moment I hear the call connect.

"Jules? Are you okay?"

"No, not really. Look, I know you said to ignore the … the emails, but—"

"Tell me you didn't …"

"I responded to the one we got last night."

"What did you say?" Her voice grows higher in alarm. I've gone off script.

"I wrote 'who is this?' Because clearly we know it's not …"

"Jenny." Tori finishes the sentence I couldn't bring myself to complete. "And did whoever-it-is answer you?"

"Yes, that's why I'm calling. She … he … whoever it is—"

"Wait, I think we should get Nessa on the line. She's going to want to hear this too."

Without waiting for my response, Tori puts me on hold. I try to collect myself as I wait, releasing the tension in my jaw that I hadn't realized I was clenching.

"Nessa, are you there?" Tori asks.

"Yes, I'm here and I'm so glad you guys called!" Nessa says enthusiastically. "I have the *best* news! I know stuff has been well, weird, but the most amazing thing just happened! My manager called and there's a record label interested in one of my tracks! Like, a real label, you guys! Can you believe it?"

"I *can* believe it," I reply. Nessa has been waiting for this moment as long as I've known her. "It's about time the rest of the world realized how talented you are." I don't want to rip her down off cloud nine with bad news, but Tori presses on.

"We're so incredibly happy for you, Ness. Seriously. You deserve this." Her words are right, but her tone isn't, and Nessa picks up on it immediately.

"Wait, why were you guys calling? What happened?" The elation I heard in Nessa's voice only moments ago has vanished.

I quickly bring Nessa up to speed on the email I sent to "Jenny" this morning.

"So what was the response?" Nessa says. A worried edge spikes her words.

I recite the latest email, my tone hushed and hurried. "And she sent a photo."

"Of what?" Tori asks.

"Of all of us. Me, you guys, Emily, and Jenny. Jenny was wearing my dress. The blue one. It must have been taken the night of the Valentine's Day party. The last time Jenny came out with us and—"

"I remember that night," Tori interjects, sparing me from having to speak the rest aloud.

"I do too," Nessa agrees, her voice soft and small.

We're all silent for a moment, lost to the past.

It's Nessa's voice that brings us back to the present. "You guys don't think it's possible that … it's really her, right?" She lowers her voice to a whisper. "Jenny, I mean."

"Ness," Tori says gently, "she's gone. We know that."

"Do we though?" Nessa responds, a worried panic infiltrating her tone. "Are we completely sure because we never actually saw—"

"She is. Jenny died," I respond, my words clipped. I don't want to indulge in the fantasy. As much as I don't want to believe that Jenny is dead, it's the truth. *Are you certain though?* a voice whispers in my ear. *How can you be sure?*

There's another pause, a silence between us that crackles with anticipation, before I speak again. "… I think it's time we find Emily."

* * *

"You're home early!" Jason says cheerfully from his spot on the sofa as I arrive back at our apartment. His feet are propped up on the coffee table, crossed at the ankles.

"Yup," I reply, trying to match his enthusiasm.

"Well I'm glad, because I have a surprise for you." He gets up from his seat on the couch and makes his way to the kitchen. Kicking off my heels and dropping my bag next to the front door, I trail behind him.

"Ta-da," Jason says with a flourish as he spreads his arms wide, gesturing to the tiny kitchen island behind him. There's a bottle of white wine, Pinot Grigio, my favorite, chilling in a silver ice bucket that's piled high with ice cubes. Next to it stands a glass vase holding a handful of pink roses surrounded by a spray of baby's breath.

"What's all this?" I say, a small smile on my lips.

"I know you've been stressed, and I thought maybe we could have a little wine …" He steps in closer to me, sliding his arms around my waist. "We could pick up dinner from that Italian place you like, maybe light a few candles … make a night of it."

He leans in even closer kissing me softly on the lips. I feel my own lips parting, my body's programmed response to him. He lifts me onto the counter, pushing himself between my legs. My skirt bunches up around my thighs and I can feel my skin growing warm with want as Jason kisses my earlobe, and then trails down my neck as he works free the top buttons of my blouse.

78

And then I freeze as Jenny's voice floats through my head: *This isn't going to end.* I can't lose myself in the moment any longer.

"What's wrong?" Jason asks breathlessly, his voice a throaty rumble.

"Nothing, like I told you, I just have a lot on my mind recently and …"

"Well then let me clear your head for you." He frees my blouse from my skirt and slides his hand underneath. His gentle fingers trail up my skin, and where I'd normally melt into his touch, my body now refuses to respond.

"Jules, what's really going on?" he asks, pulling his hand away.

"I told you last night. I have this thing at work and—"

"Are you sure it's just work? Because this isn't like you."

"Yes, Jason. I'm sure," I snap, and then immediately regret it. "I'm sorry. I don't mean to take it out on you."

Jason sighs resignedly. "It's fine, Jules. Let's just forget it. I'll go pick us up something for dinner."

He turns to leave, swiping his keys off the counter as I smooth my skirt back over my thighs. The front door closes with a loud rattle in his wake, and I'm left alone with only the sound of ice cubes clinking together in the metal bucket as they slowly melt, unused. I feel terrible that I ruined the evening after Jason had gone to so much trouble to do something thoughtful for me. I wish, not for the first time, that I would have told him everything from the very beginning.

I slide down from the counter, landing hard on the balls of my feet on the tiled kitchen floor, and head into my bedroom. I start to get undressed, undoing the remaining buttons on my blouse that Jason hadn't yet reached, when I hear the faint sound of my phone ringing.

A cold tingle shoots down my spine. I don't know why, but I have the overwhelming sense that "Jenny"—or whoever is really sending those emails—is calling. Or, perhaps, the photo she sent earlier just set me into a tailspin, a constant state of paranoia, such that the mere sound of a ringing phone is enough to make me shake.

I dash back out into the living room, clutching my blouse together, and root through my bag to find my phone. I exhale heavily, my shoulders sagging with relief, when I see Tori's name on the screen.

"Hey," I say as the call connects.

"Hey, Jules, I was just calling to check in on you. You sounded ... well, really spooked earlier."

"I was. Am. That photo, Tori ... I still can't even think about what happened at that Valentine's party."

"I know."

"It can't be a coincidence that whoever is doing this sent me *that* photo, could it?" I pad back into my bedroom, closing the door behind me and flopping back onto the bed to finish the call. I can't risk Jason walking in and overhearing anything about this. Not when I haven't even told him that Jenny exists. *Existed.*

"I don't know. I guess it *could*; there *were* rumors floating around after the Valentine's Day thing. But I'm starting to think you're right. What she said in that last email ... this isn't just some morbid weirdo who is obsessed with what happened to Jenny back then. Whoever is doing this, sending us these emails, knows something about the night Jenny ..."

"Died," I finish, my voice a hoarse whisper. "It has to be Emily. She's the only person I can think of who would have kept a copy of this photo. Have you had any luck tracking her down?"

"I have her number."

"You do? Have you been ... in contact with her recently?"

"No, of course not," Tori snaps defensively.

"Then how do you have her number?"

"I just called her parents. I knew them back in the day, remember? And they gave it to me. They were happy to hear that I wanted to *reconnect* with Emily. Though I doubt she'll be as receptive."

"Oh, I guess that makes sense …" I reply. Although I'm still doubtful. Why was she so defensive when I asked her if she'd been in contact with Emily?

I mull over the thought. I suppose Emily is probably a sore subject for all of us after what happened at Westbridge. After we cut her out of our lives. But yet, on some level, I've always suspected that Tori and Nessa held some lingering loyalty to her due to their shared past. Emily's tentacle-like grip too strong for them to ever fully break free of her hold. And now, with Jenny dragging up the past, I'm feeling more suspicious than ever.

"I mean, I know it's been a long time," Tori replies, "but you know me, Jules. You trust me, don't you?" The hurt is evident in her voice. "Because it kind of sounds like you don't."

"I do. I'm sorry. I'm just on edge with this whole Jenny thing. Plus," I add, feeling the need to make an excuse, to divert her attention, "something strange happened at work today and I don't know how to feel about it."

"What's going on?"

I debate whether I should tell her what I've learned about Barrett's file. It's been a long time since I've confided in Tori, and my first instinct is to keep it to myself. But, I just told her that I trusted her, and I want to prove to her that I do. That we're still on the same side. I can hear Emily's voice whispering in my ear, so vividly that I think I feel her breath warm on my neck. *Real friends are meant to share secrets.*

"I can't say too much, but basically, a partner gave me an assignment today, and it looks to me like he, or our client, doctored critical records in this case to conceal what could be a key witness. He didn't ask me outright to help him cover it up, but it was clear to me that he's expecting me to go along with the lie, and if I don't, he'll vote against my bid for partnership."

"Oh my God, Jules. That's awful. He never should have put you in that position. What are you going to do?"

"I don't know. I guess I know what I *should* do, from an ethical standpoint. But I also can't afford to lose this job. And if I leave my firm now, it'll probably be years before I'm in a position to make partner at another firm."

I hear the front door swing open, creaking on its hinges. "Look, I have to run. Jason just got home. But please don't tell anyone about this."

"Of course I wouldn't. It's just between us. And I'll let you know if I get ahold of Emily."

"Thanks, Tori," I rush to add before ending the call.

I quickly change into more comfortable clothes, one of Jason's old T-shirts and a pair of sweatpants. Not exactly the romantic evening attire Jason had probably been envisioning, but then again, I think that ship has already sailed.

Chapter 13

Then

"He hasn't called. It's been two days since Emily said she gave Alex my number and he hasn't called," I lamented, falling back onto my bed and pulling a pillow over my face before letting out a muffled groan.

"You're losing it, Jules. He's just a guy. There are, like, thousands of them around here. Wanna go out tonight and find another one?" Tori asked.

I ignored her question. "Why isn't he calling? Was I totally off base? Was he not really into me? What do you think Emily said to him?"

"Em said she's in the same psych class as him, and that she very casually struck up a conversation with him after class, and when he realized that she was your friend, *he* asked *her* for your number. Which, as I've told you a thousand times over the last forty-eight hours, definitely means he's into you."

"And yet ... radio silence."

"Guys are weird like that. He's probably waiting a few days before he calls, to 'play it cool' or whatever. But in the meantime, you can't just sit here and obsess over him."

"I'm not obsessing," I said, peering out from under my pillow. Tori looked back at me, her head tilted, one eyebrow raised, her hand set on her hip. "Okay, so maybe I've been obsessing just a *little*."

Her eyebrow arched even higher.

"Okay, a lot. You're right. That's enough about Alex Caldwell. I'm not going to give him another thought."

"And yet, somehow I don't believe you," Tori said with a crooked smile. "Look, I'm going to class, and then tonight we're going out. It's a Friday and I won't have you sitting home stewing over whether some idiot boy is going to call."

"You're the best," I call to the back of her head as she turns to leave the room.

"I know," she says just before the door falls closed behind her.

Maybe Tori is right. Maybe I've been too hung up on Alex. I tried to think about it rationally. It was just one night, just one boy. Just one kiss. But whenever I thought back to that night, I knew it was more than that. The sparks that were flying between us were so strong that I was sure everyone else could see them. The way he looked at me, the way my body responded to his, surely that didn't happen with just any boy, just any kiss. No, the magnetism between Alex and me was something above and beyond a random, drunken hookup. And I was certain he felt it too. Or at least I'd convinced myself that he did. He'd called me beautiful. Not hot, not sexy, but *beautiful*. "Beautiful" is a word reserved for something cherished, someone special. Tori was probably right. Alex was just trying to play it cool after how intense things had gotten at the bar. *He'll call. Eventually.*

* * *

"Wow, Jules, you're on a mission tonight," Nessa said as I threw back the shot of tequila that Tori pressed into my hand. Jenny watched me in wide-eyed amazement, (or horror, I couldn't be sure), and Emily simply offered her usual curious grin, making it impossible to tell what she was thinking.

"She's trying to get over a boy," Tori said. "Trust the process."

"I'm not *getting over* him," I corrected. "I only met him one time!"

Tori smiled as she poured another shot from a bottle she swiped off the sticky counter of the frat house. It was crowded with half-empty glass bottles in various shapes and sizes and red plastic cups discarded here and there. "Well, whatever you're calling it, tequila will help."

She tried to hand me the shot glass yet again, but I shook my head while I tried to keep the last shot from making a reappearance. Tori shrugged and drank the shot herself, throwing her head back and swallowing the gold liquid down in one fluid movement.

"Truth or dare," Emily said, a mischievous grin breaking across her face.

"Oh God, Em, not this again." Tori rolled her eyes.

Nessa turned to me and explained. "She used to do this all the time back at Brighton. Emily's favorite game, well, her twist on it. See, you can randomly ask one of us to tell a truth or do a dare, or you can ask the whole group, and whoever does it gets a free pass to ask next. Whenever they want."

"Unfortunately, we left off on Emily's turn," Tori added. "But that was years ago. We aren't sixteen anymore, Em."

"Well, any takers?" Emily carried on undeterred. "I think Jules should go since she's the newest to the group—"

"I'll go," Tori volunteered a bit too quickly. I couldn't tell whether she was excluding me from their shared ritual or protecting me from it.

"If she's going to hang around with us, I need to know if she can handle it," Emily snapped back, speaking about me as if I wasn't standing right there.

"Too late. I already called it. You know the rules, Em," Tori responded with a shrug. "I pick truth."

"Well then. Are you fucking Nate Porter?"

Tori laughed. "Not yet."

"Is that so?" a deep voice called from behind Tori and me. We whipped around to see Nate with a scandalous smile on his face as he made his way toward Tori. Emily's grin widened, her eyes trained on his approaching figure over Tori's shoulder. *Surely Emily would have seen him coming …*

I thought I saw a look of embarrassment flit across Tori's face, but it was gone as quickly as it came, her composure regained.

"What kind of trouble are you girls getting up to tonight?" Nate asked.

"None until *you* got here," Tori replied. Their eyes locked on one another's, and I could feel the tension sizzling between them.

I tried to appear casual as I looked around the room, hoping to see Alex following in Nate's wake.

"He's here," Emily whispered in my ear, as if she could read my thoughts. I blushed in embarrassment that I'd been so obvious. "Over there. In the living room."

My eyes automatically scanned the room to find him. I supposed there was no point in being discreet any longer. And there he was. With his familiar backwards hat on his head, paired with a tight black T-shirt, and a pair of faded jeans. He was talking to someone, a girl, her chocolate brown hair trailing down her back as she threw her head back in laughter at something he'd said. *She could just be a friend though … right?* She reached out her hand and touched him lightly on the arm as she took a sip from the plastic cup in her hand, her eyes never leaving Alex. *Maybe not a friend then.*

"Yikes," Emily said, following my gaze. "I'd make my move tonight if I were you."

I nodded in agreement. She had been right all along. I was out of sight, out of mind and he'd already lost interest. I had to find a way to get it back.

As the night wore on, I tried to have fun with my friends, but I was acutely aware of where Alex was at all times. I didn't think he'd noticed me in the crowd; he hadn't looked in my direction once.

The music was loud and pulsing in my ears, and the drinks I'd had earlier were making it feel as though the room was spinning. The house was packed with bodies, people drinking, dancing, and shouting, and it was all starting to feel like too much.

Emily and I queued up at the keg, waiting for another drink that I didn't need. "Have you seen Nessa and Tori?" I asked.

"No, I assume Tori is off with Nate. It's about damn time those two fucked and got it over with. And I think Jenny and Nessa went outside to get some fresh air. Jenny looked pretty drunk. As usual." Emily rolled her eyes. "Still no luck with Alex?"

"No. I haven't been able to catch his attention all night, and I didn't want to just walk up to him like some sort of desperate weirdo—"

"Well now's your chance." Emily grabbed my elbow and led me away from the keg. We abandoned our cups on the nearest table as she pulled me into the living room where people were dancing, scantily clad bodies writhing against one another in rhythm to the music.

Emily guided me to the center of the makeshift dance floor and, taking my hands in hers, started to dance. At first I felt stiff, awkward, but, following her lead, I let the music move me. Emily smiled delightedly as my hips began to gyrate in time with hers.

She moved in closer to me, her movements becoming more sensual. I could feel eyes on us, other people watching us move. Guys lustfully and girls enviously, all surely wondering who the girl was that was holding Emily Wiltshire's attention. And then Emily leaned in and whispered, "I think he's watching."

I made to turn my head to find Alex in the crowd of onlookers watching Emily's performance, but she cupped my face in her hands, her eyes locking on mine. "No, don't look now. Pretend it's just me and you. Let him watch all he wants."

I smiled wickedly in return. Emily was teaching me how to

play the game she had mastered, and I was all too happy to follow her lead. And then, to my utter surprise, she kissed me. Her tongue pressed against my lips, which parted in shock as I felt the warmth of her mouth, tasted the peppermint on her breath. I could feel her lipstick meshing with my own as she kissed me deeply, sensually, with far more passion and skill than poor Billy Matter ever had. As she pulled away, I realized that I had stopped moving. I was frozen in shock on the dance floor, surrounded by howls of approval from Emily's adoring fans.

Emily brushed a lock of my hair off my shoulder and leaned in once more, her lips still moist and full as they softly grazed my ear. "You certainly have his attention now," she purred. And with that, she turned and walked away, revealing a jaw-dropped Alex standing just behind her.

"Wow, that was ... wow," he said, removing his hat and raking his fingers through his thick brown hair, before placing it back on his head.

"I have to say that was a first for me," I replied, heat rising into my chest.

"Well, I, for one, hope to see a repeat performance." He offered me a rakish smile.

I smiled coyly in return and looked down at my shoes, too embarrassed to meet his eye.

"I was going to call, you know," he said, his voice silvery smooth. "I wanted to see you again. But this week was just so busy, and I didn't get a chance. You know how it is, right?"

I didn't. How could a whole week pass by without him finding two minutes to call me if he'd really wanted to? He couldn't even spare ten seconds to send me a text? But I didn't want to be *that* girl. So instead I said, "Totally. It's no big deal."

"Can I get you another drink?" he asked, his thumb and forefinger holding my chin as he angled my face up toward him.

I looked into his deep brown eyes, and my resolve, my feigned insouciance, was completely gone. "Sure."

After Alex fetched each of us a drink, we stood awkwardly in the living room, which was growing increasingly crowded as the hour grew later. I fidgeted with the plastic cup in my hand, rolling it in my palm as we made small talk about our hometowns and the dorms we were assigned to on campus. It felt stiff, uncomfortable, nothing like the first time we'd met when we'd been instantly drawn to each other, a tangle of wet lips and groping hands.

"What?" I shouted over the sound of the music, which had been turned up to an obnoxious level, the sound bouncing off the walls of the crowded room.

"I can barely hear myself think," Alex shouted in reply. "Do you want to go somewhere a little quieter? So we can talk?"

"Yeah, okay," I replied.

He shook his empty cup and gestured toward the keg. I assumed he was asking if I wanted a refill.

"No thanks!" I yelled.

"I'm going to get myself another drink. I'll meet you upstairs?"

I nodded in agreement, though my legs suddenly felt like Jell-O. He'd asked me to meet him upstairs ... *surely that meant he was hoping we'd do more than just talk?*

I walked up the stairs on wobbling legs, pushing through the throngs of people loitering in the hallway, toward the bathroom. I needed a moment of privacy, away from the crowds, the noise, to think. I liked Alex a lot, but was I ready for this? Emily's words floated back to me: *someone like Alex Caldwell is going to be expecting it.*

"Excuse me," I said, pushing past a couple making out against the wall. The girl had her back pressed up against the dated floral wallpaper, the guy's hand sliding up beneath her skirt. *It's so easy for everyone else; why doesn't this feel easy to me?*

I felt a hand grasp my arm, long, delicate fingers encircling my wrist and stopping me just before I could reach the bathroom. Jenny.

"Jules, I'm so glad I found you." Her words were slurred, the mascara Nessa had so carefully applied for her was now smudged like bruises beneath her eyes. I realized for the first time that she hadn't been wearing her glasses. When had she traded in the blue frames for contacts?

Jenny steadied herself on her feet, still holding my wrist firmly. "I can't find any of the others, and I think I had too much to drink. I want to go back to campus."

I pried my arm out of her grasp. "Call a cab or something." I didn't mean to sound cruel, but I'd already had my first night with Alex come to a crashing halt because of Jenny and I wasn't about to let it happen again.

"I don't want to go by myself," she whined.

"Look, Jenny, I'm sorry, but that's really not my problem." I turned my back to her and made my way into the bathroom, locking the door behind me.

I looked at myself in the dingy vanity mirror, the edges darkened with brown spots. I felt badly about the way I'd just spoken to Jenny, but why was it always my responsibility to look after her? I tried to shake off the image of her standing in the hallway, looking to me for help while she stumbled in heels that she could barely walk in. *No, tonight is about me and Alex.* Jenny could take care of herself just like the rest of us.

A loud banging on the door made me jump. "Did you fall in?" a male voice boomed. "There are people waiting out here!"

I quickly wiped away some black eyeliner that seemed to have bled under my eyes, and smoothed my hair. I still didn't know if I was ready for whatever was coming next, but it was time to find out.

When I stepped out of the bathroom, I spotted Alex leaning against the wall a little further down the hallway.

"There you are," he said as I approached. "I was looking all over for you."

I smiled shyly in reply. "Yup, here I am." *God, why am I so awkward?*

"So this is my buddy's room," Alex said, nodding toward the closed door beside him. "We can hang out in there if that's cool with you? He won't mind."

I swallowed hard, my heart fluttering in my chest. "Yeah," I said, lacing my fingers through his, "that's cool with me."

We sat on the edge of the bed next to each other, neither of us sure how to reignite the passion we felt for one another the first time we'd met. Finally, Alex put his beer down on the nightstand and reached over to me.

He gently ran his fingers across my cheek, tucking a lock of my long blonde hair behind my ear. "I meant what I said the other night. You really are beautiful," he said, his words as soft and sensual as floating feathers.

I blushed, my eyes slowly meeting his, and then he leaned over and kissed me. It wasn't like the first time, a maddening want fueling his frenzied movements. This time he was softer, gentler, as his tongue caressed mine and his hands slowly moved along the curves of my body. I lay back on the bed, allowing him to go further.

He lay on top of me, the weight of his body on mine reassuring as he planted delicate kisses along my jaw, down my neck, working his way toward my breasts, which were nearly exposed in the tight black dress I was wearing. He carefully lowered the straps of my dress, peeling it down to reveal my new lace bra. I closed my eyes and felt his fingers trail along the curve of my breasts.

"I want you so badly," he whispered. I could feel him growing hard as he pressed his weight between my legs.

I wanted to tell him that I wanted him too. A part of me *did*. I could feel my body betraying my desires when my hips arched in tune with his touch. But another part of me, a small voice in the back of my head, reminded me that this was going to be my first time. *Hadn't I always imagined it would be something more special than taking my clothes off in a bedroom of a dirty fraternity house with a boy who never called?*

I tried to push the thought from my head, to will myself to continue. I closed my eyes as Alex kissed me again, hoping my growing anxiety would subside if I focused on the feel of his touch. But when he kissed me, the image in my head was not of Alex, but of Emily. Her lips on mine what felt like only moments ago, the taste of her peppermint gum, her Cheshire-cat grin as her lips parted from mine. Emily had gotten into my head and I could no longer be present in the moment with Alex. I wondered whether she'd done it intentionally. Whether she'd known that her kiss would linger on my lips, that it would take up space in my thoughts long after it was over. I wondered if she knew that it would give her a hold over me, allowing her to possess a piece of me that she could move like a pawn on a chessboard. *Was this all a game to her? Was this what she meant when she said I had to prove myself?* All I knew for sure was that it wasn't supposed to be like this.

I sat up abruptly. "I … I'm so sorry. I … I can't do this tonight," I stammered.

"Are you okay?" Alex asked, lifting himself off me. Confusion was evident in his voice.

"Yeah, I'm fine. I've just had too much to drink and—"

"It's okay, Jules. Really. Do you want me to take you home? I can't exactly drive right now, but I could call a cab …"

"No. Thank you though. I think I should just find my friends."

I hurriedly adjusted my dress and slipped out of the room, leaving Alex kneeling on the bed, surely perplexed by my sudden departure.

Back downstairs I scanned the room for my friends but I couldn't see them. I cast a quick glance back over my shoulder praying that I wouldn't see Alex descending the stairs behind me. I was too humiliated to face him at that moment, and I just wanted to get out of there as fast as I could.

I opened our group chat and sent a text to my friends:

Taking a cab back to campus. See you later.

I didn't wait for a reply as I dashed outside and jumped into the nearest cab, catching a ride back to campus with a group of girls I'd never met before.

I squeezed into the back seat, barely making eye contact with anyone else in the taxi. In that moment, the only person I wanted to talk to was Kelly. My only friend who truly knew me, the person I was before I arrived at Westbridge. I wanted to tell her about what had happened that night, about what had *nearly* happened, but I wasn't sure she'd understand. Not anymore. In such a short amount of time, our lives had become so different to one another's. I could just picture her, still going on sweet, wholesome dates with her high school boyfriend, attending her classes at the local college, and then sleeping under her parents' roof. Exactly as I left her. But I knew I wasn't the same person I was when I left. How could she possibly understand what I was going through? *But she's my friend, isn't she? She'll at least try.*

I held my phone in my hand ready to send her a message, but then I noticed the time: three o'clock in the morning. Kelly would be fast asleep, not in the back of a cab squished between a group of giggling girls who were strangers to her. I put my phone back into my bag and sat in silence, staring listlessly out the window, for the rest of the ride home.

* * *

With my shoes in my hand, I tiptoed through the quiet halls of Nickerson Hall back toward my room.

I was almost to my doorway when I remembered Jenny. *Had she gotten home okay?* I wanted nothing more than to fall into bed and pretend this night never happened, but a renewed sense of guilt washed over me for the way I'd treated her earlier, and I decided to check in on her before going to my own room.

I made an about-face and walked back down the long hallway toward Jenny and Emily's room in the opposite wing. When I got there, I could hear muffled sounds coming from inside. I rapped on the door lightly, listening curiously to the noises on the other side of the door.

After a moment, I heard feet shuffling along the floor, the sound growing louder as they came closer. The door flew open and I was surprised to find Abby standing on the other side. She glared at me angrily.

"What do you want?" she snapped.

"I wanted to check in on Jenny. Is she here?" I asked.

"What does it matter to *you*?"

"Jenny?" I called into the room, pushing past Abby and the judgmental scowl on her face. "Are you okay?"

I stepped into the room to find Jenny hunched over on the floor, vomiting into a small, plastic garbage can, her black hair falling in a veil across her face.

"Just go away, Jules," Abby ordered gesturing toward the open door. "Jenny needs a *friend* right now."

"I *am* her friend," I replied defensively, setting my hand on my hip.

"Well you're not a very good one," Abby stated succinctly, as she turned back toward Jenny, pulling her hair back from her face as she retched again.

Her words hit me like a blow. I *hadn't* been a very good friend to Jenny. *Who was I becoming?*

Chapter 14

Now

I hug my sweatshirt tighter around my waist as I sip my coffee. It tastes slightly bitter. I'd normally add a splash of milk, watching it billow out in the black liquid, turning it a creamy hue, but—not surprisingly—we've run out. I stare out of the boxy window above my kitchen sink, watching golden sunlight striate the slate-gray sky as the first signs of early morning begin to filter through the city buildings.

I couldn't sleep last night. Every time I closed my eyes I saw an image of that photo, dragging me back to that night. And that's a place I never wanted to revisit. I wonder whether Tori got in touch with Emily. It's far too early to call and ask. And besides, she said she'd keep me updated with any news.

I look down at my phone lying on the cold, granite countertop beside me. Its dark screen looks so ominous as it stares back at me, deathly silent. I feel like I'm spinning out of control. I have no idea when I might receive another email from Jenny, and I'm constantly on edge waiting to see what else she has in store for me. *But it's not really Jenny*, I remind myself. I couldn't get Nessa's words out of my sleep-deprived mind last night: *"You guys don't think it's possible that … it's really her, right?"*

Could it be? I need to do something to distract myself before I go insane.

A rustling of sheets in the other room calls my attention. Jason must be awake. I hear his footsteps, the familiar cadence of his gait, as he shuffles into the bathroom and turns on the shower.

I refill my coffee, even though I'm not particularly enjoying it, and sit on one of the compact, cushioned stools that slide under our countertop—our makeshift breakfast table—and wait to face Jason.

After last night, I don't expect to be greeted with his usual cheery outlook. When he returned with dinner, we sat in front of the television, watching some action movie that neither of us seemed particularly invested in while we ate in near silence. Before the movie had even ended, I told Jason that I had a headache and wanted to go to bed. He asked one more time if there was anything wrong, and I, once again, lied to my husband and assured him that everything was just fine. I could tell Jason didn't believe me. He opened his mouth as if there was something more he wanted to say, a rebuttal ready to leap off his tongue, but instead he turned away from me resignedly. "Whatever you say, Jules," he muttered with a frustrated shake of his head.

When Jason finally joined me in bed hours later, I'd pretended to be asleep. I closed my eyes in the dark, my back to him, and hoped he wouldn't ask if I was awake. I hate that I keep lying to him. I sensed him looking over in my direction, but he said nothing before he turned his back to mine and went to sleep.

Jason pads into the kitchen now in a pair of shorts and a loose-fitting T-shirt with his company's logo emblazoned on the front. His hair is still damp from the shower, and the familiar citrus scent of his favorite soap filters into the room behind him.

"Have you seen my sneakers?" he asks.

"Yeah, they're in the hall closet. Are you going for a run?" I ask, perplexed. I've never known him to be a runner, especially early on a Saturday morning.

"I have the company 5k today. Remember? The fundraiser for juvenile diabetes? I doubt I'll do much actual running, but I do have to show face and help collect the donations."

I'd entirely forgotten that the fundraiser was this weekend. He must have told me a thousand times.

"Right, sorry. It completely slipped my mind."

Jason sighs. "It's fine." But I can tell that it's not. He pauses for a moment, as though considering his next words carefully before he continues. "I just feel like we've been so disconnected lately. I know there's something going on with you, and I feel like you're completely shutting me out. I just can't figure out why. I'm your husband, Jules. You're supposed to be able to talk to me. I want to be here for you, but I can't be if you don't let me in."

"I *do* talk to you," I argue.

"No. You don't. Not really. You don't think I realize that? It's like … it's like you've built this wall up around you, and I've been trying since the day I met you to scale it, to chip away at it, to dig under it, but all these years later I feel like I've barely made any progress. I love you, Jules. I really do. But I need you to meet me halfway." He seems to sag with the relief. The release of his words unburdening him of a great weight. But there's also sadness in his eyes, as though it pained him to have to unload it onto me.

I want to tell him he's right. I want to tell him that I'm guarded for a reason: because I'm terrified that someday he *will* get past the walls I've built to protect myself and that he won't like what he finds on the other side. I want to tell him that I'm scared of losing him. But I don't. "You're really this upset with me for forgetting you had a work event today?"

"It's not about that," he says with a frustrated sigh. "But I think you know that, Jules."

Jason turns away from me as he goes to collect his sneakers, pulling them on hastily.

"Jason, I'm sorry," I call after him, sliding off the stool, but he walks out the front door without so much as another look in my direction.

Damn it. I pour the rest of my coffee down the drain in frustration and suddenly realize which mug I've been using. It's a deep royal blue with the Westbridge University logo emblazoned on the side. I should have thrown this mug away years ago, as I did with most of my Westbridge memorabilia, but my parents bought it for me the day I was accepted, and I didn't have the heart to toss it out like trash.

I remember the day they gave it to me. I'd just opened my acceptance letter that morning, sliding my finger under the creamy manila envelope to find the letter, printed on Westbridge University letterhead, that I'd been waiting to see for so long: "We are pleased to inform you that you have been accepted ..." I don't think I even read past the opening words before my eyes filled with tears. My parents were elated, cheering and hugging me, but the sound of their celebration was dim for me. All I could focus on was the sight of that letter in my hand and what it meant. I'd done it. The dream I'd been chasing for so long was finally mine. I'd left for school as if I was walking on air.

I could feel the acceptance letter in my backpack all day; I carried it with me, my own little secret victory. For the first time, I didn't feel loneliness when I was ignored in the hallways, when Kelly and I sat alone under the oak tree while we ate our lunches. I had an exit ticket in my back pocket. And I'd earned it. All on my own.

When I got home that afternoon, I dropped my backpack in the foyer and walked into the kitchen. I expected the house to be empty, as it always was when I got home from school, but that day both of my parents were standing in the kitchen waiting to yell, "Surprise!" They'd both left work early, and had gotten me a celebratory cake. My feet were rooted to the floor as I took in the sight of the cake, which read "Congratulations" in shiny frosting loops, and both of my parents beaming with pride.

"Thank you," I managed, my voice choked with tears, before my dad pulled me into a hug.

"We know this is just the start of a wonderful adventure for you, sweetie. We're so very proud." I could hear the emotion in his wavering voice.

And then my mom presented me with the Westbridge mug, tied with a red bow on the handle, and stuffed with new pens and pencils.

"It's not much," she'd said, "but we just wanted to do a little something to celebrate your accomplishment."

"It's perfect, Mom," I said, accepting the gift. "Thank you."

Now, that mug has been relegated to the back of the cabinet, hidden away out of sight, but I must have accidentally grabbed it this morning in my hazy, exhausted state.

As soon as I see it in my hand, the familiar school crest printed in scrolling white ink, I drop it into the sink hastily. The ceramic mug hits the stainless steel sink basin with a clang before shattering around the drain.

Shit, I hadn't meant to break it. I begin to scoop up the larger fragments and toss them into the trash, but in my haste I slice my finger on a jagged edge. The chalky-white ceramic beneath the mug's blue enamel stains with blooms of deep red blood. I shove the pieces into the trash and grab a paper towel to stem the bleeding. With the towel wrapped around one hand, I turn on the sink with the other, watching the remaining slivers of the broken mug swirl around the drain.

With my finger throbbing beneath a Band-Aid, I try to focus my mind on work. Barrett's file. I log in to my office's intranet and start to draft the motion I don't know that I'll ever submit. The words flow naturally as if by rote; I've written so many nearly identical motions before it. I lay out the case law, and outline the arguments we'll set forth in order to hopefully convince the judge that there are no issues of fact in this case that need to be decided by a jury, and therefore an order should be granted dismissing all claims against my client.

By the time I look up from my laptop, my eyes burning from staring at the screen, I find that hours have gone by and I managed not to look at my phone once. I close my laptop and pad into the kitchen to retrieve my phone.

I have one missed call from Tori. I call her back immediately, my stomach churning in knots as I wait for her to answer.

"Hey!" she says brightly as the call connects.

How does she sound so calm when I'm barely holding it together?

"I saw I missed your call. Did something happen?"

"Oh, no. Sorry. I was just calling to let you know that I tried calling the number Emily's parents gave me, but seems that she's ignoring me."

"Typical."

"I know. I left her a voicemail telling her that it was urgent I speak with her, but she hasn't called back. You know Emily, she's probably loving the idea that she's keeping me dangling and refusing to throw me a line."

I sigh in frustration. "Some things never change."

"You know," Tori continues, "maybe we should have Nessa call her. She was always the closest to Em."

"Good idea," I agree, nodding along although I know Tori can't see me. "If she's going to answer anyone, it would probably be Nessa."

A horn blares in the background of the call and, from the sound of it, it isn't far from where Tori is standing. Then I hear a bell tinkling, the familiar tinny sound of the tangle of bells that hang over shopfront doors all over the city, followed by the sound of muffled voices coming through the line.

"Where are you?" I ask.

"Oh, I … I'm just on my way to my Mommy Meet-Up. You know, Mia's playgroup thing …" she replies, suddenly sounding distracted. "Look, I gotta run, but I'll text Nessa Emily's info and see if she has any better luck than I did."

Tori ends the call quickly, leaving me confused. *Why did she suddenly seem so preoccupied? Is there something she's not telling me?*

* * *

I pull on a light jacket over my heather-gray sweater, and zip up a pair of tall leather boots. I walk along my street where the cool air carries a whisper of the distinct scent of New York in fall: a combination of drying leaves and pumpkin spice donuts from the bakery on the corner.

I pass by a coffee shop, where two women sit outside sipping lattes, a stroller parked between them. Inside, a baby kicks and babbles as he bats at a plastic rattle suspended from the sunshade above his head. I feel a familiar twinge in my chest. The same one I feel whenever I see former classmates sharing photos of their children and their perfect families online, or pass by mothers lifting their children into the swings at the park. I know Jason is ready to move out of the city, to start a family of our own. But a baby, the one thing that would make my heart and my family feel complete, is the one thing I haven't been able to allow myself to have. Not without telling Jason the truth. About all of it.

I pull my jacket closed around me and press on with my walk. I thought that perhaps a walk would help me sort out the thoughts that are currently cluttering my head in a tangled jumble. Clearly this business with Jenny has me on edge. Of course Tori sounded distracted earlier—who wouldn't be with everything going on? I have no reason to doubt that she's been anything but forthcoming with me. The sounds of horns honking and people chatting are the normal sounds of New York City—I was just being paranoid. And besides, it makes perfect sense that Tori has her Mommy Meet-Up today; she'd even given Claire the information.

Claire. I've been rather neglectful of our friendship lately. We usually go to the gym together at least once a week, and text daily, but this week I'd completely forgotten about her.

Feeling guilty, I pull my phone from my bag and give her a call.

"Hey, Claire," I start, sheepishly.

"Hey!" she replies cheerfully. "I was just thinking about you!"

"Oh yeah?"

"What are you up to today?" she asks.

"I'm just running some errands right now. I have *no* groceries in the house."

"Well how about coming to hang out at my place tonight? Brian is out of town for some work thing ... and I have wine ..." she says enticingly.

I almost protest, knowing that I should probably be home to reconcile things with Jason tonight. But just thinking about our stilted conversations lately, and the tension that has become palpable in my apartment, makes me feel as though a heavy weight has been placed on my chest.

"Sure, that sounds great," I agree, as I step into the local grocery store. "Looking forward to it."

Maybe it will do me good to spend some time with my friend. And Jason won't mind ... *I hope.*

Chapter 15

Then

I felt my phone vibrating in the pocket of my slim-fit jeans. My hand instinctively reached for it, but I drew it back immediately.

"Are you even listening?" Emily demanded, one hand set on her hip. Nessa and I sat on Emily's bed as she paced the floor of her dorm room angrily relating the events of her day.

"Yeah, sorry, Em," I said sheepishly. "You were talking about your psych professor?"

"Anyway, he's, like, a total dick. Can you believe he called me out in front of the entire class like that? Who does he think he is?"

I could tell Emily's ire was up, and Nessa and I exchanged knowing glances. Emily's eyes shifted upwards, her head tilted, as she considered her options. "Well, I'm certainly not going to let him get away with it," she finally concluded, folding her arms over her chest.

"How are things with Alex?" Nessa asked me, in a thinly veiled attempt to change the subject.

"Oh, fine. We're just keeping it casual."

I'd hoped I sounded breezy, disinterested, but in truth things with Alex and I were getting quite serious. Ever since the night we nearly had sex, we'd been in constant contact. It started with texts exchanged. Simple things like, "How was class?", "How did you do at your track meet?" but as the days passed, the texts became phone calls, which turned into long rambling emails where we talked about our childhoods, our ambitions, our true selves. Alex had even shared with me a poem he'd written.

"No one else can know about this, Jules. It's totally embarrassing," he'd said. "The other guys on the team would make fun of me until the end of time if they knew I was writing poetry. I know we don't really know each other that well yet, but I feel like I can only share this with you."

And it was beautiful, at least to me. His gentle words making me fall for him even harder:

A last first kiss,
The first hello,
A brush of your skin against mine.
These fleeting memories, exquisite treasures
that slip through our fingers before we know they've gone.

Okay, so maybe he wasn't Shakespeare, but he'd allowed himself to be vulnerable with me, and his words opened up a window showing me a glimpse of the person he really was.

No, what Alex and I had was far from casual, but it was ours and I wasn't ready to share it with the group. The things we had said to one another felt deeply personal, but that wasn't the only thing that kept me from telling my friends about our growing relationship. I was also afraid of what Emily would say.

Ever since that night at the frat party when she saw me go upstairs with Alex, Emily had taken a sudden liking to me. Suddenly I was interesting, fun. Everywhere she went, she invited me along with her. Even, like today, when Tori wasn't around.

Last week I'd skipped class for the first time in my life to go to the mall with her.

"Come on, Jules. It'll be fun!" Emily had pleaded. "Don't make me go alone, I need your opinion." She pushed her lips into a pout.

I bit the corner of my nail nervously. I'd never skipped a class before, but just one time couldn't hurt, right? People did it all the time in college ...

When I finally agreed to go, Emily clapped excitedly, bouncing on her toes. That's how it always was with us. Emily made the plans, and the rest of us eventually fell in line, whether we'd intended to or not.

But as close as Emily and I had become, I discerned pretty quickly that she wasn't much interested in hearing about Alex.

"He sent me the cutest text," I told her one day as we walked to meet the other girls for lunch at The Hill.

Emily examined her nails, the flawless pink varnish. "Okay, but you haven't actually hung out with him again, right?"

"Well, we met for lunch once between classes, but—" I started. I wanted to explain that what Alex and I had was above making out at frat parties or even romantic dinners. We were getting to know each other, *really* know each other, and that meant something. Besides, Alex was at Westbridge on a track scholarship, and he'd been busy with practices and weekend meets for the last few weeks. But Emily was quick to cut me off.

"So a 'cute' text message is nothing. It's been, like, two weeks. If he was really interested, he'd make *sure* to get you alone."

I felt my face fall. *Maybe she's right. Maybe he's not that into me ...*

"Oh, hon, don't be upset," Emily said pulling me into a hug. "I didn't mean to hurt your feelings. I only meant that Alex is just ... some guy. What *really* matters is us. You, me, Tori, and Nessa. We'll always have each other."

I allowed myself to feel the warm glow that came with being a part of Emily's inner circle, of belonging to something. But I made a mental note not to talk about Alex too much in front of her.

"So when are you seeing him again?" Nessa asked pulling me back to the moment.

I stole a quick glance at my phone. A smile spreading across my face as I read the words:

Can't wait till we can hang again.

"Soon. He's at an away meet this weekend, but he said he wants to see me when he gets back." I stole a glance at Emily who was doing her best to appear as if she wasn't listening as she brushed her hair before the full-length mirror.

"You're so lucky, Jules," Nessa gushed. "I haven't met a single guy worth dating here yet."

"And believe me, she's been looking," Emily chided, a sneer on her face.

Nessa looked crestfallen. "What's *that* supposed to mean?"

"Nothing, Ness," Emily said dismissively. "It was just a joke—don't be so sensitive."

Nessa rolled her eyes, brushing off Emily's jab. "Anyway," she continued, turning back toward me, "call me a hopeless romantic, but I just think you and Alex make the cutest couple."

"I'm not sure we're a *couple*, exactly …" I explained shyly, though I did like the sound of it.

"All right, enough of this, girls," Emily said with a clap of her hands. "Who's coming out tonight?"

Nessa frowned. "I have rehearsal tonight for the play."

Nessa was performing in the school's rendition of *Hello, Dolly!* and, as the show was going to open in a few weeks, she had rehearsals more and more frequently lately.

"And Tori has plans with Nate," Emily said with a dramatic roll of her eyes. "Jules, you're still coming with me though, right?"

Nessa's eyes flitted between Emily and me. She opened her

mouth as if she was going to object, but she quickly closed it again. I felt a little bad leaving her behind, especially as she and Emily had always been so close. I didn't want Nessa to feel as if I was edging her out, but then again, it wasn't *my* fault that she had to go to rehearsal.

"Sure," I said. "I'm in."

Emily smiled wickedly. "Here comes trouble."

* * *

The music in the club boomed and our skin glowed purple as a hazy spotlight swept over the dimly lit dance floor. Emily and I danced, her body pressed against mine as we moved to the music, her motions free and flowing in tune to the beat. I threw my head back, feeling my hair trail down my back.

I'd drunk more than I should have, but it was so easy to get carried away when I was with Emily. She had a way of making me forget myself.

"Come on," she yelled, pulling me off the dance floor.

She led me toward the bathrooms at the back of the club. The line for the ladies' room was long, with girls in short skirts and high heels leaning against the wall. Some looked bored while others seemed as though they could barely stand.

"Follow me," Emily said, pulling me past the line. She guided me by the elbow, pushing through the crowd, to the men's bathroom. There were two guys standing outside the door, sipping from long-necked bottles of beer.

Emily leaned in to the one closest to the door, running her fingers delicately down his arm.

"You wouldn't mind letting us jump ahead of you, would you?" she purred, her round eyes wide and innocent.

"Sure, but it'll cost you," his friend replied, a lecherous grin spreading across his face.

Emily had the good sense to look appalled at the suggestion.

"Sorry about him," Emily's target said, shooting his friend a cool glare. "Go ahead."

Just then the door to the men's room swung open and Emily slipped inside, yanking me in behind her. "Thanks, boys," she said with a wink as the door slammed closed behind us.

Emily took her time studying her reflection in the mirror, touching up her makeup, adjusting her signature velvet headband, before she pulled a small plastic bag from her purse. She dangled it between her thumb and her forefinger, shaking the white powder inside.

"Let's make this night a little more exciting," she said, her eyes wild with excitement.

"Is that ..."

"Coke," Emily said bluntly as she pulled a small compact mirror from her purse and shook out some of the loose powder.

"I don't know ..."

"It's honestly not that big of a deal, Jules," she said with a shrug before leaning over and quickly sniffing a small bump, which disappeared up her nose.

She wrinkled her nose briefly, twitching it like a bunny, before handing me the mirror. "Are you in or out?"

I looked at her outstretched hand, at the invitation she was offering me. I'd never done drugs before. Not even so much as a puff of a joint passed around at a party. But I knew this was about more than whether I'd wanted to get high that night. Emily was testing me. She wanted to see how far I'd follow her.

"Well?" she said, growing impatient. There was a pound on the bathroom door, as if to emphasize her point.

I took the mirror from her hand. I looked down at my own reflection, the white powder scattered across my face like snow. I didn't want to do this, but I also didn't feel like I had a choice. I was with Emily, and I felt as though I had to run at her pace. If I didn't, I knew that her interest in me would be gone as quickly as it came.

I leaned over and very gently inhaled. I felt trace amounts of the drug enter my nose with a crisp burn that felt like I'd inhaled bleach.

I instinctively cleared my throat and reached for a tissue. After I'd blown my nose, I looked over at Emily who was watching me with a curious smile on her face.

"I'm impressed," she said with a laugh, taking the mirror from my hand and snapping it shut. "Didn't think you had it in you."

I didn't either.

Emily pushed open the door to the bathroom, looping her arm through mine.

"Thanks again, guys," she said, her head held high, as we walked past the irritated crowd now waiting outside the men's room.

We made our way back to the dance floor, where the high suddenly hit me. It felt as though my brain had been thrown into overdrive. The lights flashed around me like strobes in flashes of purple and blue, and the faces in the crowed seemed to spin around me, leering and laughing manically, like I was trapped on a demented carousel. My heart started to race, and I could feel my breathing becoming shallow.

Suddenly Emily's face was in mine. She took my face in her hands and looked me hard in the eyes.

"You're okay," she said reassuringly, as though she could see the panic coming off me in waves. "I've got you."

I started to calm down, finally able to take a deep breath.

"You're just feeling the rush," Emily explained. "You'll level out soon. But in the meantime, try to enjoy it."

She leaned into me, her arms draped around my neck, slowly bringing her lips dangerously close to mine. I didn't know what to do. I didn't know whether I wanted to move just a fraction of an inch closer, bringing my lips to meet hers, or if I wanted to push her away in protest. My brain seemed incapable of sorting out how I was feeling. In that moment, I found her both intensely mesmerizing and deeply frightening. Emily had me firmly under her spell, and all I could do was freeze and wait to see what she would do with me next.

And then she spoke. "Have you forgotten about Alex yet?" A devious grin stretched across her pretty face.

The truth was, I had. That night was the first time since I'd met Alex that I hadn't been obsessively checking my phone waiting to see if he'd tried to reach me.

"Good," Emily said, without even waiting for me to reply. She pulled away from me abruptly, breaking the spell and leaving my mind in free fall.

Chapter 16

Now

I fumble to dig my keys out of my purse. The plastic grocery bags are looped over my arms, and the handles dig into my elbows uncomfortably.

I turn the knob on my heavy, wooden front door and push it open with my foot. I lug the groceries into the kitchen and drop the bags unceremoniously onto the granite countertop.

I walk back to the coat closet and hang up my jacket, squeezing it into the tiny space among all our other coats, jackets, scarves, yoga mats, sneakers, and sports equipment that we rarely touch. I know what Jason would say ... *"If we moved to the suburbs, we wouldn't have to fit everything we own into this one little closet ..."* Maybe he's right ... If I got that promotion, we could afford the kind of house he'd always dreamed of. I know he deserves it, and I want to give that to him after all he's given me ... but I also know what it'll cost me.

After I wrestle my coat into the overcrowded closet, I head toward the kitchen to unpack the groceries. But as I walk through the living room, something gives me pause. I can't place what it is exactly, it's just a feeling, but I suddenly feel as though someone has been in the house. I know it the way an animal instinctually senses danger. It is nothing more than a scent in the air, an atmospheric change, as subtle as a draft, but I know it's there.

I quickly spin around, scanning the room. Nothing seems out of place. My laptop is still resting on the coffee table, my briefcase closed on the floor exactly as I left it. And then it dawns on me that *someone could still be in the house.* The thought makes a shiver shoot down my spine. I feel goose bumps prickling at my skin, a rush from my scalp to my legs.

I tiptoe into the kitchen and pull a large knife from the wooden knife block. The sliver blade glints in the afternoon sun that is now streaming through the kitchen window. I grip the handle tightly, my knuckles turning white, and then I creep along the wall toward the bedroom. I keep my back up against the wall, like I'm some kind of detective on an episode of *Law & Order.* I tell myself that I'm being ridiculous, but something compels me to keep looking. I know I won't be able to relax until I've checked the entire apartment. And, for the first time, I'm quite happy about its diminutive size.

I slink down the short hallway to the bedroom, where the door is ajar. The room is cast in monochrome shadows of gray, and I hold my breath as I push the door open with my foot and cautiously step inside. My eyes flit around the room, but I don't see anyone. Nothing seems out of place.

"Hello?" I call out. My voice feels flat as it carries into the empty room.

There is no response.

Next, I check the bathroom, poking my head inside gingerly, and then I look in each of the closets. Satisfied that no one is lurking about in the apartment, I trudge back out into the living room. I feel myself deflate as I drop onto the couch, loosening my grip on the knife and depositing it on the coffee table. My legs feel shaky as the adrenaline recedes from my body.

I rub both eyes with the heels of my hands. *God, I'm really losing it.* Of course no one was in the house. The door was locked when I got back, and the windows are all still intact. There's no way anyone was in here while I was gone. I sit up, collecting myself. I can't believe I just wandered through my empty apartment with a knife like some kind of paranoid lunatic.

And yet ... Just to be sure, I walk back to the front door and push it open, I poke my head outside and scan the streets. No suspicious figures in black masks darting away into the shadows. *Of course there aren't.* But just out of an abundance of caution, I check the hiding spot for my spare key: taped to the bottom of a blue plastic turtle that sits in a flowerpot on the top step of the front porch. The little turtle is cold and smooth in my hand, and when I flip him over, the key is exactly as I'd left it. The blue painter's tape I'd used to conceal the key is unbroken. Just in case, I rip it off and fold the key into my palm, bringing it back inside with me. I've only ever needed to use it once or twice when I'd forgotten my keys at work, and it will give me some extra peace of mind knowing it's safely tucked away inside.

I shake my head in disbelief as I drop the key onto the key ring and spot the knife lying ominously on the coffee table. I pick it up, this time laughing to myself at how silly I'd behaved.

I return the knife to its designated slot in the knife block, and walk over to the sink to splash some cold water on my face. *I really need to get it together.* I reach for a paper towel and blot my face dry, finally ready to put away those groceries, and then I see it: a spiked shard of shiny blue enamel lying on the countertop adjacent to the sink. The Westbridge University crest is staring up at me, and below it, a drip of crimson red.

My blood immediately runs cold. *I threw all the bits of that mug away, didn't I?* I could have sworn that I did ... *But no*, I say to myself, again shaking my head. Obviously I must have missed this piece. I can't let myself get carried away. There is no other logical explanation here. Why would anyone break into my apartment just to pull a broken mug out of my garbage can? *Unless someone is intentionally messing with my head …*

Chapter 17

Then

I stole a glance over at Alex, his arm casually draped over his steering wheel as he leaned back in the driver's seat of his car, his profile relaxed as he navigated the winding road ahead of us. I fidgeted in my seat, folding my hands in my lap, before deciding that it looked far too proper. I unfolded them again and placed them instead on top of my purse.

We were on our way to dinner. Our first *real* date. Alex hadn't exactly called it a date, but when he texted me and asked if I wanted to "grab dinner", I understood that to be college guy shorthand for asking me out on a proper date. Besides, it's not like we were just going to the dining hall and collecting fries from under a heat lamp and shuffling back to a rickety table with plastic trays in hand. No, he was taking me to a real restaurant. Off campus. With waiters and menus. Just the two of us. *It's definitely a date.*

Admittedly, I didn't know *exactly* where we were going. The waiters with menus in hand, candles flickering on tables covered with white tablecloths, and red roses in slim glass vases were all more hopeful conjecture than anything based on actual fact, but I didn't care. I was finally alone with Alex.

Not that Emily had made it easy.

"You're really not coming out with us, Jules?" she said incredulously as our friends gathered in my room to sip some concoction Tori had mixed together with a combination of cheap liquor and lukewarm cranberry cocktail from the dining hall.

They were all dressed for a night out: tight skirts, sharp heels, and thick, dark eyeliner.

Emily set one hand on her hip and waited for my reply. We'd been spending a lot of time together. By then, I rarely, if ever, turned down any invitation she extended to me, even if it meant missing a class or two. She'd grown accustomed to me being at her beck and call, a constant companion down for any adventure. I was like a loyal puppy that came running the moment she whistled.

Emily knew I had plans with Alex, but it seemed she hadn't fully accepted that answer. I opened my mouth to reply, but Nessa beat me to it.

"Aw, she has a date, Em!" she gushed, as she pulled a brush through my blonde hair until it shone.

"A long-awaited date, no less," Tori added.

"Fine," Emily relented tossing her hands up in defeat. "But try to meet up with us after."

They were heading to some club with the promise of a glow party, each of them wearing tight white T-shirts that showed the outlines of black lacy bras underneath. "You're not going to want to miss this. Nico promised us a VIP table."

I nodded in agreement, though I couldn't bring myself to get excited about another party at another club, not when the alternative was time alone with Alex.

"What's this?" Jenny said, picking up a sheet of printed paper from my desk. Her long, black hair was set into loose curls, and her dark eyes had been rimmed with thick black lines that turned up at the corners, giving her a decidedly feline appearance. And now the cat had caught her mouse.

I watched in horror as her eyes scanned the page, her lips curdling into a sneer. "Guys, I think it's a poem. Tell me you didn't write this, Jules," she said, stifling laughter.

"A last first kiss,

The first hello ..." Jenny read aloud with mock gravity in her voice.

"Give me that," I snapped, tearing the paper from her hand. "That's none of your business." I leered at her as I ripped the page into pieces. She returned the look with a wintry smile.

I knew Jenny was still feeling bitter toward me after the night I ditched her at the frat party to be with Alex. She'd pretty much been pretending I didn't exist ever since. But now she was being far more vindictive than I'd imagined she was capable of.

Although, as angry as I was, on some level I understood why she did it. Emily expected a certain level of savagery within our ranks. The occasional letting of blood. And if you weren't going to be a predator in this pack, you'd soon be the prey.

"Oh my God," Emily said with a laugh as she picked up one of the scraps of paper that had fallen from my hand and fluttered to the carpet at her feet. "She didn't write this, you guys, her *boyfriend* did." She erupted into a fit of laughter that nearly had her doubling over.

"Okay, very funny," I said, prizing the bit of paper from her hand and shoving it into the little trash bin under my desk. I could feel my cheeks burning a beet red.

"No, come on, I need to see the rest," Emily said, wiping a tear from the corner of her eye with one delicate finger.

"Oh, leave her alone, Em," Tori said half-heartedly. There was a smile playing at the edge of her lips and I could tell she was trying her best not to join in the laughter.

"Fine." Emily rolled her eyes. "We should get going anyway. Come on, girls." Emily set her half-filled cup on my desk, leaving a burgundy ring on the faux wood finish, and ushered Jenny and Tori out of the room.

Nessa's eyes followed them, but she trailed behind. Once Emily was a few steps ahead, her voice fading as she sashayed down the hallway, Nessa turned back toward me.

"Don't worry about them," she said. "I think it's sweet that he sent you a poem. Have a great time tonight, okay?" She squeezed my arm reassuringly.

Tears welled in my eyes. I wasn't sure if it was from embarrassment or from Nessa's kindness, but all I could do was nod my head as I watched her run out of my room to meet our friends.

A bump in the road jostled me in my seat bringing me back to the present. Alex looked over at me. "Sorry about that," he said with a laugh. "I think I may have lost a hubcap back there."

"It's okay, I'm fine," I said, suddenly feeling shy.

"Good, we're almost there."

My stomach churned with nerves. Both at the prospect of spending time alone with Alex, but also over whether Emily was going to hold it against me. She hadn't exactly *said* that she'd wanted me to choose her over Alex, but the message had been made clear. Bringing Jenny out in my place was a subtle jab, a reminder of how easily I could be replaced in her world. I had no misgivings about the fact that Emily had done that intentionally. She'd given me a choice, and, as far as she was concerned, I'd chosen wrong. That misstep would not come without consequences.

Emily could be so kind when she wanted to be, and so cruel when she didn't. The waves of hot and cold that she splashed over me always left me feeling disoriented about where I stood with her, always striving to stay in her good graces. Perhaps that's exactly what she wanted: the power to pull me in when it suited her and ignore me when it didn't.

"Made it," Alex declared as he steered the nose of his grumbling old Toyota into a parking spot.

I looked up at the Emperor Diner. *So much for white linen tablecloths and conversation by candlelight.*

"Wait till you try the burgers here. Best I've ever had."

"Can't wait!" I chimed enthusiastically, trying to embrace this mental shift. I was being silly. We didn't need a pretentious, stuffy dinner and forced romance. Alex and I were above all of that. I decided that it was a good sign that he'd taken me to the diner. Clearly he felt like he could be himself with me—he didn't need to put on a show. I felt a renewed warmth wash over me. *Yes, this is just perfect. This is us.*

* * *

"So," Alex said, as he chewed a bite of his bacon cheeseburger, grease dripping from his fingers. "What did I tell you? Best burger ever, right?"

"Definitely," I agreed, as I tried to nibble delicately at the edge of the massive burger that had been served in a red plastic basket on top of a pile of soggy fries.

I was severely overdressed for the Emperor Diner in my pale pink dress with the scoop neck that highlighted the curve of my breasts. Nearly everything inside the diner was made of polished chrome, which made me feel as though I was sitting in an outdated spaceship. The booths were upholstered in a pebbled, blue faux leather, and the Formica tabletops were bubbling and chipped.

"How did you ever find this place?" I asked.

"Oh, we stopped here after a track meet once, and I've been dying to come back for another one of these burgers." Alex took a massive bite of his burger. The center was a bloody red and I had to swallow back a wave of bile that suddenly rose in my throat.

"What were we talking about before the food came?" Alex pondered, a puzzled look on his face. "Oh right, Professor Perv. Anyway, I heard he's under investigation for trying to cop a feel with a freshman girl."

"What course does he teach?"

"Psych."

"Isn't Emily in that class with you?" I asked, my senses suddenly on high alert.

"Um, yeah, I think she is," Alex replied, pulling a long sip of his Coca-Cola, which was served in an old-fashioned fountain glass.

A shudder ran through me. Hadn't Emily just complained about that professor embarrassing her in front of the class? *What was it that she said again?* I felt goose bumps rising on my skin as I recalled her words: *"I'm certainly not going to let him get away with it."*

"Are you cold, Jules?" Alex asked. "You can take my jacket if you are."

"No," I said with a smile, "I'm fine." I forced myself to push all thoughts of Emily out of my head. *Tonight is about me and Alex.*

"Do you want to go out after this?" Alex asked. "I was gonna meet some friends at this glow party."

So much for tonight just being about the two of us. But I suppose it's nice that he wants to introduce me to his friends. "Sure," I replied, hoping I sounded appropriately excited. "My friends were planning on going to that party too."

"Awesome," Alex said, as he polished off the remains of his burger, licking his fingers delightedly.

* * *

"Ahh! You guys came!" Nessa squealed when she saw me and Alex picking our way through the crowd. The bar was lit by glowing purple black lights and everyone inside was laden with phosphorescent bands twisted around their bodies and splashes of brightly colored paint.

"How was your date?" Nessa asked eagerly, the glow sticks dangling from her neck swaying as she spoke.

I glanced over at Alex—we hadn't discussed whether our

dinner was actually a date. But his face remained impassive, giving me no further indication as to what he might have been thinking.

"Dinner was great," I replied.

"Good! Come have a drink with us!"

Nessa looped a glow necklace around my neck before grabbing me by the hand and pulling me toward the bar. Alex followed close behind.

"Look who I found, guys!" Nessa announced.

"Hey!" Tori said, as she collected a round of shot glasses from the bar. The liquid inside glowed an ethereal blue.

Jenny and Emily exchanged a loaded look.

"So," Emily began in a saccharine tone that made my stomach turn. "Do you think you had your *last first kiss*?"

I felt a wave of nausea rising as I looked back at Alex. I thought I saw a flash of disappointment cross his face in the darkened bar, but it was gone as quickly as it came, making me question whether I'd imagined it, whether he'd even heard Emily's pointed question.

Jenny snickered. Clearly *she'd* heard.

"Oh, don't be mad, Jules, I was just teasing," Emily said with a pout. She hugged me close to her and I could smell the jasmine scent of her favorite shampoo.

As she pulled away, she leaned in close to my ear and whispered, "I see why you're so into him." She looked over at Alex appraisingly, her teeth a flash of glowing white under the buzzing black lights overhead. "You better lock him down tonight. He's the kind of guy girls would kill for."

Chapter 18

Then

It was the early hours of the morning by the time Alex and I got back to his room. Before long, the sun would be slowly creeping over the horizon casting watery morning light over the sleepy campus.

We'd had fun at the glow party, despite my original hope that we'd be spending a romantic evening alone. He'd introduced me to his friends, and we danced all night, kissing under the glowing purple lights.

This time, when Alex asked me if I wanted to leave with him, I immediately agreed. The hesitation I'd felt the last time I was alone with him was instantly washed away under a heady mix of alcohol and the feel of his hands on my body all night as we moved to the music.

But now, as I watched Alex fumble with his door keys, I was starting to feel nervous again. *Am I ready for this? I have to be.* Emily was right, a guy like Alex Caldwell wasn't going to wait around forever. If I wanted to make him mine, I'd have to give him something in return.

Alex finally pushed open the door to his room. I don't know what I was expecting his living space would look like, but there wasn't much to it. A tiny dorm room identical to the one I shared with Tori, except it was lacking any of the softness we'd brought into our room. The tiled floor was bare in place of our white shag throw rug, and a flannel comforter hung listlessly off the edge of his unmade bed. There were no pictures tacked to the wall of Alex with his arm looped around his friends, no fairy lights strung along his headboard. The room was lifeless, unloved. Nothing, aside from the piles of discarded track clothes and sneakers, gave any indication of who might have inhabited it.

"Nate is out for the night," Alex said as we stepped inside, and he closed the door behind us. "Probably with your friend."

I tried to ignore the tangy scent of sweat that lingered in the stale air.

"Uh, sorry it's kind of a mess in here," he said, rubbing the back of his neck with one hand. "I wasn't expecting company."

I immediately felt my shoulders relax. The fact that he hadn't *expected* me to spend the night made me instantly feel more comfortable with him. Somehow it felt like less pressure. As though ending up in his bed was just the natural progression of the night.

"I don't mind," I said, stepping toward him. I rose up onto the tips of my toes, and pressed my lips to his. I could feel his mouth giving way as he parted his lips, inviting, wanting more.

He ran his fingers through my hair, gently cupping the back of my head, before sliding them down my neck and along my shoulders, taking the thin strap of my dress with him. I felt the loosened strap grazing my upper arm, a whispered reminder that the rest of my dress would soon follow.

As our lips parted, Alex's fingers nimbly worked the zipper at the back of my dress, sliding it down slowly, sensually, his hooded eyes locked on mine.

My body seemed drawn to his, a magnetic pull that made me crave his touch, the feel of his skin on mine.

My dress fell to the floor, the soft pink silk landing in a puddle around my feet, leaving me in nothing but black lace panties. Alex took in the sight of my nearly naked body: my exposed breasts, my pale skin that seemed to glow a milky white in the moonlight that flooded through his bedroom window.

"Wow," he said breathlessly. "You're so beautiful, Jules."

He gently touched my breasts, his large hands so tender and reverential, that it sent a pang of longing through my body the likes of which I'd never experienced before. In that moment, I knew I was ready.

And so, when Alex softly laid me on his bed, and I felt him push inside of me for the first time, the apprehension I'd once felt faded away, leaving nothing but love in its place.

Chapter 19

Now

Claire flops back on her cream-colored leather sofa, and brushes a lock of hair away from her face before she picks up her wineglass and takes a large sip.

"I sure do love my son, but good Lord, do I love bedtime too! Anyway," she says as she flicks on the baby monitor and sets it on the glass coffee table in front of us, "what's going on with you? I feel like I'm missing out on so much while I'm locked away up here."

My eyes automatically flit across the penthouse apartment. The soaring ceilings, the polished glass, the panoramic view of the Manhattan skyline flickering with life. A fire softly crackles in the modern glass fireplace, casting a warm glow over Claire's apartment, tastefully decorated in shades of cream and gold. I suspect that she had it professionally designed, though I don't doubt her capable of having done it herself. Claire is one of those people who seems to have a talent for everything she touches. While I'm panting at the gym, she's hardly breaking a sweat in her designer yoga pants, while I struggle to connect with people,

Claire is instantly likable, making friends everywhere she goes. If she wasn't so damn nice, I might be jealous.

"There's not really much to tell," I lie. "Same old. Crazy busy with work, as usual."

"Well what was up with you and your friends the other night when I ran into you guys?"

"What do you mean?" I push back the defensive edge that's creeping into my voice.

"I don't know. I just got the impression that I was interrupting something when I came over to say 'hello'. I could just be imagining things, but it seemed tense."

It crosses my mind that I could confide in Claire. I could tell her the truth. She's my only friend who's not associated with Westbridge. Maybe she'd understand. Maybe she'd even know what to do. But as she looks at me, all round-eyed innocence and good intentions, I know that I'm kidding myself. *How could she possibly understand?*

"Oh," I say waving my hand dismissively. "It was nothing. Just some old college drama."

I pick up my wineglass, rolling the delicate stem between my fingers. The crisp white wine inside glows a deep gold as the crystal glass reflects the licking flames from the fireplace.

"College drama? Gosh, still? Your college experience must have been far more wild than mine if you're still dealing with the drama!" Claire says with a laugh.

Claire looks over at a photograph in a polished silver frame that sits on the side table in her living room, and my eyes follow her gaze. It's a photo of her and her husband, Brian, in matching purple graduation gowns. Her face is half buried in his chest as he hugs her tightly, holding a rolled diploma from New York University over his head victoriously, a wide grin on his face. I smile to myself at how young they look. Brian in his thick, black-rimmed glasses. This would have been long before his tech company took off and he had personal shoppers at his disposal.

Claire told me early on in our friendship about how she met Brian in her junior year at NYU and knew immediately that he was the one. She speaks of her time there, her college friends, fondly, nostalgic memories of rosy days gone by. The smile fades from my face as I think of how different my college experience, my entire life for that matter, could have been, if only I hadn't met Emily.

Claire still has a large group of friends, sorority girls who remain as close as sisters. I've met a few of them. And watching how they interact with one another … it just feels so … easy. Instead of cutting one another down, they lift each other up. I wish I'd understood that distinction earlier in my life. Sometimes I think that's why Claire wandered into my life, as a cosmic reminder that things could be different, that the friendships I had before her, the ones I sometimes still thought about wistfully, were different—they'd become something venomous, dangerous, poised like coiled snakes always waiting to strike.

I take a sip of my wine, feeling the bitter bite on the back of my tongue. The baby monitor crackles with static on the table, emphasizing the uncomfortable silence. I feel like I need to offer Claire *something*. She openly shares her life with me. Her drama with her mommy friends, spats with her husband, her aspirations to someday own her own art gallery. And in return, I offer her nothing more than a surface-level view of my world. I feel a niggling guilt pulling at my mind. I like Claire; I value her friendship. But I also know that our friendship has been very much a one-way street. Even though I can't tell Claire *everything*, I need to make more of an effort to let her in. *Friends are meant to share secrets.*

"Well, there was this one thing that happened earlier today that I can't seem to shake."

Claire tucks her thin, toned legs up under her like a cat. She looks at me curiously over the rim of her wineglass, waiting for me to continue.

I hesitate a moment. It's difficult for me to take down the armor, to allow myself to be vulnerable with anyone. Claire doesn't say a word as I collect my thoughts. I wonder if she's caught on. If she realizes that she's witnessing a rare occurrence: a flash of my true self. It's as though she's watching a fawn in the woods. Fearful that the slightest sound may send me running back into the underbrush.

"This is going to sound crazy …" I start.

Claire nods subtly, encouraging me to continue.

"But when I came home this afternoon, I would have sworn that someone had been in my apartment."

Claire's eyes grow round with alarm. "Oh my God!"

"No, no, I'm sure I was just being ridiculous. But I got the strangest feeling the moment I walked in. Like something was out of place, though I couldn't exactly put my finger on what it was." I don't tell her about the mug. About the broken piece I was so sure I'd thrown away. I know exactly how insane that would sound. And so instead I force a laugh. "Would you believe I crept around the apartment wielding a knife? Like I would have had the first clue what to do had I actually found an intruder!"

"Jules, that must have been so frightening." I notice that Claire doesn't join in my effort to make light of the situation. "You poor thing. You really should have better security at your place. I can ask Brian to send someone over. I'm sure he has a guy for that at his company."

She pulls the cork out of the top of the wine bottle with a "pop" and tops up my glass. I take a grateful sip.

"Seriously, Claire. I'm fine. It just gave me a little scare. Has me a bit on edge."

"I'm sure. I'm glad you're okay, but next time, maybe just call the police instead of running around with a knife like some sort of … ninja warrior."

The thought of me creeping around in my empty apartment like a ninja makes me giggle, and soon after Claire follows suit.

128

"Anyway, enough about me, what's new with you?" I ask, in an effort to steer the conversation into safer waters.

"Oh my gosh …" Claire launches into a story about the latest dinner outing she and Brian had to attend with one of Brian's investors, who, by all accounts, has a personality as dry as burnt toast.

"It was brutal, Jules. Seriously. All that talk about software coding is enough to put any normal person to sleep. But not this guy. I think he could have gone on all night! But at least I met some nice new mom friends at the Mommy Meet-Up this morning."

"Oh right, Tori's playgroup. How was it?"

"It was great, actually! The women were all so welcoming, and it was great to meet some new people in our neighborhood. They even took me out for lunch afterwards."

I could just picture perfect, pretty Claire, with towheaded Charlie on her lap, sitting on a muslin blanket laid out under a shady elm tree. With her friendly smile and her unassuming kindness, she would have been immediately welcomed into the fold of Upper East Side motherhood, where the uniform is designer jeans, diamond tennis bracelets, and three-carat engagement rings.

"It's just a shame Tori couldn't make it," Claire said with a frown, pulling me from my reverie.

"She … wasn't there? She told me she was going …"

Claire shrugs. "I guess her plans changed. I was hoping to see a familiar face, but she didn't show. Anyway, I'll have to text her to thank her for getting me into the playgroup. I think Charlie is really going to like it." Claire begins to tell me about the other kids in the group, scrutinizing Charlie's development under a microscope in comparison to the other babies around his age. "It's just that we want him to get into a top-tier pre-school in a few years …" she says, but I only vaguely register her words.

The only thing on my mind is that Tori lied to me.

* * *

It's dark in my apartment by the time I get home from Claire's, tipsy with wine. I sneak through the house like a cat burglar, trying not to wake Jason. As I tread through the darkened rooms, our furniture only shadowy silhouettes, an image of someone else creeping through our quiet apartment flashes through my head and it makes me physically shudder.

I quickly get myself ready for bed, washing the makeup from my face and pulling my hair up into a bun, before I slip into bed next to Jason.

The lights are off, and his back is turned to me but I know he's awake. By now I know the pattern of his breaths, the sound of his sleep. But he doesn't move. It would seem that he'd rather pretend to be asleep than speak to me.

I know I should talk to him, to find a way to make things right between us, but as I lie beside my husband in the dark, I can't find the words to explain how my world has been turned upside down. This conversation is far too big, too unwieldy, to let it loose in the dark hours of the night. And so instead, I turn away from him resignedly, tucking the comforter under my chin. But just as I'm about to close my eyes, I see my phone illuminate on the nightstand with a buzz. I reach for the phone, my eyes squinting against the bright light, to find a text from Nessa:

Emily wants to meet.

Chapter 20

Then

I reached my hand into the purse in my lap and felt around for my phone. Once I felt the cool plastic case, I surreptitiously looked down into my bag to check the screen. No new messages.

"I heard he's getting fired," Nessa said, her voice a conspiratorial whisper as she leaned over the dining-hall table to give Tori, Emily, and me the latest update on the scandal surrounding Professor Perv, formally known as Professor Emmett.

All the students were talking about it, hushed whispers floated through the campus like an exotic scent swept in on a distant breeze. Everyone wanted to know which student had reported him, whether the rumors were true. And the rumors were growing larger by the day, becoming something wild and reckless as they gained momentum. I'd even heard one story wherein Professor Emmett locked a freshman girl in the janitor's closet and had his way with her. Even if he somehow managed to keep his job—which, according to Nessa, who always had her finger on the pulse of the latest gossip, was looking unlikely—his reputation on campus was in irreparable disrepair.

I assumed that on some level Nessa must have suspected Emily had a hand in this, just as I did, but she wouldn't dare say it. I looked over at Emily, her expression inscrutable, and she calmly sipped from her bottle of Evian water. She appeared, if anything, to have grown bored of the conversation. Professor Emmett's fate was of little to no interest to her. But I could just imagine the theatrics she would put on if we were to suggest she'd intentionally destroyed a man's life. The way her lower lip would wobble, her eyes clouding with tears at our betrayal. She would relish in the role of the wrongfully accused. But it frightened me, how far she was willing to go to get what she wanted. I think that was the first time I truly saw it, the dark and murky depths of her.

But I was too wrapped up in my own mess to make Emily take ownership of hers. It had been two days since I slept with Alex and he hadn't spoken a word to me since. Not unless you want to count the text I'd received moments after I left his room:

Tonight was fun. Let's do it again some time ;)

I'd read it quickly, shoving my phone back into my bag forcefully.

The sex had been quick and primal, him pushing against me feverishly, his eyes closed in pleasure, and me clutching on to his broad, muscular shoulders, my nails digging into his soft skin. I don't think he noticed that my vice-like grip was not born of the throes of passion, but rather out of how unexpectedly painful sex could be. I suppose it was because it was my first time. I didn't know what it was supposed to feel like, but I'd imagined a hedonistic rush of sensuality, an awakening of my inner goddess. Instead, it felt as though my body was breaking and tearing as he groaned with pleasure, oblivious to my pain. I lay beneath him, holding on to his back, willing away the tears that prickled at the backs of my eyes as he finally climaxed.

He rolled off me, his body glistening with sweat in the silvery moonlight. "God, that was amazing."

He looked over at me. As though he was waiting for my validation that I'd enjoyed what had just happened as much as he did. I smiled bleakly and managed a nod as I pulled his sheets up over my exposed breasts. I didn't trust myself to talk yet. I was too worried that I'd break into tears.

I hadn't expected that losing my virginity would bring with it such a tidal wave of emotions: remorse, shame, guilt, excitement, hopefulness—all mixed together into a muddled cocktail of hormones that left me feeling unmoored and slightly queasy. I felt as fragile as a raw nerve.

"You want a cigarette?" Alex asked as he lit one for himself, his lighter a quick flash in the darkened room.

I shook my head, as I watched him pull a drag from the cigarette and bend down to blow the smoke through the window, which had been cracked open.

"These windows suck," he said. The windows only opened a sliver on the upper floors of the dormitory halls, purportedly so that anxious freshman couldn't jump out of them. Some of the smoke from his lit cigarette billowed back into the room, a tangle of blueish tendrils.

"I didn't know you smoked," I managed to squeak out. My voice felt foreign to my ears, as if I'd become a new person. Someone I didn't recognize.

"Only after sex," he replied with a wink. The thought made my stomach turn. Was I, was this, all just part of a routine for him? Was my first time—an experience I'd always imagined I'd share with a boy I loved—just another notch in his bedpost?

An uneasy silence settled between us, and it made me stir. I'd noticed that he hadn't offered me anything to sleep in, and so I started to get re-dressed in the clothes I had worn earlier in the evening. The pink, silk dress I'd so lovingly selected for our date suddenly felt tawdry and cheap as I picked it up off the floor. I'd never felt more exposed than I did as I got dressed in front of Alex.

"Listen, Jules, I would love for you to stay the night. Trust me, I'd love to do that again in the morning, but I have an early practice tomorrow."

I tucked a lock of tousled hair behind my ear as I looped the straps of my heels through my fingers. "Oh. Sure. I understand," I muttered, hot embarrassment rising into my cheeks.

"I knew you'd get it. You're amazing. Like, the coolest girl ever." He pulled me into a hug, wrapping his strong arms around my petite frame. I felt stiff against his body, but I forced myself to return the gesture.

Then he held my face in his hands and kissed me hard on the mouth, his lips still full and warm from our earlier passion.

"I'll call you," he said, his voice strong and reassuring. I felt myself relax. *He's going to call. I wasn't just another conquest for him. I didn't make a mistake.*

But he hadn't called. And with each passing day, I felt myself growing increasingly bitter.

As we filtered out of the dining hall, each of us hurrying off to our own classes, Emily caught me by the wrist. "Hey, wait a sec, Jules."

I stopped and turned back to face her.

"You still haven't heard from him yet?" She looked at me pityingly.

"No, not yet."

"What a dick," she said with a scoff.

"I'm sure he's just busy."

"Busy. Right." I could feel the sarcasm dripping off her words and it made me feel defensive.

I wrapped my denial around me like a security blanket. "He has a lot going on," I replied, my tone sharp.

"Well, I think you should just text him yourself."

"You do? Really? Wouldn't that come across a little ... clingy?"

"No! You slept with the guy!" Her voice grew louder with righteousness. I shot her a pleading look, willing her to lower her voice.

"Sorry," Emily conceded, before she continued in a more hushed tone. "It's just that you *slept* with him. The least he can do is reply to a damn text."

She's right. What right does he have to ignore me? To treat me like an afterthought?

As if Emily could sense the shift she'd caused in my thoughts, my growing indignation, she pushed further.

"I mean, you were *naked* with him a few days ago, and now you're going to be shy about sending him a text?"

I wanted to rally to the cause. I wanted to feel justified in firing off a text to Alex demanding to know why I hadn't heard from him, but I just couldn't get there. Emily didn't understand. I couldn't demand anything of him. I wasn't like Emily. I didn't possess the same power she did. Emily owned the men she'd slept with. Once she was with them, she held them in the palm of her hands, toying with them like marionettes until she grew tired of them and moved on to the next. I was certain that I had no such hold over Alex.

"Maybe …" I replied. "I'll think about it."

"Well, if I was you, I'd show him that I'm not someone to be ignored."

* * *

My fingers hovered over the keyboard of my laptop wondering whether Emily had been right. *Should I reach out to him first? Will it make me look weak and pathetic, or confident in my own self-worth?* I was treading in unknown waters and I was finding the tide too strong for me to find my bearings.

I pulled up Alex's last email. Sent a few days before our "date". *If that's what it even was.* He'd been talking about his anxiety about an upcoming track meet. The pressure his coach was putting on him to beat his previous record. I had replied reassuringly, telling him I knew he would rise to the challenge. The conversation felt so distant to me, so disconnected, as if the words I was reading were not my own. I suppose in a way, they weren't. The naive, hopeful girl who'd written those emails no longer existed, at least not in me. I'd felt a seismic change happening within me, and I knew I could never go back to who I once was.

I felt a surge of anger as I thought of how trusting I'd been. I thought of all the pieces of myself that I'd given Alex, and how casually he'd collected all the precious bits I'd proffered before tossing them aside as if they were nothing. Riding the wave of my rage, I quickly slammed my laptop closed and typed out a text message instead:

Really? Nothing?

I hit send, and immediately regretted it as my anger receded like the tide, exposing a coastline of sadness and self-pity.

I sighed in frustration and pushed my chair back from my desk. Just then, I heard a rap on the door. For one brief, fleeting moment, I imagined it was Alex. A vision of him with flowers in his hand and an apology on his lips floated through my head. But then Jenny pushed open the door.

She poked her head into the room tentatively. "Jules?"

I bristled at the sound of her voice. I hadn't seen her since the weekend, when she'd maliciously read Alex's poem aloud, laughing with Emily at something I'd held most precious. My private world exposed and ripped to shreds.

"Yeah?" I replied impatiently.

She stepped into the room and perched on the edge of my bed, her shoulders hunched, making it appear as though she was shrinking into herself.

"I just wanted to apologize." She lifted her head, looking at me with pleading eyes, once again shielded behind her quirky blue frames. "I'm sorry for what I did with the poem. That was really … cruel of me. I … I don't know what came over me."

I nodded in agreement, my lips set into a hard, thin line. I wasn't ready to forgive her just yet. Even though I knew, on some level, that my anger was really at Alex. I was letting Jenny bear the brunt of it as she happened to be sitting in front of me.

Jenny fumbled to continue, to fill the silence I'd left her with. "I don't like who I am when I'm with her. Emily. I feel like she brings out the worst in me."

I felt myself softening. I knew exactly what she meant. "It's fine, Jenny. Let's just put it behind us."

"Okay … I just wanted to make sure you know how awful I feel about the way I treated you."

I knew I owed her an apology as well, for how poorly I'd treated *her*. But I wasn't ready to offer it. I was holding on to my anger toward her, stoking its flames in the hope that it would overpower the sadness I felt about Alex.

Chapter 21

Now

I knock on the door to Tori's apartment. She'd offered to drive all of us to meet Emily at her country club, just outside of the city. As I wait for the door to open, I look down at the address I'd scribbled on a sheet of torn notepaper, and then back up at the two-story brownstone towering above me. I'd heard Tori mention it back at Westbridge, the townhouse on the Upper East Side she'd been gifted by her parents at graduation, but seeing it in person is dizzying. I used to imagine what a life like that might look like, an address in the most coveted neighborhood in Manhattan. I'd always dreamed of living in New York City someday, but I think that was when the idea of it began to sparkle with an added allure. It all sounded so glamorous, that I began to romanticize what a life here could mean, how it might change me.

A man throws the front door open wide, startling me back to the moment. *Tori's husband, Matt.* His muscular chest is bare, a white T-shirt slung over his shoulder, and he's wearing a pair of gray sweatpants that hang low on his hips, revealing far more of him than I've ever seen on Facebook.

"Hey, you must be Jules. Come on in." He shakes my hand and steps aside to welcome me in. "Sorry about the informal attire. I lost a battle with some strawberries this morning."

I follow Matt into their home, trying not to stare too obviously at the grand French windows, herringbone floors, and sleek marble kitchen along the way. *How long am I going to pretend that I'm one of them, that their affluence no longer astounds me? Will I ever be enough, or will I forever be seen as the same fresh-faced girl who just stepped off the bus from Ohio …? Will I ever stop feeling like I need to prove myself?*

"This is Mia," Matt says proudly, placing his hands on the back of a highchair occupied by a beautiful brown-haired little girl with big, round eyes. She babbles happily in her seat as she smears pureed strawberries like fingerpaint on the tray in front of her. Aside from the strawberry mess, which has turned Mia's cheeks a sticky red, she looks like a clone of her mother. I feel my heart contract at the sight of her.

"Da!" she announces as she lifts her tiny plastic spoon and launches another glob onto the floor. She giggles cheerfully, her chubby legs kicking in delight, as it lands with a "splat".

Matt rolls his eyes and grabs a paper towel. "Tori will be right down," he tells me as he wipes at the floor.

As if on cue, I hear a tumble of footsteps as Tori rushes down the stairs. *She lied to me.* At the sight of her, the betrayal, the hurt washes over me anew, but I push it back down.

"Hey, Jules. Sorry. I'm just about ready," she says, fastening the back of a gold stud earring. "I see you've met the family."

She's wearing a black V-neck blouse tucked into a pair of tight jeans, paired with a blood-red leather jacket and black ankle boots with a square, block heel. I look down at my own outfit. A boxy cream-colored sweater, skinny jeans, and scuffed, brown, suede riding boots. When I left my house this morning, I'd thought I'd looked put together, edgy. Cool. But as soon as I see Tori, I realize that I'd gotten it wrong. Again. I always seem to be one step behind. Tori has, and always had, something I didn't: the air of wealth that clings to her casually, like a whiff of expensive perfume.

"Okay, let's go," Tori announces as she loops her arm through a Burberry purse and drops a kiss on Mia's head. "You be a good girl for Daddy, okay?" she coos.

Mia smiles as she splashes her hands in the mess on her tray.

"See you tonight," Matt says, kissing Tori tenderly on the temple. "I'm proud of you for doing this, babe."

She smiles sweetly and kisses him briskly on the lips. I wave my goodbyes to Mia and Matt, and follow Tori out to her car, a sleek black Lexus.

We snap our seat belts in place with a "click" in the dark underground garage.

Now that I'm finally alone with Tori, part of me wants to demand answers, to press her to tell me where she really was yesterday—why she'd lied to me about going to the Mommy Meet-Up when I know she hadn't. But if there's one thing I learned from my time at Westbridge, it's that knowing someone's secret gives you all the power. I may not know *where* Tori really was yesterday, but I do know that she's hiding something, and I don't want to relinquish the upper hand just yet. I'll let her think she's fooled me for now. Besides, there's something more pressing that I need to discuss with Tori at the moment.

"What does he know?" I ask anxiously.

"Who?"

"Matt!" *Is she intentionally being evasive?*

"Nothing really."

"Then what was he talking about? Telling you he's proud of you?" I ask pointedly.

"Oh, I had to give him a story. Some explanation as to why I'm spending a Sunday driving up to Westchester to see a woman I haven't spoken to in years."

"Well, what did you tell him?"

140

"Just that I was trying to put the past behind me."

I stare at her in disbelief. "You didn't tell him about …"

"No, NO! Not that. Look, you weren't around, Jules; you don't know what it was like for me after Westbridge. What *I* was like when I met Matt." Tori sighs. Her hands rest atop the steering wheel, but she doesn't make to leave. Instead she stares out over the dashboard as she continues.

"We all handled our guilt over what happened differently. You shut down, separated yourself from all of us. I get that, but it wasn't the same for me. I surrounded myself with other people. I had to. I couldn't stand to be alone in my own head. I went out every night, partied too hard. I drank too much, took any invitation that was offered to me, anything to avoid being alone. I got in over my head, Jules. I think I was afraid to let the noise die down, because if I did, I knew I'd have to face the reality of what we did.

"It went on like that for a few years. I was in a really bad place. Until I met Matt. I'm not proud to admit it, but I met him at a club and went home with him before I even knew his name. Although I've always seemed to have a knack for choosing the worst guys, when I woke up the next morning to find him making me breakfast in bed, I knew that he was just … different. No one had treated me that way, like I was worth more than a wild night, in years. And honestly, that's what changed everything for me. I sobered up, stopped partying. He made me want to be better. And it wasn't too long until I got pregnant with Mia."

"Wow, that's … I had no idea." From the vantage point of social media, I'd made the assumption that Tori had escaped Westbridge unscathed, that her life was perfect, that she'd let go of the past with the ease of a child releasing a balloon string. *How easy it is to make snap judgments when you're spoon-fed the highlight reel of someone else's life.*

"Of course you didn't know—you weren't there!" Tori retorts as she begins to back the car out of the parking space. She takes a deep breath, settling herself before she continues. "I don't blame you for that. I never really have. I understood why you needed some distance back then, but it hasn't been easy for any of us."

"I get that now. I'm sorry," I say gently.

"Honestly, Matt and Mia were the only things that got me through it. When I first found out I was pregnant, God, I was terrified. What if I was a terrible mother? What if I didn't deserve her? What if the relationship I was building with Matt was still too new, too fragile, to withstand the stress of a baby? But it wasn't. I should have trusted Matt more. I should have known what we had was stronger than that."

Maybe my marriage is strong enough too.

"Matt was actually thrilled when he found out I was pregnant," Tori says, a small smile edging onto her face as the memory surfaces. "He got down on one knee and proposed right there in my kitchen, and I grabbed on to that second chance with both hands."

"How do you do it though?" I ask. "How can you balance having a family, being the wife and mother you want to be, while holding part of yourself, your history, back?"

"You just do. When Mia was born, it wasn't like I had any other choice but to find a way to move forward, to make peace with the mistakes I've made, the person I was. I needed to be better … for her."

"But what about Matt? How do you manage it with him?"

"Matt's never really pried into my past, but I'm sure he's always known on some level that I was running from something when we first met. Like today, I told him that this trip was just something I needed to do, to give myself closure on some past trauma. He supported me without question."

I wonder if Jason would do the same? Maybe if I gave him the chance …

"I'm happy for you, Tori. Really," I say, and I mean it. Tori has found the kind of happiness I've been denying myself … and

Jason. I want to get to that place—I do—but while I'm happy to know that Tori found the kind of peace she needed to build a life for herself after Westbridge, I still don't know how to find it for myself.

Jason was right when he said that I've been holding myself back from him. But what if we can't survive the fallout if I take down the wall I've built, when I set free the darkness that's swirling behind it? Once something like that is unleashed, it can never be reined in again. There's no turning back. Everything changes. It has to. What if, as Tori said, our marriage is too fragile to survive it?

"What about you?" Tori asks, pulling me from my thoughts. "What did you tell Jason?"

I scoffed. "Nothing. We're not exactly on speaking terms at the moment."

"Is everything okay with you two?" Tori asks, taking her eyes off the road for a brief moment to look in my direction. "I know it's been a while since we've really talked, but I'm here if you want to. The last few days have been … a lot."

"Things are as good as they *can* be when I'm constantly lying to him," I grumble, slouching in my seat.

This morning I told Jason that I was going to meet up with an old friend from college who'd recently reached out. Not that he'd asked. He seemed content to sip his morning coffee in silence while he read the paper. It wasn't exactly a *lie*, but it certainly wasn't the truth either. I'm finding it difficult to juggle all the omissions, the sleights of hand, the lingering half-truths. It's exhausting.

"We're here," Tori announces as she nimbly navigates the Lexus into a parking spot.

"Where are we? I thought we were picking up Nessa." The squat brick building before us doesn't look like the type of place she'd live.

"Oh, she's at the studio this morning. She had an early session booked to record her single to submit to that record company that's been showing some interest."

143

Right. Nessa's record deal. I'd forgotten all about it with every-thing going on. Nessa's dreams are finally on the verge of coming true, but her good news has been overshadowed by Jenny's reap-pearance in our lives.

Tori cuts the engine and slides out of the car. "Come on. Maybe we can catch the end of her session."

Tori and I walk into the studio. The reception area, decorated with vinyl records lining the walls, is painted a bright white, and there is a sleek, glass desk along the back wall, which is currently unmanned.

"Looks like the receptionist is out," Tori says, nodding toward the empty desk. "Let's go check out the back."

"Maybe we shouldn't …" I start, but Tori is already pushing open a door at the back of the reception area. I hurry after her.

I follow Tori into a lounge of sorts, where low-slung couches in a bright pink upholstery face a glass panel. On the other side of the glass, there are two rooms.

"That's Tim, Nessa's manager," Tori whispers pointing to a large man standing in one of the rooms. His chin is in his hand and he seems to be studying an enormous switchboard with an array of flashing dials and buttons. A second man is manning the switchboard, sliding and spinning its components as though he's playing a finely tuned instrument. In the other room, there's Nessa. She's wearing tight black pants, thigh-high suede boots, and a form-fitting black tank top. The look is completed by her signature red lipstick and a pair of oversized headphones that rest on top of her long dark hair. Her eyes are closed as she sings into the microphone in front of her.

I've seen Nessa perform before, back in our college days, but never with the kind of raw passion and intensity she's displaying right now. Although we can't hear the music, it's clear that she's putting everything she has into this song. Her head is thrown back, her hair trailing down her back, and her body seems to heave with the effort of pulling the music out of her soul. Tori and I watch her in silence for a few moments before Tim notices us standing on the other side of the glass. Tori waves, and he gives us a quick nod before flicking a switch on the wall. The room is instantly filled with the sound of Nessa's melodic voice.

This song is unlike anything I've heard Nessa sing before. It's far from the upbeat pop songs she used to belt out in smoky karaoke bars. This song is deeply emotional, a ballad of sorts, which carries with it an expressive yearning for true love that stirs emotions in me that have long been dormant.

It's only now that I fully understand how much pain Nessa has been carrying with her all these years.

As if she could read my thoughts, Tori explains: "Nessa hasn't had an easy go of things either. She works really hard to look like she's okay, but she isn't. Never has been."

"What is her life like now?" I ask, realizing how little I really know about this adult version of the girl I once knew.

"Her work—the plays, and trying to write her own music—has really been her whole life. She's dated a few people here and there, but never anything serious. Looking the way she does, I'm sure you can guess there was never a shortage of suitors. But she finds something wrong with every single one of them. 'He was just too short,' 'he was *too* into me,' 'he sends smiley faces after *every* text.'"

This I can understand. Nessa found fault with anyone who showed an ounce of interest in her because it's easier to find an excuse to push people away than to face the fact that you don't like *yourself* enough to make a real connection with anyone. I'd spent years living the same way.

"Whenever Nessa lets anyone get too close," Tori explains, "they're always on borrowed time."

I nod in agreement. In this moment, listening to Nessa's song, hearing Tori's words, I feel as though I'm seeing Nessa more clearly than I ever have before. I understand why she's denied herself happiness, connection all this time. It's hard to allow yourself to be that vulnerable, to let someone else own any part of you.

Especially when there are parts of yourself that you fear might be ugly. It's far safer to loan out your heart like a well-loved library book: something worn and fragile to be held tenderly in others' hands before being returned safely back to you.

The three of us—Tori, Nessa, and I—have spent the last thirteen years hiding from our mistakes, each of us shielding ourselves from the world in our own way. I know that now. Maybe I always have.

The music ends, and Nessa opens her eyes, finally spotting Tori and me who are clapping wildly on the other side of the glass. She blushes slightly and mouths, "Thank you."

Tim's voice bellows over the intercom. "That's it, Ness. That was the one. Let's call it a wrap. I'll send you a copy of the track as soon as we're finished here."

Nessa collects her things and comes to meet me and Tori in the lounge.

"Ness, that was *incredible*," I tell her earnestly.

"Yeah, it really was," Tori agrees.

"Thanks," Nessa says modestly, waving off the compliment. "We should get on the road."

146

Chapter 22

Then

The clinking of silverware against porcelain was the only sound that filled the room as my parents and I sat down for the smallest Thanksgiving dinner I could remember.

Our holiday table was always relatively small, given that I was an only child and that most of my relatives had relocated to Florida when I was young, but this year it was just the three of us. My grandparents usually made the trip up to Ohio to spend Thanksgiving with us before giving the bigger prize, Christmas, to their favored children and grandchildren who had followed them in their move to Florida years earlier. But this year, their seats were empty.

"It's a shame Grandma and Granddad couldn't make it this year," Dad said as he helped himself to another serving of mashed potatoes.

"Can you believe we're expecting a snowstorm? It's not even December yet!" Mom exclaimed with a tut.

I rolled my eyes as I pushed a slice of dry turkey around my plate. They were acting as though we didn't see snow in November practically every year.

"You've been very quiet since you've gotten home, Juliana," Dad said, suddenly drawing me into the spotlight. "Everything okay, kiddo?"

"Yeah, fine," I replied, letting out an exasperated sigh. My parents had been asking me some variation of the same question since the minute I stepped off the bus from New York the previous day. It was as though they could immediately sense a change in me, some invisible sign that a tide had turned. And ever since then, they'd been sniffing around me like curious hounds trying to decipher what it meant.

"Why don't you tell us about your classes?" Mom suggested, an earnest look on her face. She was wearing a burgundy cotton dress, her hair swept back in a bun with escaped tendrils falling loosely around her face. Her "Kiss the Cook" apron had been discarded only moments before she sat down at the table.

I'd helped her in the kitchen, at her insistence, most of the morning as she probed me with questions about my classes, my professors, my social life. I knew she was trying to dig up clues as to why I'd returned home acting so withdrawn, but how could I tell her about Alex? How could I explain to my mother that I'd let a boy use me for sex, and even worse, that I'd been stupid enough to develop feelings for him? All I could seem to muster were one-word answers—half-truths that I was hoping would be enough to get me through the short Thanksgiving break.

"Mom, we talk on the phone all the time. I'm *always* telling you about my classes."

My mother looked crestfallen, her smile melting into a frown.

My phone buzzed in my pocket and I quickly fished it out and looked down at the screen. Emily had sent a photo of her, Tori, and Nessa, their faces huddled together beneath woolen winter hats. Emily's arm was outstretched as she snapped the photo. Beneath it, her message read, *"New York misses you."*

"No phones at the table," Dad scolded, pointing a dinner roll in my direction.

"Sorry," I muttered and slipped it back into my pocket.

"Was that one of your school friends?" Mom asked, again trying to raise my spirits. Her voice was soft and gentle, a soothing tone I remembered from my childhood—the one she'd use when I'd crawl into her arms after a nightmare, or when I'd fallen from my bike and she tended to my scraped knee.

"Yeah," I replied, my attention turning back to poking at the food on my plate.

"Do you want to tell us about them?" Mom prodded.

"They're great," I mumbled.

"Any ... boyfriends?" Mom asked. I looked up to find a conspiratorial smile on her face, as if my life was fodder for some two-bit teen drama and we were about to have a heart-warming mother-daughter bonding moment.

I snorted derisively. "No." She'd unwittingly hit a nerve, but I didn't want to show how sharply it had hurt. I crossed my arms over my chest and slouched in my chair.

"Juliana," my father snapped. "I don't have the foggiest clue what is going on with you, but there's no reason for you to be so unkind to your mother. She was—we both were—so looking forward to you coming home for the first time in months. Your mother put a lot of time and effort into making this a memorable holiday for you, and you're sulking around like a petulant child. It's enough."

I looked around at the table my mother had set: folded cloth napkins looped through gold napkin rings were arranged atop her fine wedding china, a golden roasted turkey sat at the center of the table surrounded by porcelain bowls filled with all my favorite side dishes. Candles flickered at the end of the table in crystal candlesticks that I'd never seen her use before. I was hit with a stab of guilt that almost made me double over. I hadn't intended to hurt my mother's feelings, but I also didn't know how to act as though everything was normal when my life felt like it had been turned upside down.

"I'm sorry, Mom," I said earnestly. "I'm just really tired from the trip." I stood up and kissed her on the cheek. "May I be excused?"

My parents exchanged worried looks before my father resignedly agreed.

I trekked up the stairs and into my bedroom, closing the door behind me. I leaned my back against the closed door and slid to the floor.

My bedroom was exactly as I'd left it: childish, a remnant of the person I used to be but could hardly remember anymore. This space, which was once my whole world, no longer felt like it represented me. I felt as though I was looking at it from a remove. As if I was seeing it for the first time. I took in the dated floral wallpaper, the bed, made up with a pink quilt and a matching pink ruffled bed skirt, and the horse figurines I'd lovingly collected, now sitting under a thin layer of dust on the shelf. *How would Emily see this room? Tori? I bet their Upper East Side bedrooms are sophisticated and elegantly designed—far more grown-up than this.* I imagined luxury four-poster beds and high-pile throws laid on polished floors. *Some day I'll have that life.*

I pulled out my phone and replied to Emily.

I miss New York too.

She replied almost immediately:

My dad will fly you out for the weekend if you want.

I felt a spark of excitement rush through me at the prospect of my first trip to New York City, but it was extinguished as quickly as it came. I knew my parents would be heartbroken if I suggested leaving after I'd just gotten home.

I tapped out a response:

My parents would never go for it.

Emily was quick to reply:

Shame. You're missing out.

I was hit with a wave of jealousy. *I wonder if that was the goal?* Tossing my phone on the floor, I dropped my head into my hands.

I was so busy feeling sorry for myself that I almost didn't hear my mom softly knocking on the door.

"Juliana, honey, Kelly is here."

I picked myself up off the floor and opened the door. I'd forgotten about Kelly, about our Thanksgiving tradition. Every year she walked the three blocks over from her parents' house to mine to join us for dessert, and then we would walk into town together for some midnight holiday shopping. All of the local stores were open late on Thanksgiving to let shoppers get an early start on Christmas sales.

"I'll be right down," I replied, forcing a smile. "And, Mom? I really am sorry about earlier."

Mom's face lit up immediately. "It's okay. Let's just put it behind us and enjoy the rest of the weekend together."

* * *

Plastic hangers slid across the clothes rack and collided with a *click* as Kelly and I rummaged through the sale displays.

Even though it was a desperately cold evening, we'd walked into town after shoving our feet into thick snow boots, and pulling on our new matching hats adorned with pom poms—a gift from my parents. We walked with our shoulders hunched and our gloved hands shoved into our coat pockets, too cold to even speak as we made the short journey to the shops. But now it seemed that Kelly had begun to defrost, as she spoke in an endless stream, filling me in on everything I'd missed in the months we'd been apart: local gossip, her classes, her brother's new girlfriend. It felt as though she'd been saving up the words for months, and was frantically making up for the lost time.

She finally paused to catch her breath. "I know we talk on the phone and stuff, but it's just not the same, you know?" She crinkled her nose, which was still pink from the brisk winter air.

"It's not," I agreed. I hadn't realized just how much I'd missed Kelly, her warmth, her familiarity, until I saw her. She hadn't changed at all, as least as far as I could tell, and while that filled me with a sense of nostalgia for the childhood we spent together, it also left me questioning whether we still fit together as well as we once did. "How's Owen?"

"Oh, you know, he's good." A smile spread across her face. "You have to promise you won't tell anyone, but we've been talking about getting married."

"Married?!" I couldn't believe what I was hearing. They were only eighteen. How could they already be thinking about marriage?

"I know, I know, we're too young." Kelly rolled her eyes dramatically. "But when you know, you know," she said with a shrug. "Anyway, it's not like we're going to do it right now or anything. Probably in a few years. But he gave me this promise ring in the meantime."

Kelly pulled off one of her stretchy cotton gloves and showed me a slim silver band, topped with two interlocking hearts, wrapped around her ring finger.

"Well, I'm happy for you guys …" I mustered, still feeling bewildered. I knew our lives had taken different paths, but I don't think I'd realized exactly *how* different until that very moment.

"So what about you?" she asked.

"What *about* me?"

"You told me you met a guy a few weeks ago. Alex, right? But then you never mentioned him again. To be honest, I feel like I've barely heard from you *at all* recently."

"Sorry," I said blandly. "Midterms."

152

"I figured. But whatever happened with the boy?"

Why couldn't she take the hint?

"Nothing."

"Nothing? Really? But you were so into him!"

I clenched my teeth. "It just didn't go anywhere."

There was a time when Kelly would have been the first, and, well, only person I would have wanted to talk to about boys. Especially about my first sexual experience. But it was different with Kelly. Her first time was with her boyfriend of two years, whom she was now planning to marry. How could I tell her that I'd lost my virginity to a boy who probably didn't even remember my last name? My cheeks burned with shame just thinking about it. *No, it was better not to tell her anything about it.* Besides, I had my college friends—Tori, Emily, and Nessa—who had been my shoulders to cry on every day since it happened.

I knew Emily could be a little … self-centered at times. But I had to hand it to her, she'd been so comforting to me ever since the date-gone-wrong with Alex. We'd started spending more time together, meeting up between classes, talking late into the night in our pajamas. She listened to me cry over Alex endlessly while she rubbed my back and promised me that I'd find someone who was smart enough to appreciate me someday. I knew I was probably driving her crazy. Although Tori never said it, I could tell she was growing tired of hearing about Alex. But if Emily felt the same, she never showed it. I saw a softer, kinder side of her in those weeks, and it made me feel deeply appreciative of her friendship.

"What about this one?" Kelly said as she pulled a canary yellow dress from the clearance rack and held it against my body.

I wrinkled my nose and shook my head. "Definitely not."

Kelly frowned at the dress before she tentatively put it back on the rack. "I really thought you'd like that one."

"Not really my style. Besides, Emily told me that yellow really doesn't go with my skin tone."

Kelly huffed as she continued to flick through the cheap dresses. "You haven't found a single thing you've liked all night."

I shrugged. "I've been borrowing these dresses from Emily, and they're, like, to die for. She lent me this one Oscar de la Renta—"

Kelly sighed loudly.

"What?" I asked.

"It's just that you never used to care about any of that stuff. We used to get all our clothes at this store and now you're acting like nothing in here is good enough for you."

"I didn't say that. I just think my style has changed a little since I've been at Westbridge. It's different there—"

"Or *you're* different," Kelly grumbled under her breath.

"What's *that* supposed to mean?" I asked defensively, setting one hand on my hip.

"Honestly, Juliana? You don't see it?"

"Fine, so I want to dress a little differently now; it's not that big of a deal!"

"*You* want to dress differently, or *Emily* wants you to dress differently?" She spat out Emily's name as if it tasted bitter on her tongue.

I stared at her in disbelief. How dare she judge my friendship with Emily when she didn't know the first thing about it? Kelly had no idea how Emily had been there for me in the previous weeks when I most needed a friend. While Kelly was busy picking out promise rings with her boyfriend, Emily was the one who had wiped my tears and whispered reassurances in my ear. And it made me fiercely protective of our friendship.

"Maybe we shouldn't have come tonight if that's how you feel about me," I snapped, crossing my arms over my chest.

"Look," Kelly continued, her tone softer now, "it's just that every time I talk to you lately, all I hear is 'Emily says this,' or 'Emily did that' … Maybe I'm just a little jealous of how close you are with someone else now, but I can't help but feel like I'm losing you."

"Emily is my friend. I'm allowed to have more than one, you

know. And my friends at school are a big part of my life now. Of course I'm going to talk about them!"

"I know," Kelly conceded putting her hands up in a sign of surrender. "I'm sorry, okay? I *do* want to hear about your new, exciting life at Westbridge. I guess I was just being a little sensitive about the fact that you've moved on without me. You live in New York! Just like you always said you would someday. And I'm still … here." She gestured at the provincial little clothing shop around us. "I think I'm just feeling left out."

"I'm sorry too," I replied, pushing back the anger that had so quickly swelled within me. "I didn't realize you were feeling that way. Still best friends?"

"Always," she responded definitively.

But I wasn't so sure. Being back at home only made me realize that my school friends—Emily, Tori, and Nessa—were the only ones who really knew me anymore.

Chapter 23

Now

"Of course Emily would live somewhere so entirely inconvenient," Tori grumbles as her car slowly inches forward through the infamous New York City traffic.

I look out the window from my position in the back seat. The road is congested with other cars, buses, trucks, a sea of red taillights as we head north and out of the city limits.

Westchester County is less than thirty miles away from the heart of Manhattan, but we've already been in the car for over an hour and still haven't reached the country club where Emily arranged for us to meet. Tori isn't wrong. It *is* like Emily to make this reunion as inconvenient and uncomfortable as possible for everyone except her. It's not surprising to me that she insisted we travel to her, meet her on her home turf. She probably just wanted to see if we'd still come running when she called. And here we are. Still obeying her every command.

"We should be there soon," Nessa offers, checking the GPS on her phone. "My phone is taking forever to refresh, but it looks like the traffic lets up a little further up the road." She puts down the phone and pulls her matte black lipstick tube—the same brand she's used for as long as I've known her—out of her bag and reapplies the red hue.

"Probably because we're all the way out in the sticks," Tori remarks.

Nessa sighs. "Westchester is hardly *the sticks*."

I turn back to staring out my window, watching the trees roll by, awash with an autumnal palette. I'd considered using this time to talk to Tori and Nessa about what I found in my apartment yesterday, about the eerie feeling I'm still experiencing that someone had breached my private space, but the words never formed in my mouth. I thought I could trust them, that we were in this together, a united front, but now I'm not so sure. And so instead, I sit here in silence, alone with my thoughts.

Truth be told, I don't mind the lengthy car ride. The longer I can avoid seeing Emily again the better. Not that I haven't thought of her over the years. As much as I want to tell myself that she's a long-forgotten part of my past, the reality is that she isn't. Not really. Although I haven't spoken to Emily since Westbridge, that doesn't mean I haven't given in to the temptation to look her up on occasion.

I've dropped in on her social media profiles from time to time over the years. She generally keeps her pages private, but based on the few snippets of her life that she's allowed the world to see, it would seem that time has been quite good to Emily Stafford née Wiltshire. She has a dashing husband, a sprawling colonial home, a country club membership, and from what I can tell, her looks have only become more refined with age. Her youthful prettiness has blossomed into a graceful beauty, one which is often on display at red carpet events. I've seen her pop up in the society pages from time to time, exposés on various philanthropic events—Emily in a glittering gown, languidly draped on the arm of her wealthy husband with his movie-star smile.

I don't know what it is about her, what still draws me to her, but no matter how many times I tell myself that I'm going to leave her behind me, I inevitably find myself straining to catch a glimpse of her life. It feels as though when I disentangled myself from Emily all those years ago, a piece of me stayed with her. And when I look at Emily now, my eyes scanning her glossy photos in the magazines, her perfect smile, her sparkling eyes, her waves of golden hair, what I'm really searching for is a reflection of myself, that piece of me that I could never reclaim.

"Finally," Tori says as she flicks on her turn signal and maneuvers the car off the main road and onto a wide gravel drive.

A black iron gate emblazoned with a gold crest stands before us like a sentinel as we near the end of the drive. From a small guard stand, a uniformed man in a pressed blue jacket exits and approaches our car.

"Are you ladies members?" he asks, in a way that suggests he already knows quite well that we are not.

"No," Tori replies, "but we have reservations for brunch at The Clubhouse to meet a … friend."

"Emily Wilt—er, Emily Stafford," Nessa chimes in with a polite smile.

"Oh, yes, Ms. Stafford did let us know that she was expecting guests this morning. Very well," he says as he hands Tori a parking pass. It says "VISITOR" in red block letters. A scarlet distinction between us and the people who actually belong here.

Within moments, the grand gates slowly grind open on creaking hinges, allowing us to pass through.

Tori pulls up to the main building. An enormous colonial-style mansion that sits atop a hill, complete with soaring pillars, protruding balconies, and rows of tall, paneled windows. It looks as though it may have once been a private home, although, according to the elegant script writing on the green awning that rests above the main entrance, it now serves as The Clubhouse.

Tori hands her keys to the valet, who gives us an appraising look before he slides into the driver's seat and whisks the car, and its offending visitor pass, out of sight.

"I think we may be underdressed," I murmur as we walk past a sign reading "Dinner Jackets Required" and into the main lobby. Nessa slowly nods in agreement.

The inside of The Clubhouse boasts of old-world charm. A grand, curving staircase sits at its center, which immediately conjures images of ladies in long white gloves and young women making grand entrances at debutante balls. Overhead rests a massive chandelier dripping with crystals so fine that they look like raindrops glistening in a summer sun-shower. The large space is bathed in a warm light, and a fire crackles in the sizable fireplace above a flagstone hearth.

If Tori feels out of place in her red leather jacket, she doesn't mention it, though I notice her fingers nimbly toying with her zipper as we make our way to the restaurant through the back of the lobby.

"Do you have a reservation?" the hostess asks as we step through the door. She keeps a customer-service smile on her face, but I can tell by the way her eyes rove over us that she doesn't approve of our choice in attire.

The restaurant at The Clubhouse is lovely. It is situated on a glass-covered patio off the back of the main house, and offers a panoramic view of the adjacent golf course, its lush green lawns, and softly rolling hills. A lake glitters in the distance, the sun reflecting off its azure surface in dancing sparks of light. Round tables have been set up inside, swathed in white linen, and artfully arranged with vases of fresh-cut flowers, baskets of warm pastries, tiny saucers with pates of sculpted butter, and delicate china teacups.

"We're meeting someone ..." I respond slowly as I take in the impressive sight before me. "Emily Stafford."

"She's seated in the back," the hostess advises. "I can escort you if you'd like?"

"That's all right," Tori says, her usual confidence back in her voice. "I'm sure we can find our way."

I'd forgotten for a moment that *I'm* the only one who doesn't belong here. Tori and Nessa, with their moneyed family names and boarding school charms, were raised in this world.

I feel glaringly out of place as we walk through the restaurant, passing members' tables where men in tailored suits and women in pressed dresses chat over their mid-morning brunch, pausing only to look up with raised eyebrows at the group of underdressed women making their way through to the back of the room.

"There," Nessa says, nodding toward a table along the far glass wall.

We spot Emily before she sees us. She's wearing a white sheath dress that reveals her slender arms and long legs, which are crossed at the knees, ending in distinctive, red-bottomed heels. Her elbows are propped on the table in front of her, her fingers interlaced to form a bridge that she rests her chin upon as she gazes out onto the landscape before her. The golden hair I remember so well is shorter now, cut to shoulder length, sleek and glossy. Her eyes are edged with black eyeliner below long, dark lashes, which makes them appear a startling blue.

She has all the money she needs to make sure she looks far younger than her thirty-two years. Dewy skin, courtesy of tiny pots of expensive night serums, a toned tummy, courtesy of a private yoga instructor. As it turns out, money like hers can buy anything. Even youth.

Emily turns toward us as we approach, a chilling smile snaking across her pretty face. "Hello, ladies."

160

Chapter 24

Then

The halls had been decked at Westbridge University. The ornate stone facades of its grand buildings had been adorned with evergreen boughs, crimson velvet bows, and tinkling silver bells. The air was crisp and tinged with the sweet resin of pine. It felt as though the atmosphere of the campus had changed overnight into one of festive anticipation.

The only one, it seemed, who didn't feel much like celebrating, was me. But Emily wouldn't hear of it. Ever since we returned from Thanksgiving break, she had been on a mission to help me get over Alex.

"You've been miserable for weeks now, Jules," she'd said. "It's time to get over him. And you know what they say … the only way to do that, is to get under someone else." Emily laughed as though she'd recommended something as ordinary as aspirin for a headache. I laughed along with her dutifully, but the reality was that the idea of sleeping with someone else made my stomach turn. Emily just didn't feel the same way about sex as I did. For her, sex was a transaction, an exchange of power, a give and take where she always made sure to do most of the taking. She used it like currency to get the things she wanted. She didn't understand what it was like for me—to feel like I'd given so much of myself to Alex that I no longer felt whole. But I knew that she was only trying to help.

After my falling-out with Kelly, I was all too happy to throw myself into my new friendships. The bond I shared with Tori, Nessa, and especially Emily, felt monumentally important to me. And so when Emily dragged me to party after party, I never said no anymore. Even when Tori and Nessa slowed their pace, explaining that they needed to hunker down to study for their final exams, Emily and I continued on at breakneck speed.

I felt as though I was living in an alcohol- and drug-induced haze. And there was an endless supply of anything I needed to keep the party going, thanks to Emily. It felt like she was always beside me, ready to hand me a shot of vodka or the occasional bump of cocaine from the little glass vial she kept tucked into her designer bras. If I never came down, I never had to feel anything. And that was exactly what I wanted. What I thought I needed.

But that night was going to be different. We were going to attend Nessa's play. And although I was nursing a fierce hangover, or, perhaps, what I didn't want to recognize as withdrawal, I was as sober as a judge. It left me in a surly mood, but I wanted to be there to support Nessa.

I shoved my hands deep into the pockets of my wool coat and stomped my feet in my fur-lined boots to keep my toes from going numb with the cold as I waited for Tori and Emily to meet me outside the dorms and walk over to the auditorium. I'd come straight from a meeting with my advisor who warned me that my grades on my finals had to be significantly better than they were on my midterms if I wanted any chance of holding on to my scholarship. That wouldn't be a problem though. Emily had promised she'd get me some Adderall so that I could stay up all weekend if I needed to in order to finish my final papers. I could still pull this off.

Finally, the main door to Nickerson Hall creaked open, spilling warm light and bubbling laughter out into the cold evening air. Emily and Tori stepped outside in matching tall suede boots and wool petticoats.

"Here, Jules," Emily said pulling a silver flask from her pocket. "You can catch up to us on the way."

* * *

I sat in the back of a cab on the way to celebratory drinks after the show, reflecting on the evening. Nessa was incredible tonight. Although the production of *Hello, Dolly!* left something to be desired, when Nessa took the stage, the audience—who had spent most of the night fidgeting impatiently in their seats—came to a still. The entire auditorium was captivated by her voice, her presence. The nip of bourbon from Emily's flask had done the trick to clear my headache, and the world suddenly felt sharp, focused again. And in that moment, I—along with everyone else in attendance—was in awe of Nessa's performance, her voice bellowing out to fill the enormous space.

Although the intermission nearly had as much drama as the play when Jenny unexpectedly slid into the empty seat next to me.

"I hope it's okay that I came," she said. "I know how hard Nessa's been practicing for this show. I didn't want to miss it."

"You look … different," I said.

Jenny adjusted her glasses on her nose, and looked down at her faded T-shirt self-consciously.

"In a good way, I mean," I rushed to add. "You look more like … you."

"Thanks." She smiled shyly. "I'm trying something new. And speaking of, I still feel bad about how things went down with us and I think we should talk—"

"It's already behind us." I swished my hand as if to banish her concerns. "Have you been here the whole time?"

"Yeah, my seat is in the back, but I think—"

"Why don't you join us?" I offered, extending the proverbial olive branch. "No one is using that seat anyway."

I hoped the invitation would prove to Jenny that there were no hard feelings lingering between us.

Jenny looked over at Emily, who fixed her with a cold glare.

"You know, I think I will," Jenny said defiantly, sliding into her new seat.

I thought for sure that Emily would have more to say on that matter, but she seemed to let it slide as we settled in for the second half of the show.

When it came time for the final bows, Nessa was greeted with a standing ovation. She seemed genuinely surprised at the reception as she took a humble bow. Her eyes glistened with tears as she accepted a bouquet of red roses from the director.

Things didn't start to go awry until after the show, while we were hanging around the auditorium waiting for Nessa to change. After a few minutes, she came bounding in, her long dark hair in loose tangles, and her stage makeup still on her face. The dramatic eyeliner and smoky shadow made her round eyes appear impossibly large. She looked wild, sexy, and euphorically happy.

"You're going out like that?" Emily said, studying Nessa's face.

"Sure, it's not every day I have my makeup done by a professional makeup artist."

"Let's all be thankful for that," Emily murmured, laughing to herself.

I pretended I hadn't heard the remark and instead focused my attention on the task of putting on my coat and fastening the buttons.

"I suppose you're coming too then?" Emily asked Jenny, one eyebrow raised in judgment. Probably due to Jenny's choice in evening attire.

"If that's okay with you, Nessa …" Jenny said questioningly.

"Of course! We're celebrating tonight!" Nessa's eyes dazzled with excitement.

But Emily's lips set into a hard line.

The cab began to slow, its tires crunching on the icy pavement, pulling me from my thoughts. I looked up at our destination for the evening: a karaoke bar that Nessa had chosen. The neon lights above the entrance glowed a garish pink against the inky night sky.

Karaoke wasn't really my thing, nor, I suspected, was it Emily's, given the way she wrinkled her nose in distaste when Nessa had suggested it the day before. But it was Nessa's big night, and as we slid out of the cab, even Emily seemed willing to go along with it. For the time being.

We walked into the underground bar, which was filled with a smoky haze. It smelled of stale beer. The patrons gathered around the small round tables in front of the stage seemed restless. Particularly a group of men toward the back of the room. I estimated them to be in their early twenties, in their collared shirts with their slicked-back hair. Not college boys, but not yet civilized men, domesticated by marriage and mortgage. They were downing shots and slamming them hard onto the table they were huddled around, making it rattle on flimsy legs.

One of the men raised his glass, the amber liquid inside sloshing over the rim and dripping down his wrist. "Lift them to heaven!" he shouted. "And then we give them hell!" Soon the others joined in, the toast becoming a chant. They pounded savagely on the table with their fists. *"Give them hell, give them hell!"* There was something primal about them, this group of wild-eyed men, something feral and unrestrained. They reminded me of predators, nocturnal beasts who woke to prowl in the dark of night.

The singer on stage ended a performance of "Sweet Caroline" and was met with boos and hollers from the back of the bar.

"Thank God *that's* over," Emily said.

"She wasn't that bad …" Nessa offered, trying to keep our spirits up. But she was wrong. It *had* been bad; the screech of the microphone still seemed to pierce through my skull.

"I'm going to go put in my song request," Nessa said as she turned toward the DJ booth.

"Good luck!" Tori called after her.

"Yeah! Good luck!" Jenny echoed.

Emily sidled up to me at the table, her bare arm pressed against mine. She was so close to me that a few strands of her thick blonde hair stuck to my lips, which were slicked with gloss. I could smell the subtle notes of jasmine in her shampoo.

"I think we're going to need this," she whispered, sliding her eyes toward her palm, which she'd discreetly hidden under the table.

I followed her gaze, and there, pressed into the center of her hand, was the little glass vial I'd become so familiar with.

Though tempting, I subtly shook my head. I didn't need it. *Not tonight.* Besides, I could already picture the look of judgment, of disappointment, on Tori's face. I'd seen her partake occasionally—maybe at a club where she'd dance and writhe in a corybantic sea of bodies—but not on a night like this, when we were here to sip martinis and listen to Nessa sing.

"Suit yourself," Emily said as she closed her fingers around the vial.

At that moment, Nessa stepped out onto the stage. The men at the back of the room seemed to settle, momentarily subdued by the exquisite beauty of the woman standing at center stage. As Nessa began to sing, her rendition of "Make You Feel My Love", an awed hush fell over the room.

"Is this that Adele song?" I whispered to Tori.

"Bob Dylan recorded it first, but yes," she whispered back, our eyes never leaving Nessa.

Her voice seemed far larger than her. It filled the room, reverberating off the walls. The sound left us spellbound, its coaxing melody hypnotic.

"I'll be right back," Emily said curtly, before turning on her heels. Her hand was still closed around the prize in her palm.

My eyes followed her as she passed through the room, her hips dipping sensually, garnering more than a few looks. She seemed to pause as she passed the group of rowdy men, their table littered with overturned shot glasses and steins of foam-topped beers. Her fingers gently grazed the arm of the most attractive of the group. He leaned toward her, and I thought I saw her whisper something in his ear as she passed by. A lascivious smile broke across his face in her wake.

"What the hell is she up to now?" Tori asked, nodding in Emily's direction. Evidently, she'd seen it too.

"I don't know …" I replied, but I felt a stirring of dread in the pit of my stomach.

As Emily disappeared into the ladies' room, one of the men—the one she'd spoken to—began to whistle, a wolfish howl. Soon the others joined in, all of them shouting and howling.

I watched them in horror as I heard Nessa's voice falter, just for a moment, before she carried on undeterred. She looked over at our table, where Tori, Jenny, and I nodded her on encouragingly.

The din from the back of the room soon grew to a roar.

"Show us your tits!" one of the men shouted, evoking uproarious laughter from the others.

Nessa froze. The music still played, but she stood on stage with the mic in her hand, seemingly unable to move, but for a trembling of her lower lip. She looked like a startled doe, paralyzed in the spotlight.

Emily materialized at the table as the crowd began to boo and chant for Nessa to get off the stage. How quickly their favor had turned.

"Yikes," Emily said, something akin to excitement dancing in her eyes. She always reveled in the chaos she created.

Nessa ran off the stage and out the door, a gust of cold winter air blowing in behind her.

Tori, Jenny, and I ran after her. Emily trailed behind in no apparent rush.

"Ness," Tori said pulling her into a hug. "Those guys were such assholes."

Nessa sobbed on her shoulder, her breath escaping in frosty curls. "God, that was humiliating."

"I'm so sorry that happened, Nessa," Jenny added, gently rubbing Nessa's back. "Tori's right. Those guys were horrible."

Emily laughed, the sound tinny against the stillness of the night. "Come on, it was just karaoke."

"That wasn't funny, Emily," Tori barked. "You're ... God, you're such a fucking bitch!"

Emily looked stunned at Tori's insolence. "Wait, so you mean to tell me that Nessa chokes up there and it's somehow *my* fault?" She brought her hand to her chest, a simulacrum of sincerity.

"Of course it was your fucking fault!" Tori's words crackled through the frozen air. "You really couldn't handle sharing the spotlight? You couldn't let her have just this *one* night?"

My jaw fell open, but I said nothing. I'd seen Tori and Emily butt heads before, but the gloves had never come off quite like this.

Emily glared hard at Tori and then turned her attention to me. "What about you, Jules? Do you agree with her?"

It was a test and I knew it. A line had been drawn in the sand. On one side, there was Tori and Nessa; on the other, Emily. She was asking me to decide what side of the looming war I'd be fighting for.

"Look, Emily, I don't want to take sides. I don't know what you said to those guys, but—"

"So you *are* blaming me!"

"I'm not, I'm just ... I'm just saying—"

"You're just saying *what*?" she spat.

In truth, I didn't know what I was saying. What *could* I have said, really? Emily had been so brutally cruel to Nessa, and I knew why she did it. Nessa was up there on that stage, commanding the attention of every person in the room, and Emily couldn't let that kind of power go unchecked. But if I said that, if I confronted her with the truth of it, her wrath might have been turned on me next. By then I'd become accustomed to it, the frivolity with which she could cast me aside, leaving me in the cold darkness of her shadow. All I wanted was to stay in the light.

"Truth or dare, Emily?" Tori asked, sparing me from having to reply.

"What? Now?"

"Yes, now, and I choose truth. I want you to admit what you did tonight. To explain why you're such a selfish bitch."

"You know what? Forget it," Emily said throwing her hands up. "The four of you deserve each other." She crossed her arms over her chest and headed back into the bar, her chin held high in defiance.

Tori, Nessa, Jenny, and I exchanged nervous glances. That stirring of dread I'd felt earlier began to grow, climbing over me like creeping ivy. I had no idea what we'd set in motion by aligning against Emily, but I knew with certainty that it wouldn't end well.

Chapter 25

Now

Emily sips from her cocktail—a mimosa in a long, thin flute—seemingly perfectly at ease.

"You could have at least given us a heads-up about the dress code," Tori grumbles.

Emily looks at her over the rim of her glass with one eyebrow raised. "I thought you'd have known better."

Tori responds with a wintry smile. A standoff. But Nessa squirms in her seat next to me, the judgment in Emily's remark landing squarely on her shoulders. Poor Nessa. She's always been more susceptible to Emily's sharp edges.

It amazes me how quickly we've slipped back into our old roles, the ones that were always designated for us in this group. Emily is still the queen, though she reigns over a new kingdom.

"I assume you didn't come here to discuss country club etiquette though," Emily says. "So what is it that you wanted?" She crosses one of her long legs over the other. She sits primly on the edge of her seat, her posture impeccable. She reminds me of one of the dancers in the ballet I took my mother to see at

Lincoln Center the first time she visited me in Manhattan. It's in the way she elongates her spine, pulls back her shoulders, and holds her chin aloft above her delicate, swan-like neck.

"I think you know why we're here," Tori remarks, her tone impatient.

"Well then you'd be wrong," Emily retorts with a batt of her eyelashes and a goading smirk.

"The emails. The ones I mentioned on the phone, Em," Nessa tries, her voice holding far more warmth than Tori's. *You might catch more flies with honey, Em.*

Emily pauses, her eyes sliding upwards, as though she's trying to recollect what emails Nessa might be referring to. She's toying with us. I can tell by the hint of amusement alighting at the corners of her eyes. She is a cat playing with a mouse, allowing it the faintest hope that it may escape before ensnaring it in its lethal claws.

"You know." I cut in. "The ones from *Jenny Teller*?" I've had enough of her games.

"What would *I* know about that?" Emily snaps back. "It's not like what happened to poor Jenny was *my* fault."

"Like hell it wasn't!" I grip the edge of the table as I try to rein myself in. The tips of my fingers grow white beneath my grasp.

"Settle down, Jules," Emily scoffs with a dry laugh. "I'd hate to have my guests cause a scene in front of the other members."

I understand the undertone of her message: she belongs here. I do not. The same glaring chasm that's always been between us. The one she'd never let me forget. My eyes flit to the table nearest to us, just in time to catch a gentleman in golf attire return his attention to his soup.

"Enough, Emily," Tori snaps.

Emily smiles with satisfaction, spinning the delicate stem of her champagne flute between her pink manicured fingernails.

The waiter appears at the side of our table. A palm-sized notepad in his hand, and a white apron tied neatly around his waist.

"Good morning, Mrs. Stafford," he says by way of greeting, before giving a nod to the rest of the group seated at our table. "What can I get for you ladies this morning?"

Emily orders egg whites and sliced fruit.

"Just water for me," Tori says. "I doubt we'll be staying long." She levels her stare at Emily who smiles curtly in reply.

Nessa and I both follow Tori's lead, despite the fact that my stomach is rumbling and I would love nothing more than a steaming stack of pancakes soaked in syrup and melted butter. I could only imagine the looks I'd get had I actually ordered that.

"Very well, ladies. That will be right out." The waiter walks away at an efficient clip, the soles of his shoes clicking against the polished marble floors.

"Where were we?" Emily asks, as she taps one finger against her glossy lips, a charade of thought. "Oh, right," she continues, a smug grin breaking across her lips. "I believe you were all about to accuse me of something. So come on then, let's have it."

I've had about as much as I can take. Being in Emily's presence has brought me right back to the insecure girl I was when I first started at Westbridge. The one who was desperate for acceptance, to fit in. The one who let Emily ride roughshod over my life and dictate who I was. But I'm not that girl anymore. I'm all grown up now, and I no longer have to give her a stage from which she can run the show.

"Did you send them or not?" I snap.

"Not," Emily replies calmly, casually sipping her drink. A diamond tennis bracelet glints on her wrist.

"You're lying," Tori replies. There's an edge of anger in her voice. Emily has gotten under her skin, and, it would seem, Emily knows it.

She smiles at Tori, a flash of white teeth behind glossy lips. "I'm not, actually. I know this may be hard for you to believe, but I haven't given you—any of you—a single passing thought in years. All of … that … is behind me. I have a great life, a *perfect* life, now. Why in God's name would I drag up that old drama?"

Drama. The loss of a young girl's life is nothing but ancient, silly drama to her. Akin to a spat with a best friend, a long-forgotten rumor. Though she does raise a fair point. How would bringing up Jenny now benefit Emily in any way?

"As if you ever needed a reason to be cruel," Nessa says.

"Or maybe you just wanted to get our attention," Tori adds. "You never handled being ignored well."

Emily laughs, a stale breathy huff. "You give yourselves far too much credit. I never needed your attention. It was always *you* who wanted something from *me*." She looks around the table at each of us, her hard gaze daring us to disagree.

I can't. Because she's right. I *did* want something from her: her acceptance, the social status that came with it. And I don't know that she ever really needed anything from me in return. I was nothing to her, simply a plaything she could use to pass the time. I suspect the same was true for all of us.

"Truth, Emily," Tori says.

Emily smiles mischievously. "I believe you had the last ask ... which would mean it's my turn ... If we're going to revive childish games."

"Not so fast. You never answered the last time. You owe me a truth, and I'll take it now."

They lock eyes, Emily's lips pressed into a firm, hard line.

The waiter arrives back at our table. He quickly slides our glasses in front of us and jaunts away, as though he can't escape the tense silence that hovers over our table fast enough.

"Look," Emily says, her voice warmer now. Her eyes have grown round, a picture of innocence. "I'm sorry you guys are going through this. I really am. But whatever emails you got, they didn't come from me. That's the truth."

It's amazing how she can still do that. Turn on the charm like one might flick on a light switch. It's one of the things I most remember about her. The way she seemed to be able to get away with anything just by timing her mood swings with razor-sharp precision. She was always at her most charming immediately after saying something unfathomably cruel. With Emily, even kindness was weaponized.

"Who else could have sent them?" I ask.

Emily shrugs her slim shoulders. "From what I remember, I wasn't the only enemy you three made back at Westbridge."

Tori, Nessa, and I exchange a look. We know she's right, but I think we'd all been hoping that Emily was behind all of this. A nice, easy explanation wrapped with a pretty bow. The more frightening alternative—the one we're forced to face now—is that we have no idea who's targeting us, and the realization sends a cold shiver down my spine.

"What about Nate?" Emily suggests, eager to pick at the open wound. "From what I recall *that* didn't end too well." She holds her chin in her palm.

"It's not him," Tori snaps back almost immediately.

This catches Emily's attention. She raises one eyebrow inquiringly. "Well, you sound pretty *certain*."

There's something that pulls at the back of my mind. A small niggling, a flash of something unknown, that warns me that there's a familiarity about the way Tori and Emily exchange jabs—like rival boxers in a ring, they seem to know exactly where to land each blow. And it makes me question, yet again, whether these two women have been in closer contact than Tori has been willing to admit to.

"Have you … spoken to him recently, Tori?" Ness asks bewilderedly.

"No, I just know that he wouldn't do something like this. And besides, why would he go to all this trouble to bring up … Jenny? He hardly knew her."

"You're probably right," I concede. Although Emily has planted the seed of doubt in my mind. After all, when Nate and Tori's relationship went up in flames, all that was left in its wake was scorched earth. "But I don't think we can rule *anyone* out just yet." I level a glare at Emily.

"I agree with Jules," Nessa says, nodding along. "We have to consider all possibilities." She seems pleased to have another potential suspect on the table. It is, admittedly, easier to imagine a face, any face, behind the emails. Anything but the dark void of the unknown.

Tori sighs. "I'll see what I can do about getting in touch with him."

We sip at our drinks uneasily, none of us certain where we go from here.

"I'm surprised you didn't get them too, Em." Nessa finally says, breaking the uncomfortable silence. "The emails, I mean."

"Who said I didn't?"

My eyes snap up from the table, where I'd been anxiously rolling a straw wrapper into a tight little ball. Emily is smiling, a coy, lopsided smirk.

"Why the hell didn't you just tell us you'd gotten them too?" Tori barks.

Emily's smile widens. "You didn't ask."

"Is this some kind of game to you?" Tori's voice grows louder.

"Of course not, but I also don't see why you're making such a big deal out of some silly little email. To be honest, I assumed it came from one of you, and so I deleted it the second I got it. Easy." She flicks her hand as if swatting away a gnat, the diamond rings on her finger catching the light and throwing off a shower of sparks.

"So … you only got the one then?" I ask.

"Yes. Why?" Emily's voice takes on a solicitous tone, as if she's savoring the details. "Have you been getting more?"

I hesitate. I don't know whether I should trust her with the contents of Jenny's other emails. I'm still not entirely convinced that Emily isn't behind this whole thing. But Nessa cuts in. She's always been far too trusting.

"Yes, and Jules got a photo too. You're in it. Here, look." Nessa pulls her phone out of her bag and aims the screen at Emily.

"Interesting," Emily says. "Strange that whoever is doing this would send a photo from *that* night. Don't you think, Jules?" She turns her gaze on me and I feel myself shrink beneath it.

"You're the only other person who would even understand the significance of this photo, who would know it from … that night." I aim to sound confident, but my voice wavers, betraying my uncertainty.

"Evidently not." A vindictive grin breaks across Emily's face. "Besides, these two were there too, weren't they?" She tips her glass in the direction of Tori and Nessa. "Surely *they* haven't forgotten what happened. Did you ever think to question your dear, loyal friends?" Her face is beautiful and cruel.

My mind is reeling. I was sure, I was *so* sure, that these messages were coming from Emily, but now … now I can't be certain. She could very well be lying, *but what if she's not?*

Tori has known me for long enough that she can see my thoughts spinning out of control. "Don't let her get in your head, Jules. This is what she does. Don't give her the satisfaction."

"We shouldn't have come here …" I murmur as I push away from the table and lock eyes with Emily. "I should have known you wouldn't be honest with us anyway."

"Oh, I *have* been honest with you. Someone is coming for you, Jules. But it looks like it's someone far more dangerous than me."

Tori rushes to my defense. She was always my greatest protector. "You seem very sure of yourself, Emily. But that certainty that hangs around your head like a crown, someday it's going to come crashing down around you. I'll make sure of that."

176

Chapter 26

Now

I sit at my desk on Monday trying to think about anything but Emily's haunting words. *Someone is coming for you, Jules.* But I'm finding it almost impossible. It seems that lately all I do is try to stave off the inevitable.

Jason and I ordered in Chinese takeout last night, after my day spent visiting Emily and running errands specifically designed to keep my mind distracted from all that's been going on. We made small talk over the dinner we ate out of plastic containers. Neither of us seemed to have the energy to pick up the argument we'd started the day before, and so we politely stepped around it. "Pass the lo mein," "It's supposed to rain all week." But marriage is like that, isn't it? When you know you have a lifetime to spend together, it sometimes feels as if there is no rush to work on it. Sometimes it's easier to hit "pause" than it is to unpack complex emotions, to mend hurt feelings. I do worry, though, that if we let so many things pass between us, like a swelling river it's eventually going to erode the banks of our marriage, the murky waters growing turbulent and destructive.

With a sigh I turn back to my work.

"You okay over there?" Andrew asks.

"I'm fine ... just working on this motion for Barrett."

"You're working with Barrett now?" Andrew asks incredulously.

I'd forgotten that I hadn't mentioned it to him. "Yeah, lucky me ..."

"Well, he might be a nightmare to work for, but that should go far in locking down your bid for partnership. If he likes you, you're basically a shoo-in."

I chew my lower lip. Andrew is right: I need Barrett's support, but I know I won't get it unless I do his bidding and submit this motion—and the falsified operating report along with it.

"Hypothetically ..." I begin, "if you thought a client had, say, lied to you, what would you do?"

"They *always* lie," Andrew replies with an exaggerated roll of his eyes.

"I mean ... what if you thought critical records had been tampered with. Possibly concealing an important witness."

"Yikes." Andrew thumbs his chin. "Have I *hypothetically* discussed this with the senior partner on the file?"

"Yes."

"And he, hypothetically, wants me to go along with it?"

"Yes."

"Then I'd want to know for sure what I'm being asked to overlook before I put my career on the line."

I nod in agreement. Andrew is right. I should at least know what Barrett is expecting me to cover up for him.

"Do you want to tell me what's going on?" Andrew asks.

"It's probably best if I don't ..."

"All right, well, I'll be back in a little while if you change your mind. I'm just going to go pick up lunch. Do you want anything?"

I shake my head.

Andrew heads out of our office and pulls the door closed behind him.

I immediately pick up my phone and dial Barrett's extension. "Hi, Mr. Barrett. It's Juliana Daniels. I just wanted to talk to you about some inconsistencies in—"

"There are no inconsistencies," he snaps.

"But—"

"I said there *are* no inconsistencies." He ends the call without warning.

But of course I know that's not true. *Unless something has changed ...* I need to see those medical records again.

I make my way down to the file room and dig out the original hospital chart. It's exactly where I left it on Friday afternoon. But when I flip to the operating report, I find that it's been replaced with the altered version, listing Gabriella Marion as the surgical nurse. By all appearances, Nurse Nancy Ravit never laid eyes on this now-deceased patient.

I rush back to my office and sit down in front of my computer. I minimize the motion I've been working on, and pull up Google to run a search for Nancy Ravit.

I find her rather quickly: Nancy Ravit, RN. Employed at Austin General Hospital in Texas.

I pick up my cell phone and dial the number listed for the hospital's nursing station. I decide not to use the office line in case Barrett ever decides to poke around in the firm's phone records to see how well I followed his directive to forget all about Nurse Ravit. I wouldn't put it past him.

The line rings three times, and I'm about to hang up before a woman answers.

"Hello?" she says in a harried voice.

"Oh, um, hi," I stumble. "I'm calling for Nurse Nancy Ravit, please?"

"She's doing rounds. Let me see if I can get her."

The line goes silent and I toy with a pen on my desk, pressing its end over and over again. *Click, click, click.*

Finally, someone returns to the line.

"This is Nancy Ravit. Who's calling, please?"

"My name is Juliana Daniels. I'm an attorney at Miller & Marquee, and—"

"Is that Mark Barrett's firm?" she interjects, her voice an aggravated whisper.

"Yes, it is. I'm working on a case with Mr. Barrett and—"

"Listen, I don't know why you're calling me, here, of all places, but you tell Mr. Barrett that I did everything he asked of me. I held up my end of the deal, and I never said a word to anyone, and I'm not about to now. Now please hold up *your* end and don't ever call me again."

The call ends abruptly, the line going dead. But it doesn't matter because she already told me everything I needed to know. The only question now, is what I'm going to do about it.

* * *

I tentatively knock on the door to Barrett's office, the finished motion for summary judgment cradled in the crook of my other arm. "Mr. Barrett?"

"Come in." He barks it at me, more of an order than an invitation. "Did you finish that motion?" he asks before I even fully step into the room.

I pull the door closed behind me. "That's what I wanted to talk to you about. I drafted it, but I don't know if we should submit this. In light of the ... issues with the hospital chart."

"I see," Barrett says slowly, pressing his fingers into a steeple. "Well, here's my position, Ms. Daniels. If you want to be a partner at this firm, I need to know that you will put our clients' interests first and foremost. And believe me when I say that it is in *this* client's best interest that this motion be submitted exactly as I directed. Am I making myself clear?"

"Yes, but—"

"Good. And if you decide that you'd rather *not* become a

partner with Miller & Marquee, or if you, say, decide that you'd like to create obstacles for me to defend this case as I see fit, I wish you the best of luck seeking other employment without a recommendation from this office. My pull in this town is quite strong. If you would like to continue to practice law in New York, my suggestion would be to submit that motion by day's end."

I open my mouth to reply, but the words don't form on my tongue. Barrett has left me little room for negotiation.

"That'll be all," he says with a flippant flick of his wrist. "I believe you have work to do."

* * *

Back at my desk I stare at my computer monitor, the court's e-filing system loaded on the screen.

I bite my bottom lip, mulling over my options. On the one hand, I know I shouldn't submit this motion. It's ethically, and legally, wrong. On the other hand, my career that I've worked so hard to build hangs in the balance.

I could get away with it though. The thought trails across my mind like a whisper. If by some remote chance anyone ever found out that the operating report had been altered, it wasn't done by my hand. I could pretend that I'd never seen the original record. It's long gone by now anyway.

I tap "submit" on the screen. For better or worse, it's out of my hands now. "Ugh," I mutter under my breath. *What have I done?*

"You okay over there? Hypothetically, of course," Andrew says between bites of his lunch.

"I'm not sure." I drop my head into my hands, my mind spinning with all the eventualities I may have just set into motion, when I hear my cell phone buzz on my desk.

One new email from Jenny Teller.

I open it quickly, nearly dropping the phone from my shaking hand:

Liar, liar.

Attached is a photo of the original hospital record, Nurse Nancy Ravit's name circled in blood-red ink.

I've just handed Jenny everything she needs to destroy my career.

Chapter 27

Then

A few days after the karaoke incident, Emily sat down at our table in the dining hall. None of us had spoken to her in days, and the more time that passed, the more anxious we grew about what the repercussions of our falling-out with her were going to be.

"Hey, girls. It's been a busy week. I feel like we haven't seen each other at all!" she said cheerfully.

Tori, Nessa, and I exchanged confused looks. Of all the ways I thought Emily would react to our perceived betrayal, completely ignoring it was not one of them. I felt wrong-footed, flustered by this surprising turn of events, and I couldn't formulate a response.

"By the way, Nessa," Emily continued, as she popped a French fry into her mouth, "I told my father about how amazing your performance in the play was the other night. He said that if you're really interested in pursuing a career in show business, he can hook you up with a friend of his who does the casting for Broadway shows."

It wasn't exactly an apology, but I figured it was the closest Emily would ever come.

"Oh my God, Em! Seriously?!" Nessa squealed delightedly.

"Yeah, he said he'll set you up with an audition, and if you impress the guy, he can get you a summer internship working on one of his shows. And maybe something more permanent after graduation."

"Emily … I don't even know what to say. This is so amazing. Thank you." Nessa wrapped her arms around Emily's neck.

"We need to stick together," Emily said. "This friendship, the four of us, this is what matters the most."

Tori caught my eye, a worried expression on her face. I understood her concern. Nessa may have been willing to put the past behind her, but I wasn't sure I'd be able to forget what I saw in Emily that night so easily. The dark and vicious side of her.

"Good, now that that's settled," Emily said, "let's make plans for tonight. It's our last night on campus before winter break."

"Speaking of last nights on campus …" Nessa began, leaning over the table, a scandalous smirk on her face. "I heard that Professor Perv was asked not to come back next semester. There were moving vans up by Faculty Row this morning. Rumor has it that even though the school couldn't prove he was messing around with a student, his whole family was ordered to leave campus immediately."

I felt my stomach turn over. He had a family. A wife, maybe even children.

"Well, good," Emily said casually. "He was a dick anyway. But about tonight: it has to be epic. Let's close out the year properly."

"What did you have in mind?" I asked.

"There's going to be a big party on Main Street tonight. All of the frat houses are involved. We should go."

"Sure, that sounds okay …" Tori replied, still sounding unsure about Emily's newfound penchant for forgiveness.

"I invited Jenny along, by the way," Emily said, offhandedly.

Tori looked over at me and shrugged. It wasn't like Emily to spring an outsider on us unplanned. But perhaps this was her way of apologizing to Jenny as well.

"That's not a problem, right?" Emily added. It was more of a statement than a question. We knew we were in no position to question her anyway, to challenge the unexpected benevolence she'd shown.

"No problem at all," Nessa replied.

"Good." Emily smiled to herself as if she was on the inside of a joke that the rest of us had not yet been privy to.

I swallowed hard and tried to steady the feeling of unease that was listing in my gut.

* * *

We got ready for the night in Nessa's room. Slender hips wrapped in short skirts, leather boots over long legs, and lips slicked with shimmering gloss. Tori made us her version of Cosmopolitans and passed around the pink drinks in plastic martini glasses. It all seemed very grown-up, very sophisticated. I felt my apprehension about the evening, which was bunched up around my shoulders, start to loosen, softening like butter the more I drank.

Even Jenny seemed to be having a good time. She sipped delicately from her drink and smiled far more than I was accustomed to seeing from her.

"Are you going to meet up with *Nate* tonight?" Nessa teased, jostling Tori with her elbow.

"Maybe ..." Tori replied, an air of mystery twisting in her voice.

"You should," Jenny added resolutely. "He's, like ... really fucking hot."

It was so unexpected, so shockingly uncharacteristic, of sweet, innocent Jenny, that we all paused for a moment after she spoke the words, before falling together into a fit of laughter.

"We should get going," Emily reminded us. "The cab will be here any minute."

"I'm coming too," a voice chimed in. Abby. Nessa's roommate. I'd almost forgotten she was there, her nose buried in her computer screen in the corner. The sound of her voice caught me by surprise. Abby hardly, if ever, spoke to us, given a choice, and she'd refused to so much as taste Tori's Cosmos that night, even when Jenny had tried to coax her into it.

Emily rolled her eyes, an exaggerated loop. "You *never* go out."

"Well tonight I am," Abby replied pointedly. "Whenever Jenny goes anywhere with you people, it always ends up in some sort of a disaster for her. Not that any of you seem to care. This time I'm coming with her."

Jenny's cheeks burned a scarlet red. "Only if you want to come, Abby. You don't have to babysit me …"

"I'm coming."

"Well, you better get ready then," Emily said, her eyes scanning up and down Abby's form: her untamed curls, the baggy jeans with the frayed bottoms, the dingy hue of her sneakers, and her Care Bear T-shirt that strained to cover the bulge of her stomach.

"I *am* ready," Abby replied undeterred.

Emily threw up her hands in exasperation. "Let's just go then."

* * *

Main Street was a sea of bodies, a drunken bacchanal accented with the glow of holiday lights. Every fraternity house on the street opened their doors, Christmas music wafting out from inside. Girls in skimpy dresses and Santa hats flitted from house to house savoring the warmth and sampling what each had to offer. Some houses handed out spiked ciders, others red and green holiday punch.

I looked over at Emily as we stood at the center of Main Street, ready to take on the night. A sliver of moonlight reflected in her glassy blue eyes, giving them an almost menacing glint.

"Shall we?" she asked, looping her arms through mine and Nessa's.

"Let's do this," Tori replied.

We walked down that street like we owned it, heads held high, stilettos clicking against the pavement. In a way, we *did* own it. People I'd only met in passing waved at us, Westbridge's very own glitterati.

"Hi, Emily!", "Hey, Jules!" voices chimed as we made our way down the crowded street. Faces I hardly knew smiled at me, called me by name. It was a surreal and heady experience, this notoriety that came with being in Emily's orbit. *But what price did I pay for this?* I pushed the thought out of my head. I was precisely where I wanted to be.

Jenny and Abby trailed behind, their heads together, whispers passing between them, seemingly in their own little world.

* * *

The music pulsed through me, more punch was poured, bodies moved together on the dance floor, flesh on flesh. Somewhere along the line, the tone of the night shifted from festive excitement to one of minatory debauchery.

Emily draped her arms around my neck. Her body felt loose, languid, her eyes wild and wide. I wondered what she'd taken.

"We're okay, aren't we, Jules?" she asked.

"Yeah, of course."

"After what happened at that hateful karaoke bar ..." Her nose wrinkled in disgust at the mere mention of the place.

I heard the undercurrent of her question. It floated to my ear as soft as a whisper. *Are you with me or against me, Jules?*

"We're fine, Em. I promise."

"Good," she replied, her cheek grazing mine.

I looked over Emily's shoulder and caught sight of Tori and Nessa standing by the bar, chatting with a few guys, the houses' Greek letters proudly displayed across their chests.

"Where are Jenny and Abby?" I asked. "I haven't seen them in a while."

"Who cares?" Emily replied with a derisive scoff. "It's better when it's just us. The four of us, I mean. I think it's time we got rid of her."

"Got rid of who?" Nessa asked. She and Tori had materialized next to us, fresh drinks in hand.

"Jenny, of course," Emily replied, peeling herself off me. "She's been nothing but a problem for us. A bit like feeding a stray cat. Show it kindness once and it never goes away. Besides, you all saw what happened the *last* time she tagged along with us … She's coming between us."

I should have known that Emily would have found someone, anyone else to blame for our falling-out after what she did to Nessa.

"Emily …" Tori said, an edge of warning in her voice.

"What? That was the plan all along, remember? Build her up and break her down."

"What are you *talking* about?" Tori demanded, setting a hand on her hip.

"It was Nessa's idea. Catching flies with honey and all that."

"You can't be serious," Nessa said, her eyes wide with incredulity. "That wasn't what I meant! Is this really still because she wouldn't move out of your room!?"

"It was never about the fucking room!" Emily shouted, her voice rising over the music. Her eyes burned with a vicious intensity, her hands pulled into fists at her sides. She lowered her voice, but the calm and intense way she spoke next felt even more chilling. "It wasn't about the *room*. It was because she actually thought she could *be* one of us. She needs to be taught a lesson."

What she really meant was that Jenny had to be punished for standing in Emily's way. That Jenny, shy, awkward Jenny—a nobody—had dared to stand toe-to-toe with Emily Wiltshire instead of cowering in her presence. Emily, who prided herself on having anything and everything she set her mind to, had inadvertently met her match in the most unexpected of places:

188

Jenny Teller. But what Jenny didn't know, was that there would always be a price to pay where Emily was involved.

"Well whatever the hell this is," Tori said, "I want nothing to do with it."

"I'm sorry, Em, but I don't either," Nessa agreed.

Emily looked at me. Her glare hard and focused. "At least *you* have my back, don't you, Jules?"

I thought of the way she'd turned on Nessa, her oldest friend, the bite of her tone when she argued with Tori, how vindictive she was being toward Jenny over the smallest perceived slight, and I suddenly realized that I had to distance myself from her before I was the next to fall. I felt like I'd finally opened my eyes only to realize that I was the frog in the pot who hadn't felt the temperature steadily rising until the pot was boiling over. I knew then that my only hope was to jump.

"I ... I can't be a part of this either, Em."

Emily's gaze turned cold, a hailstorm of anger raging behind her eyes. "You all choose *her* over me?"

"It isn't like that, Em," Nessa tried.

"Oh, but it is. And after everything I've done for you. You especially, Jules," Emily said, her tone glacially cold as she pointed one manicured finger at my chest. "I made you. You were no one, nothing before me. You've all made a very grave mistake."

Emily turned on her heels, and sauntered away without so much as a backward glance.

"We should probably go," Nessa said nervously.

"Yeah," Tori agreed. "Let's find Jenny first though. God knows what Emily is going to do."

I texted Jenny:

Are you still at the Omega house? We need to go. Meet us by the bar.

Jenny replied quickly:

189

Be right there.

Tori, Nessa, and I stood anxiously by the bar, my fingers drumming on the sticky wood surface, waiting for Jenny to appear.

When she finally did, she stumbled into the room, beer sloshing over the rim of her cup. Abby had her arm hooked around Jenny's waist. They were both giggling as Abby helped her regain her balance.

"Are you guys really wanting to leave?" Jenny asked. "We're having such a good time!"

"We actually are," Abby agreed. "I don't know why I didn't do this sooner!"

That may have been the first time I ever saw Abby smile.

"I think it's for the best ..." Nessa offered gently.

Jenny took a gulp of her foam-topped beer. "Well, you guys can go if you want, but I'm finishing my drink first."

"Me too," Abby agreed with a shrug. She turned toward Jenny, hanging heavily on her arm. "Do you know that you're my best friend?"

Jenny giggled. They were both too drunk to sense the danger heading their way.

My eyes automatically scanned the room for Emily.

"Shit. There," Tori whispered as she nudged me in the ribs and nodded to the far corner of the crowded room.

Emily was standing next to a guy in a fraternity jacket, a backwards hat on his head. She was raised up onto the tips of her toes, whispering something in his ear, a wicked smile playing at the corner of her pretty, pink lips.

Emily traded in secrets and rumors. Poisonous whispers formed with a serpent tongue. She would spill them into your ear, igniting a spark and letting you fan it into a wildfire while she danced in the glow of the flames. To Emily, people were merely pawns, players in a game that sometimes had to be forfeited.

Word about Jenny slithered through the room like a snake,

snickers and whispers in its wake. Jenny, oblivious to all of it, didn't see the stolen glances in her direction, the twisted smiles, until it was too late.

A pair of large hands grabbed Jenny's waist, firm hips pressed against her lower back. "Hey," a deep voice said. "You're Jenny, right?"

Jenny seemed to freeze in shock for a moment before trying to wriggle out of his grasp. "Get off me," she said, her voice a cocktail of anger and fear.

"What's your problem?" the guy asked, a hint of jest in his voice. "I was only trying to have a good time."

"Well she's *not* having a good time, so fuck off," Tori interjected.

"What's the matter, Jenny? You only put out for the Beta guys?" The guy laughed, a deep guttural laugh that seemed to reverberate off the walls of the crowded room.

Others joined in as Jenny spun around, finally taking in the intensity of the attention of her, the sideways looks, the creeping sensation of eyes on her back.

"What's going on?" she asked, looking from Tori, to Nessa, and finally to me.

"I … I don't know exactly …" I started.

Snippets of conversation floated in our direction. Harsh words spoken far too brazenly.

"… *slept with half of the Beta house …*"

"*All in the same night …*"

"*… Total slut.*"

"*I heard they took her two at a time …*"

"*… She came tonight to see how many Omega guys she could land …*"

Emily leaned against the far wall, her arms crossed over her chest, a mischievous smile on her face, as she watched the chaos unfold.

"Oh my God," Jenny said, her lower lip trembling. "They're all talking about *me*?"

"Emily—" I started, but Abby was quick to interject.

"This is why you wanted to leave, wasn't it?" she snapped, suddenly sober as she pointed an accusatory finger in my direction. "You all knew she was going to do something like this and you did nothing to stop her. This is just as much your fault as it is hers. Come on, Jenny, let's go." Abby grabbed Jenny by the arm. "And you three tell Emily that Jenny is moving in with me. She's not spending one more second around that fucking monster."

Abby yanked Jenny in the direction of the front door, pushing past anyone who stood in her way. The crowed jeered and laughed as they passed through the room. Their words seemed to pile up on Jenny's shoulders, which sank lower and lower as she disappeared into the night.

Chapter 28

Now

No, no, no, this can't be happening. I stand on the sidewalk outside of my office pulling in big gulps of the cool air, but I still can't seem to catch my breath. It feels as though I'm trapped on a spinning carnival ride, the city swirling around me, a blur of yellow cabs, faded gray cement, and reflective glass windows glaring down at me like angry eyes.

How could Jenny possibly know that I submitted the falsified record with that motion? Her email came almost instantaneously after it was submitted, as though she was just waiting to see what I was going to do.

But the only person who knew about my dilemma with this motion, aside from Barrett who *clearly* wouldn't have brought the truth to light, was Tori. Was Emily right? Could these emails be coming from one of the few people I trusted? Did I fail to see what was right in front of me all this time because it was too awful to even consider? Or—the thought occurs to me all at once—could Tori have sold me out to whoever is doing this? Traded my secret like currency?

My phone starts ringing, its vibration in my hand grounding me. I hope it's Tori calling, maybe to offer some sort of explanation, but when I look down at the phone, it's Nessa's name that I see flashing across the screen.

"Jules," she cries the instant I accept her call. I can hear her sobbing, imagine the tears streaming down her face.

"Ness, what's happened?" I grip my phone so tightly that I can feel the blood draining from my fingers.

"It's ... I got another email from Jenny." She sobs again, trying to catch her breath. "She ... I did something I shouldn't have ... It could ruin everything ..." Her words come out in a broken tangle.

"And Jenny knows, doesn't she?"

"Yes! But I don't know how it's possible," Nessa laments.

"Where are you?"

"I just left rehearsal. I just couldn't stay after ... this."

"I just left work too. Is there somewhere near you where we can meet?"

"Yeah," Nessa sniffles. "There's a café right near the theater. I'll text you the address."

"I'll be there as soon as I can."

* * *

I find Nessa sitting at a small, round table near the back of the café she'd chosen. She stares out the window as if in a daze, a haunted look on her face, with her fingers wrapped around a mug of tea, letting it warm her as it slowly goes cold in her hands.

"Ness?" I say softly as I approach her table.

Nessa startles at the sound of my voice and a splash of tea escapes her cup and lands on the table. She grabs a napkin and blots at the spill. "Jules. Thank God you're here."

"What's going on?" I ask.

Nessa runs her slender fingers through her shiny brown hair.

"I made a mistake." Her chin wobbles as tears collect in her big, round eyes.

"What happened?" I ask gently. "Whatever it is, you can tell me. We're in this together." *At least I hope that's true.*

"I …" she starts, swallowing hard before she can continue. "You know that song that I submitted to the record label? The one they wanted to sign me for? Well, it's … it's not exactly mine."

"What do you mean?"

"The lyrics are mine. I really did write them. But the melody … it's … it's sort of … borrowed? I swear I didn't mean for this to happen." The words start to come faster now, rushing from her tongue. "I went to this open mic night a few months ago and I saw the most incredible songwriter singing all of these amazing original songs. This one in particular got into my head. I even recorded a clip of it and listened to it over and over again, hoping it would inspire my own writing. I was struggling to find the right melody for the lyrics I was working on at the time." She gazes out the window once more, lost to the memory or to the guilt. I can't be sure.

"But when I went back to the studio and started playing around, trying to write my own music, I found myself singing to the tune of her melody. Overlaying the lyrics I'd been writing on top of her song. And it was magic. It worked *perfectly*. The thing is, I didn't realize that Tim had stepped into the control room and was listening to the whole thing. He *loved* the song and insisted we record a track. He said we'd found the song that was going to finally get me that record deal. And I … I …"

"You didn't tell him it wasn't yours."

Nessa shakes her head sadly, her eyes not meeting mine. "I let him think I wrote it. And now Jenny, or whoever she is, knows about it somehow."

"Did you get another email?" I ask.

Nessa nods and pulls her phone out of her bag. "Here, see for yourself," she says as she hands it to me.

Jenny's email is open on the screen. The message is eerily familiar:

Liar, liar.

Below is a video of a young girl with an acoustic guitar strapped across her chest.

"She's singing … that song. In the video, I mean," Nessa explains.

"I know this isn't ideal, but can you pull the song now? Take it back before you sign?"

Nessa sighs. "I signed with the label this morning. It's too late. If they find out about this … I'm ruined." Her voice is heavy, her head hanging in shame. "Even if I were to somehow get the rights to the song, if they find out that I palmed it off as my own, the fact that I lied will probably get me blacklisted in the industry." She drops her head into her hands.

"I got one too," I say meekly. I need to take a leap of faith; I have to trust her. Because there's something I need to know …

Nessa's head snaps up. "You got what?"

"An email from Jenny. 'Liar, liar,' the same as yours. She knows about something I did at work. Something that could cost me my career … my license."

"Oh my God …" Nessa's eyes grow round.

"I have to ask, Ness … did Tori know? About the song?"

"Yes." She thinks for a moment. "I told her about it after I first recorded the track with Tim. I couldn't keep it all in—I just needed to talk it through with someone … Wait, why are you asking about Tori?"

"Because she knew about my case too … and she's the only one who did."

Nessa and I lock eyes over the table, a frightening reality settling over us.

"Have you told her about this latest email?" I ask.

"No, not yet. I called her right before I called you, but she didn't pick up."

"Good. Maybe it's best that you don't. Not yet."

"You don't really think she could be involved in this ..." Nessa says, her voice barely above a whisper. She doesn't want to believe it, but I can tell that there's a part of her that is already questioning everything she thought she knew.

"I don't know *what* to believe anymore."

Chapter 29

Now

When I get home, after finagling the lock that always seems to get stuck at the most inopportune moments, I find the apartment empty. It takes me by surprise, the stillness of it, although it shouldn't. It's still early in the evening and Jason isn't usually home by this time. And yet, the fading evening light—which casts long, angular shadows across the empty space—gives me a distinct sense of unease.

Maybe I should call Claire and get the name of that security company after all. Just to give me some peace of mind. I wish I could talk to her too. Talk to anyone really. Anyone who might be able to help me sort through what's been going on, to come up with a solution. I try to envision what it might be like to let someone in for the first time in so long. *But isn't that exactly what Nessa did with Tori?* She'd confided in her about the song she recorded, and look where that got her. No, I've known for a long time that putting my trust in anyone is far too dangerous. I've been conditioned to believe that my closest friends are also my most powerful enemies.

Maybe I just wasn't cut out to have real friends. Things always seem to fall apart. Just like with Kelly. I couldn't be the innocent girl from Ohio that she remembered, and also the person I was becoming at Westbridge. With the benefit of hindsight, maturity, I can see now how I was trying to straddle two worlds, to be everything to everyone, and somewhere along the way, I lost sight of who *I* wanted to be. We slowly grew apart over the years, Kelly and I, until the chasm that opened in our friendship eventually became too wide to cross. Maybe if I'd held on to that friendship, if I hadn't taken it for granted, I wouldn't feel so alone right now.

I walk through the apartment, flicking on all the lights as I go. The apartment is suddenly flooded with light. I imagine that it must look like a glowing lantern from the street, and, with a shudder, I wonder whether anyone is being drawn to its light.

I close myself in my bedroom and start to undress. I just want to wash this day off me, and I'm hoping that a hot shower will help me clear my head enough to sort out what to do next.

It occurred to me, after Nessa and I left the café, that we know Jenny has all the ammunition she needs to shatter our lives into pieces. And yet, she hasn't used it yet. Which leads me to believe that Jenny, too, understands the immense power that comes from holding someone else's secret in the palm of her hand.

Friends are meant to share secrets. Emily's voice ringing in my head again. But what happens when they decide to use that secret to destroy you?

I turn on the tap and let the hot water wash over me. My skin burns with it, turning a soft pink, a sort of purging of the sins of the day.

"Jules?" a voice calls out.

It startles me so much that I let out a strangled yelp. It takes a moment for the familiar voice to filter through my brain, which has been running on hyper-speed since I got Jenny's latest email. It's only Jason.

199

He steps into the bathroom, his form blurred and obscure through the foggy glass of the shower door.

"Hey, didn't mean to startle you," he says. "But why is every light in the place turned on? You suddenly scared of the dark or something?"

Maybe.

"Very funny," I reply, trying to keep my tone light and jokey. But it comes out all wrong. High-pitched and strained.

"I'm going to make myself a cup of tea," Jason says. "Would you like me to make one for you for when you're finished?"

"Yes, please." A warm cup of tea might be exactly what I need to settle my nerves right now.

I finish my shower quickly, and change into a comfortable pair of sweatpants and a T-shirt. As I turn to leave the room, something catches my attention. Or, more accurately, the lack of something. Missing from the top of my dresser is a slim silver frame that holds a photo from our wedding day, Jason and me, hand in hand, staring into each other's eyes. It was one of our favorites from the day, taken just before we slipped carefully chosen rings onto one another's fingers.

It's strange that it's not in its usual place. I guess Jason could have moved it, maybe while in one of his rare cleaning frenzies. *How long has it been missing?*

Funny, I pass by that photo every day, but I hardly notice it anymore. Not until I feel its absence do I start to think about it. The photo is a lot like my marriage itself, I suppose. I took it for granted. I'd become so accustomed to the idea that it would always be there, that I didn't feel the need to inspect it too closely.

I quickly scan the room, looking atop Jason's dresser, peering beneath my own in case the photo had fallen, all the while thinking back to the day it was taken. Our wedding day, and what it meant to me.

I remember peering through the doors of the church, my stomach in knots. Jason looked nervous too, shifting his weight from one foot to the other as he stood at the end of the long aisle, waiting for his bride. I nearly turned around; I nearly ran from that little white chapel that we'd so lovingly chosen together. *Can I really go through with this without telling him the truth about who I was, what I've done?* I'd tried so hard to become someone new. Especially since meeting Jason, all I wanted was to be the kind of person he thought I was. I shoved my past into shadows, and I shone a light on the best pieces of myself. But a part of me knew that the slate can never really be wiped clean.

Jason deserved to know the truth about the woman he was about to marry. I watched him standing there at the end of the aisle, adjusting his bow tie, sweat breaking on his brow. *He thinks he's marrying the girl of his dreams, but am I really that girl, or is it all just a glittering facade? An act I've convinced myself is true?* I wanted this life, this marriage, more than anything, but I also knew it was selfish to allow myself to have it. Jason deserved more.

My dad held my arm, ready to escort me to the altar. "You okay, sweetie?"

I cast my eyes down the aisle, strewn with pink rose petals, one last time, and Jason and I locked eyes. He smiled then, as though he was lit from within, and I knew it was too late to turn back. The time to tell him had passed. The truth, in that moment, would have crushed him.

I smoothed the smile on my face. "Yes, I'm ready." And I walked down that aisle to stand next to the most wonderful man I'd ever known. Jason slipped his hand into mine, the familiar weight of it a reassurance, and he gave a gentle squeeze. "I can't wait for forever," he whispered. And I thought maybe, just maybe, this was the start of a new life, one where the past would no longer haunt me every day. Maybe it would all be okay.

But I should have known that it couldn't last forever, that all that happiness was never really mine to keep. It was always just a matter of time before my past caught up with me, the immense weight of it pulling both of us under.

The smell of peppermint tea floats through the apartment, grounding me back in the moment. I breathe it in deeply, savoring the coolness of the scent on the back of my throat. *I'll have to ask Jason what happened to that photo.*

I walk into the kitchen, barefoot. My hair is still wet and the back of my shirt is damp and clings to my skin. I find Jason at the counter, his back turned toward me.

"That tea smells like just what I need tonight," I say, already feeling slightly calmer. "But it's the strangest thing. You know that photo in the bedroom, the one from our—"

Jason turns to face me, and I gasp in horror at what I see in his hand—my Westbridge University mug. The very same one my parents gave me the day I got my acceptance letter. The same one that shattered into a million pieces when I dropped it into the sink.

But how is that possible? I look down at my fingers, which tremble slightly. The cut on my index finger is still there, as I knew it would be, the edges of the torn skin an angry red.

"What's the matter?" Jason asks as he rushes over to me.

"That mug ... where did you get it?"

He looks at me as though I've lost my mind. *Maybe I have.* His brows knit in confusion. "The mug? From the cabinet. It's been there forever."

"But ... I broke it the other day ..."

"Evidently not," Jason replies, still looking perplexed. "Or maybe you had two."

"No, I only had the one. I'm sure of it."

"I don't understand ..." he says.

"Neither do I ..." My voice sounds vacant, distant, as if someone else is speaking these words. Someone had to have been in the apartment. Replaced the mug. Taken our wedding photo. It's the only explanation I can think of. *But ... why?* It just doesn't make any sense. I feel like I'm losing my grip on reality. I don't know what's real and what's imagined anymore. First I suspected Emily, and then Tori, and now it feels as though I can't even trust my own mind to tell me the truth.

"Look, Jules, I don't know what's been going on with you lately, but I'm worried about you … You've been acting very strangely."

"It's just …"

"It's what? Please talk to me." His eyes are pleading as they lock onto mine.

"It's nothing."

Jason sighs. "We can't just ignore this anymore," he says resignedly. "I've been waiting for you to come to me. I know how you are—if I pushed you, you only would have shut me out further. And so I tried to give you the time and space you needed to feel ready to talk to me about whatever is going on, but I don't think it can wait any longer."

He reaches into the kitchen drawer. I hear the stack of paper takeout menus and the odd bits and bobs of our lives shuffling around inside. He pulls something out and places it on the counter before me.

I feel the world tilt, the blood rushing from my head.

"Where … what are those doing here?" The words seem to fall out of my mouth as I stare at the familiar blue eye glasses frames now resting on my counter.

"I found them the other day. They were just sitting here on the counter when I got home from work."

"I don't … I don't understand," I stammer. But a part of me does. I know exactly who these glasses once belonged to, where I last saw them: on a dead girl's face. My hand reaches out to touch the frames to prove to myself that they're real, that they're here, but before I reach them, I physically recoil, a shudder running through my veins.

"Whose are they, Jules?" Jason asks.

"I don't know," I lie. "Maybe they're one of your old pairs?" As far as lies go, it's a weak one and I know it, but in this moment with Jason staring at me, waiting for some kind of explanation for the impossible, it's all I can think of.

Jason shakes his head in frustration. "They're not *mine*. Look, at first I didn't think much of it. I thought maybe you had a friend by or something and they got left behind. I just tossed them in the drawer meaning to ask you about them when you got home the other night, but then you were late getting back from Claire's and I completely forgot about them. But now … well, I got to thinking, and things with us have been really tense lately. Distant. You haven't been acting like yourself and I just thought … well … I have to ask, Jules … is there someone else?"

I almost laugh. A nervous burst of it bubbling to the surface. If only the explanation were as simple as an affair. "No, Jason," I say instead. "I swear to you there's no one else. I would never do that to you." I reach out to take his hand in mine, hoping he will feel the sincerity in my touch, but he pulls back.

"Then why did you react like that when I showed you the glasses? You looked … terrified," Jason retorts. "If these glasses mean nothing, why did seeing them upset you so much?"

"I wasn't—"

"You were. Don't even try to deny it. I could see it all over your face; and it only made me more certain that you're hiding something. If it's not an affair, then please, explain to me what exactly is going on here."

"I think someone has been breaking into the house." The truth rushes out in an outburst. It's a relief to finally tell him something true, something real, but I also know how crazy, how desperate, it must sound to him.

"What?!" Jason exclaims. "What do you mean?"

"Strange things have been happening lately." The words are coming faster now, the truth breaking free of the lies that have constrained it for so long. "The mug returning, there's a photo missing from our bedroom, and now these glasses that don't belong to either of us …"

Jason folds his arms over his chest, his head tilted, eyeing me appraisingly. He wants to believe me, I can see that he does, but

I can also see that a part of him, a big part, isn't convinced. If only I'd told him everything earlier, maybe he'd understand. But how could I possibly explain now that I'm being stalked by a girl who died over a decade ago? That I think a ghost from my past has been skulking around our apartment while we've been going about our normal lives? *Hasn't that always been true though? Jenny's ghost has been here with us all along.*

"This doesn't make any sense, Jules. You mean to tell me that someone has been breaking into our place to do … what? Replenish our drinkware? And they happened to leave their glasses behind?"

"I don't know. I really don't." I suddenly feel so tired, so drained, from all of the surprises that have bombarded me at every turn today, that I can't muster up the strength to convince him. "All I can tell you is that it's not what you think, okay? There's no one else."

Jason nods, but his upper lip remains stiff, his eyes don't meet mine. "I think I'm going to go to the gym."

"Now? Please don't walk away …" I hate the pleading tone that's crept into my voice. I reach out for him once again, but he steps away.

"I need some time to cool off, think this through. I don't want to say something I'm going to regret later."

"Are we okay?" I ask feebly. We've had our arguments, like every married couple does, but never like this. Never where he hasn't even been able to look at me. Never where I've doubted the security of our marriage.

"I don't know," he replies, his voice heavy. "I hope so."

As I watch him leave, the front door falling closed behind him with a "thud", I know that something needs to change. I may have cowered in fear when the ghost of Jenny Teller threatened my career, but I won't let her destroy my marriage too. I need to find out what she wants from me and put an end to this once and for all.

Chapter 30

Then

I was happy to be back on campus, on my way to meet Tori and Nessa for lunch, after what felt like a very long winter break spent at home in Ohio. My mom had done her best to fill our days with shopping trips in town, dinners at my favorite local restaurants, and Hallmark movie marathons over bowls of buttery popcorn, but I very quickly found myself yearning to return to my newfound home at Westbridge. In Ohio, I was a nobody. Another familiar face in the grocery store where the girls I went to high school with still largely ignored me. But at Westbridge, I mattered. I was seen. And I found myself counting down the days until I'd be back on campus. It didn't help that I'd barely even seen Kelly while I was home. She left right after Christmas to spend two weeks on a ski trip with Owen and her future in-laws.

I pushed open the doors to the dining hall and quickly spotted Tori and Nessa at our usual table. The familiarity of it felt immediately comforting to me. Of course we'd all exchanged texts and photos during the break, but seeing them again in person felt like coming home.

Nessa sprang up from the table and enfolded me in a long hug. "I've missed you!" she said, her face buried in my hair.

"You too!" I sat down across from Tori. "What did I miss?"

"We were just talking about Nessa's new room situation ..." Tori began.

"Yeah, when I got back to my room earlier, Jenny had already moved in. All my stuff was tossed into boxes and stacked up in the corner. She's still pretty upset. She barely even acknowledged me as I was moving out."

That's right. Abby had told us to relay that message to Emily. That Jenny would be moving in with her. We, of course, had never done it. As far as I knew, none of us had spoken to Emily at all during the break.

"So that leaves you ...?" I pondered aloud.

"With Emily," Nessa groaned. "But better me than Jenny. That poor girl. I don't know how she's going to show her face on campus again after what happened."

"I know," I agreed. "I feel awful for her." But in the back of my mind, a small, selfish part of me also couldn't help but feel relieved that it hadn't been *me* that Emily went after that night.

"So ... have you seen her then? Emily?" Tori asked.

Nessa shook her head. "I don't think she's back yet. I moved all my stuff in as quickly as I could and then got out of there. I'm dreading seeing her again to be honest."

"Maybe some of her anger will have passed ..." I suggested lamely. Even I didn't think that would be true. If anything, a month spent without her friends would only give Emily more time to think about how she was going to make all of us very sorry for having crossed her.

Tori let out a sardonic laugh. "I find that extremely doubtful."

"Do you know Hadley Richards?" Nessa asked.

I shook my head.

"She lives on the third floor? Her father owns, like, half of LA?" I shrugged.

"Well anyway, I heard that she and Emily spent the entire winter break together at Hadley's family's ski chalet. They're, like, best friends now."

Tori laughed. "Then I wish the poor girl the best of luck."

How quickly we'd been replaced. Of course Emily would have another minion lined up, just waiting to fill the vacancy we'd left in her social circle.

We finished our lunches, depositing the scraps into the garbage cans, and made our way outside. Wind whipped around my legs, picking up a trail of snow, icy crystals as fine as sand, from the graying mounds that sat rumpled along the shoveled walkways. I hugged my jacket close to me, bracing against the violent freeze.

The wild landscape surrounding Westbridge University could be as unforgiving in the winter as it was beautiful in the fall. The sky above us was a slate gray, brimming with a heaviness that threatened snow. The mighty hills, once covered in rolling green pastures and clusters of brightly colored trees, a wash of fiery oranges, and sunny yellows, had frozen over. Gashes of limestone now tore through the mountain plains like exposed bone, the earthy flesh shorn away. The graying land was cross-hatched with the skeletal branches of barren trees that looked like gnarled hands winding up from the wind-whipped ground, black and foreboding in the distance.

I saw her then, her hair an unmistakable flash of gold against the rinsed-out sky. I wanted to look away, I wanted not to care, but the truth was that I did. I stood there as though transfixed as I watched her talking to a guy wearing a blue and white Westbridge jacket. Though I couldn't hear what she was saying, her body language, the way she seemed to lean toward him, the way her hand rested gently on his arm as she laughed, suggested Emily had him firmly in her sights. And as we all knew by then, Emily always got what she wanted, one way or another. I was about to turn away when realization dawned on me, the scene sliding into painful focus before my eyes. The guy she was talking to, was Alex. *My* Alex.

"What the hell does she think she's doing?" I snarled.

Tori and Nessa followed my gaze, taking in the sight before us: Emily slipping her hand into Alex's back pocket, Alex looking down at her, his eyes wide with awe and want. He seemed mesmerized, dazzled by her, as though he was already swept up under her spell.

I could see it so clearly then, I could feel their awareness of one another. *How did I not see it sooner?* To Emily, nothing was as appealing as possessing something someone else coveted.

I felt rage settle over me like a fog, a red mist rising behind my eyes. "How dare she," I growled.

"She went too far this time," Tori agreed.

"Maybe it's not what it looks like …" Nessa offered lamely. I knew she was trying to spare my feelings. But I couldn't feel anything but anger, as though the burning intensity of my hatred had already reduced the rest of me to ashes.

"Look, Jules," Nessa continued. "I'm living with her now, for better or worse, so I might as well use it to our advantage. I'll do a little digging and see if they're really … together … or whether she's just trying to get a rise out of you."

I nodded tersely, feeling the red mist slowly start to recede. Maybe this was all an act for my benefit. It was entirely possible that Emily had seen us in the dining hall and orchestrated the scene before me just to push me over the edge. *I certainly wouldn't put it past her.* I latched on to that thought. I wanted to believe that's all this was: nothing but smoke and mirrors. Another of Emily's games designed to break me. But as I watched Emily and Alex together, a small voice pointed out that Emily didn't even seem to notice I was standing there, my heart shattering right in front of her.

* * *

It was late in the evening when I heard a gentle knock on our dorm-room door.

"You guys still up?" Nessa called through the closed door, her voice an elevated whisper.

Tori slid off her bed and flicked on the lights, making me wince. I'd nearly been asleep. Then she pulled the door open to reveal Nessa standing in the hallway in her pajamas.

I could tell from the moment I saw Nessa's face, her nervous, watery smile, that whatever she came to tell us was not something I'd want to hear.

"What is it?" I asked, sitting up in my bed and hugging a pillow to my chest. A barrier between me and the rest of the world. I ran one hand through my tousled hair, trying to tame my tangled locks.

"So Emily is asleep and ... I ... I might have taken her phone ..."

"Let me see," I replied, instantly reaching for it, but Nessa pulled her hand back.

"The thing is, Jules, I looked through it, and there's some stuff on here that is going to be ... difficult to see."

"Ness, whatever it is, I need to know. Just show me."

Nessa sat down next to me and swiped at the screen on Emily's phone, bringing it to life. She opened her recent text messages and tentatively handed it over to me.

"You might not want to—" she started, but I wasn't listening. I was already furiously scrolling back through hundreds of text messages between Emily and Alex, going all the way back to the beginning of the year. *How could I have been so blind?*

Tori sat down next to me, looking over my shoulder as I began to read.

Emily: *She has such a crush on you. It's actually kind of cute.*
Alex: *I'm not in the market for "cute" ;)*

"We don't have much time, Jules," Nessa reminded me. "Emily could wake up any moment, and if this phone is not on her nightstand … all hell will break loose."

I scrolled a little further.

Alex: *What's up with your friend? She went upstairs with me last night. She seemed totally down for anything, just like you said. And then she just freaked out.*

Emily: *She was probably just intimidated. I'm sure you're the hottest guy who's ever even looked at her. Maybe ask her out?*

Alex: *Like, on a date? I'm not really looking for a girlfriend or anything right now.*

Emily: *You don't have to make her your girlfriend, you loser. But if you really want to get her in bed, show her a little attention. Tell her she's beautiful, buy her some shitty dinner and I guarantee she'll put out.*

My stomach somersaulted. Was this the only reason he asked me out? Sent me all those emails? The ones that made me feel so special? It was all because Emily told him I'd put out? The betrayal felt like a stab in the gut. Especially after Emily had been the one who made me feel like I needed to sleep with Alex in the first place. I nearly stopped there. It was so hard to read on. But I did.

Emily: *Did you sleep with Jules last night?*

Alex: *So what if I did? Jealous? ;)*

Emily: *Of her? Never.*

Emily: *Are you two together now then?*

Alex: *It's not like that. Just keeping it casual.*

Emily: *You must not know then …*

Alex: *Know what?*

Emily: *That she is … was … a virgin. Before you, that is.*

Alex: *SHIT! I didn't know. Why didn't you tell me?!?*

Emily: *I didn't know until after the deed was done.*

Alex: *I can't believe SHE didn't tell me! That's like a really big thing.*

Emily: *She was probably embarrassed to tell you that no one ever wanted her before. But now I think she's expecting that you're going to be like a couple or something.*

Alex: *What the hell am I supposed to do now? I wasn't trying to make her my girlfriend or anything.*

Emily: *I'd just ignore her if I was you. Between you and me, she's getting totally obsessed. Even talking about how she thinks she's going to marry you right after graduation.*

Alex: *I feel bad blowing her off, but I wouldn't even have slept with her if I knew. I'm just not looking to be tied down right now, ya know?*

Emily: *Don't feel bad. It's best for both of you if there's a clean break. She's a smart girl. She'll catch on eventually.*

I skipped forward, reading ravenously despite the pain it brought me. I was punishing myself for ever having trusted Emily. Every line a new lash on my back.

Alex: *I blew off your friend, just like you said, but I think she's pissed.*

Emily: *Did she text you?*

Of course I had, Emily encouraged me to. Making me feel justified, empowered in doing it.

Alex: *Yeah.*

Emily: *God, she's such a desperate loser. I told you she was obsessed.*

Alex: *This is a mess.*

Emily: *She's super clingy. Even with me. It's SO weird. Sometimes I think she wants to BE me or something.*

Alex: *What girl wouldn't?*

Emily: *Just hold strong. She'll get over you eventually, Casanova.*

Soon the nature of their conversation began to change. I checked the date. Just before winter break.

Emily: *I finally got rid of the clinger.*
Alex: *Oh yeah?*
Emily: *Yup. Only wish I'd done it sooner. Oh well. At least she introduced me to you ;)*
Alex: *In that case, we should hang out sometime. If you're down?*
Emily: *Totally.*
Alex: *Over break? We can meet up in the city.*
Emily: *I'd love that.*

Was I no different than Jenny to her? Just another loser on the periphery of her world who needed to be taught a lesson?

Nessa pried the phone from my hand. I hadn't realized how hard I'd been gripping it. "I have to get this back, Jules," she said gently. "Are you going to be okay?"

"No … not really," I murmured as if in a daze.

"I've got her," Tori told Nessa as she put her arm protectively over my shoulder.

"She can't get away with this," I said, my voice growing stronger. "I'm going to make her pay for this. One way or another."

"We'll help you," Tori assured me, her tone certain.

"Yeah," Nessa agreed, nodding along. "We're with you, Jules. Whatever you need."

Chapter 31

Now

We need to talk.

That had been the text Tori sent to me and Nessa in the late hours of the evening last night. It could mean so many things, but none of them good. We'd agreed to meet at Tori's apartment after work, but the growing anticipation of it has only served to make the work day feel as though time has slowed down, dragging itself along at a glacial crawl.

I still don't know whether I can trust Tori, but either way, I need to hear what she has to say. I need to get to the bottom of this Jenny thing before it destroys me. My career, my marriage, feel as though they're hanging in the balance, barely clinging to one tenuous thread.

Andrew breezes into our office late in the afternoon, a pair of aviator sunglasses pulled over his eyes. The scent of winter clings to his wool coat. "Freezing out there today," he says by way of greeting. "I can't believe it's only October and it's already this cold."

I nod in agreement, the white oval of my face reflected in his sunglasses bobbing up and down, but the snap freeze every news outlet had been talking about this morning is currently the least of my concerns.

"You had a deposition today?" I ask. I feel as though I need to partake in the small talk, this ritual of normalcy that already feels like a distant memory from a past life: my life before Jenny Teller rose from the dead.

"Yup. It was brutal. I couldn't wait to get out of there. Any word from Barrett? On your motion?"

"No, he hasn't spoken to me all day."

"That's probably a good thing," Andrew replies. "That guy creeps me out."

"I think that's the general sentiment around here."

Andrew starts to unload his briefcase, busying himself with work, and I turn back to my computer screen, trying to force myself to draw out a few more billable minutes. It's been a struggle to get anything done today. Between everything going on with Jenny, plus the added knowledge that I may soon be stripped of my license and perpetually unemployed, I've found it rather difficult to concentrate on any of the work that's piling up on my desk.

What feels like an eternity later, six o'clock rolls around and I immediately pack up my things to leave. It's time to meet Tori, to face my problems head on.

* * *

Tori, Nessa, and I assemble ourselves on Tori's sofa, which is upholstered in a subtle champagne-tinted leather. A bottle of chardonnay sits on the glass coffee table in front of us, above a high-pile white rug. The lights are dimmed, giving the room an almost sleepy feel. Pillar candles flicker in decorative crystal jars, casting a spray of dancing lights across the walls. A constellation of refracted warmth.

Tori pours each of us a glass of the pale gold wine. I take a small sip, savoring it on my tongue. It tastes expensive, with none of the usual bitterness of the bargain bin whites I usually buy. Or perhaps it's all in my head, my expectation to taste elegance from Tori's crystal wineglasses.

There is a familiarity to this. To sitting here with these women as we'd done so many times before in what feels like a previous life. But now, there is none of the old laugher, the trading of stories, the fierce loyalty I once felt toward them. I try to imagine what it might be like if we could pick up where we left off, if we'd come back to one another by choice and not by the force of Jenny's hand. What, besides the past, do we have in common anymore? And is a shared past, especially one we've all adamantly refused to acknowledge, enough to form the basis of a friendship in the present?

But if I don't have them, if Tori and Nessa aren't on my side, then I really am alone in this. And that's a prospect that's too frightening for me to even consider. And so I don't. I wash down my concerns, the niggling doubts scratching at the back of my mind, with another gulp of wine.

"Where are Matt and Mia?" I ask, suddenly realizing how empty, lifeless, the house feels.

"Matt took Mia to visit his mother for the night," Tori replies.

"Oh, that's nice."

We fall into an uneasy silence. So many things left unsaid hanging between us.

"So what's going on, Tori?" Nessa finally asks, her feet tucked up under her, a chenille throw cast over her lap.

Tori looks nervous. Her red varnished nails tap against the side of her wineglass. *Clink, clink, clink.* "I have to tell you guys something. Sort of a … confession." She winces as she says this last word.

This is it. This is where she admits that she traded our most valuable secrets to Jenny. *But I wonder what Tori received in exchange?* I wait for her to continue, my breath held in my lungs, as though the simple act of exhaling might whisk away this fragile promise of truth. Such a rare and exotic thing to pass between us.

"I got another email from Jenny," Tori says. "She's ... she knows something."

I hear Nessa let out a long burst of air. She must have been holding her breath too.

"Neither of you look surprised ..." Tori says.

"We got them too," Nessa explains, unable to keep the relief out of her voice. "She knows something about all of us."

"Why didn't you tell me?" Tori asks, putting her glass down on the table.

"It just happened," I cut in before Nessa has the chance to tell her even *more. How can she trust Tori again so quickly?* But I should have known that Nessa would side with Tori at the first available opportunity.

I feel myself unraveling. Reverting to the girl I was at eighteen, when I was so desperate for their acceptance, to be one of them. When, no matter how hard I tried, I always felt as though I didn't quite belong. *It's only my own insecurities talking*, I remind myself. It's because I'm perpetually the "new girl". The last added to the group. No matter how many years I've known these women, they'll always have known each other longer. They'll always have a history that existed before me. *And so, if push comes to shove, who do you think will be shoved?* The thought is mine, but it's whispered with Emily's voice. Another gulp of wine. Another worry swallowed down.

"What does she know?" I ask, suddenly desperate to know. Desperate for Tori to give me something I can latch on to, some way that I can know for sure that I can trust her, that we're still in this together.

Tori blows out a long plume of air. "She knows about someone I was with. Before Matt."

Nessa stiffens in her seat, and I notice the way Tori's eyes seem to avoid her.

"Is that all? An ex-boyfriend?" I ask. It hardly seems fair. Some ancient fling compared to my career, my marriage, and Nessa's dreams, on Jenny's hook.

"The thing is ... it was right before Matt. Like, the night before." Tori fusses with the edge of her thumbnail. "I told you how quickly I got pregnant with Mia after I met Matt ... It's just that ..." Tori's voice begins to waver. She lifts her wineglass from the table and takes a long sip. "Well, I just ... I could never be sure that she's ... his. Biologically, I mean."

My eyes round with shock. I want to ask if Matt has any idea, but I'm pretty sure I already know the answer to that.

Tori presses on. "Like I told you the other day, Jules, I was in a bad place before Matt. There was this other guy. Damian. Total waste of life." She swishes her hand as if repelling the very thought of him. "I kept falling in with him for some reason. We partied together a lot, hit all the same clubs, moved in the same circles, and it just kind of happened. We had this on-again off-again thing going, where we'd hook up and then not talk to each other for weeks. It was a pretty toxic relationship, to be honest."

Nessa nods along in agreement. "I remember Damian. He was a mess."

"So was I," Tori reminds her. "I don't know what was wrong with me, but I always went for the bad boys back then. The ones I knew would break my heart."

Like Nate, I think to myself.

"Anyway," Tori continues, "even though I knew Damian was an awful decision, and I hated myself every time I woke up in his bed, I let it go on for too long. The last time I was with him was ... the night before I met Matt."

She sighs heavily, blowing a plume of air toward the ceiling.

"The guilt I've been carrying over this for years ... God, it makes me sick to my stomach. I know it must sound so selfish that I've kept this to myself. And it *was* selfish, in a way. Matt has a right to the truth, I know that, but ... it's just ... he's been

218

hopelessly in love with Mia since the moment he found out she was coming into this world. I couldn't bring myself to take that away from him. *Or* from her. He's an incredible father and Mia adores him. How could I risk taking him away from her for some guy who would be furious if he knew she existed?"

"So Damian doesn't know about Mia?" I ask.

Tori shakes her head, her nose crinkling in disgust. "No. He was very clear on his stance on children. Never wanted them. I had a scare once while we were together. I remember telling him that I was going to take a pregnancy test. And do you know what that asshole said to me?"

She doesn't wait for us to answer. "'If it turns out to be a problem, handle it.'" She says it with a mock voice, deepening the timbre. "That wasn't going to be Mia. She was never someone's *problem*. Especially when she had Matt for a father, someone who loved her, wanted her. So yeah, maybe it was selfish not to tell Matt the truth, but I wasn't just thinking of myself. I was thinking of Mia too." Tori's voice begins to crack. "I just wanted her to have a family, to feel loved. Even if there's a chance that Matt's … he's … not really her father." She speaks these last words as a whisper, which float through the silent, empty house.

"How did Jenny find out about this?" I ask gently.

"I have no idea. I've been racking my brain about it since I got the email last night, but I feel like I'm just spinning in circles."

"Did anyone else know about … Damian? About when you ended things?"

"No. Our relationship wasn't exactly public knowledge. We treated it more like the shameful secret that it was." Tori shakes her head slowly, as if in thought. "So no, I don't think anyone would know, except for Damian, obviously, but I doubt he's given me so much as a passing thought in years. Oh, and, well, Nessa." Tori nods in Nessa's direction. "Of course I told her about meeting Matt, and how I knew I needed to end things with Damian right away. But obviously the email didn't come from Ness."

Nessa nods solemnly. "I remember how happy you were about Matt. How you said that the night before was the last time you'd ever see Damian, but I swear I never said a word about your thing with Damian to anyone. I was just glad he was going to be out of the picture. And, to be honest with you, I never did the math … about Mia. By the time you announced that you were pregnant, you and Matt had already been together for a few months. It never occurred to me that she might not be his. After seeing how good you two were together, how well you were doing, I'd forgotten all about that loser Damian."

"If only *I* could forget him," Tori says, toying with the stem of her wineglass, rolling it rhythmically between her fingers. "This can't come out. Not now. Even if Matt *is* Mia's father, I don't know that he'd ever forgive me for keeping this from him. The time to tell him was before we got married. Now, no matter how it turns out, it will feel like a betrayal to him."

It's the same fear that's kept me from telling Jason about my past as well.

Tori sinks back into the couch, and pulls her hand through her hair.

"Can I see the email?" I ask. "The one you got last night?"

"I deleted it," Tori says, a little too quickly. "I couldn't risk Matt finding it. All it said was 'Liar, liar,' and there was a photo of me and Damian attached, Mia photoshopped into the frame. I don't even remember taking that photo with him, to be honest. But there we were, two drunk idiots smiling for a selfie." She drops her head into her hands.

I want to believe Tori is telling the truth. I want to believe that she's deep in the hole with Nessa and me, because the alternative—that she's the one throwing dirt on our graves—is far more frightening to me. But, it would seem, Tori deleted the evidence that could prove which side she's really on.

I need to find out if I can trust her. One way or another.

"How was the Mommy Meet-Up the other day?" I ask.

"Huh?" Tori sits up, her brows knitted in confusion at the change of direction. *Which is precisely what I wanted.*

"You know, your playgroup thing with Mia."

"It was fine ... I'm not sure why you're asking about that right now though—"

"So you went then? Because my friend Claire was there. The one you gave the information to, and she said you didn't show up."

Tori's face goes pale. She pulls a sip of her wine before responding.

"I did go. I swear. I just ... I got there pretty late. Some of the moms had already left to take the new members for lunch. Claire was probably with them."

Claire had *mentioned going out to lunch* ... But there's something else bothering me about Tori's story. Something that doesn't quite add up. And then it dawns on me.

"Fine, but when we spoke on the phone that morning, you said you were on your way there. What could possibly have delayed you that much?"

A trip to my apartment maybe? I told her I was out running errands. She could have been the one who snuck in. *No. I'm being ridiculous.* Tori broke into my apartment and did what? Pulled a broken mug out of the garbage? Why would she do that?

"I was going to tell you guys ..." Tori says, her voice wavering.

"Tell us what? What's going on, Tori?" I ask, growing impatient.

"I went to see Nate Porter that morning."

"What?!" Nessa exclaims.

Tori rushes to respond, her words quick and harried. "I thought it was possible that he had something to do with these emails. I knew he wasn't happy about the way things ... played out, and so I called him, just to rule it out. He refused to talk to me over the phone, but I convinced him to meet me for coffee. He didn't want to at first, but I told him it was an emergency." Tori swallows hard.

"Why didn't you tell us this before?!" I ask, my voice rising in anger.

"After seeing him again, I didn't think it was important. I really don't believe that the emails are coming from him. I told him what's been going on. Not all of it, of course, but just that we've been getting emails from someone who's calling themselves Jenny Teller. He got really angry. He said he wanted nothing to do with any of this. With any of *us*, actually, and told me never to call him again."

"Certainly doesn't sound like someone who's doing everything they can to insert themselves back into our lives ..." Nessa murmurs.

"My thoughts exactly," Tori concurs. "That's why I didn't mention it. It was a dead end."

"You still should have told us," I say. "We're supposed to be in this together." *At least I hope we are.* "Is there anything else you're not telling us, Tori? No more secrets."

"Well ..." She picks at her thumb again. "Nate did mention one more thing when I saw him ... He's a detective now. For the NYPD."

We grow quiet while we consider the implications. If the truth about that night *does* come out, it's rather unsettling to know that we have an enemy in law enforcement who would be all too happy to see us in handcuffs.

Chapter 32

Now

When I get back to my apartment, my head swimming with the rich wine, I find that it is, once again, empty. It takes me a moment to recall that it's the first Tuesday of the month, Jason's standing poker night with his buddies. I don't know why they bother. None of them are any good. But at least they don't play for money. It's supposed to be all in good fun. Maybe I just don't understand it. When my friends played games, the stakes were always deathly high.

I sigh as I push open the front door. Even though I know there's a good reason Jason isn't home tonight, I still can't help but feel like it was intentional. Like Jason would rather be anywhere but home where the tension in the air has grown so thick that it can sometimes feel suffocating.

The moment I step inside, I know something is amiss. I feel a rustling at the back of my mind. *The lizard brain.* I'd heard the term on a documentary once—a reptilian name that conjures images of prehistoric beasts, all scales and sharp claws—fitting for that ancient part of the human psyche that is responsible for our primitive survival instincts. A holdover from our days of hunting and being hunted. I feel a primal stirring, one that alerts me to danger before the rest of my brain has formulated a logical reason for the sounding alarms.

I fly through the apartment turning on every light once again. Nothing appears to be out of place, but that dark corner in the back of my mind still shouts its ancient wail: *There is danger here.*

Finally, I reach the bedroom, flicking on the light switch and spinning around in the flood of light it brings. And that's when I see it.

"Truth or Dare? xoxo" written in a bloody red scrawl across the mirror of my vanity.

My breath catches in my throat, as if the words themselves had leapt from the mirror and wrapped themselves around my neck, slowly draining me of life. I feel the blood rush from my face, a dizzying tingle racing down my spine.

"Is someone here?" I shout, my voice escaping in a strangled croak. The skin prickles on my arms as I await a response. Both praying that there is one and that there is not. But I'm met only with a deafening silence.

I race through the apartment, checking every closest, every window, every shadowed corner. But I am alone.

I make my way back into the bedroom, and slowly approach the mirror, tentatively lifting one hand to touch the burning scarlet letters. I swipe my finger along the glass, leaving a trail of red behind it. I roll the waxy substance between the pad of my thumb and forefinger. It has a familiar scent, a soft floral undertone, currents of violet and rose. *It's lipstick.* I feel some measure of relief in this, and yet my hands still tremble, the sight of the red stain on my fingers a macabre reminder that an intruder has been here. There is no denying it now. Someone has been inside my house. *You're not safe here*, my lizard brain hisses. *You're not safe anywhere.*

I'm so distracted with the mirror, with the malevolent thing that seems to have flown into my home on dark, leathery wings, that I almost miss it. Lying atop the vanity, is an envelope. Neatly folded, creamy white stationery, tied with a royal blue satin bow.

I grasp one end of the ribbon and slowly pull until it unties and flutters down onto the glass surface of the vanity. I open the card, my eyes scanning the words hastily:

You are cordially invited to Homecoming Weekend at Westbridge University.
Hosted by the University Alumni Association for the class of 2009.
Festivities shall commence on the twelfth day of October, 2019.
This year's theme is A Midsummer Night's Dream, and in keeping with the great comedy, we invite you to lose yourself in the blurring of fantasy and reality at the Welcoming Dinner Masquerade Ball.
(Black tie preferred)

And then, in red ink, at the bottom of the printed card, someone has written: *"I'll see you there, xoxo."*

I look from the card back to the mirror, my face pale and drawn, reflected between the menacing red print. The letters are neatly formed in a looping scrawl, as if whoever did this had put great effort into the calligraphy. Carefully composing each character. The dichotomy between the sinister intent and the elegance of the lettering could not be more representative of Emily. Who, but she, would have written those words: *"Truth or dare, xoxo"*? Such malice signed with a pantomime of affection.

I notice the way the word "truth" has been underlined, the lipstick crushed into the glass as if for emphasis. I understand then that the card in my hand is not an invitation at all. It is a summoning. And should I fail to comply, my truth will be told for me.

Chapter 33

Now

I swipe at the mirror, swirls of red smearing across its surface. I catch sight of my reflection through the mess, a bold streak of blood red is slashed over my mouth giving the appearance of a demented, wicked smile. I wipe harder, determined to rid my life of any trace of those words.

My phone buzzes on the table and I glance down at it briefly, scanning the flood of incoming texts.

> **Tori:** *I just checked my mailbox and got an invite to homecoming?*
> **Nessa:** *There was one on my doorstep when I got home too!!*
> **Tori:** *Are we going?*
> **Nessa:** *I don't think we have a choice.*

I can't respond right now. Jason could be home any minute and this mess needs to be gone before he gets back. Besides, I know it's a petty thought, but I also can't deny that I'm feeling a bit resentful that Tori and Nessa's invitations were politely placed by their front doors while I'm over here cleaning up the results of a home invasion. In this moment it feels profoundly unfair.

"Jules?" Jason calls out, followed by the sound of his keys jangling on their ring as he hangs them on the hook by the door.

"In here," I call back. I quickly wad up the paper towels I've been using, now stained with patches of bleeding red dye, and toss them under the vanity, stepping in front of the mess just before Jason breezes into the room.

"What are you up to?" He seems to sniff the air. The astringent smell of glass cleaner hanging over us.

"Oh, just cleaning up a bit," I say, offering him a smile that I hope appears genuine.

He steps toward me and kisses my cheek, the stubble on his chin rough against my skin. I'm surprised by the intimacy of the gesture after our argument the other night. It feels like an olive branch.

"What's this?" he asks, reaching behind me. He picks up the invitation to homecoming, which is lying innocently on my vanity.

My first instinct is to snatch it from his hands, to rip the offending thing from his grasp before it can leach its poison into him, the past tainting my future. But I refrain, and instead steady my hands in fists by my sides, my nails digging crescent moons into my palm.

"It's homecoming at Westbridge this weekend," I say lightly. "The invitation just came today." *Via hand delivery.*

"We should go," Jason replies, his eyes scanning the text.

"Oh you don't want to go to that," I say with a swish of my hand. "I skip it every year."

"Looks like this is a big one—the ten year reunion with a fancy dinner and everything. It could be fun," Jason says, his eyes rising to meet mine. "And I think a weekend away could be good for us." He reaches for my hand, squeezing reassuringly.

Not this *weekend.*

"I don't know if—" I start, but Jason pulls his hand away. I

227

instantly feel a coldness settle between us. *Jason is giving me a chance to make things right. How can I shut him down?*

"You know what," I say instead, "you're right. A weekend out of town *could* be just what we need." It's not like I have any other choice. I have to go to homecoming. Jenny has made that clear. She has my marriage, my career, in the palm of her hand, and this invitation feels as though she's begun to squeeze. If I want to get to the bottom of this, to take my life back, I have no choice but to go. And now that Jason's seen the invitation, there's no way I can go without him. Not without putting a further strain on our marriage. He already suspected that I was having an affair—I can't imagine that an impromptu overnight trip without him would do much to dissuade him of that notion. But the very thought of Jason inside Westbridge's gates is enough to make me lightheaded.

Jason nods, the coolness lifting ever so slightly. "Great," he says. "I'm just going to take a quick shower and then we'll figure out dinner?" There's something in his voice, a cautious hopefulness, that feels like a knife twisting in my gut.

"Sure, that sounds great," I reply.

Jason closes himself in the bathroom, and I get down on my hands and knees. I feel around under the vanity for the paper towels I'd tossed there earlier. It's time to get rid of the last remaining evidence of "Jenny's" latest visit. I grope along the wall, my fingers sliding along the hardwood floor, when suddenly I feel something cold and hard under my fingers. I close my fingers around the object and pull it into the light.

A lipstick cover. Matte black. Exactly like the one I've seen in Nessa's hand so many times before.

An image begins to form in my head now, blurry at first and then with startling clarity: Nessa standing before the mirror in my empty apartment, red lipstick in her hand, slowly applying it to the contours of her lips with delicate care before penning a message she knows will point me directly at Emily.

Chapter 34

Then

"What should we do tonight?" Tori asked. She was sitting on her bed, her back resting against the wall, her hair in a messy bun that was bunched up near the top of her head.

"We should go out," I replied.

"Oh thank God. You've been so mopey these last two weeks. It's time to get back on the horse. Maybe even meet a guy who isn't a total lying dick."

"I'm beginning to suspect that they're *all* total lying dicks."

"Touché," Tori conceded with a nod. "But I'm glad to see you getting back to your old self."

My old self. I don't even remember who she is anymore. Certainly not the girl who barely did well enough on her finals to hold on to her scholarship by the skin of her teeth.

"Speaking of guys, shouldn't you be with Nate tonight?"

"Hardly. Valentine's Day isn't really our style. And we're not really a couple. Or maybe we are. Who knows? But no, there will be no heart-shaped boxes of chocolates or romantic candle-lit dinners here."

I was relieved to hear that I wasn't the only one who was feeling particularly bitter about the garland hearts strung up all over Nickerson Hall, and the school newsletter highlighting college sweethearts now married for twenty-plus years.

"Where do you want to go then?" Tori asked.

"Anywhere Emily and Alex *won't* be."

"Then the Tau house it is," Tori concluded. "Emily hates it there."

"I know. She says it smells like a locker room."

"She's not wrong." Tori laughed. "I think it'll be just what we need tonight though. I heard they're throwing an anti-Valentine's party. Wear anything except red and no couples allowed."

"Yes, that sounds perfect. But are you sure Nate won't care if you go to a singles party?"

Tori flicked her wrist dismissively. "If he misses me that much, he can come find me."

A knock on the door pulled our attention.

"Come in," Tori yelled, then cracked the gum between her teeth.

The door opened slowly, and Jenny lingered in the doorway. It was the first time I'd seen her since we got back from winter break. I'd thought about reaching out to her so many times, but I wasn't sure how warm a reception I'd receive. *This is just as much your fault as it is hers.* Abby's words swirled around in my head. The truth was that I *did* feel some level of responsibility for what Emily had done to Jenny, and I was finding it hard to traverse the landscape of my own guilt and make things right with Jenny. But then there she was. Standing in my doorway, and I couldn't shy away from it any longer.

"I just came to give you guys this," she said, her eyes avoiding ours. She thrust a bright pink flyer toward the center of the room, making no effort to venture inside.

I lifted myself off the bed and took the paper from her hand. "I hope you're not angry with us … We didn't know about what Emily was going to do and—"

230

"No. I'm not mad. Just completely humiliated." She lowered her voice to a whisper. "I feel like everyone is still talking about me."

"I'm sure they're not," Tori said reassuringly. "Most of the idiots around here have the attention span of a gnat. Everyone is probably already on to the next big scandal."

"That'll be the first time I'll be glad to be old news," Jenny replied, cracking a small smile.

I looked down at the paper in my hand and read the bold-faced title aloud: *Nickerson Hall Valentine's Gala.* "A *gala*?" I said skeptically. "I'm not sure 'gala' and 'Nickerson Hall' should exist in the same sentence."

"I know. Lizzy and Beth organized it though and I told them I'd help hand out the flyers. It's tonight in the student lounge."

I groaned.

"I assume you guys aren't coming then?" Jenny asked.

"We were just talking about going to the singles party at Tau tonight …" Tori began.

"You're welcome to come with," I jumped in hastily. I was eager to make things up to Jenny, to prove to her that I wasn't like Emily, that she wasn't a pariah, as least as far as we were concerned.

Jenny hesitated as she seemed to mull over the invitation, and I rushed to fill the uncomfortable silence. "Unless, of course, you already have Valentine's Day plans. I didn't mean to assume you wouldn't—"

"It's fine," Jenny replied. "I don't."

"No special man for you either then?" Tori said lightly, comically batting her eyelashes.

"Er, no. I thought there was maybe one guy that I might have been interested in, but it … didn't work out." She shrugged. "Feelings weren't mutual."

I was surprised to hear that Jenny had boy troubles of her own. I suppose, in a way, I was finally seeing her as her own person. Not just Emily's pet project, but a whole multi-dimensional person with a real, complex life that I knew nothing about. *A life not unlike my own.*

"You have to come with us then," I concluded.

Jenny ground the toe of her sneaker into the carpet. "I'd like to, but I have to go to Lizzy and Beth's thing first. I promised them I would."

"We could maybe stop by too ..." I suggested, casting a glance in Tori's direction.

Tori laughed. "Fine, first we go to the Valentine's Gala and then we hit the singles party. This is going to be an interesting night."

* * *

A few hours later, Nessa, Tori, Jenny, and I huddled in my dorm room to get ready for the night ahead.

Nessa and I chose matching black dresses with plunging necklines, which we paired with red lipstick, and dramatic smoky eyeshadow. Tori, on the other hand, dressed in jeans, a midriff Johnny Cash T-shirt, and a black choker necklace. She looked Nessa and me over appraisingly, one finger pressed to her lips.

"Do you know what you two look like? Mistresses at a funeral. You know, the ones who stand mysteriously in the back looking all sad and sexy and making the poor widow wonder if she ever really knew her late husband at all."

Nessa laughed. "You watch too many bad movies."

"I think you mean *classic* movies," Tori replied.

"Well I like it," I said. "Exactly the kind of vibe I need tonight. The opposite of happily ever after."

I pulled my hair back from my face and fixed it in place with a black velvet headband. I checked myself in the mirror—the tight dress, the blonde hair, the makeup—and for one brief, chilling moment, I could have sworn that it was Emily's face that I saw staring back at me. I pulled the headband off and tossed it onto my bed behind me.

Jenny was still pawing through my closet, touching each of the dresses in turn.

"Still didn't find anything for tonight?" I asked.

"What about this one?" she said pulling the sapphire blue bandeau dress from my closet. The same one I'd worn out on my first night at Westbridge.

"That would look great on you," I told her.

And it did. When Jenny shimmied into the dress and stood before the full-length mirror I could swear that I saw something come alive in her. A dark and seductive spark ignited behind her eyes. "It's perfect," she said.

When we arrived at the student lounge, the walls were festooned with an explosion of paper hearts and red and pink streamers. Students milled about the room drinking punch from red paper cups. As I looked around, I realized there were so many faces I didn't recognize. People who lived in the same hall as me that I'd never given so much as a passing glance to.

"How soon can we leave?" Tori whispered, leaning in my ear.

"Not soon enough," I grumbled back.

"Jenny! You came!" Lizzy ran up to us and wrapped Jenny in a hug.

"And you look *hot!*" Beth said as she followed closely behind Lizzy.

Jenny blushed a sweet petal pink. "I told you guys I'd be here."

"I know," Lizzy said. "I just didn't know if a Valentine's party would be your thing what with … everything." She placed her hand gently on Jenny's arm.

The pink blush in Jenny's cheeks now burned red. "Is Abby here?" she asked, probably desperate to push the spotlight off her.

"Yeah," Beth replied. "She's here somewhere. Though she doesn't seem too happy about it. Valentine's Day is *definitely* not her thing."

Jenny craned her neck to look over Beth's shoulder. "I should probably go say 'hi' before we leave. We can't stay too long."

"At least let me get a photo!" Lizzy said, tapping the boxy, black camera that was strapped around her neck. "I'm on the yearbook committee now, and this would be a great shot." She lifted the camera to her eye. "Squeeze together, girls."

Tori, Nessa, Jenny, and I looked at one another. *I guess it will forever be documented that we attended a Valentine's Day Gala in the student lounge.*

The four of us huddled close, our arms thrown around one another, our faces pressed together, polished smiles plastered in place.

"I think you're forgetting someone," a familiar voice said just as the whirr of the camera's shutter sounded.

Emily. She'd positioned herself next to Nessa on the end of our group, her own teeth bared for the camera's lens. To anyone else, it may have looked as though she was smiling, but we knew that she meant it as a threat.

"I'd *love* a copy of that," Emily crooned.

"Sure thing!" Lizzy said happily before she walked off, ready to capture more humiliating moments for the yearbook.

"Funny story," Emily said. "I was just walking past the student lounge on my way to meet my *date*, and I see you four losers attending ... whatever the hell *this* is." She gestured around the room with a sweep of her arm, at the handmade decorations taped to the walls, the group of misfits huddled around the punch bowl, unable to secure proper dates for Valentine's Day.

We heard someone snicker from outside in the hallway. *That must be Hadley.* She bore a passing resemblance to Nessa, but wasn't quite as pretty. It was as if there was a dullness to her; she was lacking Nessa's shine, the thing that drew people to her. A fact that I was sure Emily was rather pleased with.

"We were just stopping by ..." Nessa started.

"Whatever you say, hon," Emily replied, her voice dripping with feigned pity. She laughed as she turned to leave. "You're all even more lost without me than I'd imagined."

In that moment, I felt as though I was seeing myself through Emily's eyes. Suddenly, the outfit I'd meticulously chosen for the evening felt cheap, the makeup tawdry. It was the first time I saw myself for what I truly was: a pale imitation of Emily Wiltshire. *Maybe we all were.*

I gritted my teeth as I watched Emily saunter away, my replacement at her heels, on her way to spend a romantic evening with the boy that should have been mine.

* * *

The frat party was everything the Valentine's Gala was not.

"Welcome to the den of sins," a boy wearing devil horns said in a deep voice as we'd entered. His lips curled into a lecherous smile, and his face took on an eerie white glow in the frosted moonlight.

Tori rolled her eyes at the time, but as it turned out, it hadn't been an inaccurate description.

As the night grew dark, the party devolved into hedonistic revelry. Gyrating hips came together on the dance floor, hands roved over bodies, everyone touching, everyone longing to be wanted, to feel seen. Even Nessa, who normally acted as though she was saving herself for Prince Charming, seemed to have lowered her standards for the evening. I spotted her dancing with some frat boy in a wrinkled shirt—letting him run his hands along her hips, as he pressed into her back and kissed her neck so enthusiastically that I wondered whether he was a vampire hoping to draw blood.

Nate had, unsurprisingly, come in search of Tori and so she'd been preoccupied for most of the evening with her tongue in his mouth. Which left me and Jenny to fend for ourselves.

"Need another drink?" I yelled to her over the roar of the music. Jenny nodded. It seemed that we both needed a little extra help getting through the night.

We wandered into the kitchen to top up our lukewarm beers.

"Sorry, keg's kicked," one of the frat guys said, one foot resting atop a dented keg. "Can I interest you in some punch?"

I remembered Tori's cautionary words on my first night at Westbridge. *Never drink the punch. You don't know what's in it.* But in that moment I didn't care what was in it. Not if it would take the edge off. I wanted to be like everyone else around me. All of them uninhibited, so cavalier with their sexuality. But most of all, I wanted to stop the thoughts that were running rampant through my mind about what Emily and Alex might have been doing at that very moment.

"Yeah, sure," I said. "Fill me up."

"You got it," the boy said with a wink that made my stomach churn.

"Me too," Jenny said, handing him her cup.

The boy swirled the bowl of red punch with a ladle before scooping some into each of our cups.

"Enjoy, ladies," he said. That wink again. The curdled grin. I pretended I didn't see it as I swallowed a large gulp.

What came next felt like a series of snapshots. Me on the dance floor, the smell of cologne in my nostrils—a cloying musk that made my stomach feel queasy. A boy with his hands on my waist, laughing, his face too close to mine in a distorted blur. Me on a couch that smelled of mildew and rot, the feeling of teeth clashing against mine, a suffocating weight on top of me that made me feel as though I was drowning.

"Stop," I said, as I sat up feeling disoriented and lightheaded. I pressed the palm of one hand to my temple as I pushed whoever-he-was off me. I faintly registered his disappointment, his calls for me to come back. But I didn't.

I wandered through the room looking for my friends. I couldn't find Tori or Nessa, but I saw Jenny pressed up against a wall, making out with some guy I didn't recognize, her hands gripping his hair. I wondered whether I should intervene, ask if she was okay, but she seemed like she had the situation under control, and I was hardly in a position to help anyone.

And so instead, I went upstairs in search of a bathroom, my fingers dragging along the banister for support as the room spun around me.

As I waited in line for the bathroom, my back pressed against the peeling wallpaper, I was bombarded with images of Alex and me, at a frat party very much like this one. The feeling of his hands on my skin, the way he looked at me with such longing, such deference, that it made my heart feel as though it was shattering all over again. *Had it really all been an act? Had I imagined the spark between us?* I felt a wave of bile rising up in my throat. Whatever had been in that punch had only made my thoughts of Emily and Alex more vivid, more pervasive. I slid to the floor, my back scraping along the wall, and screwed my eyes shut; but I still saw them, their laughing faces twisted in a grotesque distortion.

"Hey." *Jenny.* She sat down next to me on the floor. "Quite a night, huh?"

I nodded. "You seemed to be having a good time though …"

Jenny laughed, a breathy huff. "I guess. I've never done anything like that before, ya know? It was kind of … empowering. To be wanted like that."

I tried to listen to what she was saying but my head was pounding. It felt as though her words were pelting me.

"It's just that after what happened with that other guy I told you about, the one who didn't work out, it felt really good to be in control. I think he wants to have sex."

"Who?" I managed, digging the heels of my palms into my eyes, trying to stop the cloying pain that was throbbing behind them.

"The guy downstairs. The thing is, I've never done it before." She started speaking faster, her voice piercing my brain, an endless assault. "I think I might want to. Sometimes I think I should probably get it over with. Get the first time out of the way so when I finally do get together with the right guy, he doesn't think I'm some inexperienced loser. But on the other hand, I don't want to be the kind of girl who loses her virginity to some guy who probably won't ever think about her again."

Like me. A vision of Alex sparked in my brain: his bare chest silver in the moonlight, his strong arms holding him over me, his hips pressed to mine, and another wave of nausea washed over me.

I felt a rush of anger toward Jenny, a stabbing resentment that she'd forced me to face my own regrets. But even then, somewhere in the deep recesses of my alcohol-steeped mind, I knew it wasn't entirely her fault. She was just as messed up as I was. And besides, she couldn't have known exactly how close her words were hitting to home, how she was prodding at a raw and open wound. I hadn't told her what happened with Alex. That he'd used me for sex and then cast my feelings aside as though they meant nothing. And I certainly wasn't about to tell her that Emily had merely loaned him to me and then taken him back, as though he'd been a borrowed toy. It was all far too humiliating.

But it was more than that. I didn't want to see how alike we really were, Jenny and I. The parallel between our lives was undeniable in that moment, and I didn't want to face it. A mix of resentment and jealousy bubbled up within me as I realized that Jenny was standing on the precipice of a mistake I'd already made, and that, unlike me, she still had the chance to turn back.

A snapshot of the last time I'd been with Alex floated through my mind unbidden: him bending down to blow a plume of smoke out of the bottom of his window, me slinking back into my rumpled silk dress, embarrassed and exposed, as he waited for me to leave.

"What do you think?" Jenny said.

"About what?" I muttered. I felt so disoriented, my thoughts snapping back and forth between the past and the present in a dizzying blur. *What was in that drink?*

"About sleeping with him. Should I do it?" Jenny turned to me; she was sitting too close. I could feel her breath warm on my cheek. And in that moment all I wanted was for her to stop talking. For her to stop reminding me of my own regrets. To stop conjuring images of Alex.

I leaned my head against the wall, clenching my eyes shut. I didn't even look at her as I snapped, "It's just sex, Jenny. It's not that big a deal, okay? Just sleep with the guy and get it over with."

I pushed myself up to my feet, stumbling on my heels as I walked into the now unoccupied bathroom and slammed the door behind me.

* * *

I wiped the vomit from my mouth as the remains of the punch, frothy and pink, swirled down the drain. I felt a little better now that whatever poison I'd drunk had been expelled from my body, but the aftermath was starting to set in. I'd sent Jenny, who'd taken whatever drug I had, off with some man she didn't know.

I walked out of the bathroom, my body aching and sore, and made my way back downstairs.

"There you are!" Nessa yelled as I reached the living room. The red lipstick was fading from her lips; her hair was mussed. "I've been looking everywhere for you. You haven't been answering your phone."

"Sorry," I replied. "I wasn't feeling well. Where's Tori?"

"She just left with Nate. I told her I'd hang back and wait for you and Jenny. Speaking of, have you seen Jenny anywhere?" She looked around the room.

"Not for a while," I said. *Though I have a strong suspicion about where she is.* "Maybe we should check upstairs. I saw her with some guy earlier."

"Tori and I saw her too. She didn't seem … like herself." Nessa bit at her thumbnail.

We ascended the stairs, pushing past a couple sitting on the steps, lips locked, cups of punch resting in their hands. "Maybe we should have checked on her earlier," Nessa said nervously. "I think the punch was spiked. Everyone seems really fucked up …"

I'll say.

When we reached the hall at the top of the stairs, most of the bedroom doors were closed. I pushed the first one open, now desperate to find Jenny. For all I knew, she could be passed out, some predator taking advantage of the drugs coursing through her system. I didn't think Jenny had ever willingly taken drugs before. I doubted she'd have any kind of tolerance for it.

The lights were off in the bedroom and my hands shook as I groped along the wall to find the light switch. Finally my fingers found the switch and the room flooded with light. On the bed in the center of the room were two naked bodies tangled together like a two-headed beast. It took my drug-addled brain a moment to process what I was seeing. A muscular back, thrusting hips, a girl lying on her bed, her pale breasts exposed.

I froze in shock at the primal, carnal scene before me. The man turned to look at me then, in what felt like slow motion, a salacious grin creeping across his face. My stomach lurched.

"Get the fuck out!" the girl yelled, snapping me back to reality. I retreated back into the hall and slammed the bedroom door.

"Wasn't Jenny," I muttered to Nessa.

Just then, the door to another bedroom flew open and Jenny came bounding out, her dress a familiar blur of blue. She ran toward us, barefoot, holding the top of her dress up with one hand. One of the straps was torn, and it trailed behind her helplessly as she ran.

"Hey! Where are you going?" a voice called from the bedroom. A shirtless boy, fist holding up the front of his jeans, lingered in the doorway. "I heard you were supposed to be a sure thing!"

Jenny didn't look back. She kept running in our direction, nearly collided with Nessa and me at the top of the steps. Mascara ran in streaks under the eyes, her lipstick was smeared around her mouth, and her face was contorted with racking sobs.

240

"You're just like her," she cried, pushing past me. "I can't believe I thought you were different."

"Jenny, wait!" I called. But she didn't stop. She never even looked back.

Chapter 35

Now

We whizz past rows of tall, elegant pine trees that blend into a blur of deep, hunter green outside my window. Jason's fingers tap a beat on the steering wheel in the seat next to me, calmly syncing with the rhythm floating from the radio. But the closer we get to Westbridge, the faster my heart thrashes in my chest.

This drive is exactly as I remember it. For a moment I feel like that same eighteen-year-old girl with her nose pressed against the car window, giddy with anticipation and raw nerves to find out what Westbridge would hold in store for me. The wild terrain here is nothing like New York City, the ever-evolving organism that it is. The city is forever changing; new shops popping up every week, familiar restaurants stripping their names from their awnings and shuttering their doors. Nothing ever stays the same for long in Manhattan, and I find comfort in that, in the assurance that change is possible. But here, nature rules the land. Thickets of ivy spread across the ground and wrap around the rough tree trunks, thorny briars rise from the dense underbrush. It is a reminder, one that is all at once humbling and frightening, that the forest was here before me, and it will be here long after I'm gone. I wonder, if in a place like this, the past can ever really be forgotten.

"I'm so glad we're doing this, Jules," Jason says, placing one hand on my thigh. His eyes never leave the road as he maneuvers our little rental car along the winding pavement.

"I am too," I agree. Even though that couldn't be further from the truth. In reality, I'd spent the better part of the last three days trying to think of a way to avoid this trip, but it was of no use. Deep down I knew that the only way to put an end to this dangerous game with Jenny was to accept her invitation to homecoming. It seems almost fitting, poetic in a way, that this should end where it all began: at Westbridge University.

I think back to my first homecoming, freshman year, how I'd tried to imagine what it would be like to go back there as an adult. I never could have imagined *this*.

"It'll be great to meet some of your old friends too," Jason says, giving my thigh a squeeze, a gesture that might once have sent a pang of longing through me. "I'm happy they all decided to come."

As if we had any choice. I'm not quite as enthusiastic as Jason is about spending a weekend with Tori and Nessa. I've been avoiding them since the night "Jenny" left her menacing invitation on my vanity. *"I'm so busy at work."* (A lie.) *"Jason is home. Can I call you later?"* (Another lie.) It feels like I'm lying to everyone these days, but after the most recent break-in, I don't know that I can trust them anymore. It could just be paranoia, the stress of Jenny's sudden return making me see things that aren't there, but until I know for sure who is behind this, I can't trust anyone.

My phone pings with a text and I fish it out of my purse, happy for the distraction.

Claire: *Brian has to work AGAIN this weekend. Do you want to keep me company?*

Me: *I wish, but I'm going to homecoming at Westbridge this weekend.*

Claire: *Who knew you had so much school spirit?! Guess all is okay with the college drama then?*

Me: *Yup. All worked out.*

Claire: *Glad to hear it! Have a great time!*

I grimace as I close the conversation. More lies, more lingering half-truths. There is a familiarity in this. I recognize this battle raging within me that feels as though I'm being torn in two. I felt the same way when Kelly and I drifted apart so many years ago. I am once again straddling two worlds, my past and my present, and I know that I won't be able to keep my foothold in both places much longer. I can feel it happening, the tectonic plates of my life as I know it are shifting beneath my feet. The worlds I've worked so hard to keep separate all these years are about to collide, and I don't know what the new terrain will look like when they do.

I bounce my heel in the footwell of the rental car. I just want to get this weekend over with. To take back control of my life. Knowing "Jenny" is out there, somewhere, has me constantly looking over my shoulder, checking for ghosts in every shadowy corner. As I left work yesterday, I could have sworn someone was following me.

I felt my skin prickle, the sensation of eyes boring into my back as I walked down the crowded city sidewalk. I picked up my pace, my panic rising, my palms tingling. I'd nearly reached a sprint as I bolted for my train, but I still couldn't outrun the feeling that someone was bearing down upon me, weaving through the crowd to catch up to me. But when I turned around, there was no one there. No ghost-like girl with long black hair reaching out for me with cold, spindly fingers. *The only thing chasing me is my own guilt.*

I think it's the silence that has me so on edge. I haven't heard from Jenny since she left the invitation. In a sense, her sudden absence has felt even more threatening than any of the messages she's sent. She has me under her thumb now and she knows it. I am returning to the one place I never wanted to see again. But it seems that Jenny is determined to make me face the past I've been running from for so long.

I pull out my phone in an effort to distract myself. I type in the web address for the e-courts website and check to see if there's been a decision on the motion I filed for Barrett. I know it usually takes weeks, even months, for a motion like this to be decided, but it can't hurt to look. *But what am I hoping for, really?* Regardless of whether the motion is granted or dismissed, the damage is already done. I knowingly submitted falsified records to the court, an offense that could cost me my license, and Jenny knows it. E-courts takes forever to load. It must be the service up here. It's always been unreliable. But when the screen finally blinks to life, I see that my motion is still pending. Undecided. Hanging in purgatory. Just like the rest of my life.

"This is it, right?" Jason says, pulling me back to the moment.

I look up at the familiar wrought-iron gate, its dark, twisted metal soaring up toward the sky in pointed spires. At its center, is the Westbridge University crest in a scrolling, gold filigree design, and on either side, great stone pillars serve as a perch for two fearsome-looking hawks, the school's mascots. They stand at the ready, their talons curled around the stone ledge, their shoulders hunched, as if they're bracing for an impending battle.

"Yup. We're here," I reply.

As our car makes its way up the cobblestone drive, the grand gates seem to loom over us, a menacing warning. The hawks—huge, winged beasts with blank, stony eyes—stare down upon us like gargoyles. Their gazes, cold and unforgiving, seem to follow us as we pass onto their hallowed ground. I remember reading somewhere that gargoyles were once thought to frighten away evil spirits and protect the buildings they guard. In the case of

245

Westbridge's stone guardians, they've failed. An ancient evil has already made its home here. I can feel it hovering in the air, a ringing echo, a remnant of the past that never left these walls.

"Where to?" Jason asks.

My mouth goes dry and my voice catches in my throat as I answer. "I think we need to go to the student center to check in for the weekend's events, and then we can go find our hotel."

I direct him toward the student center, passing the clusters of buildings that once made up my whole world.

I thought I remembered Westbridge, every detail of my time here, but being here now makes me realize that my memories of this place have faded, the color of the place, the texture of it, rinsed out like an old photograph. Driving through campus, the memories come back to me in full technicolor clarity. Suddenly I can see again Tori smoking by the center fountain after dark, hear Nessa laughing as she climbed into an idling cab, feel the coldness of the metal stadium benches beneath my fingers. It was real. We were here. And now we're back.

"Maybe after we check in, you can give me a tour of the campus," Jason suggests. "There's no rush to get to the hotel, and it's incredible here."

I look out the passenger window. At the stately brick structures surrounded by leafy maple trees, resplendent in their autumn tones, at the cobblestone paths, the bubbling fountains, the ivy-covered walls. For a brief moment, I see this place as Jason does. As I once did. It's almost romantic, the collegiate elegance of it all—this idyllic patch of academia seemingly untouched by the outside world. But I know better. I know that there is something sinister that hovers over this place like a specter. A dark malevolence that casts its long shadow over Westbridge. I recognize the darkness here; it is as familiar to me as an old friend, and I fear it recognizes me too.

Jason pulls into the lot for the student center and we step out into the brisk fall air.

"Wow," he says. "It's a lot colder here than in the city."

I force a smile. I don't want Jason to see how much being here has already rattled me. "Hard to believe we're still in New York, right?"

"That's for sure." Jason wraps his arm around my shoulders, pulling me close to him as we walk into the building. He seems so much calmer here, more willing to forgive, as though our being here in the fresh country air, away from the stagnant gloom that was building within the confines of our apartment, has given us a fresh start. *If I can just make it through this weekend, if I can just find out what Jenny wants, maybe we can go back to the way things were before. Maybe my marriage will survive it.*

We walk into the student center. It's different than I remember it. I'm struck by the same feeling I had when I was in high school and we took a class trip to the elementary school to read to the younger children. From my vantage point as a near-adult, my old desk, the little cubbies, suddenly felt so much smaller, so much more childish, than they did in my memories of my time there. Although I'm sure the difference here is more than just a matter of perspective clashing against my faded memories of Westbridge. The student center has probably been renovated since I was last here, not that I'd know as I intentionally "forgot" to send my contact information to the Alumni Association after I graduated. I didn't want the monthly newsletters, the fundraising emails, the constant reminders of my time here.

"Oh, there's the check-in station," Jason says, nodding toward a folding table that's been set up at the far end of the lobby under a blue and white tablecloth. A sign reading, "Homecoming Headquarters, Check-In Here," has been affixed to the front.

We approach the table, which is being manned by two women: a blonde with a severe, blunt bob wearing a fitted, sleeveless dress, and a brunette with stylish side-swept bangs and a chic V-neck blouse. The scent of Chanel No. 5 greets me before they do.

"Hi, we'd like to check in for the weekend, I'm Juliana Da—"

"I know who you are, Jules," the blonde interjects coolly. She folds her thin, wiry arms on the table in front of her.

My eyes fall to the name tag on her chest. *Elizabeth*. "Lizzy?"

"I go by Elizabeth now."

"I'm sorry," I say. "I didn't recognize you!" I'm shocked by her transformation. I never would have imagined that the meek, mousy Lizzy I knew back in our school days would become the polished woman sitting before me in the designer sheath dress with the diamond bracelet encircling her wrist.

I look over to the brunette, to the nameplate pinned to her blouse. *Beth*. "Hi, Beth. You look incredible!" I say. She does. The shy girl with the rosy cheeks and the flute case swinging from her arm has become edgy, trendy with a high-end sheen. Her dark hair bears no resemblance to the drab, lank locks of her youth. It is now a carefully crafted array of colors that blend together to create a rich, dimensional chocolate hue. Beth smiles but it doesn't reach her eyes.

"You guys look so different!" I say brightly.

"And you appear to be exactly the same, Jules," Lizzy remarks with a wintry smile.

Jason snakes his arm around my waist proprietarily. He smiles broadly, blissfully unaware of the undertones of the conversation, the entire exchange that's occurring beneath our words. *Men*. "She never seems to age, this one," he says with a laugh. "Still as gorgeous as the day I met her."

Lizzy ignores him. "Did you register online?" she asks me instead.

"Oh, no, I uh … I didn't know I was supposed to …"

"The invitation we got in the mail didn't say anything about registering online," Jason adds, confusion in his voice.

"We didn't mail paper invitations," Beth remarks. "It was all done over email."

"Did you get an email too?" Jason asks me, his brows pulling together quizzically.

"No."

"It would have gone to whatever email address you gave to the Alumni Committee," Lizzy says. The look in her eye leads me to believe that she knows very well that I hadn't given them one.

"Oh I, uh …"

Jason offers her one of his patented, charming smiles, the one that shows off the dimple in his left cheek. I silently pray his charms will work on Lizzy. "Sorry for the mix-up," Jason says, his voice as smooth as velvet. "Is there any way we can register now? We're already here, after all." That amiable smile again, a flash of the dimple.

Lizzy sighs. "Fine. Just fill out this form." She thrusts a sheet of paper in my direction.

"Do you … have a pen?" I ask feebly. "I left my bag in the car."

Lizzy sighs again and hands me a blue pen with the Westbridge crest printed on the side.

"Thanks." I lean over the table and begin to fill in my contact information. Name, current address, phone number …

"I have to say, Jules, I'm surprised you came," Beth says. I don't meet her eyes as I continue writing.

"Yup, it's been a long time," I reply lightly. I clench my teeth as I finish filling in the form as quickly as I can, hoping that we can get out of here before Beth or Lizzy say something that I'll have to explain to Jason later.

"I had to talk her into coming," Jason says warmly, placing his hand on the small of my back. "She never wants to tear herself away from work these days."

"Funny," Lizzy says, holding her chin in her hand as she leans on the table in front of her. "The Jules *I* remember never needed to be talked into a party."

"Here," I say, my lips pressed into a firm line. "The form's done." I shove it in Lizzy's direction and hook my arm through Jason's ready to pull him out of the danger zone.

"Lovely to have met you, ladies," Jason says with an endearing wink.

Lizzy hands him an itinerary of the weekend's events as I lead him away.

"See you at the welcoming dinner," Beth calls after us. "It's a masquerade. In case your *mysterious invitation* hadn't mentioned."

"Well, *they* were delightful," Jason whispers with a laugh as we mercifully approach the exit.

I laugh along with him, but inside my heart is racing. "Welcome to Westbridge."

"It's funny though," he says, playfully bumping his shoulder against mine. "They made you sound like some sort of party girl. I can't picture it."

"I'm glad," I say. "Stop trying." Jason laughs again.

"It's kind of hot," he says, his voice a deep purr.

It feels good, this fleeting second of normalcy between us. Even though I know it can't last.

Jason and I climb back into the rental car and click our seat belts into place, and I pull out my phone to look up the address for the hotel I've booked for us.

When I look up from the screen, I have to stifle a gasp.

"What is it?" Jason asks, his eyes snapping toward me. "You look like you've just seen a ghost."

"No, not a ghost …" I watch as Emily walks past our car. Even with the dark, round sunglasses pulled over her eyes, it is unmistakably her, striding across the campus, the kingdom she once ruled with an iron fist, now with her handsome husband on her arm. "Just someone I used to know."

If Emily is back at Westbridge, it can only mean one of two things: she was forced to return … or she's the one who lured us here.

Chapter 36

Then

Nessa arrived at our room with a duffel bag slung over her shoulder and her laptop tucked under her arm. "Can I spend the night with you guys?"

"Missing our slumber party days?" Tori asked.

Nessa giggled. "Yes, but that's not why I'm here. My delightful roommate jammed the lock on our door." She rolled her eyes. "Emily's key broke in the lock and now the door keeps getting stuck. I called maintenance, but the guy who showed up said they had to order some new part or something and he can't fix it until tomorrow. He told us we should stay elsewhere tonight so we don't get, like, locked in, or something." She shuddered. "Imagine being locked in a room with Emily? I'm not sure we'd both make it out alive. So it looks like I'm homeless for the night unless you're willing to take in a stray?" She looked at us with her best puppy dog eyes.

"Of course you can stay here," Tori said. "It'll be just like old times."

Nessa dropped her bag to the floor and plunked her laptop down on Tori's desk. "Thanks, roomies!"

"Where is *Emily* staying?" I asked Nessa, spitting the name out with a grimace.

"Who knows," she answered vaguely. "Maybe with Hadley."

"She'll probably end up with Alex," I grumbled.

"I *did* hear her on the phone with him earlier …" Nessa confessed.

I flopped back on my bed. "I still can't believe they're together. It's *so* obvious that she's just doing this out of spite. It's not like she even *liked* him. It's just so unfair. Emily gets to do whatever she wants and there are never any consequences."

Tori perched on the edge of her bed, a scandalous grin spreading across her face. "There *can* be …"

The truth was that I'd spent an inordinate amount of time fantasizing about how I could make Emily pay for everything she'd taken from me. I wanted her to feel the same betrayal that I did, but I didn't know how to do it. As far as I could tell, Emily was invincible.

"How? I can't think of a single thing I could do that would faze her."

Tori and Nessa exchanged a knowing look. "If there's anything I know about Emily," Nessa began, "it's that she hates rejection. It's like she'd die if she didn't feel as if the whole world was revolving around her for one damn second. One time, at Brighton, a guy she liked was twenty minutes late picking her up for a date and she had a *total* meltdown. I guess she thought he was going to stand her up? She was so mad that she wouldn't even go out with him after that. And then the next day at school she started a rumor that he had herpes, and for the rest of our junior year none of the girls would go anywhere near him."

An idea was starting to form in my mind, slowly taking shape like clay in a sculptor's hands. "Tori, I need you to do me a favor …"

* * *

Tori hadn't wanted to do it. I noticed her hesitation about getting Nate involved, but I pretended I hadn't. It was the perfect plan. I just needed all the pieces to fall into place if it was going to work.

"Nate was pretty pissed," she said as she returned to our room, where Nessa and I eagerly awaited the news. "He said he felt like a rat giving us intel behind Alex's back."

"Did he tell you anything though?" I asked, trying not to sound impatient.

"He did." Tori sighed as she sat down on her bed. "Sort of. The most he would tell me was that Alex is going out tonight with 'some girl he's seeing'." She put the last bit in air quotes for effect with a roll of her eyes. "And then he kindly suggested we find a new hobby."

"*Some girl he's seeing?* Alex and Emily really don't think we know about their little love affair yet?"

"Seems that way," Tori replied with a shrug.

Nate hadn't given us much but it was enough. *So Emily thinks Alex is taking her out tonight? We'll see about that …*

Chapter 37

Now

I catch my reflection in the polished glass window of the Great Hall where the welcoming dinner is to be hosted. My floor-length black dress, in a tapered silhouette, drapes flatteringly over my body, and the black and silver Venetian mask affixed over my eyes catches flecks of the chilled moonlight.

Jason stands next to me, his reflection materializing beside my own.

"You look stunning," he says, his eyes sparkling.

"You don't look half bad yourself," I reply with a wink. Jason went with a black tux, which highlights his broad shoulders and the clean cut of his jawline. A simple, black satin mask over his soft hazel eyes completes the look.

"I feel like James Bond," he says with a laugh.

"The masks are a bit much."

"Hey, you two!" a voice calls from behind us. *Tori.* I hesitate for an awkward moment as she approaches. Unsure how to bridge the gap, savoring the last fleeting moments before Jason is thrown into this world.

"I'm Tori," she says, taking over. She shakes Jason's hand, and introduces Matt. The men greet each other warmly, with firm handshakes and broad smiles.

I turn to see that Nessa is following closely behind. She and Tori are each in black dresses, not too dissimilar to my own, although Tori has chosen a silver mask with a metallic sheen, and Nessa's is a delicately woven black lace, the silky strands gossamer thin, laid over the bridge of her nose.

"Jason, this is Nessa," I say as she joins our group, finally finding my voice.

"Pleasure to meet you," he says, his eyes lingering on hers just a beat too long as she delicately places her hand in his. Or maybe it's all in my head. Nessa is as stunning as I've ever seen her tonight, and I can't help but feel like I pale in comparison. Being back here, at Westbridge with these women, has me feeling wrong-footed. The insecurities of my youth rising to the surface. Probably because this is where they were cultivated in the first place—the seeds tenderly planted and watered in the private garden of Emily's kingdom.

"Shall we?" Tori says, looping her arms through mine and Nessa's.

"After you, ladies," Jason replies with a deferential bow and a sweep of his arm.

I can feel the tension in Nessa's arm as though it's radiating off her as we walk into the hall. Tori, on the other hand, walks confidently into the lion's den.

I'm taken aback when we step into the reception. I don't know what I'd been expecting, but it certainly wasn't this. The cavernous hall, which always felt stuffy and dated to me with its dark wooden rafters and stone floors, has been transformed into a Renaissance garden. Tea lights flicker from just about every surface in the dimly lit space, giving the room a soft, warm feel. Wisteria vines hang from the vaulted ceilings in romantic, sweeping boughs dotted with thousands of fairy lights that resemble a sky full of twinkling stars. An arched trellis, covered with sprays of pink roses, greets us at the entrance, and tables have been set up throughout the length of the room, adorned in crushed velvet tablecloths in a deep midnight blue. At the center of each table, stands a gold lantern. Flickering candles enclosed inside cast the tables in pools of warm light and reflect off the grand, arched windows that line the walls of the Great Hall. As much as I don't want to be here, I have to admit that the space is enchanting.

"Damn, you ivy leaguers really know how to host a soirée," Matt says as we all huddle at the entrance to the room, taking in the scene. I look over at Jason. The twinkling fairy lights are reflected in his eyes, making them dance.

"You're at table six," a familiar voice says in a clipped tone. I turn to see Lizzy standing behind us in a dark blue dress and a gold mask (a perfect match to the decor).

"Thanks, Lizzy," Nessa says.

Lizzy's eyes harden. "It's Elizabeth now," she admonishes before she turns on her heels and walks away.

"Still just as pleasant as she was at check-in," Tori says with a roll of her eyes.

"I think I see table six in the back," Jason says, nodding toward the far end of the room. He places his hand gently on the small of my back and escorts me in the direction of our table. Nessa, Tori, and Matt follow closely behind us.

It's not until we near the table that we see who is already seated there.

"Hello again," Emily says, a wicked smile inching across her face. "Long time no see." She's wearing a deep crimson dress that hugs her toned, sculpted body-by-yoga, and a black satin mask with an extravagant plume of feathers that curve around one side of her face.

I freeze in place. For one painful, awkward moment Nessa, Tori, and I fall silent. *Does this mean that Emily was the one who summoned us here?* Jason breaks the spell and extends his hand to introduce himself.

"Hi, I'm Jason," he says, placing his hand in Emily's. I'm immediately hit with the compulsion to tear their hands apart, to grab him and run from the room. But this is my only chance to find out who has been blackmailing me. I have no choice but to see it through.

"Emily," she purrs. "And this is my husband." She places her hand on her husband's thigh, and nuzzles gently against his shoulder as if she's a cat making its territory known.

There he is: the perfectly styled hair, the chiseled jaw, the movie-star smile, the same face I've seen splashed all over Emily's social media profiles. *Hashtag blessed.*

"Brett," he says, his voice deep and sure.

"Nice to meet you, man," Jason replies, giving his hand a firm pump before sitting down next to him.

"And I'm sure you all remember Hadley," Emily says, placing her hand lightly on the shoulder of the willowy brunette sitting to her right. Hadley smiles coolly beneath her jeweled, burgundy mask, a glass of red wine resting between her fingers. "Hello," she says, bitterness leaping off her tongue.

"And this is her husband, Blake," Emily adds, gesturing to the blond-haired, wiry man to Hadley's right with the pinched face and the rodent-like eyes, small and beady. Blake's reception is just as cold as Hadley's was—he hardly looks up from his drink to greet us.

Tori, Nessa, Matt, Jason and I say our hellos and arrange ourselves around the table. The men are already ordering glasses of whiskey, loosening their ties. But it's as though the women are at an entirely different party. One that could determine the course of our futures.

* * *

Jason twirls me in his arms. The faux stars above swirl into a blur.

I steady my hands on his shoulders, my body moving with his,

257

while I steal glances around the room, looking for familiar faces behind the sea of masks. *Could "Jenny" be among them?*

I've seen a few other people I recognized so far, nameless faces that I could still picture as younger versions of themselves. People I shared a residence hall with, classes with, who have faded into the distant recesses of my memories. I'm fairly certain that they've recognized me as well. I can feel the whispers flitting around the room like a hummingbird, landing here and there to gain momentum.

"Why are they here?"

"I'd never show my face on campus again if I was them."

"Everyone knows they had something to do with what happened."

"You all right?" Jason asks, his fingers gently tucking a stray lock of hair behind my ear. I hadn't realized I'd stopped dancing.

"Yeah, I'm fine. I think I just need some water." I lead him away from the dance floor, from the rumors I don't want him to hear.

We walk back to our table, arm in arm. Matt has pulled up a chair next to Brett and they seem to be deep in conversation, their heads angled together, as we approach. Blake watches on with thinly veiled contempt for the interloper.

Emily and Hadley have taken up a similar position, whispering among themselves, as far as they could possibly sit from Tori and Nessa, who are at the other end of the table starting on yet another round of drinks.

"Ah, there you are, man!" Matt says as he sees Jason resume his seat. It seems they've already become fast friends, in that easy, uncomplicated way that men can.

I reach for my glass of water, savoring the coldness on my tongue.

"Brett was just showing me his secret stash," Matt continues.

Brett holds up a slim silver box, and flips it open to reveal a row of papery cigars, wrapped with gold and red foil bands. "Care to partake?" he asks.

"Absolutely," Jason replies almost instantaneously. I'm a bit surprised at his enthusiasm as I've never seen him smoke a cigar before, but I suppose sometimes a cigar is not just a cigar. He'll have been happy to be included in this male bonding ritual. It would seem that Brett has the same natural magnetism as his wife.

"Excellent." Brett stands from the table and brushes off his crisp, pressed pants. Jason, Matt, and Blake rise in unison after him as though paying their respects to royalty. I suppose I can see the allure. Brett's tux, though similar in style to Matt and Jason's, is a world apart. The expensive fabric, the satin lapels, have been cut to precision to compliment his physique. The other men suddenly looked like little boys playing dress-up beside him.

Brett leads the way to the back patio, where heat lamps casting patches of orange light have been set up under a wooden pergola. I watch through the plate-glass window as they go about the ritual of cutting the tips off their cigars and lighting the raw ends, the embers glowing red against the velvety darkness of the night.

I suddenly feel exposed without Jason. I'd been hiding behind him like a shield all night, using him as a distraction to shut out the sensation that Jenny is here somewhere, circling like a shark in murky waters.

I look around the table, at the women who were once my closest friends, and wonder if any of them could be the person destroying my life.

"Any sign of *Jenny*?" Tori asks, a bit too loudly, the ends of her words clumsy and slurred as she pulls another sip of her drink through her straw.

I risk a quick glance at Emily as I sit down next to Tori and Nessa. She looks amused, one eyebrow raised.

"Nothing yet," I reply, keeping my voice low.

"I guess I'd expected that *she'd* find *us*," Nessa replies.

"Maybe she already has," Tori says. "But if we're going to start looking, we should probably start with *her*." She tosses a nod in Emily's direction.

"Start *what* with me, exactly?" Emily says, her bare arms folded neatly in front of her on the table, a smirk playing at her lips.

"Why are you here?" Tori asks, hostility rising in her voice.

"Because it's homecoming, obviously," Emily replies. "Fairly certain that's why *all* of us are here." Hadley giggles dutifully, her slender fingers rising to her lips, her enormous engagement ring twinkling in the candlelight.

"Right, because this is the year you just *happened* to discover your school spirit. Go, Hawks!" Tori raises her glass in a mock toast before downing a gulp of the clear liquid inside, ice cubes clumsily clinking in her glass.

"I'm afraid I don't know what you're implying," Emily says, the picture of innocence wronged. "Perhaps you've just had a bit too much to drink. You're sounding a little ..."

"Nuts," Hadley finishes.

Tori's eyes harden and Emily smiles deviously. They stare each other down over the length of the table.

Nessa gently places her hand on Tori's shoulder. "She's not going to tell us anything," she says, her voice just above a whisper. "It's not worth engaging."

"You're right," Tori concedes, turning away from Emily. "It's just ... God ... she really knows how to get under my skin. I'm seriously convinced that this is all her doing, you guys. I can't think of anyone else who could possibly be this vindictive." She slumps back in her chair and runs her hand through her hair. "I just keep thinking that this could be it. This could be my last night with Matt. If Impostor Jenny tells him what she knows ... it's over. I just know it."

She seems so genuinely distraught. Could it really all be an act?

"I know how you feel," I respond. "If the truth about that night comes out, I'm afraid I could lose Jason too." *Translation: I want you to know that if you sold me out to save your marriage, you've risked mine in the process.*

"It's all so messed up," Tori says.

"It is," Nessa agrees. "And is it just me or is everyone talking about us?"

Nessa looks over toward Lizzy's table and my eyes follow her line of sight, just in time to see Lizzy snap her head away, pretending she hadn't been staring in our direction. "They definitely are," I agree.

"Lizzy … er … Elizabeth has been acting like we're evil incarnate since the second we arrived," Tori grumbles. "Her other little friend too. What was her name?"

"Beth," I reply.

"I don't know that they're capable of something like this though. They were never exactly the … confrontational types."

"Who knows," Nessa says. "We haven't seen any of these people in over a decade. They could be totally different now."

She has a point. We don't know any of these people anymore. *Maybe we never did*. We thought we had them all figured out. Nerd, jocks, band geek, popular girls—we thought we had them all pegged, all tidied into neat little boxes that they could never escape from. But what did we ever really know about any of our classmates? It's not like we ever tried to get to know them.

"Have you seen anyone else you recognize?" Nessa asks.

"No one I remember too well," I reply. "But there are so many people here, and these ridiculous masks don't help."

It dawns on me then. The one person who is conspicuously absent in all of this. The one person who was the closest to Jenny. Not that I could picture her at an event like this, but now that the thought is in my head, I can't shake it. "What about Abby?" I ask, my voice a strained whisper. "I don't know why I didn't think of it sooner. She could be the one—"

"No, Jules, she couldn't," Nessa says gently with a slow shake of her head.

"She could! She's the only one not here and—"

"That's because she's dead, Jules," Tori interjects.

I feel myself deflating. For a moment there I thought I had

261

the answer. Abby seemed like the perfect solution. And then the weight of Tori's words fully register in my mind.

"Wait, she's ... dead?" I ask incredulously. "How? When?"

"Don't you get the alumni newsletter?" Nessa asks. I shake my head. "They wrote a memorial piece for her a few months back. They didn't go into detail, but I got the impression that she took her own life."

"Oh my God ..."

"I know," Tori remarks. "But I heard that she was never quite right after what happened to Jenny."

I'm hit with a pang of guilt. Is what happened to Abby on our hands now too?

"So, like I said," Nessa adds, interrupting my thoughts, "Abby can't be behind this."

I look around the crowded room. At the nameless, faceless people milling around us and I suddenly have the feeling that I'm being watched. Observed like a fish in a tank. Evil eyes behind a mask watching my every move. Jenny could be any of these people.

"I know you guys think I'm crazy ..." Nessa starts, "but I just keep looking for Jenny ... Like, the real Jenny."

Her words make me shudder. I pick up my water glass, suddenly desperate for a cold drink, but it's empty. "I'm going to get some more water," I say, pushing away from the table. "And I'm getting you some too," I add, directing my attention to Tori. She huffs but doesn't object.

I pick my way across the dance floor in the center of the room. Elegantly dressed couples sway gracefully to the soft music that floats through the room. I'm so busy watching the crowd, my paranoid mind now searching for the familiar veil of black hair, that I run directly into the hard, muscular chest of Nate Porter.

"I'm sorry," he says. "I wasn't looking where I was going, and—" He looks down, realization dawning, his eyes narrowing. "Oh. It's you."

"Nate ... I ... I wasn't expecting to see you here." After what

Tori had told us, it didn't seem that Nate would have any interest in revisiting his days at Westbridge.

"I come back for homecoming every year," he sneers, crossing his arms over his chest. "It's *me* that wasn't expecting *you*."

Or was he? "Nate, listen, I know Tori told you some of what's been going on, and maybe we should talk—"

"No." His voice is firm, final. "Listen to me carefully, Jules. I never told anyone about … what I know, but I paid a price for that. I always knew there was more to what happened that night than Tori would admit, and now I'm even more certain of it. Why don't you all just stay the hell away from me before I decide to start asking all those questions she never wanted me to ask." Nate pushes past me, his shoulder bumping mine, making me stumble in my heels.

"You all right?" Jason catches my upper arm, righting me on my feet.

How much did he hear? "Yeah, I'm fine," I reply, trying not to sound as flustered as I feel.

"Who was that guy?" He shoots an angry look at Nate's receding figure as he blends into the crowd.

"Some guy Tori used to date back in the day. I think he's had too much to drink." I roll my eyes.

Jason nods, his shoulders softening, but his eyes linger on Nate's back as I lead him off the dance floor.

We make our way to the bar, where he orders himself another whiskey and two glasses of water for Tori and me. He shoves a twenty-dollar bill in the tip jar. Jason has always been a good tipper. It was one of the things I loved about him when we started dating. He may not have been rich, but he was generous with what he did have, which made it all the more meaningful. "A product of my teenage years spent slinging pizza and beer," he once told me. But I've noticed over the years that he becomes more generous the more he drinks. A twenty-dollar tip for one drink at an open bar probably means he's reaching his limit. Or maybe he's just spent too much time with the crowd here tonight, the ones who can throw money around like confetti. Maybe he's forgotten we aren't like them. I know how easy it is to get swept away in it all, but this tide is a dangerous one—one that can quickly pull you under like a rip current.

* * *

"Are you ladies about ready to call it a night?" Matt asks, yawning. "I'm beat."

"Yes," Tori replies quickly. "Let's get out of here."

"Shall I go find us cab?" Jason asks. I nod.

"I'll go out to the valet with you," Brett chimes in. "I wanted to show you guys the new wheels anyway."

"Awesome," Matt replies, excitement in his eyes. "Brett just got the new Porsche," he explains animatedly.

Jason looks at me expectantly, like a child who wants permission to go to a sleepover. I roll my eyes. "Go see the cool car. We'll get our coats and meet you outside."

"You're the best, babe," he says, planting a kiss on my temple.

It occurs to me that Brett shouldn't be driving after all the whiskey he's had tonight, but people like Brett, people like Emily, they don't play by the same rules as the rest of us. So sure are they that the consequences of their actions could never reach them atop the lofty height of the pedestals they hold themselves upon.

The men gather their things and make for the exit, Emily and Hadley in tow.

"Convenient that we haven't been able to get Emily alone all night," Tori grumbles.

Nessa nods. "I'm sure that was intentional."

We collect our purses and rise from the table, just as a server approaches. A young man, probably a student from the local community college earning minimum wage to pour coffee to the wealthy Westbridge alums.

"Are you Juliana Daniels?" he asks.

"Yes, that's me …"

"And Tori and Vanessa?" he adds, looking at the wide-eyed women in question.

They nod.

"Um, I think these are for you guys then." He hands us each an envelope, sealed with a drip of red wax that had been pressed with a circular stamp, featuring an intricately carved "J".

"They were delivered to the hostess station," he adds before walking away.

Each cream-colored envelope is printed with our names in a familiar looping calligraphy, a perfect match to the invitations we'd received earlier in the week.

Juliana Daniels
Tori Sullivan
Vanessa Holland

My hand shakes as I slip my finger under the flap of the envelope bearing my name, cracking the red wax seal.

Meet in the basement of Nickerson Hall
Tomorrow. 4:00 pm.

We stand there a moment. All of us speechless.

"I guess this is where it ends," Tori says somberly. "One way or another."

I shove the envelope into my purse, and we collect our coats from the coat room as if in a trance.

When we make it outside, I'm hit with a rush of cold air that sends a chill straight through to my bones. I wrap my coat tighter around myself as I look for Jason. It's a clear night, the black sky above speckled with stars like silver paint flicked from an artist's brush. I'd almost forgotten what the night sky looks like outside of the city, where the indomitable lights make it impossible to see the celestial display above.

I spot Brett's new car pulled over to the side of the valet station in the center of the circular drive in front of the Great Hall. It's impossible to miss. Glossy black paint, headlights glowing, grown men gathered around, slack-jawed with awe as though they were viewing a priceless work of art. But I don't see Jason among them. I squint my eyes to get a closer look in the dim light. There are plenty of men in tuxedos, but I don't recognize the familiar slope of his shoulders, the unmistakable shape of my husband.

Where the hell could he be? I cast my eyes along the expanse of the drive, the black asphalt graying with a layer of frost. *There he is.* Standing in the shadows, set back from the spectacle that is Brett's new Porsche, and draped on his arm is none other than Emily. Her head is thrown back in laughter at something Jason must have said, her breath escaping in a smoky veil against the dark, velvety sky. I watch as she leans into him, as though she's about to whisper something in his ear.

Get away from him. It's the only thought running through my head on a loop as I stalk in their direction. I feel it happening again, the red mist descending. The rage, the jealously, the hatred taking over. *Get away from him.*

"Daniels!" the valet manning the cab stand calls out. "Your taxi is ready."

"That's me!" Jason replies as he drops Emily's arm unceremoniously and jaunts over to the cab station. His hand reaches into his pocket, probably looking for his phone to call me. But there's something I need to do first.

I march over to Emily, fury burning in my eyes, hands clenched at my sides. "What the fuck do you think you're doing?" I growl.

"Me? Oh, just chatting with your charming husband. He's quite funny, once you get to know him."

"You don't know the first thing about him." I feel my nails digging crescents into my palms.

"I wonder though, Jules, does he know the first thing about *you*?" A sinister smile spreads across her face as she crosses her arms over her chest defiantly.

"Stay the hell away from my husband," I spit through gritted teeth.

"Why, hon? Are you afraid I'll tell him what you did, who you *really* are? Or are you just worried that he'll want me more than you? That your sweet husband will realize that you're nothing but a sad imitation of me? Just like Alex did."

"I'm nothing like you," I say stepping toward her until we're toe-to-toe, acerbity leaping off my tongue.

Emily's eyes widen, just a fraction, but she recovers quickly, the fear gone and replaced with something else: hatred. "I think we both know that's a lie."

Chapter 38

Then

"Do you really think this is going to work?" Nessa asked.

"Of course it will," I replied confidently. "No one ever says no to Emily."

"Hurry up," Tori hissed, her eyes trained on the girls' bathroom across the hall. "She could be back any second. I don't hear the shower running anymore."

Nessa fumbled with Emily's phone, tapping out the message we'd rehearsed so many times.

Meet me at my room tonight, 7pm ;)

"She's coming," Tori warned, her head poking into Nessa's room. "Send it now, and then delete the message from her phone."

"What if Alex texts her back?" Nessa asked nervously.

"We don't have time to figure that out now. Just do it."

"Done," Nessa said, dropping the phone onto Emily's desk with a clatter.

Just at that moment, Emily pushed past Tori, her nose held high, and waltzed into the room. "What are you losers doing here?" Her hair was damp from the shower, a pink caddy holding her hair products dangling from her arm. "I thought you already left for the night, Vanessa."

"Just forgot a few things," Nessa said. I could hear the nerves rattling in her voice. She never was a good liar.

"Whatever. If you could all get out of my way, I have places to go."

"Like where?" I asked.

Emily's lips curled into a vicious smile. "Wouldn't *you* like to know."

"Fine, we'll go," Nessa agreed. "But leave the door open when you leave. I haven't finished getting what I need before we lock up for the night."

"Whatever," Emily said again, sounding bored.

We turned toward the broken door, which had been propped open with a doorstop, but it seemed that Emily wasn't quite finished with me yet.

"By the way, Jules," she said, brushing her wet hair before the full-length mirror. "I heard some really messed-up shit happened with Jenny at the Valentine's thing she went to with you. Everyone's talking about it."

The blow landed hard. I hadn't seen Jenny since that night, but I felt terrible about what happened. I'd tried to go talk to her, but Abby stood in the doorway blocking my entrance. "Jenny never wants to see you again," she'd said, her arms folded over her chest, eyes hard and full of disgust, before she slammed the door in my face.

"You don't know what you're talking about," I barked at Emily.

She shrugged. "I'm just saying, nothing like that ever happened when *I* was in charge." The brush glided through her silky hair, and I had the sudden urge to grab it with both fists.

"Come on, Jules," Nessa said, pulling me by the elbow. "It's not worth it."

But tonight will *be worth it.* I was sure of it.

* * *

My heart was racing by the time seven o'clock came around. Tori and I stood watch in the hallway, waiting to see if Alex would appear.

"Maybe he's not coming," I said, biting the edge of my thumb.

"Will you chill?" Tori said. "It's, like, one minute past seven. Give the guy a second."

And, lo and behold, within moments, I saw Alex's familiar form sauntering down the hallway. I felt a twinge in my heart just seeing him again, a stabbing pain from an open wound.

Tori grabbed me by the wrist and pulled me into the girls' bathroom just across the hall from Nessa and Emily's room. With our backs pressed against the cool tiled wall, she lifted one finger to her lips. "Shhh."

We heard Alex rap on the door to Emily's room.

"Come in," Nessa said.

Tori and I crept out of the bathroom and took our positions outside of Emily's door, listening intently to what was going on inside.

"Oh, hey, Nessa," we heard Alex's deep voice say.

"Hey, yourself."

"Is Emily here? She asked me to meet her."

"No, just me," Nessa purred, her voice silky and seductive.

I peered around the door just in time to watch her step closer to a very confused Alex, and snake her slender arms around his waist.

She deftly plucked his cell phone from the back pocket of his jeans and made for the door.

All we have to do now is close that door and Alex will be locked inside, and Emily will think he stood her up. I felt giddy with anticipation as I envisioned how crushed she'd be when she realized Alex was never coming. *Serves her right.*

"Have a nice night," Nessa said as she jaunted out of the room and joined us in the hall.

Tori kicked the doorstop out of place, and I was about to slam the door on a bewildered Alex, his mouth forming a perfect "O" as his eyes met mine, but I was startled by another voice behind me.

"Alex? What are you doing here?" *Jenny*. She stood next to me, her head tilted to one side curiously. "Did you forget that my room is down the hall now?"

Alex ran his fingers through his thick brown hair. His eyes flitted between me and Jenny, assessing the landscape as though he was picking his way through a minefield. "Hey, Jen. I know we had plans tonight, but I got this random text from Emily asking me to meet her here for some reason."

"Wait ..." I said. Time felt as though it was slowing down around me as the pieces slotted into place. "*Jenny* is the girl you're seeing?" I was lightheaded with the realization, leaning on the edge of the door I had tightly grasped in my hand.

The boy Jenny liked ... all this time it was Alex?

"But I thought you and Emily ..." I started.

"Er, I think she's seeing some guy named Nick ... Nico ... something like that. She mentioned something about hanging out with him tonight?" Alex replied, his inflection rising at the end, making it sound like more of a question than a statement.

The club owner. That's who Emily has plans with tonight. Has it been Nico all along?

"But you and Jenny ..." My mind flashed back to the night of Nessa's play, how Jenny had told me she needed to talk to me, but I waved her off, not wanting to hear it. "How long?" I asked, anger bubbling in my throat. The tips of my fingers turned white under my grip.

"Oh, uh, it's new ..." Alex stammered, shifting his weight uncomfortably.

Jenny shouldered past me and laced her fingers through Alex's. "Not that it's any of *your* business, Jules," she said coldly. "It's not like we're *friends*. I think you've made *that* pretty clear."

I felt a blinding rage rising, the crushing weight of their betrayal, and without a second thought, I slammed the door shut.

"The two of you can go to hell!" I yelled through the locked door.

Chapter 39

Now

Jason flops back onto the fluffy white duvet atop our king-sized bed, his jacket falling open, his bow tie pulled free and hanging limply around his neck. His feet hang over the edge of the bed, his dress shoes still on, the untied laces dangling toward the floor.

I do a quick inventory of the room. It's nothing fancy, four white walls, a bed in the center of the room, a pair of tiny end tables. It smells faintly of bleach and carpet cleaner. I'd rented a room at the Starlight Hotel, which actually resembles more of a motel. It's only one level, the rooms arranged in a horseshoe shape, each with a door opening directly onto the parking lot. It's certainly not the Four Seasons—the real appeal of this place is the massive lake behind the hotel. It's supposed to be quite scenic during daylight hours. We caught a glimpse of it as we pulled in, its silvery surface as still as glass, the knotted pines surrounding it like bristles against the night sky.

"Care to join me?" Jason asks as he sits up, kicking off his shoes and yanking off his tie.

Part of me wants to tell him I'm too tired. After all, it's kind of hard to think about sex when I'm being stalked and blackmailed. But he's in such a good mood, tipsy with whiskey and on a high from the night. I don't want to take a step back with him, not when things are finally starting to feel normal between us again.

"Definitely," I say instead, pushing a smile onto my face. "I just forgot one of my bags in the car earlier, so I'm going to grab it first." It's another lie, but only a small one. I just need a moment alone to collect myself, to settle my mind before I can pretend that everything is okay.

"Just leave it," Jason implores, his voice a husky growl.

"I'll just be a minute. Why don't you slip into something more comfortable while I'm gone?" I throw him a playful wink.

Jason grins and tosses me the car keys from his jacket pocket. "Fine, but hurry back."

I drop the keys into my evening bag and step outside, back into the cold dark night. A gust of wind lashes against my bare arms and I fold them over my chest, hunching my shoulders and bowing my head as I dash across the parking lot toward our car.

I see something then. Out of the corner of my eye. A subtle movement along the tree line that surrounds the hotel. It could be a deer. I saw plenty of them during my time at Westbridge. They're quite used to being around humans and have grown pretty brazen. I ignore it as I click the door fob, unlocking the car doors.

I grab my gym bag from the trunk—I don't really need it, but I can't go back inside empty-handed—and then I settle into the passenger seat of the car to think. The world is suddenly quiet as I close myself inside. I hadn't remembered the sound of the forest, how it can come alive at night when the rest of the world falls silent: the lake lapping at the land's edge, bullfrogs croaking in the distance, crickets crying out from hidden crevices.

I reach into my evening bag and quickly peek inside. The strange note is still there. Exactly where I left it. I lean my head back against the seat with a sigh. I know I have to go back inside. To pretend, for the sake of my marriage, that my life as I know it may not be coming to an end tomorrow. I just hope I can pull it off.

I climb out of the car and turn on my heels, prepared to run back to the warmth and safety of our room, but then I see it again: a dark form moving among the trees.

I freeze. I can feel the tension vibrating through my body, as though every fiber of my being is coiled and ready to flee, yet my legs feel like they're locked in place. *Fight or flight.* I'm suddenly back in freshman psychology.

"Fight or flight," the professor said, his hands tucked into his pockets under his tweed blazer as he paced the floor of the lecture hall. "How many of you have heard of that term before?"

A gaggle of hands lazily rose into the air. "But I propose to you, that there is a third, equally likely, physiological reaction to danger: *freeze.* Fight and flight are *active* defense responses, where your body prepares to *do* something in the face of a perceived threat. The heart rate increases, pain perception drops, and even your senses of sight and hearing improve. But I, and many experts far smarter than me, would agree that another perfectly normal response to fear is to freeze. Your body feels stiff, your heart rate may slow, you may even hold your breath. We see this kind of response often in the animal kingdom. The startled deer, the rabbit hiding in the tall grass, knowing the fox will surely spot it if it tries to run toward the safety of its den. The way the human body will respond in the face of danger is a complex, and often unpredictable thing."

I remember thinking, "Who would just stand there as danger approaches?" Surely I'd run ... *wouldn't I?*

But I don't. Not now. Not when I'm truly faced with it.

I feel my vision growing sharper, my hearing amplified in the silence of the night. I hear footsteps approaching on the spongy land, downy with a bed of fallen pine needles.

A figure steps out of the woods, onto the pavement of the parking lot. Tall, male, I think. Broad shoulders, an imposing build. I will myself to run, to scream, but my voice is trapped inside of my stiffened body.

The figure stops, seems to consider me. *He knows I've seen him.* My legs suddenly jolt back to life as though they've just broken through a block of ice. I start to run, a messy trot in these godforsaken shoes, the heels clicking on the pavement.

I can hear his footsteps picking up pace behind me. I quickly glance over my shoulder as I run, certain that the man from the woods is right at my heels. But he isn't. He's stopped now, standing on the periphery of the parking lot in a pool of light cast by one of the hotel's streetlamps. Harsh shadows obscure his face. But there is something about him, something so familiar, that it makes me stop in my tracks. I turn to face him, squinting my eyes to get a better look.

The man takes another step toward me, bringing him fully into the light.

My breath escapes me in one long burst, a deflated sigh. "Nate? What the hell are you doing here?"

"I didn't mean to frighten you," he says, lifting his palms in a sign of surrender as he approaches me.

"Well, I hate to break it to you, but I'd be willing to bet that being stalked in a dark parking lot is pretty frightening for most people." I fold my arms over my chest defensively, but also to stop him from seeing how much they're shaking.

"I'm not stalking you," he says, sounding indignant.

"Then what exactly would you call this?"

"I don't know, okay?" He edges closer, and suddenly his presence feels suffocating, threatening. I take a small step back.

"All I know is that there's something you never told me," Nate continues. "Something about what really happened ... that night, and I think it's time—"

"Jules?" It's Jason's voice. I turn in time to see him step out of our room. He's jogging toward Nate and me now, in the shadows at the center of the dark parking lot. "Are you okay?"

I open my mouth to speak, but nothing comes out.

"She's fine," Nate says sternly.

"I didn't ask *you*," Jason growls in reply. He wraps his arms around me protectively. "Come on," he says, leading me away from Nate. "Let's get you inside." I cast one last look back over my shoulder. Nate is still standing there, unmoving. He watches us leave, never taking his hard, cold eyes off me.

* * *

"What the *hell* was that, Jules?" Jason says, his hands balled into fists at his sides as he paces the floor of our small, rented room.

"I already told you. Nate just showed up out of nowhere while I was getting my bag from the car."

"Convenient timing, don't you think?"

"Well, no, not really. It wasn't exactly *convenient* for me to be scared half to death."

Jason scoffs. "Maybe so, but I saw you talking to him earlier in the night too, and—"

"Like you were talking to Emily?" I interject.

"Emily? Brett's wife? What does she have to do with anything?"

"I want to know what you were talking about."

"You. If you must know. She was telling me how close you two were, how much fun you had in college. But that's not really the point here, Jules. You're deflecting and we both know it."

"What *is* the point then, Jason? I already told you that I have no idea why Nate showed up here tonight."

"It seems that you have no idea about a lot of things lately. First the glasses, and now this …"

"I already told you that I don't know where those glasses came from. I don't know what else you want me to tell you!"

"I want you to tell me the truth for once! I'm not stupid. I can tell something is going on. You've been on edge since the second we got here. And, frankly, for the last few weeks. I've tried to get you to talk, but you insist on shutting me out. I think I've been patient, Jules, I really do, but this time I need answers—I need you to tell me something, anything, that makes sense. Are you having an affair with Nate? Just tell me the truth."

"Of course not! I haven't seen Nate in nearly ten years!"

"And yet, you two were arguing about something earlier. And then he shows up at your hotel in the middle of the night. Coincidentally at the same moment that you decide to go get a bag from the car that we both know you didn't need."

I know how bad it all must look to him, but the truth would look even worse. "It's not what you think, I swear, Jason." I'm begging him, pleading with him to believe me now.

"I don't know what to think anymore!" Jason shouts. In all the years I've known him, I don't think he's ever raised his voice with me. Not like this. It makes me wince to know I've pushed him to this point.

Jason softens slightly. "Listen, I know something is going on here, and if you don't want to tell me what it is, then I can't make you. But this is supposed to be a marriage. A partnership. And it just doesn't feel that way lately. You're constantly closing me out, pushing me away. And to be perfectly honest with you, I'm afraid that someday you're going to push me too far and we'll never be able to come back from it."

"There's nothing—"

"Save it, Jules. Please, spare me another lie." He sits down next to me on the bed and takes my hands in his, one last desperate plea for our marriage. "You said you're not having an affair, and I want to believe you, I really do. But if it's not that, then there's something else going on, and I just want to be here for you. If only you'd let me in. I want to help. Whatever it is, we can get through it. We can handle anything together. But only if we're really in this together. Just let me help you."

I want to believe him. I want to fall into his arms and beg him to help me. But I'm afraid that if I do, if I show him who and what I am, we won't be able to get through it. He says we can handle anything, but he doesn't know what we're up against.

"Jason … I … I can't." I squeeze his hands; my eyes plead with his. "Just please trust me. Give me just *one* more day, twenty-four more hours, that's all I'm asking, and then things will be back to normal. I promise you."

Jason drops my hands. "I just wish *you* trusted *me*."

He turns away and lies down, his back to me, and pulls the duvet up over his shoulder. That's when the tears come. Silent streams sliding down my face.

Chapter 40

Then

I leaned against the window of the taxi, hoping the feel of the cool glass on my forehead would make the world stop spinning.

"Jenny," I lamented. "*Jenny*. I can't believe he chose *her*." *I thought I was better than her.* That was the dark and glittering truth of it. How could Alex have chosen Jenny? On some level, when I thought he was seeing Emily, I could understand it. I wasn't happy about it, but I knew why he'd chosen her. In any competition between the two of us, she'd be the clear winner. But Jenny? It didn't make sense to me. It wasn't how things were supposed to be.

"Maybe he's into that whole 'babe in the woods' thing," Tori said. "You know, that wide-eyed naive girl you see in, like, every Nineties rom-com movie, who's in serious need of a makeover."

Wasn't that me though? At least it was, once upon a time. I didn't know who I was anymore.

My mind couldn't hold the thought. Couldn't process what Tori was telling me. I knew drinking was a bad idea tonight. Tori and Nessa insisted that after a few drinks, some dancing, I'd feel better, things wouldn't seem so dire, but I only felt worse. The alcohol seemed to amplify my emotions, giving them a tar-like stickiness that I couldn't break free of. If anything, I was sinking deeper, lower, the darkness threatening to consume me.

"I probably shouldn't have locked them in that room," I said with a sigh. "I don't even know why I did it. I was just so *mad*."

"Whatever," Tori said. "They deserved it. Jenny looked so ... smug." She pulled a look of disgust. "And they're probably out by now anyway. I'm sure someone will have called maintenance to set Romeo and Juliet free."

"Did you see Alex's face as you closed the door though?" Nessa said with a giggle. "Priceless."

The taxi pulled onto the campus, and I could already tell that something was wrong. There was a stillness to it, a ghost-like vacancy. No students walking along the cobbled paths, no late-night pizza deliveries or idling cabs with their exhaust trailing into the frosty, black sky.

"Afraid this is as far as I can take you," the cabbie said as he approached an emergency barricade. He shrugged and turned to us to collect his fare. We fished handfuls of singles out of our purses and quickly handed them over before sliding out of the back seat.

"What's going on?" Nessa asked as we stepped around the barricade and walked, as quickly as we could, toward Nickerson Hall.

There was a crowd of students on the lawn in front of the building. All of them looking ghostly pale in the moonlight, some with quilts draped over their shoulders, others barefoot in the stiff, frozen grass, their breath escaping like puffy white clouds. Everyone was eerily quiet, staring at Nickerson Hall.

We pushed toward the front of the crowd. Police cruisers, ambulances, and fire trucks were parked haphazardly in front of the building, fallen leaves stuck to their slicked tires. Plumes of dark, black smoke rose from the windows of the fourth floor, as though the building was breathing it out, a dragon rising from an ancient grave.

"Oh, God," I wailed. "No, no, no. Please tell me they got out."

I took off running, darting through the throngs of students.

"Jenny!" I shouted. "Alex!" But I felt as though I was screaming into a dark abyss, already knowing that they'd never answer.

That's when I started to hear the whispers. They rose from the crowd as if spoken from a collective consciousness:

"Emily Wiltshire is dead. They found her body in her room."

"I heard it was Jenny Teller."

"Did you know she was dating Jules's ex?"

"Everyone knows that Jules hated Jenny anyway. Did you hear what she did to her at the Tau party last week?"

"Do you think Jules and her friends could have started the fire?"

Tori grabbed me from behind, wrapping both of her arms tightly around my chest. "Breathe, Jules. You need to breathe."

I sucked in big gulps of the cold night air. I felt wild, raw. My entire body quivered like an animal in a trap. "This can't be happening," I sobbed. "I never meant—"

"I know," Tori said. "But not here. Come."

Tori guided me through the crowd, her arm protectively slung over my shoulder. But it didn't stop the whispers:

"I bet they'll be arrested."

"And I thought Emily *was evil."*

"She is, but at least she's not a murderer."

Tori led me around the side of the building, into the woods, where Nessa was already waiting for us, tears streaming down her face. "What have we done?" she cried.

"We didn't do this," Tori said, a false confidence in her wavering voice. "We couldn't have known there would be a fire."

Nessa's lower lip quivered. "Then why do I feel like this is all our fault?"

I watched my friends helplessly, their faces illuminated with splashes of red and blue light, their eyes wide and glassy. Nessa was wrong, it wasn't *our* fault. It was mine. *I* locked Jenny and Alex in that room in a moment of selfish anger. And it may have got them killed.

"Oh God, I still have Alex's phone," Nessa sobbed. "He couldn't even call for help."

"We'll get rid of it," Tori said. "We have to."

"Everyone thinks we did it," Nessa cried into Tori's shoulder. "They think we started the fire."

"But we didn't. They're just rumors," Tori consoled her. "No one knows what really happened, what we … did. And Alex and Jenny might still be okay … we don't know for sure that they're … gone." Tori looked to me as if for reassurance, but I just stood there. Frozen. Unable to find the words she needed to hear.

A guttural wail cried out from the main lawn. In the distance I saw Abby, her hair a familiar tangle of curls, drop to her knees as a stretcher was carried out of Nickerson Hall. A white sheet over a slim figure. "Jenny," she cried. "Not Jenny."

I looked on in horror, in disbelief, at what I was witnessing. *Jenny can't really be dead. She just can't …* I felt my body go numb with shock as I waited to see if another stretcher would follow.

A figure emerged from among the trees then, a black shadowy form that moved on graceful, cat-like feet. It weaved between the trees, taking shape as it approached. A flash of golden hair that seemed to take on an ethereal glow beneath the moonlight. *Emily*.

Her pretty face was marred with soot and the smell of ash clung to her. "Is it true what they're saying?" she asked, her words flat and distant, as though she was in a trance. Her arms hung limply at her sides. "That you … killed them?"

I didn't answer. I couldn't.

"You really did this, didn't you?" she speculated, my silence only making her more certain. "You're a … a … murderer."

I stood there in silence, letting her words strike me like lashes from a whip. Even though Emily didn't know exactly what I'd done, she'd been right to blame me.

Something in me died that night alongside Jenny. All of my aspirations, my dreams for the future, visions of the girl I thought I was, of the woman I hoped to be, reduced to ash.

"No one can ever know," I said breathlessly.

Chapter 41

Now

I wake slowly, my eyes gritty and raw after a fitful night spent tossing and turning. Between the argument with Jason last night, and the knowledge that I'm about to come face to face with Jenny, I could hardly sleep. I was delirious with exhaustion, old ghosts haunting me in the night. Every sound from the forest outside was an otherworldly intruder, every spindly shadow on the wall a specter come to call.

I sit up, rubbing my eyes. Jason is perched on the edge of the bed tying his shoes. He's already dressed for the day in a pair of khakis and a pale blue polo shirt, tucked neatly into his pants.

"You're up early," I say, my voice wooly.

"Yeah," he mutters in reply. He doesn't even look in my direction.

"Any special reason?"

"I'm going to the golf outing today. It's on the itinerary."

"By yourself?"

"No," he replies. "With the guys."

"The guys?" I raise one eyebrow.

Jason sighs and turns to face me. "Yes. The guys. They're all going. Matt, Brett, Blake … I thought I'd join them. Brett said I can use his spare clubs."

"But … do you even know how to play golf?"

He huffs. "Don't worry. I won't embarrass you in front of your fancy friends."

"Jason, please. That's not what I meant." What I *really* meant was that I hated the idea of leaving Jason alone with the Westbridge wolves. I don't know who else might be at that outing, what they might tell him. But it's not like I have a choice. And at least he'll be distracted while I handle the Jenny issue.

"Look, Jules. You asked me for twenty-four hours and I'm giving it to you. I still wish you'd just *talk* to me, but I'm giving you the time and space you asked for. I'm doing my best to trust that you know what you're doing."

"Okay," I say, my voice soft and small. "Thank you for that."

He shakes his head in frustration and turns back to collecting his things.

"Where is this golf thing anyway?" I ask.

"There's a shuttle leaving from the student center in about a half-hour. I'll call a cab."

"No," I rush to add. I can't have him running around the campus alone. "I'll drive you."

Jason shrugs and I rush to get ready for the day: brushing my teeth, untangling the mess of my hair, and pulling on a pair of slim-fit jeans, an emerald green cable-knit sweater, and chocolate brown leather boots. Finally, I apply a touch of makeup to cover the dark circles under my eyes that look like pressed bruises, two purple crescent moons.

"Ready," I say.

The ride to campus is silent, Jason looking distractedly out the window while I drive. I turn on the car radio, but it's nothing but static. Service is notoriously unpredictable on the mountain roads.

I park outside the student center and Jason climbs out of the car before I've even cut the ignition. He walks a few paces ahead of me and I jog to catch up. "Come on, Jason, it doesn't have to be like this," I say.

"No, it didn't. But you chose this," he replies coolly. "You insist on leaving me in the dark, and then wonder why things have grown cold."

I feel my lower lip start to quiver, tears pricking at the backs of my eyes. *You can't cry. Not here. Don't give them something else to talk about.* But it takes a great effort for me to swallow back the emotions. I can't lose Jason. He's the single most important thing in my life. *This has to end today.* I discreetly pat away the moisture from my eyes with my sleeve.

When I look up, I find that Jason has busied himself looking at a blown-up print of the weekend's order of events, ending with the homecoming game tomorrow afternoon, which has been propped on an easel. And, to my horror, right next to him is another easel bearing a poster-sized image of Jenny and Alex.

Please join us for a candlelight vigil as we
remember our classmates,
Jennifer Teller and Alexander Caldwell.

Because, of course, even though Jenny is the one who has come back to haunt me, it was never only her death that I was responsible for that night.

Chapter 42

Now

I loop my arm through Jason's, hoping to pull him away before he sees the memorial poster, starts asking questions that I don't want to answer. But I'm too late.

"What happened to them?" he asks, nodding toward the over-sized photo of a smiling Jenny and Alex, the immortalized young lovers. In the wake of their tragic deaths, their relationship took on a romanticized lure on campus. It grew to epic proportions, becoming this golden and glittering thing that could never be tarnished. And Alex and Jenny became Westbridge's very own Romeo and Juliet.

Looking at their faces now, I'm taken back to that night. I can smell the ash, see the trails of smoke snaking their way through the trees, as if it was happening all over again right before my eyes. We stood there. All of us—Tori, Nessa, Emily, and I—holding our breaths waiting to see if Alex would be carried out of the building … dead or alive. I knew it was too late for Jenny. I knew I'd never forget the sight of the stretcher, the white sheet, the sound of Abby's wails. That would be burned into my memory for as long as I lived. But maybe there was still a chance that Alex would make it out alive. *Please let him live, please let him live.* The thought ran through my head on repeat, like a scratched vinyl record, the needle stuck in place, doomed to never move forward again. I prayed. For the first time in a very long time, I prayed.

I was raised Catholic, my parents taking to me church every Sunday, but as a child I was far more interested in the cake and juice served after the children's mass than I was in the actual sermons. And as I grew older, I stopped attending services with my parents altogether. I knew the church, the sense of community my parents found there, brought them some comfort, but it never held the same appeal for me. I understood why they were drawn to believe in a higher power, but I just wasn't sure that I did. I wasn't sure that things like God or miracles really existed. But that night, as we waited to see what Alex's fate would be, I prayed to a God I couldn't be sure was real. I bargained and I pleaded, and I waited.

When the firemen, laden with heavy black suits and soot-covered boots, finally emerged with a second stretcher, I was so overcome with relief to see them putting an oxygen mask over Alex's face that I fell to my knees in the wet earth. I cried out, an animalistic whimper, a sound that barely sounded human to my ears. It was a release of so many things: fear, remorse, sorrow, relief. He was alive. He had to have been if they were giving him oxygen, right? There was no white sheet, no hidden face. Not like with Jenny. There was nothing but darkness there, a loss of all hope, but Alex could still survive. Maybe all was not lost.

It felt like the entire campus sat vigil while Alex was taken to the hospital. It was eerily quiet at Westbridge, as though everyone was afraid to speak the wrong combination of words, the one that would take all hope away. But all of our silent prayers were for nothing. Alex passed away within hours. "Smoke inhalation," I heard was the official cause of death. Jenny's as well. It gave me some modicum of relief to know that they hadn't been burned alive, an unspeakable and gruesome death. But rather I liked to imagine that they'd fallen unconscious in the dark, black smoke, like drifting off to sleep, before leaving this world within hours of one another. *Romeo and Juliet.*

But I knew. Deep down I knew it was my fault that they were gone. And I knew I'd never be able to forgive myself for my role in it. I was a monster. *Maybe I still am …*

"Jules?" Jason's voice shocks me back to the present. "I was asking what happened to them?"

"She would know," a familiar voice mutters behind me.

I wheel around to find Lizzy glaring at me, her lips curled into a knowing sneer.

Chapter 43

Now

"Could that be her?" Nessa leans toward the windshield and points at a figure in the distance approaching Nickerson Hall.

"I don't think so," Tori replies, squinting. "Looks like a student."

From my position in the back seat I could hardly be of any help.

It was Tori's idea to arrive early and stake out Nickerson Hall. It was a good idea in theory; however, from our vantage point at the edge of the nearest parking lot we don't exactly have the best view. And we don't even know what we're looking for. We see Jenny in every person who walks by. But at least I feel like we're *doing* something. We're *trying* to stay one step ahead.

And besides, being here is better than pacing my hotel room alone as I'd done most of the day. I felt like a caged animal, my mind racing as the minutes slowly ticked by, every second bringing me closer to meeting my fate. I flipped through the few cable channels that the Starlight Hotel had to offer, but I couldn't focus on the mindless dramas on the screen. All I could think about was Jenny. And Jason.

After Lizzy's comment this morning, it was hard to get him to drop the subject.

"What was that supposed to mean? '*She would know*'?" he asked, a puzzled look on his face after Lizzy sauntered away, her hips dipping with satisfaction.

"I don't know. Probably because I knew her. Jenny, I mean. She was sort of … my friend, freshman year. Before she … died." I felt the words tumbling out, a tangle of lies and half-truths, as I fingered the sleeve of my sweater.

"What happened to them? You never answered me before."

"There was … there was a fire," I replied. I bowed my head, keeping my eyes on the ground. *Don't cry. Not now.*

"You had a friend who died in a fire?" Jason said incredulously. "And you never told me?"

"It's not exactly a topic I like to revisit." I traced tiny circles on the floor with the toe of my boot. Something to focus on other than the lies I was telling my husband.

"I guess I can understand that," Jason said, still sounding bewildered, "but I'd think that would be the kind of thing you might mention. How horrible that must have been for you." He placed his hand in mine, and I felt a bout of nausea rising. He was feeling *sorry* for me. Here we were finally reconnecting after our argument, and it was all based on lies.

My stomach rumbles, bringing me back to the present. I press my palm to my abdomen to settle the noise. I try to think of the last time I ate a real meal. I picked at the dinner last night—overcooked chicken and some soggy asparagus—and the only thing I've eaten today was a bag of chips from the Starlight's vending machine that I could hardly keep down. My stomach roils with nerves now and I worry that the chips are going to make a reappearance in Tori's back seat.

"It's just about four o'clock," Nessa says defeatedly, her voice small and quiet in the silence of the car. "I guess we'd better go in."

We walk up to Nickerson Hall like death row inmates awaiting execution. It looks quite different than when we lived here. Gone are the bricks and ivy. Instead, a modern metallic structure with harsh angles and glass walls has risen in the footprint of the old Nickerson. It stands out like a sore thumb on the rest of the campus, which is only slowly crawling toward the modern world.

A girl with a swinging ponytail and an overstuffed backpack approaches the front door and scans her keycard to unlock it. I break into a jog to catch up to her before the door closes and locks behind her.

My fingers wrap around the edge of the door just as it begins to close. The girl is caught by surprise, and she wheels around to look at me with sculpted eyebrows raised.

I offer her a pretty-girl smile. *I'm one of you*, it says. *You can trust me.* "Hey ... I know this is silly, but my friends and I are here for homecoming"— I nod toward Tori and Nessa —"and we used to live here back in the day. We were just hoping to revisit our old dorm while we're in town. Is that cool?"

The girl relaxes, her shoulders falling. *She knows us. She is us. Or so she thinks.* "Oh, sure, no problem. Enjoy homecoming!" she says before happily jaunting up the central staircase.

Tori, Nessa, and I file into Nickerson Hall. Even though the building is new—no trace of the old Nickerson left behind—there is something that still lingers here. A darkness in the atmosphere. As though the land remembers what happened all those years ago. The lives that were lost. And although it must surely be in my head, I think I can still smell a hint of ash, the smoldering scent of death. It's nothing more than a wisp in the air, as faint as the scent of lemongrass carried in on a summer breeze, but it's enough to instantly conjure memories of that horrible night. The sound of the sirens, the flash of the lights, the dark clouds of smoke billowing into the night air, so thick and so dark that they blocked out the starry night sky overhead. I shudder, my entire body shaking with a deathly chill. I heard somewhere that a sudden chill means a ghost has passed through you. Maybe one has. Or maybe it never left. I can feel Jenny in my bones as I stand here, in the place where she died.

"Let's go," Tori says, leading the way to a metal door at the far end of the lobby reading "Stairs to Basement. Staff Only".

We walk down the stairs slowly, our footfalls echoing in the cement stairwell.

At the end of the stairway is a rusted metal fire door that has been propped open. We pause at the bottom of the dimly lit staircase, the only sound the whisper of our nervous breaths.

I step into the basement first, feeling along the cold cinderblock wall for a light switch. I find one, a large industrial black switch, and with some effort, I lift it to turn on the hazy overhead lights.

"Have you ever been down here before?" Nessa asks the group. She speaks in a whisper although there's no one else here. It just seems fitting that we don't disturb the quiet of the dusty, open space.

I look around the underground room. The cement walls have been painted a dingy gray, although it's unclear if that was the chosen color or whether they've taken on some of the gloom of the space over the years. The ceiling is unfinished, a network of criss-crossing pipes and wires between tubes of dim fluorescent lighting. There's a utility sink in the far corner, its exposed plumbing coated with flaking rust, a few mop buckets, and stacks of sagging card-board boxes, their contents roughly labeled: *floor cleaner*, *bleach*, *toilet paper*, *paper towels*. There are two small, rectangular windows near the ceiling, mostly obscured by long tufts of grass.

"No, never," I reply. "It doesn't look as new as the rest of the building though."

"It's probably not," Tori says. "I bet this is the original base-ment. They just built the new Nickerson on top of it."

The lights overhead flicker and then buzz like a looming swarm of bees as Tori and Nessa follow me deeper into the room.

"Do you hear that?" Tori asks. She freezes in place, her eyes roving over the room.

"I think it's just the lights," I say.

293

"No, not that. Listen."

Nessa and I still. I feel like a prey animal, waiting to sense an approaching threat. *Fight, flight, freeze? Which will it be?*

"There! I heard it!" Nessa whispers, her voice strained and hoarse.

I heard it too. The sound of feet on the stairs. The footfall grows louder, closer. My hands shake and I press my sweating palms against my thighs, rubbing them against my jeans to steady them. This is it. This is where we find out who has been haunting us with the ghost of Jenny Teller.

I risk a quick look at Tori and Nessa. I wonder, briefly, whether one or both of them already know who is about to walk through that door. I wonder how much I can trust them. But right now they look just as nervous as I feel. Their eyes round with horror, Nessa bites at the edge of her thumb.

The footsteps draw closer and I hold my breath in my lungs as the toe of a shoe steps out of the dark stairwell. The world begins to swim as I take in the familiar face.

"Did you miss me?"

Chapter 44

Now

"Emily?!" Nessa says incredulously, her mouth agape.

"I *knew* you were behind this," Tori sneers. She clenches and unclenches her fists at her sides.

"You don't *know* anything," Emily says flippantly. "I'm only here because I got a note telling me I was supposed to meet someone here."

"And you came," I reply pointedly.

"Obviously," she retorts with a scoff and a roll of her eyes. "Since, here I am."

"How did she get you here?" I prod. "What does she have over you?"

"If I wanted that to get out, I sure as hell wouldn't be here now, would I? And I'm certainly not about to tell *you* anything." Emily glares at me, her stare glacially cold as she folds her arms over her chest.

"*Only the truth will set you free.*" The words seem to rise out of nowhere, a disembodied voice floating through the room, followed by the sound of the heavy metal door to the basement slamming shut and a lock turning over and sliding into place.

Chapter 45

Now

Tori runs for the door, first yanking on the handle, the sole of her boot pressed against the doorjamb for leverage. It doesn't budge, and before long she begins to pound savagely on the door with both fists. The metallic thud of her hands colliding with the door reverberates through the room.

"What the fuck do you want?" she screams, but no reply comes from the mysterious voice.

Emily and Nessa seem to have frozen in place, huddled in the center of the room, wide-eyed and terrified.

"We're trapped," Nessa cries, her voice a desperate whimper.

"Someone will come for us," Emily says. Her tone has taken on an air of confidence, one that is not entirely convincing.

"Does anyone know you're here?" Nessa asks hopefully.

Emily shakes her head. "No, but someone will figure out we're missing and come look for us … won't they?"

"Well, I'm not just going to sit here and wait to find out," I remark. I fish my phone out of my pocket and hold it out in front of me, arms outstretched, praying for service. But there is none. Not a single bar. "Do any of you have service?"

Emily, Nessa, and Tori check their phones. "Nothing," Nessa says.

"Of course not," Emily retorts. "We're underground."

Tori shakes her head in frustration, and resumes pummeling the door.

"Just perfect," I mutter. I begin pushing the boxes of cleaning supplies toward the far wall next to the sink. They're heavy and it takes a great deal of effort to drag the first one across the cement floor. I turn, sweat breaking on my brow, and look back at the others. "A little help, please?"

They turn and look at me, as though they hadn't noticed my efforts. "What are you doing?" Nessa asks.

"Trying to reach the window. We might not be able to fit through it, but maybe I'll at least get some cell service if I get close enough. I'll call Jason and tell him where we are."

Tori finally stops beating against the door, the sides of her fists red and raw, and she marches toward me and begins pushing the next box. Nessa and Emily silently follow suit.

We work together to build something of a makeshift staircase from the old, drooping boxes.

"This is all your fucking fault," Tori growls at Emily as she pushes a box, which is digging into her shoulder, above her head.

"*My* fault?" Emily retorts, bending over to catch her breath, resting her palms on her thighs. "*I'm* not the one who killed Jenny Teller. From what I heard, you three had something to do with that."

"It wasn't our fault," Nessa snaps back. "We didn't know the building was going to go up in flames!"

"If you say so," Emily quips. "Plenty of people think one of you set that fire."

"Well they're wrong," Tori snaps.

I begin to climb the wobbling pile of boxes. "That's not helping." I stand on the first box. Still no service, so I climb higher still.

"Be careful," Nessa cautions. The boxes sway beneath my feet. The old, soft cardboard threatening to give way under my weight.

"I just … have to … get … a little … higher …" I muster as I rise onto my toes, holding my phone high above my head like a torch. I'm almost to the window now, and my heart flutters in my chest. *Please find service.* "The call still isn't connecting." I sigh. "I'm going to try a text, maybe it'll get through."

I tap out a text to Jason: *Stuck in basement of Nickerson Hall. Need help.* I hit send, but it doesn't go through. "Shit," I grumble. "I have to get higher." I press my body against the cold, cement wall, stretching my arm as high as I can. *Maybe if I can get my phone onto the window ledge, it will—*

I feel the box under my feet cave in and I begin to fall. I scramble to keep my balance, but it's no use. The boxes begin to tumble like dominoes, and I fall to the ground, striking my wrist on the edge of the old metal sink on my way down. Luckily, a box of paper towels breaks my fall as I land, splayed out on my back, or I may have injured a lot more than my wrist.

I moan, holding my injured arm to my chest as I sit up.

"Oh my God! Are you okay, Jules?" Nessa rushes to my side, helping me up.

"Yeah," I say, looking back up at the window ledge. "It's just my arm." It's already swollen, my fingers tingling. I'm pretty sure it's broken. "I lost my phone though. And my message never went through."

"It's here," Emily says, digging out my phone from among the fallen supplies. "The screen is shattered. It's not turning on."

"Fuck. That was our best shot," Tori says. She looks toward the door. "What do you want?!" she yells again at the top of her lungs.

This time the voice answers. "I want the truth," it says through cracking static. The voice is mutated, tinny and metallic, as though whoever is speaking is intentionally disguising their voice. "None of you will leave this room until you admit what you did to Jenny Teller."

Our heads whip around the room looking for the source of the voice. Then I see it. A small camera mounted to the ceiling, partially hidden between the exposed pipes, a small red light blinking.

"She's watching us," I whisper to the others nodding in the direction of the camera, the all-knowing eye in the sky.

* * *

We're exhausted, our throats raw from screaming for help, our limbs tired from trying to pry open the door. Nothing worked. No one is coming. And my arm is throbbing, the pain nearly unbearable.

We sit along the back wall of the basement, as far away from the ominous camera and its beady red light as we can get.

"We're never getting out of here," Nessa laments, her head in her hands.

"You've always been such a drama queen," Emily says.

"And *you've* always been a bitch," Tori retorts.

Emily shrugs, unfazed by Tori's insult. "People may not have liked me, but they respected me."

"Alex didn't," I snap. "Did you know about him and Jenny?"

"No," Emily admits, her voice less confident now. "Not until ... after. Did you know? Is that why you killed them?"

I look up at the tiny sliver of window near the ceiling. It's getting late, the evening light waning. I take in the sight of my old friends. The ones I wasn't sure I could trust. A tear slides down Nessa's pretty face. Tori stares off into space, a haunted, vacant look in her eyes. *This is my fault. I'm* the one responsible for Jenny's death. It's time to tell the truth. I have to. For their sakes.

I sigh. It's harder than I thought it would be to dig up the words I've kept buried for so long. "I didn't mean to, not in the way everyone thinks. But what happened that night *was* my fault," I begin, my voice soft and small. "Only mine. I ... trapped Jenny and Alex in your room. I knew the lock was broken. And then they couldn't get out when the fire started."

"But ... why?" Emily asks incredulously.

I swallow hard. Telling myself that I need to continue. I have to finally say the words aloud. "It wasn't supposed to be that way." I turn toward Emily. "I found out about you and Alex. About how you'd been pulling the strings all along, convincing me to sleep with him and then yanked him away. I thought I loved him. At the time I really did believe that. It wasn't until years later that I realized that I didn't love Alex, I loved the idea of being wanted, of being loved. But he didn't want me. He wanted you. And I couldn't handle that. I thought it was *you* Alex was supposed to meet that night."

"That bit was my doing," Tori confesses. "I asked Nate to find out what Alex was doing that night. When he said he had a date, I assumed it was with you, Emily."

"And so," I continue, "I arranged for Alex to meet you in your room."

"Actually, that was me," Nessa admits, placing her hand on top of mine. "I texted Alex from your phone. I told him to meet you in your room."

I feel gratitude welling up inside of me. That these women, my friends, refuse to let me take the blame for that night alone. Even when the stakes are so high. But I know that I'm the one who is truly to blame. And now is the time to confess the rest.

"The plan was to lock Alex in the room so that you'd think he stood you up, Emily. It was just a prank, something harmless. But then Jenny showed up, and I realized that *she* was the one he was actually seeing. And I was angry. *So* angry. When I thought about it later, I realized that what I was really feeling in that moment was a mixture of betrayal, humiliation, shame, foolishness. But at the time, all I saw was white-hot anger. I was blinded with it. I slammed the door, locking them both inside. I don't even know what I was thinking. Truthfully, I guess I wasn't thinking at all. I just did it." I pause, steadying myself. "I didn't know there would be a fire that night. I swear I had nothing to do with that. I wasn't even on campus. None of us were." I look over at Tori and Nessa who are nodding along.

"It's true," Nessa says. "We left campus right after we closed the door on Jenny and Alex."

Now that my story is finally coming out, it pours out of me like water breaking through a dam. I can't stop the cascade of truth. "I'm so sorry about what happened to them. I can't even put into words how sorry I am. I've thought about them every day. *Every single day*. I've never forgiven myself. But I didn't mean for them to die. I never wanted that. I didn't think anyone would get hurt."

"Wow," Emily says. She pauses for a moment as if pondering how to respond to all I've just confessed. "So you really did kill them."

The tears break through, hard and fast. I bow my head in shame, crying into my one good hand. The other is so swollen now that I can barely move my fingers—the pain excruciating if I try. But Emily is right. I'm responsible for their deaths. If it hadn't been for my selfish, stupid actions, Jenny and Alex may have survived that fire.

Tori lunges at Emily. She's on her knees in front of her now, one hand around Emily's throat, pushing her head back against the wall. Emily's eyes grow round, wild.

"What the fuck is wrong with you?" Tori yells. "After everything Jules just told you, you feel the need to make her feel *worse*? You're sick!"

"Get off me," Emily hisses, pushing Tori hard in the chest. The two women rise to their feet. Emily looks up to the camera. "You heard her. Jules killed Jenny. She admitted it. Let me out of here now."

"Not just yet," the voice replies. "Not until I hear the rest."

"There's nothing else," I lament, as I stand, cradling my injured arm against my chest. "I told you my secret; I told you what I did to Jenny and Alex. And I'm sorry. I'm so very sorry for what happened to them, for what I did. But please let the others go. This wasn't their fault."

"One of you is lying," the voice replies. The words seem to ring in the air after they're spoken, like struck glass.

We look at each other—Emily, Tori, Nessa, and I. *Which of them could possibly be hiding more secrets about that night?*

"Well it isn't me," Tori remarks. "You know that, Jules. Nessa and I were with you all night."

Nessa nods in agreement. "We have nothing else to hide, I swear."

And I believe them. For maybe the first time, I know—beyond a shadow of doubt—that I'm one of them. We're in this together. And we always have been.

"Which just leaves Emily," Tori says.

The three of us look to Emily, who crosses her arms over her chest defiantly. "Don't look at me. I had nothing to do with any of this. You three saw me leave campus that night, remember? I spent most of the night with Nico. You can check the police reports if you want. We both gave them a statement during the investigation. By the time he brought me back to campus, Nickerson was already on fire. Frankly, I could have been killed when I tried to go inside. So I really have nothing else to say," she replies, looking down her nose at us. "I'm just an innocent bystander in all of this."

"Innocent?!" the mysterious voice says, incredulously. But this time it's not coming through the intercom. It's closer now. Just on the other side of the door. "You think you're innocent?!" the voice bellows.

I feel a chill run down my spine. *I know that voice. Why do I know that voice?*

And then we hear the lock disengaging, the door slowly creaking open on rusted hinges. Someone is standing on the other side, their face hidden in the shadows. But all I can focus on is the shiny, silver glint of a gun, pointed directly at us.

Chapter 46

Now

My entire body shakes with fear as the figure hovers in the doorway. The four of us huddle in the center of the underground room, brought together once again by the uncertainty of what's coming next.

"I don't know what role you may have played that night," our captor says, anger interlacing the words, "but I know you have never been *innocent*."

A woman steps into the light, allowing the heavy door to slam closed behind her. She glides in confidently on thin legs, her blonde hair shiny even under the dull fluorescent lighting, the barrel of her gun leveled at Emily's chest.

"Claire?" I say, my voice strangled and unfamiliar.

"You *know* her?" Emily asks. I can hear the fear in her voice: the feral, primal fear of death.

Claire arches one professionally sculpted eyebrow. "You don't remember me, Emily?" she says as she approaches our group, her cold eyes trained on Emily's face, which has gone deathly pale.

"Or maybe you'd remember me better by the nickname you gave me? Flabby Abby?"

My jaw falls open and my tongue trips over itself to form words. "But ... that's ... that's not possible," I stammer. "We met at the gym ... I ... would have recognized you ..."

"But you didn't, did you?" She swings the gun toward me, and my body tightens with terror. "That's because you never noticed me. You never even *looked* at me. Not until I looked like you, talked like you, moved through the world like you. Not until I was one of the pretty ones. It took some time, but after what happened to Jenny, I became someone new. I transferred to NYU. Did you even notice I was gone?"

No one answers. What could we possibly say? We were all too wrapped up in ourselves, in our own fears, our own self-pity at that time to have felt Abby's absence.

After what happened to Jenny, I did everything I could to keep my head down, to make myself invisible on campus. I took extra classes, focused solely on bringing my grades up, kept to myself. Everyone already hated me anyway. I felt like I couldn't escape the rumors that milled around the campus. If I could have, I would have transferred schools like Abby did, but it would have looked too suspicious, especially as we'd already been questioned by the police about our whereabouts that night. We'd lied. Of course. Except to prove that we weren't anywhere near Nickerson Hall when the fire started. But I was afraid that if I left Westbridge, it would have raised even more questions. Besides, how could I ever have explained to my parents that I'd given up a scholarship at my Ivy League dream school? I was so busy worrying about myself and keeping my secret hidden, that I hadn't given Abby another thought. I hadn't noticed that she was gone.

Claire snorts derisively. "I didn't think so. But being at a new school gave me the chance to be a new person. I had a clean slate, and I was never going to be Flabby Abby again. I shed every trace of that person. I lost a ton of weight, probably from the stress of losing my best friend, so thanks for that. I had my teeth whitened, my hair straightened, my vision corrected, and even a nose job. It's amazing what a little money can do to your image if you really care to try. I never cared about those things while I was at Westbridge, but I couldn't risk becoming the new Jenny of NYU. And so I started to become a different person. My mother, for one, was thrilled. She could finally take me on those mother-daughter shopping sprees she'd always imagined. Fitting me in designer dresses made for the size-zero mannequins. But a new me needed a new name. And so I became Claire."

"But …" Nessa stammers. "I thought you … Abby … was dead. The alumni newsletter …"

Claire shrugs. "She *is* dead, in a way. It took me all of twenty minutes to type up a sappy obituary and email it to you and Tori from a fake Alumni Association email address. I was willing to bet you'd never notice that it came from a different account. Just in case you put the pieces together, I didn't want you looking too hard for me."

I clutch my throbbing arm against my chest. "But … why … why did you do this? Why pretend to be my friend?"

Claire grins, a frosted sneer. "You're really going to cast judgment on me for pretending to be someone's friend? Isn't that what you, all of you, did to Jenny?"

"It wasn't like that," Tori ventures, her voice calm and placating. But Claire isn't buying it.

"It was *exactly* like that," she snaps before turning her attention back toward me. "I found you by accident, Jules. I didn't plan for any of this. But when I saw you at the gym that day, living your picture-perfect life, I felt something snap inside of me. I remember just staring at you, at your pretty, blonde ponytail, thinking about how unfair it was that you got to live the kind of life where you had the luxury of dropping in on a yoga class to find your inner peace or whatever, not when I knew that you were somehow responsible for ending Jenny's life. She was my best friend. Did you know that? Did you even care? Jenny was the only real friend I'd ever had, and you took her away from me."

"Did you know then … about what I did?" I ask.

"I had my suspicions. I heard the rumors, just like everyone else, but I couldn't be sure. No one knew exactly what happened that night. And so, I approached you. At first I just wanted to see if you'd notice me. I wanted you to see the person I'd become, how different I was. I wanted you to know that I became all the things you never thought I could be. But, to my surprise, you didn't seem to recognize me at all. You didn't have a clue. And so I went along with the ruse that I was your new bestie. I thought maybe you'd eventually confide in me about what had happened to Jenny. Maybe it was weighing on your conscience, and if I got into your good graces, you might unburden yourself onto me. But you didn't. You never even mentioned her. And so I kept pushing the envelope further: inviting you to my penthouse, which I knew would make you drool with envy, arranging dinners with our husbands. But the more time I spent with you, the more I realized that you were never going to tell me anything. You never even cared about her."

"I did care, I swear I did, Claire," I plead.

"Shut up," she snaps. "You've never cared about anyone but yourself." She sweeps the gun in an arch, pointing it at each of us. "None of you have."

"Please don't do this, Claire," I beg.

Claire narrows her eyes, two vicious slits. "You know, Jenny told me all about her thing with Alex. She even felt bad at first. Because of you. She thought you were different, that you weren't like the others. She thought you were a nice girl." Claire huffs, shaking her head in disbelief. "It wasn't long until you started to prove her wrong though. Do you remember the night you abandoned her, left her drunk and alone at some awful frat party so you could be with Alex?" Claire pauses, waiting for my response.

I open my mouth to speak, but my tongue has gone dry and the words stick in my throat. I nod instead.

"She was so disillusioned with you after that. And then Emily here …" Claire's eyes, hard and furious, flit over to Emily before training their gaze back on me. "Well, she told Jenny that the best revenge would be to talk to the boy you found so much more important than her. Jenny didn't want to do it at first. She said it felt mean. Even after how horribly you'd treated her. Because that's the kind of person Jenny was. But, as we all know by now, Emily has a way of getting people to do her bidding.

"The problem was that Jenny fell for Alex and his lies. He made her think he was actually into her. Maybe he was. Jenny was an incredible person. None of you would ever have known that because all you saw was a project. Some sad little girl you could dress up in pretty heels. None of you ever really knew her. But Alex did. She opened up to him, and she thought he was opening up to her too. That's why she was so angry when she saw that he was sending you poems, Jules."

I think back to that night. How Jenny had scowled at the type-written page. I assumed she was trying to get back at me, that she'd read them aloud to hurt me. *But maybe she was the one hurting.*

"He'd been sending them to her too," Claire continues. "After that, she cut him off for a while. Which only made him pursue her more. That boy must have spoken with a gilded tongue, the way he had all of you falling at his feet. But despite that fact that Jenny still had feelings for him, she chose you over him, Jules. Even though you never chose her. She tried to come clean with you."

"When?" I ask, my voice coming out in a croak.

"At Vanessa's play." She rolls her eyes. "Before that turned into a whole different drama."

That's right. It all comes back to me now. Jenny wanted to talk, but I didn't listen. *I'm trying something new*, she'd said.

Claire scoffs. "Would you believe that after that night she thought maybe you guys might have actually been good people? Not Emily, of course, but the rest of you. Jenny resolved never to talk to Alex again; because she thought you were her friends."

So that's why Emily was in such a rush to get rid of Jenny after the night at the karaoke bar. She was worried that if we let Jenny get too close, she'd tell us the truth about what she'd asked her to do.

"But then, of course, Emily destroyed her with those disgusting rumors," Claire adds. "And none of you lifted a finger to stop her. I told Jenny it was a bad idea to hang around you. Any of you. But she so desperately wanted to believe you were her friends. Some friends you turned out to be. Do you know that Alex was the only one who bothered to check in on her after what Emily did? And yet, Jenny still felt like she owed you her loyalty, Jules." She shakes her head at me in disgust. "I don't know how you did it. How you kept convincing her that she owed you anything. Did you even know you had that power over her?" She pokes me in the chest with the gun. "Did you?"

I feel as though the blood is draining out of my body; my toes tingle and my head swims. The most I can muster is a small shake of my head.

"The last straw was the night of that horrible Valentine's party. You were so cruel. Throwing Jenny to the wolves, knowing she was drugged and vulnerable. You cast her aside again as though she meant nothing to you, when you were the only thing standing between her and the boy she thought she loved."

Because of course Jenny didn't know that Emily was also standing in her way.

"You know what happened to her that night," Claire adds, her eyes locking on mine, "I know you do."

I shake my head. "No, I … I couldn't be sure, I thought maybe she—" I start, tears welling in my eyes, but Claire cuts me off.

"Jenny may not have told you, but a part of you has always known, Jules."

"Oh God," I cry, swiping at my tears with my one good hand. "I never meant—"

"The only good thing to come from that night was that Jenny finally saw the selfish, careless person you really are, and she was finally free to be with Alex. And so the next time he asked her out, she said yes. She fell for him pretty quickly after that. She was head over heels. He said he felt the same, but who could be sure with him? Maybe he said that to all of you. But it doesn't matter now, does it? Because you got your way, Jules. You're more like Emily than you ever knew. You found a way to make sure that if you couldn't have him, no one could."

The room falls silent as Claire finishes. All of us fitting together the pieces of our past that we'd been missing for so long.

"How did you know all of those things about us though?" Tori finally asks. "The things you used to get us to come here?"

"Oh, I cloned your phones," Claire says casually, the gun in her hand cocked to the side now. "My husband owns a technology company. It wasn't really all that hard. And suddenly I had access to all of your texts, emails ... everything I needed. The only trick was getting access to your phones. Jules's was easy. I grabbed her phone in the locker room at the gym. With Nessa, I snuck backstage at one of her plays. I pretended I was going to the ladies' room. They could probably benefit from some tighter security, honestly.

"Tori, yours took a little more work. I was hoping to do it at the Mommy Meet-Up, but then you didn't show. Not at first. I was getting ready to give up and leave for lunch with the other moms, when I saw you running in late. I told the others that I wasn't feeling well, and while you were distracted with your kid, I snuck back to the playgroup and plucked your phone out of your stroller. I installed the software and put it back where I found it before you even noticed it was gone. You really shouldn't leave that expensive stroller unattended, by the way. People like you, people who have always had everything, take it all for granted. You assume nothing can touch you. But you're wrong.

"I'll admit, I had to dig pretty deep through your old messages to find your secret, but all the pieces I needed were right there waiting for me when I did. I just had to put them together.

Meeting Matt, breaking things off with that loser ex of yours after you were *clearly* with him the night before ..." Claire shifts her weight to her hip, the gun looking heavy in her hand. "I mean, I couldn't know for *sure* that your kid isn't Matt's, but—after reading all of the texts you exchanged with him during your pregnancy—I gathered pretty quickly that you never told him it was even a possibility. The timeline just fit so perfectly, I had to take that gamble."

"What about *my* phone?" Emily asks, her voice quaking. "I haven't seen you since Westbridge."

Claire smiles deviously. "I didn't have to clone your phone to find out *your* secret ... That your husband is having an affair. That you're not enough for him."

Emily's cheeks burn a scarlet red. *She'd never want anyone to find out that her perfect life is all a sham, that her carefully curated Instagram is nothing but a cover story.*

"All I had to do was sit outside your house a few times, and he brought her right to me. Kind of tasteless to bring your mistress to the house you share with your wife, but whatever." Claire shrugs. "Anyway, at first I thought cloning your phones would be all I'd have to do. I'd have recordings off all of your phone calls, copies of your photos and videos, access to your texts and emails. I thought I'd snoop around a bit and somewhere someone would surely have mentioned Jenny. But none of you ever did. You never spoke about her, about what you'd done. It was as though she never even existed. But you told each other plenty of other things. You were so careless with your secrets. And soon enough I confirmed what I had suspected all along, that you're all still exactly the same—liars who will do anything, and destroy anyone, to get what you want. I knew if I applied the right pressure, if I threatened to expose you for what you are, you'd all come running when I summoned you here."

Claire must have broken into my apartment too. While she was lecturing me about tightening up security, all this time she was th

310

one invading my private space. It dawns on me now that that must be how she had the photos of the altered medical records. I'd taken them home with me that weekend, the first time I suspected someone had been inside the apartment. And then I told Tori about my dilemma. Claire must have come looking for evidence.

"You were in my apartment too, weren't you?" I ask gently, more of a statement than a question. I don't want to provoke Claire any further by pushing too far, but I have to know for sure. "How did you do it?"

"I didn't have to break in, per se. You trusted me, *your friend*, so much, that you showed me where you kept your spare key. Under that ridiculous plastic turtle. Do you remember? We went back to your apartment after happy hour one night and you said you'd left your keys at work so you pulled the spare out of its hiding spot. I went back the next day while you were at work and made a copy for myself just in case I ever needed it. Truth be told, that was my favorite part of all of this. Probably unnecessary, but so worth it to mess with your head. I honestly wish I could have seen your face when you found that the Westbridge mug had been replaced. Oh, and the glasses! That was just genius. I'd found them after the fire, when I was clearing out my room. Jenny had been living with me by then. And, I don't know, I just held on to them, something to remember her by. But it was worth parting with them for this. You must have been terrified."

She laughs then, a menacing chuckle. "That was some of my best work. That, and the photo I sent you. I knew that would mess with you too. It was never printed in the yearbook for … obvious reasons, but I was there when it was taken, and Lizzy was all too happy to give me a copy when I asked." Claire takes one hand off the gun and wipes her palm on her jeans. I see her finger trembling on the trigger.

"Claire, p-please, let's just talk," I squeak out between my chattering teeth. "You don't have to do this."

"Yes, I do!" she shouts, her voice rising with rage. "For Jenny.

I couldn't save her that night. I tried. I really tried. When the fire alarms started going off, I couldn't find her. I didn't want to leave without her, but what choice did I have? It was chaos that night. Total chaos. The student lounge was up in flames, and the rest of the floor was filling up with smoke. It burned my lungs, stung my eyes, as I pushed down the hallway in the mass of coughing, spluttering students who were shoving one another out of the way, everyone trying to save themselves, to hell with everyone else. I don't even know how I heard her, but as I passed by Emily's room, I heard Jenny's voice rise over the din. She was pounding on the door, screaming that she and Alex were trapped.

"I heard Alex inside trying to break the glass, but he was already coughing and frantic by then. You must remember how those windows barely opened."

My head fills with an image of Alex, the one night we'd spent together. How he'd complained about the windows, bending over to blow the smoke from his cigarette out the bottom, the tendrils of blue smoke spilling back into the room.

"I tugged on the doorknob," Claire continues, "and I kicked and beat on the door, but it wouldn't budge. Jenny was pleading with me to help her, but I couldn't. I just couldn't. Soon I was the last one left on the floor, and I knew that if I didn't get out of there, I'd die too. And so I had to leave my best friend behind." Claire's face remains hard, determined, but fat tears slide down her cheeks. "How was I ever supposed to be the same again after that? How was I supposed to be okay? My mother sent me to a therapist, thousands of dollars for me to sit on his couch over the years pretending that I was 'coping', but how could anyone ever really cope with the fact that they had to make a decision to leave their only friend to die?" The gun trembles in her hands, and my eyes are glued to her finger, which is wobbling dangerously on the trigger.

"I'm so sorry, Claire," Nessa offers gently. But Claire just scowls.

"A part of me died in that fire with her, but what was left of me was reborn. I rose from the ashes a new person: Claire. And now, finally, I have the chance to do something for Jenny. I knew the second I saw you, Jules, that the universe was giving me a second chance to do right by her, and this time I'm not going to let her down. It wasn't supposed to be like this. I hadn't set out to kill anyone. I just needed your confessions. You were never even meant to see my face, but you, all of you, you're just so selfish. So *horrible*. You couldn't tell the truth even to save your own lives."

"We did though," I plead. "We've told you everything there is to know!"

"That's not entirely true though, is it?" Claire replies with a shake of her head. "I've spoken to nearly everyone who was in the dorm that night. I managed to track most of them down. And while your confession was a good start, Jules, there is still one thing that doesn't add up from that night."

Claire shifts her attention to Emily, righting her grip on the gun. "You. You're the only one no one could account for that night. I know your alibi, your night with some club owner, was a lie. And so it's finally time to tell the truth, Emily."

Chapter 47

Now

"I ... I ..." Emily stutters.

"NOW!" Claire shouts. "You tell me everything, now, or I will kill you, I swear it."

Emily falls to her knees, her eyes pleading with Claire, her palms raised in surrender. "It ... it was an accident. I swear to you that it was. It just got out of control."

"What did, Emily? Say it," Claire barks.

"I ... I started the fire. But I didn't mean to! I didn't know what would happen!"

Emily started the fire that killed Jenny and Alex? No wonder she was so quick to point the finger at me, to call me a murderer in the dark anonymity of the woods that night. She couldn't face what she'd done. She had to find someone else to blame, just as she always did.

"I found out that Jenny was with Alex," Emily continues. "I really did have plans with Nico that night, but I'd forgotten my purse. I went back to my room. It must have been just after the others left because Jenny and Alex were already locked inside. A:

soon as I heard them together in there, I knew what had happened. I knew that he'd chosen her. Alex and I had been secretly flirting all semester, but it never really went anywhere. I always suspected there might be someone else. I started seeing Nico just to see if it would get under his skin.

"But it didn't work. Not like I'd hoped it would. I don't think I was what Alex was looking for. I wasn't exactly a … nice girl back then. Not the kind you make your girlfriend. But he'd led me on. Passing me notes during lectures—stupid, handwritten copies of his shitty poems, suggestive messages, long rambling narratives about his life. And I'd kept them all, stuffed into the notebook I kept hidden in my backpack.

"I guess he liked the attention. I did too. I liked that he'd chosen me when I knew Jules wanted him. I liked the idea that I could have what she couldn't. And so when I found out he was with Jenny, I couldn't stand the thought that he'd played me. That he'd chosen *her*—just like my friends had. I was furious. Livid. And so after I found them together, I went back to Hadley's room where I'd been planning to stay for the night. I grabbed the notebook from my backpack and decided to destroy everything he'd ever given me." Emily looks at the ground.

"Finish it," Claire growls, her gun leveled at the crown of Emily's pretty blonde head.

Emily whimpers, yet she has no choice but to continue. "It was a Friday night and the student lounge was empty, so I ducked inside and closed the door. I didn't want anyone to see how upset, how hurt, I was. I shook out my notebook into the garbage can."

I can picture it. All of Alex's love notes, soft and worn at the folded edges, fluttering out liked dried leaves.

Emily pauses there, and lets go of a deep breath. "And then I lit a match. Ironically it was from Alex's matchbook. He'd given it to me after class once when he offered me a cigarette. I didn't even smoke, but I'd kept the matchbook, like everything else he'd ever given me, tucked into the notebook. I didn't know the fire would get so out of control. I guess I just expected that the paper would burn and it would be forever gone from my sight. I just wanted to be rid of it so I could pretend none of it ever happened. But that's not how it turned out. The fire started sparking, smoking. Tiny bits of papers floated up through the air and landed on the carpet. I stomped out the first ember … I remember staring at the singed black mark it left behind in disbelief. But soon there were too many little fires for me to put out. Those damn streamers from the Valentine's party … they were still hanging on the walls. Why hadn't anyone taken them down? One caught fire, and before I knew it, the curtains were burning too. It all got so out of control! I panicked, I ran—"

"And you left the rest of us to die," Claire says, a cold finality to her voice. She switches the gun to her other hand, her sharp eyes never leaving Emily. "You know, I spent years looking at that night from every angle. My therapist told me it was becoming an obsession, that I needed to stop. And I did … for a while at least. But after I ran into Jules here at the gym," she explains, nodding in my direction, "the thoughts started up again. Maybe it was because I knew that our ten-year reunion was coming up, but I couldn't get them out of my head. I always knew what happened to Jenny wasn't just some freak accident. *Someone* started that fire. The police may not have been able to prove who did it, but I became determined to. I asked Jenny's parents for copies of the police reports from back then. I must have read them a thousand times. But I knew there had to be more to the story. Something that wasn't in those papers. And so, I tracked down that ex-boyfriend of yours, Emily." Claire pauses, casting the room in a deathly silence broken only by the buzzing of the lights overhead.

"How … how did you know?" Emily croaks.

"I didn't." Claire scoffs. "I had no idea how important Nico would turn out to be. He wasn't the first person I'd spoken to. I tracked down plenty of our old classmates—I wanted to talk to the same people the police did, to find something, *anything* they missed. But with all the rumors that were passed around about the four of you, I knew I had to hear for myself where you were the night my best friend died." She smiles, a vicious grin breaking across her face. "As it turns out, whatever hold you had over Nico didn't withstand the test of time, Emily. When I found him, he was feeling a lot less loyal to you than he once did. As soon as I asked him about the night of the fire, he was all but tripping over himself to tell me the truth: that you weren't with him that night; that you'd lied to the police; that you'd begged him to do the same. At the time, he didn't think you'd really been involved in what happened on campus, he thought the lie was harmless—just something you'd wanted him to do to spare you the trouble of having to be questioned by the police any further."

I can picture it all with vivid clarity. I can see Emily's lips curling into a pout, hear her voice purring in Nico's ear: *"You'll do that for me, won't you, babe? It's not like it's a big deal or anything. You know I had nothing to do with the fire. Besides, I've already told the police I was with you; it would just be a mess if we changed our story now."*

Claire shakes her head slowly in disbelief. "Not a particularly bright man, our Nico. But I guess thirteen years was enough time even for *him* to think things through, and he was done lying for some girl who never cared about him at all. It was like he was just waiting for a push, for his chance to come clean. All he needed was for someone to ask. And I finally did."

Claire's eyes narrow to angry slits as she straightens the gun in her hand, leveling it at Emily. "Once I learned that you'd lied to the police about where you were that night, I knew there had to be a reason. That you'd been involved in what happened to Jenny one way or another. I just didn't know how or why. But now, after what Jules told us tonight, it all finally adds up. You intentionally set a fire right down the hall from where you *knew* Jenny and Alex were trapped and helpless because you were jealous, because Jenny took something you thought you deserved. *You* killed them, Emily. *You*. You *wanted* them to die that night.

"I didn't! I swear!" Emily cries, her hands covering her face. Her entire body shakes.

"You killed my best friend, and you don't deserve to live," Claire says plainly. A judge delivering a sentence of death.

Tori, Nessa, and I huddle together, our trembling bodies pressed together as one as we watch the scene unfold before us in horror. It feels as though time is moving in slow motion as Claire's finger tightens on the trigger, and Emily lifts her head, her eyes clenched, waiting for the inevitable crack of the shot that will end her life.

A loud bang reverberates through the room, but it isn't from Claire's gun. The sound startles Claire and she whips around, gun held out in front of her.

"Jules!" a voice calls through the door to the basement that's been kicked open.

Jason. He's come to save me. Realization dawns just as I hear the deafening blast of Claire's gun.

Chapter 48

Now

I drop to my knees as Jason falls to the floor. I scream, a guttural moan summoned from the depths of my soul.

Claire looks shocked, her arms shaking, the gun hanging limply in her hands, her eyes wide with panic. "I … how …"

Nate bursts through the door and tackles Claire to the ground. The gun flies from her hands and skids across the cement floor.

But I don't care about the gun, about Claire. Not anymore. I feel my world going black, my head wobbling on my shoulders. *Jason can't die. He can't. I never should have brought him here. This is all my fault.*

Tori kneels behind me, holding me up.

"He's okay," she says. "Jason is okay. The bullet missed him. Look, Jules. He's okay."

I stare at him, forcing my eyes to focus. There is no tell-tale puddle of crimson red spreading beneath his fallen body, but I still can't quite make myself believe it. And then Jason pushes himself up off the floor.

"Jules," he cries as he rushes toward me. "Are you okay?"

He kneels in front of me, taking my face in both of his hands. He kisses me, fervently. I can taste his tears, salty on my lips as they mix with my own. "I thought I'd lost you," he says, breathing the words into my mouth.

"I love you," I say. "I love you so much." I collapse into his arms, my tears wetting his shirt, just like they did the first day we met. My own injured arm hangs limply by my side. The pain doesn't matter now. Nothing matters except Jason. He's okay.

"I'm so sorry, Jason," I cry. "I'm just so sorry. For all of it. I should have told you everything sooner. You could have been killed!"

"It's going to be okay," he says, holding me close to him, his hand cupping the back of my head. "We're going to be okay."

"I can't lose you," I sob, my shoulders heaving.

"You won't, I promise you, sweetheart. I'm here now, and I'm not going anywhere."

Tori stands, just as Nate snaps a pair of silver handcuffs behind Claire's back. Claire doesn't move, doesn't resist. She's frozen in shock. *Fight, flight, freeze.*

"How did you find us, Nate?" Tori asks, her voice flooded with relief.

"Matt and Jason have been looking for you guys all afternoon. Jason approached me on campus and asked if I'd seen Jules. Poor guy looked really worried. Apparently, he couldn't reach her since he got back from this morning's golf outing. I already knew something strange was going on with you guys—I just wasn't sure exactly what it was. So I told him I'd help him look for you. We were in my car when he got a text from Jules telling us you were trapped down here. You know how service can be around here. In and out."

My text must have eventually gone through. We'd gotten so lucky.

"And how much did you hear?" Tori asks Nate.

Nate eyes Emily coldly. "Enough to know that she killed my best friend." He produces another set of handcuffs, and Emily begins to back away.

320

"No, I … it wasn't my fault!" she cries.

"We'll leave that for the district attorney to decide," Nate says s he grabs hold of her wrist. "The local police will be here any minute."

He looks around at the rest of us—Tori, Nessa, and me—all waiting to see if we'll be next. "You three will need to stick round and give your statements," he says as he clicks Emily's uffs into place.

* * *

son sits next to me in the back of an ambulance while a para- edic applies a splint to my arm. "You'll have to go to the hospital r a proper cast once you're done talking to the police," the EMT ays as he drapes a blanket over my shoulders.

The scene reminds me of that awful night, the red emergency ghts bouncing between the trees of the cold, dark woods.

A man in a suit, a gold badge affixed to his breast pocket, limbs into the ambulance, and the paramedic jumps out, giving s some privacy.

"I'm Detective Bently," he explains, his voice warm and coaxing. Can you tell me what happened here tonight?"

I look over at Jason, and he gives me a reassuring nod. And en I tell them. All of it.

Jason sits by my side, holding my hand in his. I half expected im to drop it in disgust, to tell me that he can't believe he's arried to a monster, but he doesn't. If anything, he moves even loser as I tell my story. His presence an anchor.

"She videotaped it. Claire. She set up a camera to record the whole thing," I conclude. I wonder whether Detective Bently is oing to arrest me, but I don't think he can. Especially not after mily admitted to starting the fire.

I know from my days in law school that I couldn't be charged rith Jenny's murder, as Emily had suggested all those years ago.

Maybe that's why I was drawn to study law in the first place—subconscious need to examine what I'd done under an academic microscope. Locking in Jenny and Alex may have amounted to false imprisonment, but the statute of limitations for that offense has long since expired. Although I've always understood that couldn't be held legally responsible for my actions that night, that knowledge never made me feel any less *morally* responsible. It was never a fear of arrest that kept me quiet all these years, it was fear of the ugly truth coming out into the world. Of Jason seeing me in a harsh and unforgiving light, of having him know that I'd gotten an innocent girl killed all because I was jealous of her.

"Thank you," Detective Bently says, his face impassive. "That'll be all I need for now. You go get yourself fixed up, and I'll likely be in touch soon." He hops out of the ambulance, slapping his hand once against its metallic side, prompting the driver to start the engine.

"All this time ..." Jason says, "you thought you'd killed that girl?"

"I did," I say, dropping my eyes to my lap and tugging at the edge of the bandage wrapped around my wrist. "Sort of. She might have survived if I hadn't locked her in that room."

"You don't know that, Jules. And you couldn't have known that Emily was going to start a fire that night." He cups my chin in his hand and angles my face toward his. "You were just a kid really. It was a terrible thing that happened, but I think you owe yourself some forgiveness."

I look into his eyes and I can feel how much he loves me, how much he believes the words he's saying. I don't know that I'll ever be able to forgive myself for my role in what happened to Jenny, but for the first time, I know I'm not alone. I've shown my husband the darkest parts of me, and yet when he looks at me now, he doesn't see a monster, he doesn't see the mask, he just sees me. The broken, flawed, complicated person I am underneath it all. And somehow he still loves me.

I rest my head against his chest and I feel home.

Chapter 49

One Week Later

sit at our kitchen counter, my fingers wrapped around a warm mug of tea, one wrist still in a plaster cast. My hair is still damp from my shower this morning, and I'm feeling content, sitting here in a pair of soft leggings and one of Jason's faded cotton t-shirts. No makeup, no pretenses, just me.

"Are you going to miss this place?" Jason asks as he stretches out a length of tape to seal yet another box full of our belongings. He's hardly let me lift a finger to help with the packing, in light of my injured arm. It's as though he expects me to break at any moment. But I won't. I know I'm not that fragile anymore.

"Not really," I reply. I'm not the same person I was when we rented this apartment, and I'm ready to leave this part of my life behind me. To build something fresh and new with Jason. "I'm ready for a change."

Jason smiles, and rips the tape off the roll.

The doorbell rings and Jason and I look at one another curiously. I didn't think we were expecting any visitors today.

Jason shrugs. "I'll get it."

I swivel in my stool, and my eyes follow him to the door.

Jason pulls it open, letting in a stream of watery mornin[g] sunlight, and a burst of crisp fall air.

"Nate," Jason says, "come on in." He steps aside, letting Na[te] enter our apartment, which, by now, has mostly been tidied awa[y] into boxes.

"I hope it's okay that I dropped by," Nate says, wiping h[is] boots on our doormat.

"Of course," Jason replies. "After what you did for us, you'[re] welcome anytime."

"Thanks," Nate replies, running his fingers through his hai[r] which is still as thick as it was in college.

Nate and I lock eyes and I smile warmly. "Would you like [a] cup of tea? As you can see most of our stuff has already bee[n] packed, but I think I can rustle up a tea bag."

"Uh, sure," he replies. "That would be nice."

Nate sits on one of the stools at our counter while I prepa[re] the tea. He and Jason get to chatting, about the weather, ou[r] move. How easy it all seems now.

"Sugar?" I ask. Nate nods.

I dip the tea bag into the hot water and watch it steep, turnin[g] the water a warm amber hue.

"Here you go." I slide the cup onto the counter in front of Nat[e].

"Thanks," he says, almost sheepishly. I can tell there's somethin[g] he wants to say, some reason he came here today, other than fo[r] a cup of Earl Grey tea.

"So what's going on, Nate?" I ask as I lower myself back ont[o] the stool next to him. My tea is only lukewarm now, but I cradl[e] it in my hands anyway. The weight of it a comfort to me.

"Well, for one thing, I wanted to give you an update on Clai[re] and Emily. I thought you might want to be kept in the loop."

I nod, encouraging him to continue.

"Claire—or, Abby I guess—was charged with quite a fe[w] offenses. The most serious of which is kidnapping in the fir[st] degree, which, I'm sure you know, is a felony in New York. I think it'll stick too, what with the video evidence. She recorded everything that happened in the basement that night, and the local cops were able to get the footage off her phone when they officially arrested her."

I nod. "And Emily?"

"After reviewing her confession, the district attorney determined her actions the night of Alex and Jenny's deaths constituted, at best, a minor arson offense and manslaughter in the second degree."

I don't practice criminal law, but I think back to my law school days, to the lofty lecture hall, my criminal law professor in his signature bow tie quizzing us on the degrees of common felony offenses as we prepared for the bar exam:

"Juliana Johnson, what constitutes manslaughter in the second degree?"

I remember it so vividly. It felt as though he could see right through to the core of me, to what I'd done. I rose from my seat and responded by rote, the words carefully memorized: "Manslaughter in the second degree is when the defendant recklessly causes the death of another person."

"Very good, Ms. Johnson. And define the term reckless for us?"

"When the defendant is aware of, and consciously disregards, a substantial and unjustifiable risk."

"Precisely."

I shake the memory from my head, coming back to the present. "But wait, the statute of limitations on man two in New York is only five years ... It's expired. She can't be charged with that now."

Nate sighs. "I know."

"And the district attorney doesn't want to pursue a more serious intentional homicide charge?"

"No," Nate replies, the corners of his mouth pulling down into a frown as he slowly shakes his head. "They don't think they can prove that Emily *intended* for Jenny and Alex to die in the fire."

"Oh, Nate," I say, placing my hand over his on the counter. "I'm so sorry. I remember how close you and Alex were. I'm sure it would have given you some closure to have been able to hold someone legally responsible for what happened to him."

A small, begrudging smirk edges its way onto his face. "All is not *completely* lost. Even though it may be too late to charge Emily for her actions that night, while the district attorney's office was looking into her, they came across some … financial irregularities. It seems her husband has been embezzling funds from his company for quite some time, and they've been hiding the funds in offshore accounts in Emily's name."

"What?!" I exclaim, my jaw falling open at the implications.

Nate nods. "It looks like they're going to be bankrupt quite soon. And they're both facing the possibility of some serious charges: embezzlement, criminal conspiracy, tax evasion … by the time the DA's office is through with them, I wouldn't be surprised if they both end up doing jail time."

"Wow … I … I can't believe it," I stammer. It looks like Emily's dangerous games, her love for skirting the rules, have finally caught up with her. But Emily isn't the only one who was responsible for what happened to Alex and Jenny.

"I know none of this will bring Alex and Jenny back, but, Nate, for what it's worth, I want you to know that I'm truly sorry for the role I played in what happened to them. I never meant for anyone to get hurt."

"I know," Nate says, his eyes falling to his lap. He sighs again. "For so long I wanted to blame you, and Tori and Nessa too, for what happened. I didn't know exactly how you were involved, but after Tori had come to me to ask me what Alex's plans were for that night, I knew there must have been more to the story. I should have pushed. I should have found out the truth. But, at the time, I felt like I was just a kid. I thought the police would handle it.

"I let it go. Or at least that's what I told myself. I'd just stay away from all of you, and I'd never have to revisit my own regrets about that night. That was, until Tori came to see me a few weeks ago, telling me that someone calling themselves Jenny Teller had come back into her life. I knew then that I had to find out the truth. I'm not a kid anymore; I'm a detective now. I thought maybe I could finally do right by my friend. And so I decided to find out for sure what happened to Alex, even if it meant facing my own demons. He wasn't perfect, Jules. I know that. But he was my best friend. I felt I owed it to him." Nate lets out a long breath. "I kept an eye on the three of you after Tori came to see me. I thought that maybe I could piece together what was going on."

So someone was *following me. I'd convinced myself that it was all in my head.*

"That's why I went to homecoming," Nate confesses. "To find out what I could. And why I followed you to your hotel after the masquerade. The three of you had been acting strangely all night, and I could sense that something bad was about to happen. But it's also why I happened to be on campus when Jason came looking for you. In truth, I was looking for you too."

"And thank God you were," Jason says, as he comes to stand behind me and gives my shoulder a squeeze.

"Did you really think we set out to kill them?" I ask Nate, trying to keep the hurt out of my voice. Nate knew us. He *loved* Tori. How could he have believed such a horrible thing? I pull my hand off his and wrap it back around my mug.

"No," Nate says, shaking his head sadly. "The truth is that deep down I never really believed you three were capable of taking someone else's life. It was just easier to blame you than to blame myself."

"Yourself?"

"I just kept thinking … if I stood my ground, if I hadn't been so head over heels for Tori, if I just hadn't told her about Alex's plans, maybe none of this ever would have happened."

"I understand," I say softly. "More than you know. But you

can't do that to yourself. You can't punish yourself with 'what ifs' forever. As much as I wish we could all go back and change what happened that night, the truth is that we can't. And, Nate, what happened wasn't your fault."

Nate looks up, his eyes meeting mine again before he runs his fingers through his hair, raking it back from his face. "That's the other thing I wanted to talk to you about." He pauses, releases a deep breath. "I know you've been blaming yourself for what happened to them too. I watched Abby's tape. I heard every word."

I feel a heat rise into my chest at the thought of Nate watching me confess to the actions that led to his best friend's death. *How awful that must have been for him.*

"But there's something I think you should know." He lifts himself from his stool and pulls a folded piece of paper out of his pocket before smoothing it out on the cool granite surface of the counter. "I got a copy of the fire marshal's report from that night. Jenny and Alex weren't in Emily's room when they died."

"What …?" I ask incredulously. It feels as though the breath has been drawn from my lungs. "How …"

"They were found in the stairwell. Together. Jenny had already passed from smoke inhalation by the time the firemen arrived, and Alex was alive but in pretty bad shape."

"But that means …"

"They got out," Nate replies, a finality to his voice. "And there's more. I spoke to the fire marshal myself. I told him that one of the victims was a friend of mine and I asked his thoughts about what happened that night. He told me that had Alex and Jenny stayed in the sealed dorm room and breathed through the window, had they not gotten the door open, had they not run out into the smoke-filled stairwell, they probably would have survived."

"But, we can't know for sure … If they hadn't been locked inside in the first place, maybe they would have left the dorm before the fire started. Or maybe Emily never would have found out about them, and maybe she never would have started it at all

328

or … or …" My mind is reeling, spinning out with the possibilities.

"You can't punish yourself with the 'what ifs', forever," Nate replies. He pauses, as though choosing his next words carefully. "I don't blame you for that night, Jules. Not anymore. And I'm learning not to blame myself either. I've carried around the weight of my guilt for far too long. And I think you have too. Maybe it's time to set it down."

Epilogue

Eight Months Later

"Who wants cheese on their burger?" Jason calls out. He stands in front of the shiny silver barbecue on our deck, in the sprawling green yard of our new house on Long Island. After resisting it for so long, I finally see the appeal of the suburbs. The relative quiet, at least compared to Manhattan, the slower pace of life, the space and freedom to grow into something new, something larger than ourselves.

My hand automatically lifts to my belly. I'm not showing yet, but the instinct is already there, to protect the tiny little life inside of me. Today is the day we're going to tell our friends that we're expecting, and I can feel the excitement bubbling in my stomach. Or perhaps ... could that be the first little kick, the first tiny flutter from the daughter I've yet to meet?

"I'll take cheese!" Tori calls from across the yard. She and Matt have set up a little paddling pool for Mia on the grass and she's splashing and kicking happily, covering her parents with droplets of water that glint on their skin in the afternoon sun.

Tori decided to tell Matt everything after what happened with

Claire. She didn't want there to be any more secrets between them, anything that could ever tear them apart. He was hurt at first, mostly that she hadn't told him sooner, but in the end, he decided he didn't need a paternity test to know that Mia is his daughter, his reason for living. As far as I can tell, their marriage is stronger than ever.

As is mine. Jason and I have been like newlyweds again, getting to know each other all over, or, maybe for the first time. It's made us closer than I ever thought possible. And when our little girl arrives, our family, and our hearts, will be full.

"Add cheese to ours too, please!" Nessa replies. She and her boyfriend, Grant, watch Mia splashing in the pool, his arm around her waist, her head leaning on his shoulder. It's nice to finally see Nessa allowing herself some happiness, some peace, after all she's been through.

"Oh my God, turn that up!" Tori yells to me, and I spin the dial on the radio.

Nessa's song floats through the yard on the warm summer breeze. It still feels surreal hearing one of my closest friends on the radio. I'm not sure I'll ever get used to it. In the end, Nessa came clean about the origins of her first song with her manager, Tim, and he went to great lengths to finagle a deal with the record company to sell them one of Nessa's other, completely original tracks instead. It hadn't been easy, and took months of negotiation, but in the end Nessa did the right thing and refused to sell the rights to a song she knew wasn't truly hers.

As for my career, as soon as I returned from Westbridge, I quit my job at Miller & Marquee … but not before reporting Barrett to the Ethics Committee for what he'd coerced me into doing for him. The motion I filed at Barrett's behest was withdrawn by the managing partner of the firm, and Barrett's employment was terminated immediately. They offered me a raise to stay on at the firm, but I decided it wasn't for me. I no longer wanted to work at a firm that would allow someone like Barrett to reign unchecked for so long. I was certain that I wasn't the only one who knew that he was skirting the edges of the law. Instead, I've taken a job at a smaller firm on Long Island. The pay is significantly lower, but the hours are far more reasonable, and now with the baby coming, I know I've made the right choice. Last I heard, my old officemate, Andrew, was thinking of making the switch as well. I'll put in a good word for him with my new boss when the time comes.

My phone buzzes in my pocket and I fish it out, reading the text message on the screen:

Can't wait to see you next weekend!

Kelly. I reached out to her a few months ago, unsure if she'd want to hear from me. But I was surprised to find that she was *thrilled* to reconnect. I should have known she'd welcome me back into her life with open arms. That's just the kind of person she is.

We've been exchanging texts and photos ever since, pictures of her two kids, our weddings, my new house, just filling each other in on all the years we've missed. Next weekend will be the first time I'm seeing her in person in over ten years, and I smile to myself at the thought. This is the life I never thought I could have again.

I don't think I'll ever completely be able to forgive myself for what happened to Jenny and Alex, but I'm slowly starting to try. Tori, Nessa, and I have set up a scholarship fund in Alex and Jenny's names. It's not much, certainly not enough, but it's something we *can* do where there is so much we can't.

When I look back at that time now, I still feel the guilt, the hollow remorse that sometimes feels so deep it might swallow me whole. But sometimes, on rare occasions, I catch a glimpse of something else: a hurt eighteen-year-old girl who slammed a door in the heat of the moment—a lost girl who didn't yet understand that consequences could be dire. I'm trying to learn to forgive her.

I've come to accept that a lot of people played a role in what happened that night, and that I'll always feel regret for my part in it. But I realize now how much I've been punishing myself all these years. I held myself back from my husband, and even from my friends, the people who knew the truth about that night and never judged me for it.

But I think it started even before Jenny, my decision to hide myself from the world. I see now how my insecurities, my need to question myself, to compare myself to everyone around me, robbed me of years of seeing what was right in front of me all along: that I had found true friends in Tori and Nessa. These are the kind of friendships that last a lifetime, the kind that can surpass the bounds of friendship and grow into family. We're closer now than we ever have been. And when I think back on it now, I can't believe I ever suspected that they would have done anything to hurt me. I make a silent promise to myself here and now that I won't take everything I have for granted again.

Because if there's one thing I know for sure, it's that life can be far too short.

Acknowledgments

Writing can sometimes feel like a solitary experience, but in reality there are so many people who help take a story from an idea in the author's head to the book in your hands. I'd like to thank my editor, Belinda Toor, for helping me to make it the best it could possibly be. Thank you also to the marketing team, design team, editors, and all of the other people who work behind the scenes at HQ and HarperCollins who made this book a reality.

A huge thank you is also owed to my writing friends. Tanya (the genius behind The Book Is Better Editing Service), thank you for being the best pen pal. As much as I love being a writer, it doesn't come without its tough days. Thank you for always answering my frantic texts and for never failing to have the perfect sitcom quote to get me back on track. Shelby, the best critique partner there is, I'm so glad we connected. This book would not be what it is without your thoughtful advice.

Lauren, I also owe you a big thank you for the late nights spent plotting and for never asking questions when I ask you to help me figure out how to kill someone. That's the sign of a true friend right there. Jess, thank you for reading the completely random passages I sent you while writing this book, and for always having words of encouragement at the ready. Your unconditional support means the world to me.

To my mother, thank you for always being the first set of eyes on my finished manuscripts and for finding every plot hole along the way. I wouldn't have the courage to put my writing out into the world without knowing that you're always standing behind me. (Also thank you for making everyone you've ever met buy my books. You should really be getting a commission.)

I'd also like to thank my cousin Ali, who is completely convinced that everything I write is going to be a best seller. Thank you for helping me iron out the details to get the ending of this book just right, and for always believing in me even when I have moments of doubt.

To my brother, Steven, I hope you noticed that I put your name into this book. You can stop being jealous of Brittney now. Thank you both for shouting about my books from the rooftops.

And to my early readers, Annalisa Oppedisano, Erin Prunty, Kathy Rowan, Sarah Formont, and Marilyn Boake, thank you for taking the time to read my manuscript and for all of the invaluable feedback you provided along the way. This book is far better because of each and every one of you.

I'd also like to thank Randee Watson at the Westbury Fire Department for his expert advice on all things fire and smoke, and for not being (too) alarmed when I asked him to help me kill off a few people. I know that I took a few creative liberties with this book (sorry, Randee), and I assure you all that any mistakes are purely my own.

My apologies to Tompkins County as well for moving Westbridge and its mean girls into your neighborhood. I spent my college years at Binghamton University and fell in love with the area, and so when I thought of the idea for this story, I knew it would be the perfect setting for a murder in the woods.

Giancarlo. Thank you for being you. I couldn't do what I do without having you in my corner. From entertaining the kids to

336

give me time to write, to listening to me read random paragraphs aloud, completely out of context, thank you for being so endlessly supportive of my dreams.

And now for my girls. My reason, my inspiration, my everything. Juliana, thank you for letting me borrow your name for this book. Even though this character wasn't based on you in any way (and not just because you're only two), I thought that someday you might appreciate seeing your name in print. And Christina, don't worry—your book is coming …

And finally to you, my readers: thank you from the bottom of my heart. I couldn't continue to do what I love without your support. I hope you loved reading *Deadly Little Lies* as much as I loved writing it.

Keep reading for an excerpt from
The Guilty Husband ...

STEPHANIE DeCAROLIS

THE GUILTY HUSBAND

It only takes one lie
to destroy a marriage...

Chapter 1

Vince

It started, as so many things do, with a choice. Though it wasn't one consciously planned—a decision made, a line drawn in the sand. No, this felt more like something that happened while I wasn't looking. The gentle pull of the tide that sweeps you out to sea while you're preoccupied with the feeling of sunshine on your face. It all happened so slowly, and yet all at once. It started so small, a glance exchanged, a word whispered, but somehow, it's grown into something so large that it now looms over my life, casting a shadow on everything I once thought I'd die to protect.

I don't even know who I am anymore. I've become someone I barely recognize, making decisions I never thought I would make. What started with one mistake, one bad choice, has become many. One following the next until I could no longer keep up, I couldn't set it right. But in truth, I didn't really try. Not until it was too late anyway. I didn't know, in those glittering early days, what malevolent thing would curl around me like smoke, so thick and so dark, that soon I wouldn't be able to see my way through it any longer.

I need to snap out of it. I need to focus. I stare at the spreadsheet on my computer screen, the cursor blinking at me impatiently. I know I should be working. I'll need these quarterly numbers before the board meeting this afternoon, but I'm distracted today.

I glance down at my cell phone that's resting, face down, next to my keyboard. I try to resist the urge to flip it over, again. To check for new messages. But the pull is too strong. Disgusted with my own disappointing lack of will power, I check my home screen. No new notifications. This is what I wanted, right? *Don't contact me again*. Then why does this silence feel like the quieting of birds before an impending storm?

"Vince?"

The voice rattles me and I drop my phone like a child caught sneaking sweets before dinner.

"Sorry," my assistant Eric says, "didn't mean to startle you."

"No, no, I was just lost in thought for a moment. What's up?"

"There's someone here to see you," he replies.

"Really? I don't see a meeting on my schedule. I'm supposed to sit down with the board in about an hour and I thought I had cleared my morning to finish up the quarterly reports." We're about to launch a new branch of the company, expanding from software development into producing video games. It's a huge step for KitzTech and I have a lot riding on it.

"It's not a meeting … It's a detective," Eric says.

"A detective? Do you know what it's about?"

"She said it's about one of our interns. Layla Bosch. She's … she was killed last night."

I feel the blood rush from my face, the periphery of my vision start to blur. My stomach drops and I have the strange sensation that I'm suddenly in free fall.

"Do you … want me to send her in?" Eric asks.

"Of course, yes, send her in right away." I straighten up in my seat, willing myself to regain my composure.

Eric leaves my office, closing the door softly behind him.

I rake my hands through my thick, wavy hair. I've started to notice that it's thinning lately, but Nicole says she can't see any difference. *Nicole.* What am I going to tell her? Do I have to tell her anything? I guess I'm about to find out.

I hear a quick rap on the door; a courtesy before Eric swings it open. We have an open-door policy around here, and even though I'm the CEO, I constantly have consultants, associates, and my production teams coming in and out of my office throughout the day. I try to keep a relaxed and open feeling in our company; I think it's essential to keep the employees happy and the creativity flowing. But today Eric escorts the detective into my office and shuts the door behind him.

"Mr. Taylor, I'm Detective Allison Barnes," the detective says, extending her hand to me. I'm taken aback for a moment when I first see Detective Barnes. I suppose I've always imagined detectives the way I've seen them portrayed on television—middle-aged, paunchy, rough around the edges. Detective Barnes is nothing of the sort with her thin frame, glossy brown hair pulled back into a smooth bun, and her rich olive skin. In another version of my life, I might have found her attractive, but today all I can focus on are her sharp hazel eyes, which are already looking me up and down, seeking out my cracks and flaws.

I walk around my desk to shake her hand, and offer her a warm smile. "Come on in, take a seat."

I gesture for her to sit in one of the low-slung leather chairs situated across from my desk. I walk back to my own chair and sit behind my large glass desk, assuming a position of power, confidence. It's all part of the show.

"Thank you," Detective Barnes says, sitting primly on the edge of her seat as she takes in my spacious, modern office. My office is of a minimalist design, and, like the rest of our corporate headquarters, it's painted a bright white. I notice the detective's gaze lingering curiously on the only splashes of color in here, the assortment of beanbag chairs and yoga balls that also serve as seating options in my office. "I'm sorry to interrupt your morning, but unfortunately it seems that one of your interns, Layla Bosch, was killed last night."

"Yes, my assistant, Eric, just told me," I reply. "That's truly awful. May I ask what happened to her?"

Barnes nods curtly. "We found her body in Central Park this morning. I'm afraid that's all I'm able to tell you at this time."

I feel my pulse quicken, my heart beating rapidly like a bird futilely thrashing its wings against a metal cage.

"My partner, Detective Lanner, and I are here to interview anyone who may have known Ms. Bosch. We're trying to sort out if there was anything going on in her life, if there was anyone who may have wanted to harm her. Detective Lanner is meeting with your assistant at the moment."

"Of course," I say. "Unfortunately, I personally didn't work too closely with Ms. Bosch, so I'm afraid I won't be of much assistance to you, but I can have Eric pull up the names of her direct supervisors for you."

"I figured as much. I didn't expect that the CEO of a big company like this would have much day-to-day contact with the interns, but I would certainly appreciate that list of her supervisors."

I nod, and jot down a note to have Eric pull the names of everyone that Layla Bosch was assigned to work with.

"So," Barnes continues, "did you know Ms. Bosch?"

"We like to call ourselves a family here at KitzTech, and that includes the interns. I make it a point to try to get to know everyone that works for me, but from what I recall Ms. Bosch hasn't been with us for very long. She would have come in with the new class of interns only about five months ago, so I didn't have the chance to get to know her as well as I may have liked."

"What can you tell me about her?"

"Well, like I said, I didn't have much opportunity to work with her personally, but I've heard great things through her supervisors. I hear she was a very ambitious and intelligent young lady that likely would have been offered a full-time position after the completion of her internship. But I'm afraid that's all the information I can offer you, Detective. I wish I could be of more assistance."

"Thank you, Mr. Taylor," Barnes says.

"Just call me Vince. Everyone around here does."

"We would like access to Ms. Bosch's personnel file if you'd be so willing."

"Of course. Anything you need. I'll have Eric pull that for you as well. And if there is anything else we at KitzTech can do to assist in your investigation, please don't hesitate to ask." I slowly rise from my chair. "I don't mean to rush you out, but I'm scheduled to meet with my board in just a moment unless there is anything else you need?"

"No, thank you, Mr. Taylor. Vince. That'll be fine for now. I appreciate your time this morning, and I'm sure we'll be in touch." Detective Barnes pulls herself up from the chair and dusts off her perfectly pressed pants.

I smile and extend my hand across the desk, hoping that she hasn't noticed the sweat beading along my collar. It's only a matter of time before she finds out that I'm lying.

Chapter 2

Allison

DAY 1

He's lying. Or, at the very least, there is something that Vince Taylor is not telling me, something hiding beneath his flawless smile. Vince was not at all what I was expecting when I asked to speak to the CEO of KitzTech. For one thing, I didn't expect him to be so startlingly attractive. My hand automatically goes to check my hair just thinking about him, and I can sense the color rising into my cheeks as I recall the tiny gasp I was unable to suppress when I first saw him walking toward me in his expensive jeans and crisply pressed shirt. He smelled of citrus and sandalwood, of exotic currents from faraway places.

Vince is casually handsome, as if he's become accustomed to how good-looking he is, but yet I suspect he's still very much aware of the charming effect his tall stature, broad shoulders, and honey-brown eyes have on everyone else around him. He's younger than I imagined he would be too. I'd guess he's around forty, with gentle laugh lines around his eyes and an easy, languid confidence that comes from living on top of his world.

Vince sat behind his fancy desk, in his absurdly large office, looking appropriately concerned about the death of his young intern, but something about him struck me as odd. I can't quite put my finger on it, but I have a gut feeling that there is more to him than the relaxed jeans, finger-combed hair, and movie-star smile. I make a note to myself to look into Vince Taylor.

I walk down the large, glass spiral staircase at the center of the KitzTech corporate headquarters and into the brightly lit white lobby to meet my partner, Jake Lanner.

"Can you believe this place?" Lanner asks, gesturing at the grand, minimalist lobby. It's all polished glass and pristine surfaces. "Did you notice they don't even have light switches?"

I quickly scan the walls. He's right. Not a single light switch, outlet, or wire in sight. I try to think back to the inside of Vince Taylor's office. Much like the lobby, his office was white and sparsely furnished, with the exception of a few brightly colored beanbags and yoga balls that seemed a bit ridiculous for a CEO's office. It was obvious that he tries to be the "fun" boss that lets his employees call him by his first name and "hang out" in his office that is easily larger than my apartment. But Lanner is right. I didn't see the familiar tangle of wires coming from the back of his desktop computer.

"I'm telling you, Barnes, the entire place is wireless. Everything is controlled by these little panels that blend into the walls. Watch," Lanner says as he walks toward a glass doorway reading "Café". He places his hand on the outside of the doorframe and a control panel illuminates asking for an employee ID.

"Can I help you?" a chipper young woman asks. Thick, trendy black glasses are perched on the bridge of her nose and she's wearing a form-fitting, yet professional, black dress.

I turn and introduce myself and Lanner.

"Yes, you're the detectives here about Layla, right? Such a

shame. I'm Rachael. I work at the front desk. Sorry to have missed you earlier but I was giving a tour of the facilities to some new applicants. Is there anything I can help you with?"

"No," Lanner responds. "We were just admiring all the tech around here." He's in his element. Lanner loves anything techie.

"It's very cool, isn't it?" Rachael says, nodding. "There's a panel like this outside just about every door. You just have to touch the panel to light it up. To get in and out of any of the community spaces around here you need to scan your employee ID, and to get into any of the restricted spaces you need to scan your fingerprints. We get a lot of people who stop in just to see the facility and we found that this was the best way to keep them out of the areas we don't want them wandering into. Would you like something from the café? I can scan you in."

"No, thank you," I respond. "We were just leaving."

"Okay, good luck with the investigation. I hope you find whoever did this," Rachael says solemnly as she scans her ID, prompting the glass doors of the café to slide open before her.

Lanner and I begin walking toward the exit. "So what's the deal with this place?" I ask him.

"What do you mean?"

"KitzTech. I know it's a technology development company, but this office doesn't exactly give me the 'nerdy computer programmer' vibes I was expecting."

"Nerdy? Come on, they created Friend Connect!" Lanner exclaims, evidently surprised at my lack of familiarity.

"That stupid social media site?"

"I swear, Barnes, I think you're the last person on Earth who still doesn't use social media. Even my grandmother has a Friend Connect page! But, yes. Friend Connect is a social meeting space where you can post pictures, connect with video calls, send messages, that kind of thing. It's crazy popular. KitzTech also put out Date Space. Do you know that one?"

"No, what the hell is that?" I ask.

Lanner rolls his eyes. "It's another app where you can connect with singles in your area and it gives you a private, virtual space to connect before you meet in person. Slightly less sleazy than other dating apps. Trust me. I've tried out a few. But if sleazy is your thing, KitzTech also created Secret Message. It's an app that you can download on your phone to send discreet messages with anyone else using the program. The messages automatically disappear after they're read. You can imagine what that one is used for ..." Lanner explains with a goofy smile.

"So, basically what I'm hearing is that Vince Taylor is probably pretty wealthy?"

"Try extremely wealthy," Lanner replies. "You gotta see his house."

Lanner pulls out his phone and quickly taps away at it before turning it around and showing me a photo of what could easily pass for a luxury resort. The house, or I should say mansion, is incredible. An expansive villa set against a wooded backdrop. The aerial view Lanner found highlights the private pool, tennis courts, and long winding drive. The large property is extremely secluded and bordered by a stately stone wall—the only thing separating the grandeur of the home from the tangled woodland surrounding it.

"Just a touch larger than my apartment," I scoff with a roll of my eyes, as I envision my tiny one-bedroom rental with the rattling air-conditioner that can't seem to keep up with the suffocating heat wave we've been experiencing.

"I'll say," Lanner agrees. "But if it makes you feel any better, his commute into the city from Loch Harbor probably sucks."

That earns him another eye roll. "You know, somehow that doesn't make me feel any better at all."

"Anyway," Lanner continues, "did you get anything good from your interview with him?"

"Not really. He didn't seem to know the victim too well. She was just an intern and she's only been here a few months, but there was something about him that didn't sit right with me. I'm gonna scope him out later. You get anything good?"

"Not much. The vic worked with the development team. They were working on some new app or something. All very top secret," Lanner says. "Pretty much everyone on the team had the same things to say about her though: she was a quiet girl, kept to herself, but very bright and very ambitious. Apparently she showed a lot of promise."

"Any luck getting in touch with her next of kin?"

"No," Lanner explains, "but I had Kinnon drop by her address this morning and he got in touch with her neighbor. She's on her way down to the morgue now to ID the body."

"Let's meet her there," I say.

* * *

I hate the morgue. I can't count how many times I've been here during my years on the job, but it never gets any easier. The cold metal slabs, the blue-gray lifeless bodies, and the smell of formaldehyde make me shudder every time. But I have to keep it together. I've only recently been promoted to detective and this is the first major homicide investigation that I've been put in charge of, and so I don't want to show any signs of weakness.

Lanner and I have worked together for a long time. Although he made detective almost a year before I did, we more or less came up the ranks together, so he already knows my feelings on hanging out with dead bodies. But still, as lead detective on this case, I feel like I have something to prove. Lanner is a good guy, but he's still exactly that ... a guy. In a male-dominated police force, I can't afford to look like I can't handle the gore that comes along with the job.

"You ready?" Lanner asks.

"Of course."

I pull back my shoulders, shake off the eerie chill that this place gives me, and walk into the lobby to meet Layla Bosch's neighbor.

We find her sitting on one of the small wooden chairs in the waiting room under a mop of frizzy black curls. She seems almost folded in on herself, making herself appear as small as possible, while she nervously picks at the skin on the side of her thumb.

"Hi, I'm Detective Allison Barnes," I say gently as I approach. "And this is my partner, Detective Jake Lanner."

"I'm Mindy," the woman says in a small voice, as she brushes a rogue curl away from her face. "I can't believe this is happening. Are you sure it's Layla?"

"We think so," Lanner says. "We found her work ID badge on her when we arrived at the scene this morning. But we need you to identify the body, if you can, so that we can be sure the woman we found is Layla Bosch."

"Yes, I can do that," Mindy says, pulling herself to a stand. It looks as though she's doing her best to brace herself for what's to come.

"Follow me," I tell her as I lead the way to the viewing room.

"Do I have to … go in the room?" Mindy asks, her eyes widening. "You know … with the body?"

"No," I assure her. "The coroner will go into the autopsy room and he'll pull back the sheet, just away from her face. You'll see her here," I explain, indicating a television monitor in the center of the room.

"And all you'll have to do is tell us if you recognize the body. If it's Layla," Lanner adds.

"Okay. I can do that," Mindy says, but she can't seem to stop her hands from shaking.

The television flickers to life and the familiar face of the coroner, Dr. Allen Gress, appears on the screen. "Are you ready?" he asks.

Lanner presses a button on the intercom next to the screen. "We are," he says. "Go ahead."

Dr. Gress gently lifts a white sheet away from the victim's face. He's cleaned her up a bit since we've last seen her. Her face is no longer splattered with dirt, and her hair, which was matted with blood this morning, has been carefully brushed away from her face. The red dress, mottled with dark red blood, that she was wearing when we found her, has been cut away and replaced with a clean white sheet tucked neatly under her sides.

I hear Mindy take a sharp breath, and then she covers her mouth with her hands. "That's her," she says. "That's my neighbor. Layla Bosch," she manages before she begins to sob. Her hands tremble in front of her face and I can see red splotches blooming on her cheeks underneath.

"Thanks, Dr. Gress," Lanner says through the intercom. The coroner nods and pulls the sheet back over Layla's face as I switch off the screen.

I lead a tearful Mindy to a seat while Lanner goes to talk to Dr. Gress about his findings thus far.

"Do you mind answering a few more questions for me?" I ask Mindy gently.

"Of course. Anything I can do to help." Mindy's eyes fill with tears again and I hand her a tissue from a box on the small end table situated next to us.

"We've been trying to track down Layla's family," I explain. "We haven't been able to find any next of kin for her."

"She doesn't have any family, I don't think. She told me that her parents and her only brother were killed in a car accident when she was very young. She was raised by her grandmother who recently passed, which is how she ended up moving to Brooklyn in the apartment next to mine. After her grandmother died she wanted a fresh start. Oh my God, I can't believe she's really gone." The tears in Mindy's eyes begin to fall.

"Were you two close?"

"We were becoming pretty good friends, I guess," she replies. "Layla only just moved to town but I made an effort to get to know her. I live alone too, and I figured two single girls should look out for each other. She was kind of shy at first, kept to herself but lately we've been spending more time together. Having a glass of wine after work, that sort of thing."

"Did you ever meet any of her other friends? Boyfriends?"

"I don't think she had anyone else," Mindy explains. "She was new to town and really only ever talked about people she worked with. It didn't seem like she socialized with them much outside of the office though. I don't think she was seeing anyone either. If she was, she never mentioned it. I told her about my love life, or lack thereof, all the time. I think she would have told me if she was dating."

"Thanks, Mindy. You've been really helpful," I reassure her, handing her my card. "If you think of anything else, you can call me any time."

* * *

Lanner folds himself into the passenger seat of my car, his long lanky legs pressed up against the glove compartment. He slams the door behind him, making me wince. He always slams the damn door. It's infuriating. He immediately rips open a bag of chips, shoving a handful in his mouth. I watch the greasy crumbs fall onto the passenger seat of my car. Also infuriating. I don't know how Lanner manages to stay so thin with all the junk he eats.

"What did Dr. Gress have to say?" I ask.

"He hasn't finished his autopsy yet," Lanner replies while munching away, "but his initial impression is that the cause of death was blunt force trauma to the back of the head. He's putting her time of death at approximately 9.30 last night. Give or take about a half-hour."

"That's consistent with CSI's initial findings. When they looked at the site this morning they said that the blood spatter along the jogging trail looked like it came from a blow to the head. They're still canvassing the area, but no sign of the murder weapon yet."

"What's the plan?" Lanner asks.

"I've asked Kinnon to put together a team to check CCTV footage. There are no cameras in that area of the park, but maybe we can pick her up somewhere heading into the park. See if anyone was following her."

"Good idea," Lanner agrees. "Where to now?"

"Let's go see what we can find at her apartment."

Dear Reader,

We hope you enjoyed reading this book. If you did, we'd be so appreciative if you left a review. It really helps us and the author to bring more books like this to you.

Here at HQ Digital we are dedicated to publishing fiction that will keep you turning the pages into the early hours. Don't want to miss a thing? To find out more about our books, promotions, discover exclusive content and enter competitions you can keep in touch in the following ways:

JOIN OUR COMMUNITY:

Sign up to our new email newsletter:
http://smarturl.it/SignUpHQ

Read our new blog www.hqstories.co.uk

🐦 https://twitter.com/HQStories

f www.facebook.com/HQStories

BUDDING WRITER?

We're also looking for authors to join the HQ Digital family!
Find out more here:

https://www.hqstories.co.uk/want-to-write-for-us/

Thanks for reading, from the HQ Digital team

HQ

If you enjoyed *Deadly Little Lies*, then why not try another gripping thriller from HQ Digital?

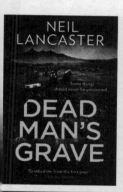